You Never Know

Melinda Harris

To my husband, for loving the fangirl in me.

To my family, for supporting the fangirl in me.

To my soul sister, for understanding the fangirl in me.

I love you all.

TABLE OF CONTENTS

CHAPTER 1

I can honestly say that tonight, I'm glad to see the filming finally coming to a close.

I push my hands deeper into my jacket pockets, as yet another shiver runs through me. I eye what is now probably lukewarm coffee in my chair's cup holder, but I decide against it. It's not worth taking my hands back out into the cold.

Earlier today, I was in shorts and a long-sleeved t-shirt for an afternoon jog. But as soon as the sun sets, the temperature drops with it. Now I'm sitting outside in jeans, two pairs of socks, Converse, long sleeves, a hoodie, my winter jacket, gloves and a scarf, and I'm still freezing.

You gotta love autumn in the South.

Trying to pass the time, I take a quick look around at what's left of us. The crowd's a little larger than usual, which will be disappointing for some. A big crowd usually means we have less of a chance for a meet-and-greet later on with the actors.

But the big crowd won't make a difference tonight for me. The person I want most to meet won't be showing up – not that he ever mingles with the crowd anyway – which makes nights like tonight very hard to justify.

We say we're "set stalking", but I think I may be starting to take the "stalking" part a little too far.

My most reliable sources told me he would be here tonight, so I made all the necessary arrangements: begged to get off work a little early, saddled my eight year old with his grandma and packed some snacks and a thermos full of coffee.

The rainy weather has been keeping the cast and crew away for a week and a half, so we've all been looking forward to this – myself, more so than the others, I fear. But late this afternoon, I was told there was a change in schedule and that meant bad news for me.

"Sorry kiddo," my friend Rose pats my arm as she stands to fold up her chair at the end of the last scene.

"It's okay," I say, as I get up as well and start packing my things, eager to be out of the weather.

"That was awesome!" the newest addition to our group, Sydney, says as a "That's a wrap!" is announced from the director. "Do you think they'll come over here and take pictures with us?" Sydney asks.

I see Rose give me a sideways glance and a smile, before she explains to the newbie how things work.

"It's a big crowd tonight, girl," Rose tells Sydney. "Plus, Luna and Vick rarely come over for autographs and such anymore."

Sydney's excitement reminds me of the first time I watched the filming. I remember how it felt.

I don't care who you are, it's exciting. That's the draw. It's a little piece of Hollywood right here in our tiny town.

Seeing all of the lights, the cameras, the action...I've never seen anything like it. And the crew is amazing to watch – carrying gear all over the place, setting up cables and wires, marking spots for the actors, putting up tents for the director, the food, the clothing. Plus, you have the thrill of possibly meeting a real life celebrity! You can't beat that, especially if you're a true fan, which I am. I think. Honestly, I'm not sure what I am anymore.

All I know is that I want to meet him. I want to see him, up close, and I want him to see me. I don't need an autograph or a picture. I just want to introduce myself, "Hi. My name is Samantha. It's great to finally meet you." And then he would say, "My name is Ethan. It's great to meet you too."

I've played and replayed this conversation over and over in my head, but it's yet to happen because Mr. Ethan Grant is rather...well, I like to call him shy and mysterious, but most people would just say he's an asshole.

I've seen him film several scenes at this point, and I've even been an extra on a few episodes. My friends and I have met most all of the actors now at least once, except for one.

Ethan's a very serious actor, script with him constantly, studying, brooding. He rarely even acknowledges the crowd, especially when it's larger like tonight. He gets out of the white passenger van with the other actors in the scene, does his part, and then he's back in the van and out of our lives.

Actually, only a couple of the actors from the show will risk a large crowd gathering. I look at Sydney's face, and I can tell Rose has recently filled her in on this fact.

"So they won't even come and say hello?" Sydney asks Liz, another friend and regular in our "stalking" group.

Sydney looks like she may start crying at any moment.

"No dear. I'm afraid not." Liz smiles at her. "But we may catch them next time. You never know."

As predicted, the two celebrities we watched film all evening graciously wave to their fans and blow some kisses, before hopping into their white vans and heading back to their trailers.

My friends and I grab our things and start walking toward our cars parked outside of the town square. I smile as Rose and Liz try to console a heartbroken Sydney.

"Do you think they'll come out tomorrow?" Sydney asks, hopefully.

"Maybe," Rose says, with a warm smile.

I take a deep a breath and hitch my backpack a little higher on my shoulder.

The weather wasn't ideal, and Ethan never showed, but I will definitely be back tomorrow. I'm not ready to give up quite yet, because Liz is right. You just never know.

ॐঔৎ

Even though I got to bed rather late after our stalking adventures last night, I decided to leave for my mom's house early this morning.

It's a nice day, and the deserted, winding roads make for a very peaceful and relaxing drive. I roll down my windows and turn up the music, enjoying nature and some much needed alone time.

My mom lives about twenty minutes outside of town in an old, two-story farmhouse that has been in her family for years. I love it. It's small and a little rundown, especially since my dad's been gone, but my mom does the best she can.

There haven't been animals on the farm since I was around eight years old, but there's still a pretty large garden, which my mom takes care of with the help of some neighbors.

"Did you ladies you have fun last night?" my mom yells to me from the kitchen, as I walk in her front door.

It's early and the clean living room tells me Jake isn't up yet. I can smell breakfast sizzling in an iron skillet.

"Yes ma'am. How about you?"

The delicious smell gets stronger as I round the corner from the living room to the kitchen.

"I always have a good time with my little man," she tells me, as she watches me walk to the refrigerator to grab a drink. "So, did you finally meet him? Was he there?"

"Not last night."

I can't hide the disappointment on my face, but I really don't want to get in to this with my mom.

"Mom, when are you going to start cooking healthier?" I ask her, in an effort to change the subject.

"What? Bacon and gravy's not healthy?" she says, teasing me as she turns back to the stove to finish up breakfast.

"You should let me cook for you some time. I'm not bad."

"You're too fancy for me," she says as she slides homemade biscuits out of the oven.

"Spaghetti's too fancy for you, mom." I smile at her.

"You're right. I'm just a simple meat and potatoes gal."

My mom turns to me again smiling, but I sigh as her smile slowly vanishes. "Hun, you know I love you, right?"

"Yes," I say, rolling my eyes at her, knowing where this conversation is headed. "Do we have to go over this again?"

"I just think this is a little crazy. That's all."

"I know mom. I do too."

I open the can of Coke I pulled from the fridge and take a swig.

"So, what are you doing then?" my mom asks. "You've told me that you don't want to date the guy or anything. You said you just want to meet him, but I'm sorry. I don't get it."

She goes back to her bacon, turning her back on me.

"I mean, it's one thing to go watch the filming a few times," she continues. "I understand the excitement, but every single time? For a grown woman, I think that's a little overboard."

I know my mom isn't trying to be hurtful. She's just worried.

"It's okay, mom. Not a lot of people would understand."

I sit down at my mom's small kitchen table and rest my head on my hand.

My mom sits a plate full of eggs, bacon and a biscuit in front of me then sits down beside me at the table. "Well, explain then."

I sigh as I look down at my plate, trying to think of how to explain this to her...*again.*

The thing is, not a lot of exciting things happen around here. We got a Wal-Mart a few years ago. Most people thought that was pretty intense. And that's about it.

So, when we heard that a fancy new TV show would be filming in our fair city of Delia, imagine the excitement.

The Mayor called a huge meeting at the courthouse to announce the news and let us all know what to expect, but most people didn't care about the type of show or who the actors were. Everyone was just excited about the opportunities and the money it would bring our town. For a town with a population of around 8,500, a dollar can go a long way.

My friend Rose and I were just as excited as everyone else, but we couldn't have cared less about the money.

The minute I found out what show was coming and who would be in it, the money ceased to matter. All I knew was that Ethan Grant would be starring in this show. *The* Ethan Grant.

He's my age, and I've been in love since I first laid eyes on him in *Jimmy's Story* almost 10 years ago. Ethan played a troubled teen with a dark past, and I thought he was an incredible actor. I was instantly smitten.

"I know how you love to put your heart into things, pumpkin," my mom says, interrupting my reverie, "but you're missing work and staying away from your own son. I've never seen anything like it."

I can tell she's getting frustrated now, as she normally does with this conversation.

"Besides, most people think he's an ass," she makes sure to tack on at the end.

"He's not an ass," I say, always defending him, as I stab at my eggs, not feeling very hungry.

"So you say," my mom replies, but she's smiling. "I'm just worried about you. That's all. You don't usually get in this deep, and I personally think that boy's got some dirty secrets."

I roll my eyes. "We all have secrets mom."

My mom is right though. I'm not usually in quite this deep, but Ethan is different. The truth is I tend to obsess over things. That's just what I do. I personally like to think of it as being "passionate" about things, but let's call a spade a spade. Shall we?

I've done it before with random actors and musicians in my past. I think it started with Luke Perry when I was in the first grade. But I feel like this time is different. At least, that's what I keep telling myself because it allows me to continue my crazy obsession with him, but I'm not so sure this is any different from the others any more.

From the first time I saw Ethan, I did the usual and went nuts trying to find out everything I could about him. To my dismay, I found very little.

He rarely does in depth interviews, so no one knows him all that well. There are a couple of fan sites online now, but as I mentioned before, most people think he's a jerk, so he doesn't have a ton of devotees. Most of his fans only like him because they think he's some kind of bad boy.

I thought about starting my own fan site for a while, but that would be like officially admitting I'm an addict. I guess you could say I'm not ready for the "Ethan Grant Twelve Step" program quite yet.

"Personally, I don't think he makes little effort – okay zero effort – to meet his fans because he's an ass," I tell my mom, who is now rolling *her* eyes at *me*. "Maybe it scares him," I continue. "Or maybe he likes to concentrate solely on his work, while he's working. Is that such a crime?"

"Whatever you say," my mom says, and I sigh.

I can defend him all day, and I normally have to with anyone who knows about my little crush, and I don't mind. I can see it in Ethan's eyes. There's more to him than most people think.

Maybe I relate to him because I feel the same way about myself at times.

I think everyone is subject to labels at one point or another in their life. I come from a tiny town in South Georgia, so to most, I'm just a simple country girl. Maybe that's partly true, but in my heart, I know I'm more than that. I've just never had the opportunity to prove it. I was at the top of my graduating class in high school. I was going places. We all had high expectations.

Then I found out I was pregnant.

"Mom, I know you don't understand. No one does, including me." I take another sip of my Coke. "I just feel some kind of weird connection to the guy."

I wince knowing how crazy that sounds. I hate saying it out loud. It makes so much more sense in my head.

"Connection, huh?"

My mother's tone confirms that it sounds crazy to her too. I take a deep breath and exhale in a huff.

"Look mom. I can't explain it. Okay?"

I stand up because I'm tired of this conversation, but also because I can hear Jake rustling around upstairs.

"Let's just drop it," I say, exasperated.

"Do you think you're in love with him or something?"

My mom's voice is quiet, like she is uttering something too horrible to say out loud.

"No," I answer quickly, but I'm not completely convinced.

Do I think I'm in love with him?

I see my mom is definitely frustrated now. As if trying to drive the point home, she throws her hands on the table. "Well, I wish I could understand. I mean, what do you expect to get from this?"

I frown at her because I have no idea. That's the million dollar question.

"Mom," my voice is quiet now, and sincere. "I just want to meet him. That's all. I'm a big fan. I want to introduce myself and then walk away."

My mom giggles, which throws me off guard.

"So you're not looking for him to whisk you away in his arms to the nearest wedding chapel?"

"I promise. My expectations extend no further than meeting him," I assure her, but it's not like I haven't fantasized about the other. The truth is I want to meet him because it will finally confirm the fact that I can never be with him. There. I said it.

In my head, believe it or not, being with Ethan is a possibility. But in reality, he's a famous actor and I'm nobody, and it's never going to happen. Of course I continue to have my ridiculous fantasies about us being together, but they are what they are – fantasies. I am certain after I meet him, I can get over him. At least, I hope that's how it works.

My mom stands up now too, probably also hearing Jake coming toward the stairs. "Well dear, I can't say I understand fully, but I've never been opposed to what makes you happy. You keep doing what you're doing, if that's what you want."

About fifteen seconds later Jake comes running into the kitchen.

"Mommy!" he yells as he jumps into my arms.

This is when the true guilt hits me. Instead of spending time with my son, I'm spending long nights – risking frost bite – waiting to meet a perfect stranger for what will probably be the first and last time.

CHAPTER 2

I drop Jake off at school after I leave my mom's house, and I reluctantly make my way to work.

I've spent the last six years of my young life working for the city of Delia. The job is horrible, but it's steady work and the health benefits are great.

These are the types of things you have to think about when you're twenty-six with an eight year old. Instead of college, you have to think about daycare, and instead of a career you love, you have to think about finding a reliable job that will pay your bills and provide for your family.

I turn up the radio in my car, upset with myself for thinking ill thoughts about my son. There's nothing I love more than him, and I'm confident there never will be. He's my own personal angel here on Earth, and I love him with everything I am. I just have a tendency to feel sorry for myself from time to time.

I pull into the courthouse parking lot at the same time as Rose.

"Mornin'!" she yells from her car a few spaces down. "Feels like we were just here!" she adds with a smile.

Rose and I work together at the Delia courthouse in the square, where we happened to be set stalking last night.

"I know," I say, as Rose makes her way over to me so we can walk in together.

"Sorry again about last night, girl. What a disappointment."

"It's no big deal," I say, lying. "Maybe he'll show up tonight."

"Well," Rose starts, and I know what she's about to say. "I didn't see them adding any new trailers when I drove by this morning, so I don't want you to get your hopes up."

I look up at her as we walk up the courthouse steps and into the building.

"It's a long shot, but a girl can dream, right?"

I try to smile, but from the pitiful look on Rose's face, I realize it must have fallen a little short.

"Is there something else bothering you, Sam?" Rose asks, as we sit our purses on the conveyor belt at the metal detector.

"No. I'm fine."

I don't want to burden Rose with my issues, which I'm sure to be over in the next couple of hours anyway.

"It's just been a long time since I've seen him," I confess, which is true. "I need a fix," I add, with a more genuine smile this time.

Rose laughs. "Maybe he'll show up tonight."

"Maybe," I say, as we walk into the small room of cubicles where Rose and I spend eight hours of the day, Monday through Friday.

I put my purse in my desk drawer, take a deep breath and turn on my computer, poised for a brand new day, already starting to push my poor excuse for problems to the back on my mind.

☙❧

After work, Rose and I go straight to our cars and grab our chairs.

They've been filming in the city since noon, but they just made it to the square.

It looks like they're going to redo or continue a scene from last night. I recognize some of the props and outfits from the night before. Plus, they're starting to set up some elaborate lighting in the middle of the square.

As we sit down in our usual spot, I call my mom to check on her and Jake.

"Will you be late tonight?" my mom asks before we hang up.

"I don't think so," I answer honestly. "I should be over to get Jake before bed time."

"All right then. You ladies have fun."

God, I love my mother. No one else on earth would ever do something like this for me. An obsessed fangirl at twenty-six? That's something only a mother could love.

I turn back to Rose and we finish watching set up. It's only Rose and me tonight. Sydney decided to bow out, disappointed about not getting to physically meet any of the actors last night, and Liz had an appointment in Atlanta.

Rose and I chat and stay until a little after filming is over – Rose has a pretty serious crush on Vick. And since the crowd is surprisingly thinner tonight, Luna and Vick come over to meet with the few of us remaining. Sydney will be so disappointed.

I'm not sure whether I should be embarrassed or not, but most of the cast knows my crew by name. We've been pretty dedicated fans since the start of filming, and since we're not obnoxious and loud like some, we've become pretty well respected among the show's actors.

I watch as Luna and Vick bypass a few fans to come and say hello to Rose and me. I feel kind of bad, but not too bad. Rose and I have earned our stripes, so to speak.

Despite that fact, Rose and I don't take up too much time with actors. At the end of the day, we are all just fans of the show, and we want to make sure everyone gets pictures and autographs.

My friends and I – minus Sydney – don't do pictures or autographs anymore. How many photos do you really need with the same actor? Now, it's more about coming out, saying hello and letting the actors know we love and support the show and everything they're doing.

Plus, you could say it's our way of having girlfriend time. It's something we all enjoy, and it's our time to sit, chat and catch up.

"See you tomorrow, girl," Rose says, as we part ways near the courthouse to go to our cars. "Maybe next time."

I just smile and nod, feeling the now familiar wave of disappointment settle in.

He wasn't there again tonight. He never showed up.

On the way to pick up Jake, I try to shake off the bad mood that seems to have melded itself to my person today.

By the time I get to my mom's house, I'm feeling a little better, having listened to some favorite tunes on the ride over.

"Hi mom!" Jake greets me at the door.

"Hi sweet angel!" I reply and grab him up in my arms.

He'll be bigger than me soon, which wouldn't take much, but for now, I'm still able to lift him with no problem. I hope he always wants a place in my arms. I don't care if he's thirty.

"What did you have for dinner?" I ask, as I put my purse on the desk by the front door.

"Pizza!" he says excitedly. "Grandma made it! It was delicious!"

I have to smile at what little it takes to make an eight year old happy. I can't help but be a little jealous of that kind of innocence.

"Great!" I say, as I walk toward the kitchen with Jake's hand in mine. "Did you save any for me?"

I see my mom's in the kitchen, where she spends most of her time, already pulling out a slice for me and putting it in the toaster oven. I study her for a moment, once again feeling so thankful to have her in my life. She has her graying hair pulled back in a clip, and her glasses are hanging off her nose as she bends over to try and see the dial on the toaster oven.

My mom and I didn't look much alike when I was younger, but people say we favor more now. I'm glad.

My mom is still a beauty to me, even at fifty one years old, and in faded sweatpants and a t-shirt. She's a little rough around the edges – a typical Southern woman – but if I have half the guts and heart she has when I'm her age, I'll be more than satisfied.

"Thanks for the pizza, mom," I say, as I walk in and sit down at the table with Jake.

It appears he's been coloring. The table is a mess of half used papers and scattered crayons.

"You're welcome, hun," she says, smiling over at me. "Did you have fun?"

"It was okay."

I pull off my jacket and place it on the back of the chair. My mom smiles as she brings me a glass of sweet tea.

"I take it Prince Charming didn't show?"

I smirk at my mother. "No." I pause. "At least I don't think so. I never saw any white horses."

"Smarty pants."

"Smarty pants!" My son happily mimics my mother's name calling.

"Nice mom," I say to her, but I'm not mad, of course.

I eat my pepperoni pizza as my mom sits by Jake and helps him color the red race car he just finished drawing.

I frown as I think about all the time I've been missing these last several months. Watching Jake sitting here, coloring, smiling from ear to ear, I'm reminded once again that it isn't worth it. My obsession has gotten really out of hand this time.

I miss my son, and I'll never get this time back with him. It's time to give up Ethan Grant for good. My mom is right. It doesn't make any sense. It used to, but I can't pull any logic out of it lately.

"Whatcha thinking about?" my mom asks, pulling me from my deep thoughts.

"I was just thinking," I pause, still unsure on whether or not I want to give up on Ethan, "I was just thinking that I may quit this set stalking stuff for a while."

I don't want to look at my mom because I know she'll be smiling. I look at my half eaten piece of pizza instead.

"Are you sure about that?"

Huh? I look up at my mom. She's not joking. I can tell by the look on her face.

"I'm sure." I say it this time with a little more conviction. "I miss this." I gesture to her and Jake sitting shoulder to shoulder over his drawings. "And you're right. It doesn't make any sense. Not anymore."

My mom doesn't say anything at first, and I start staring at my pizza again, but I can tell she's looking at me.

"Okay then," she finally says. "If that's what you want, that's fine by me."

I look back up at her, eyes wide with disbelief. This morning, I felt like she was reading me the riot act for my little hobby, and now it seems she's defending the other side. My anger quickly subsides though. This has nothing to do with my mom.

"It's what I want," I say firmly.

I look down at my watch. It's already past Jake's bedtime, and he needs a bath tonight.

"Buddy, you ready to go?" I ask Jake, as he finishes up his red race car.

"Sure mom."

He packs up his papers and starts putting his crayons back in the box. I can't help but smile at what a good kid he's turning out to be.

"You don't have to clean this up, sweetie. I'll take care of it." My mom takes the crayons from his hands. "Go upstairs and get your back pack, okay?"

When Jake starts upstairs, I help my mom pack the sixty four crayons back in the box.

"Sam, baby?"

I flick my eyes to my mother, and see the concern on her face. "Yea?"

"Are you sure about this?"

"Mom," I sigh. "You basically told me this morning that all of this was ridiculous, and now you're changing your mind? What's going on?"

My mom puts down the crayons, leaving that task to me, and takes my plate over to the sink.

"I do think it's ridiculous," she starts and then turns to me. I continue to concentrate on the crayons and try to place the remaining few back in the crowded box.

My mom goes on, quieter now, like she doesn't want Jake to hear. "You're a smart girl, so I always trust you know what you're doing."

I have to smile at the irony in that statement. Most *smart* girls don't get themselves knocked up at seventeen.

"Just because I don't understand something you're doing, doesn't mean I think it's wrong," she tells me. "You've just been going about this for so long. I guess I'm just a little surprised you're giving up."

I can hear Jake coming down the stairs. "Mom, this is what's best for me and my family. Okay? Trust that decision."

"Ready mom?" Jake asks at the end of the staircase.

"Yep," I say, surprised to find I'm fighting back tears. "Let's go."

"Goodnight, my babies." My mom kisses us both before we walk out the door.

It's another cold night outside. Jake jumps in the back seat and I look back at him in the rearview when I get in the car. I can tell he's tired.

"How was your day, sweet angel?"

"It was good, mom. How was yours?" Jake lets out a huge yawn, confirming my suspicions.

"It was good. Long, but good. I missed you."

"I missed you too. Did you meet Ethan today?" Jake asks excitedly, and I feel bad, like I've passed on some defect to him.

"Nope. Not today."

"Oh well," he says, eyes heavy. "Maybe next time."

I smile back at him, but I can feel my heart breaking. There won't be a next time.

CHAPTER 3

I pull into a parking spot in our apartment complex feeling kind of strange. I can hardly remember the drive home. I shake my head trying to get my bearings, and I realize I must have been so lost in thought that I forgot the ride. That's pretty scary.

I look in the rearview again to find Jake sound asleep. It's not a long drive from my mom's, but Jake must have been beat. I guess we'll be skipping the bath tonight.

I open the back door quietly, and grab Jake out of the car. He wakes briefly, but then lays his head back on my shoulder as I struggle to carry him up the three flights of stairs to our apartment.

After I get Jake in his pajamas and under the covers, I go into the kitchen and crack open a beer. I'm normally not much of a drinker during the week, but it sounded good, and I think it may help me calm down. I'm feeling kind of jittery and I can feel a headache coming on.

I move into the living room, turn on the small lamp on the end table and plop down on my couch.

It's been five years since Jake and I moved out of my mom's house, and it still doesn't feel like home here. I'm yet to put any real decorating touches on the place. Plus, it has a tiny kitchen with zero counter space. I wish I had a better place to cook.

I'm not crazy about apartment living, but it's the best I can do for now. There are just so many disadvantages, like noisy neighbors, a lack of privacy and strange odors. For example, I now have the scent of rubbing alcohol and anti-septic in my living room. That can't be good.

Another problem with an apartment is it's such a transient place. Or maybe it's because I still think of my mom's house as home. Whatever the reason, I never feel truly comfortable here.

I keep telling myself home is wherever my son is, and that thought normally makes me feel better about the situation.

I finish my beer in silence, never turning on my TV or radio. I just rest on the couch, thinking about the decision I made earlier tonight at my mom's and laughing a little at myself for letting it go on as long as it has.

It seems utterly ridiculous now, sitting here in my quiet living room. I imagine all of the things I could have been doing with the past eighteen months of my life, and I'm disgusted.

I brush off the thought. Nothing good ever comes from reliving the past. Tomorrow is a new day. Maybe I'll enroll in those college classes I've been thinking about. I should be spending my nights doing something like that instead of chasing after some fantasy that will never come to life.

The next thing I know, I'm asleep and dreaming about Ethan.

In my dream, I meet him for the first time, and it goes exactly like I always hoped it would. He comes over to me after his scene, walks directly up to me, bypassing the other screaming fans and says, "Hi. I'm Ethan." I reply, staring straight into his beautiful green eyes, with "I'm Sam. It's nice to meet you." He takes my hand then and kisses the top, like some gentleman from an old black and white movie. Then he's gone. And I wake up.

I look at the clock hanging on the wall in my kitchen. It's five A.M.

I get up, feeling a crick in my neck, obviously from my awkward position on the couch, and I massage it as I walk back to my bedroom. I don't bother with my pajamas. I just take off my pants and crawl into bed in my t-shirt and undies. I still have at least another hour of sleep.

But before I close my eyes again, I think about my dream. It was one of those that seemed so real, like when you have a dream that someone hugs you and you can almost feel it.

I start crying softly then. They're irrational tears, since I'm still half asleep, but they come anyway – mostly because I suddenly realize that my dream is as real as it's ever going to get.

❧

Thank God it's Friday, was all I could think of on my drive to work this morning after dropping Jake off at school.

I'm feeling a little better about all of my silly issues from yesterday. Now, I just have to break the news to my friends.

It's tradition for us all to meet for lunch on Fridays at a Chinese restaurant in the square. It's the only nice restaurant in town, and it isn't anything special. The only thing that really makes it *nice* is the fact that it's a Chinese place in the middle of nowhere Georgia, so people think it's *exotic*.

"Hi Sam!" Sydney calls from the table, as I walk into the poorly lit restaurant.

The dim lighting is a scary fact in itself. Either the owners are trying to make it romantic, or they don't want you to get a good look at the food.

"Hi ladies." I wave at them. It seems I'm the last to arrive today.

Rose smiles at me, as I sit down, but my attention is immediately drawn to Sydney, who is literally bouncing up and down in her seat.

"Okay gals..." Sydney starts, as soon as I sit down, but before she can continue, the waiter comes by to get my drink order.

I order water and then look to Sydney, encouraging her to continue, but Sydney is watching the waiter walk away, an annoyed look on her face.

"Okay, look. I have it on very good authority that the cast will be at a party in Atlanta tomorrow night!" Sydney says eventually, once again bouncing in her seat.

None of us get overly excited by this news. Who cares if they go to a party? Surely they go to parties all of the time.

The waiter comes back with my water then and takes our lunch orders.

"And? Who cares if they're going to a party?" Liz says, after the waiter finishes with our orders, obviously sharing my thoughts on the issue.

"Let me finish, please?" Sydney throws up her manicured hand towards Liz's face. "I happen to know where the party is, *and...*" she pauses, obviously for dramatic effect. "I have us on the guest list!"

Okay, so she got us on that one.

Rose, Liz and I are all momentarily shocked into silence. No one says a word, as we start looking at each other in turn, total disbelief in our eyes.

Sydney's annoyed again. "Isn't anyone going to thank me?"

"You're kidding, right?" Liz is laughing.

"Nope. Totally serious." Sydney is beaming.

"And how did you manage this?" Rose asks.

It seems Liz and Rose are starting to come around. I'm still feeling like my heart may beat its way out of my chest. I look at Sydney and she's busting at the seams to tell her story.

"Well, I started dating this guy named Scott about a month ago. Remember Sam? I told you about him?"

Sydney looks to me for validation, but I still can't speak. Scott doesn't sound familiar at all, but I nod in confirmation any way so she'll continue.

"Scott works for The World Wildlife Federation," she tells us, "and they're hosting a celebrity fundraiser, in partnership with the YA network, tomorrow night in Atlanta. Well, of course I was curious about who was coming, so I asked him. He shared most of the guest list with me, and I freaked out when I heard that the cast – *our* cast – would be making an appearance! *All* of them!"

Sydney looks at me directly for that last sentence.

"How are we getting in? Where's it at?" Liz asks – the first to completely absorb the story.

"I have all of the details handled, including a limo to pick us up," Sydney says nonchalantly, like she does this sort of thing all the time.

Rose nearly spits her Diet Coke on the table. "A limo?"

"That's right!" Sydney is gloating. "Scott hooked it up. The limo will be at my house at six P.M. and will take us to the conference center downtown where the fundraiser's being held."

All of us are shocked once again. I'm yet to speak a single word since Sydney started in about the party.

The waiter comes to bring our food, which gives everyone another minute or two to absorb the news.

"So, when are we going shopping tomorrow? I have to find something excellent to wear! I was thinking about making a trip to Bristol. We'll never find anything decent in this shitty town." Sydney is talking mostly to herself, as she starts shoveling in her Lo Mein.

"Let me get this straight," Rose starts. "We are going to a formal, celebrity fundraiser tomorrow night in Atlanta, where the cast of our favorite show, *Stephen's Room*, will be in attendance, whom we will all have a possible opportunity to meet?"

Sydney smiles. "That's correct, my friend!" she nearly shouts, obviously glad this is finally sinking in for the rest of us.

Liz and Rose exchange smiles, and then both look at me. I haven't touched my lunch. My stomach is in knots, and I'm sure I'm as pale as the white linen tablecloth on our table.

I also feel very odd, like I'm sitting inside a glass jar. I can hear people talking, but it's muffled. *Please don't let me faint!* I shake my head to try and dislodge the feeling.

"Sam? Are you okay?" Rose asks me, suddenly clear as a bell. I'm happy to see my head shake worked.

I look up at her and answer honestly. "I'm not sure if I can make it."

Sydney's face immediately falls. "What? You're kidding me, right?"

"I don't know if mom can keep Jake, and I have nothing to wear and no money to spend on something new."

I'm being honest, but I'm dancing around the real reason for my hesitancy. The idea of finally getting a chance to meet him is inconceivable. I've dreamed of it for so long, but now that it may come true, I'm scared stiff.

"Nonsense!" Sydney nearly yells again.

I look around, sure to see people with their eyes now fixed on our table. Luckily, the restaurant is pretty loud from the lunch crowd, so we're not being ogled too badly.

"I'll talk to your mom myself! And as for the dress, I know we can figure out something. You're going!" Sydney slams her tiny fist down on the table for emphasis.

"I'm sorry to say, I have to agree with Sydney on this one," Liz says, shrugging her shoulders.

I sigh in defeat. Liz is the oldest of us at twenty nine, and she's also the strongest of us all. There's no fighting Liz once she makes up her mind. Her decision is normally the final one.

"You can't afford to pass this up, Sam," Rose adds. "It's a once in a lifetime opportunity."

Her eyes are full of things she isn't saying, and it makes me frown. *I just gave up on him yesterday!*

"Fine," I finally say, closing my eyes. "I'll go, but I can't afford a dress. Sydney, I may need to borrow your closet."

"No problem!" she says, happy again. "Liz? Rose? You guys want to go shopping tomorrow?"

The excitement at the table is now tangible.

"I'm game!" Rose says, with a smile. "I'm not sure how Danny will like this, but who cares? He'll get over it!"

"Damn right he will!" Sydney confirms.

"I'm all for shopping tomorrow too," Liz says, and then looks over at me. "And I think you should come along as well Sam, even if you don't plan on buying anything."

Once again, Liz's decision is normally the final one. That trait must come with being a lawyer.

"Okay. I'll go," I reluctantly agree.

We finish lunch and eventually leave the restaurant, having made plans to meet at Liz's house for shopping tomorrow at nine A.M.

It's a thirty minute ride to Bristol, and Sydney wants to make sure she has plenty of time to pick out the perfect gown. Sydney would look great in a trash bag – with her size four frame, wavy blonde locks and C-cup – but the girl loves clothes, and shopping is definitely a sport for her.

Now back at my desk, I find I can barely think of anything but the party. Rose keeps passing my cubicle, giving me loaded looks. I smile, but my heart is racing. This is impossible.

"Rose, I have a confession," I say to her, as we walk toward the front doors of the courthouse to leave for the day.

Rose nods, looking fearful, probably from the tormented look on my face.

I'm truly grasping for a good reason to get out of tomorrow night, but it's a complete tug-of-war inside.

"I kind of decided last night that my set stalking days were over," I tell her.

Rose stops in her tracks. "You're serious?"

"Yes, I'm serious." I start walking again.

Why is this so hard for people to believe? I'm beginning to feel like my infatuation with Ethan has been even worse than I thought. I thought it was only real for me, but I've apparently been so immersed that I made it real for everyone else too.

"I'm sorry." Rose says, jogging a bit to catch up, as I walk out the front doors. "I was just a little shocked by that statement. Why the sudden change of heart?"

I stop on the steps outside to explain.

"It's ridiculous Rose. Isn't it? You're my friend. Tell me the truth. I'm crazy, right?"

Rose looks into my eyes and laughs softly. "I'm in no place to judge," she says with a smile, "but honestly? The craziest part is that I don't think it's crazy at all."

I glance down at the pavement of the courthouse steps, and then back up at my friend.

"Thanks Rose."

"Any time, darlin'," she says, as she walks to her car. "See you tomorrow morning!"

"See you tomorrow," I say happily, as I walk to my own car.

All my thoughts about last night suddenly have new meaning.

Maybe my set stalking days are over, but I can't give up on meeting him. Not yet. If it's not crazy to Rose, then I won't let it seem crazy to me.

I start my car with a renewed sense of hope, thinking about the possibilities tomorrow night may bring.

CHAPTER 4

A nine o'clock meeting time is early for me on a weekend. Instead of my usual Saturday morning routine – a cup of coffee, a book and lounging around in my pajamas until at least ten A.M. – I'm dropping Jake off at my Aunt Clara's house, bright and early. She's taking her grandson, Sean, to a birthday party today and said Jake could come along. I feel really guilty for the lack of time I've spent with Jake this week, but it will all be over after tonight.

"Will I see you this afternoon?" Jake asks with sad eyes, as I pull into Clara's driveway. This does not help my guilt factor.

"Yea, buddy. I'll see you some time after lunch," I say, as I lean in to give him a kiss, "but remember, I'm going to a party tonight, so you're staying at Grandma's."

"I remember," he says, eyes still sad.

"What's the matter Jake?" I can't let him leave the car in his current mood.

"It's nothing," he says, looking down at his feet.

"You're not being honest with me." I lift his chin so he'll look into my eyes. "Please tell me what's wrong?"

"I was just thinking about Pops last night, and it made me sad."

Oh. This is a little out of left field. My dad passed away over a year ago, and we're all still dealing with it.

Jake was very close to him, and is having an especially hard time, since he's still too young to truly understand.

"I know baby. We all miss him," I say, trying to make him feel better, but my own grief surfaces any time I bring up my dad. It's hard to be encouraging.

"I told you that he's always watching over you from heaven, right? He is always with you in your heart and your memories," I tell him. "No one can take that away, ever."

Jake smiles. "Thanks mom."

"You're welcome, Buddy," I pause. "Are you sure you're not upset about me being gone so much lately?" I have to ask. My own guilt is overwhelming.

Jake looks surprised and confused about my question. "No, Momma. Why would I be mad at that?"

I'm glad he's not mad at me, but I suddenly feel sad because it seems he doesn't miss me as much as I miss him.

"I just haven't been around much this week, so I thought you may be upset about that," I explain.

Jake rolls his cute little blue eyes at me. "It's not like you're gone all of the time, Mom. We spend lots of time together," he says, seeming a little peppier as he opens the car door. "Besides, I like Grandma's house. She's fun."

"She *is* fun," I agree. "I love you son," I call to him before he shuts the door.

To my surprise, Jake makes his way over to my window. I roll it down.

"Yes sir?" I ask.

"Don't worry so much, Mom, okay? Grandma said worrying is not good for you," he tells me. Then he gives me a kiss on the cheek and runs toward the front door.

I smile, waiting for my Aunt to open the door before I drive off. It's amazing how smart kids are, yet they get so little credit for being such brilliant gifts.

I wave to my aunt when she opens the front door, and then I pull out of her driveway and turn up my radio. As long as Jake's okay, I'm okay.

For the first time, I allow myself to get a little excited about tonight.

❧

Sydney is a ball of energy by the time I roll into Liz's driveway. She's standing outside with Rose, hands wrapped around what I'm sure is probably her third cup of coffee at this point. This is way too early for her.

Once again, it seems I'm the last to arrive.

I get out of my car and start walking down the curvy walkway toward Liz's front door.

Liz is the only wealthy person I've ever known, and she probably wouldn't be considered much outside of our small town.

She's also the only one of us who didn't grow up in Delia. Liz grew up in Atlanta, in a wealthy family. Why she chose to move here is a mystery to all of us, but we're all glad she did. She's a good friend and definitely someone you want on your side. She makes a great lawyer.

"Finally!" Sydney drags out the word in exasperation, and I smile. Sydney's the newest member of our group, but she fits in fine. She's also the youngest at twenty-two, but she's the only one of us with enough fire to go up against Liz. It's fun to watch.

"Ready to do this?" I ask. "Where's Liz?"

"She's on a call inside. She said she'd be right out," Rose answers.

"Like forever ago!" Sydney adds. "I'm freezing!"

Just then, Liz walks out the door and locks it behind her. "Ready!" she says, clicking the button to unlock her Mercedes SUV.

The energy in the car on the way to our shopping extravaganza is electric. Put a sad person in this car, and they're sure to leave with a smile on their face.

We spend the ride making jokes and talking about all of the hot cops that we like to gawk at in the courthouse from time to time. We also get our digs in on the few not so attractive ones. Both groups have googly eyes for Sydney.

"They do not!" Sydney interjects as Liz is making this point, but she knows we're right.

Sydney works at the ticket office in the courthouse, and the cops always seem to find a reason for unnecessary visits to her desk.

"Sgt. Tanner is just a friend!" she exclaims. "He stops by to talk to me about his family drama. That's all."

"Whatever," Liz says smiling; looking over at Sydney in the passenger's seat, out of the corner of her eye. "You keep telling yourself that."

Rose and I laugh at the entertaining banter.

"Either way," Sydney starts, "I'm not interested in any boys in this dumpy town. I've got my sights set on bigger and better."

"Scott?" Rose asks, raising her eyebrows.

"Scott works...for now," Sydney says, turning around to smile at Rose.

By the time we reach the mall in Bristol, I'm in a great mood. It's amazing what some time with girlfriends can do. Oh, that *and* a fabulous party where I'm sure to meet the object of my longtime affections.

We start our search at Belk, the only department store in the mall, minus Sears.

Sydney has her arms full of things to try on before I can make my way through one rack. Like I said, shopping is like a sport for her. If it were an Olympic event, she would most definitely be a gold medal contender.

Once everyone gets a few to try on, I follow them to the dressing room to observe.

Rose comes out first in a long Kelly green number with a wide strap on only one shoulder. It's beautiful, and a perfect color for Rose, with her deep brown eyes and flaming red hair.

Rose has a great figure like Sydney, but she's a little more hesitant to show it off. I give her the thumbs up on the green and she makes her way back for more.

Liz comes out next, and Sydney's close behind.

Liz is wearing an elegant, long black velvet gown. It has a vintage style – very simple, with Liz's name written all over it.

"What do you think?" Liz asks, spinning in the three-way mirror so she can see her backside.

"I love it!" I say. "It looks awesome on you."

Liz also has a great shape, but she's not as conventionally pretty as someone like Sydney or even Rose. Liz is tall and slim, with jet black hair to her shoulders and fierce brown eyes. She has perfect olive-colored skin and undeniably looks like she belongs on the cover of *Forbes* magazine, or in the Oval Office. The best part is that she certainly doesn't act the part, at least not around us.

"How about me?" Sydney asks, spinning around like a ballerina and drawing my attention to her.

She's in a pale pink strapless dress, covered with iridescent sequins at the top to just past her waist. The bottom is a fuller skirt, in layers of chiffon and tulle. It's nothing I'd choose for myself, but it's surprisingly elegant on Sydney. It definitely has a princess feel, which is perfect for her.

"I love that one too!" I tell Sydney with genuine excitement.

I feel like each of my friends has picked the perfect dress on the first go around. They're all going to look gorgeous. I hope Sydney can pull something together for me in her closet later.

Both Sydney and Liz go back to their dressing rooms to try on more, as Rose comes out again in a royal blue, knee length number. She and I both quickly agree it's not as good as the green, so she goes back to try on what she says is her last pick.

Pretty soon, all of the ladies appear again in the waiting area at the same time.

Sydney's second choice is short, and peach colored, with a bow around the waist that makes me immediately turn my nose up. Luckily Sydney agrees, but she waits around to give opinions on the other two's choices.

We both look to Rose. Her final choice is a little black dress that looks great on her.

"I like it," I tell her, "But I would still go with the green."

"Green?" Sydney asks, hands on her hips. "I didn't see green! Go try it on again, please?"

Rose smiles and heads back to the dressing room as I turn my attention to Liz.

My mouth pops open. I can barely take my eyes off of the dress.

Selfishly, all I can think about is how perfect it would be for me. If there were a million dresses for me to choose from to wear tonight, I would have picked this one.

It's long, classic and deep purple, which is my favorite color. It's a layer of soft chiffon over satin, with a slightly deep V-neck, but still respectable. It's sleeveless – the fabric gathered at each shoulder to create a small, rope-like strap. The bodice is fitted to the hip, where the fabric gathers again to the left and hangs elegantly to the floor. It's the most beautiful dress I've ever seen.

Liz watches me eye the dress longingly. "So, what do you think?"

I look up at her, and she has a suspicious glint in her eye. Sydney's watching the exchange as well, but I'm sure she's mostly picking over the dress in her mind, waiting for her turn to critique.

"I love it," I say in a small voice. "I absolutely love it."

Liz looks at herself in the mirror. "Yea, but I'm just not sure it's me," she says, brushing the fabric at her stomach. "What do you think Sydney?"

About that time, Rose comes back out in my favorite green dress. Sydney turns to look at her first before answering Liz. "*Love* that!" she says to Rose. "It's perfect for you!"

Rose smiles. "I think this one's a keeper," she says, before looking over at Liz. I notice Rose's face is confused, probably because neutral-colored Liz is in a deep purple gown.

Sydney turns to Liz then. "I like it," she says, in a very non-committed way, "but I like the black better, I think."

"Rose?" Liz asks. "What do you think?"

"It's not really you." You can always count on Rose for honesty. "Actually, the color looks like something Sam would pick out." Rose looks over at me. "Sam, did you pick that one?"

"I didn't pick it," I say, "but I do love it. And I think it looks great on Liz."

"I think it may look better on you, now that I think about it," Liz says, casually looking at herself again in the mirror, this time pulling up her hair to simulate an up-do. "I know! How about you try it on? Just for fun?"

Liz is obviously trying to get me involved in the dress hunt, knowing I can't afford anything. Why would she do that? Is it that important to her that I participate? There's no way I'm trying on that dress. I'll love it, and I can't have it. God only knows how much it cost. Liz doesn't have much regard for price tags, so she probably has no idea herself.

"No thanks," I say, sullenly. I'm disappointed that she isn't being a little more understanding.

"Oh," Liz says, seemingly taken aback by my reply. "Well, I guess I'll just get them both. I can't decide."

It all comes together for me then. Liz is buying the dress for me. I can't let her do that, but I'm too embarrassed to acknowledge my epiphany out loud.

"I really liked the black one best," I say, trying to communicate to her with my eyes that she doesn't have to do this. I can't let her do this.

Sydney and Rose look confused, noticing our private exchange. Sydney rolls her eyes and goes back to her dressing room to try on what will probably be number three of the thirty we will have to look at today. Rose sits down next to me on the bench.

"No, I think I'll do both," Liz says, still obviously not getting it. "I may need something extra for the holidays."

"Liz," I plead, "please just get the black one, okay?"

Rose grabs my hand, finally understanding what's going on.

"No Sam. I want both, and you can't stop me," Liz says, which is her final word. She smiles and winks at me then, before making her way back to her dressing room.

"No one argues with Liz," Rose says, her eyes soft, probably about to spill over with tears.

"I know," I say, feeling so guilty for what Liz is doing, but also so grateful for my amazing friends.

"So," Rose says standing and walking up toward the mirrors, "I think this one is the ticket!"

"I agree!" I say, more excited now than ever.

"Did I miss anything?" Sydney asks, as she comes around the corner in a horrible bright yellow dress that makes her skin a lime green color.

"No," Rose and I say in unison, as we eye her up and down.

"I know." Sydney beats us to the punch. "It's horrid, but I didn't want to miss any other dresses."

I tell Sydney that Rose and Liz are both done, and she heads back to the dressing room to try on more.

We all three sit and watch the Sydney fashion show, until she finally ends up with the cute pink strapless number she tried on first.

As everyone is standing in line with their dresses, waiting to check out, Liz gets my attention. "Sam? I have a great idea!" I look at her, confused by her excitement, but she continues before I can say anything. "Why don't you just borrow this purple dress tonight, and I'll wear the black? Great idea, right?"

"That's an awesome idea, Liz!" Sydney is clueless, as usual. "Sam, that's much better than anything you'd find in my closet. And it will look awesome on you!"

Rose and I exchange glances, and I push down the tears that are threatening my eyes. "I would really appreciate that Liz, more than you know." I have to figure out a way to pay her back.

"Don't mention it," she says, winking again in her conspiratorial way.

Everyone spends the next couple of hours trying on shoes and accessories to go with their new gowns. Liz uses very little tact while purchasing things to go with the purple gown. She holds the earrings and necklaces up to me, acting like she needs to see them from a distance. She asks my opinion on everything, and she even purchases shoes that are way too high for her, but they'll make up the difference in height for us so the dress will fit me better.

It isn't a very good show, especially since everyone is in on it – except Sydney, who never seems to catch on.

Sydney makes everyone promise to get ready at her house tonight, since the limo is coming there. Liz promises to bring the dress and accessories over with her.

We make it home from Bristol around one, so I'm at my Aunt Clara's at one thirty to pick up Jake.

"Hi Buddy!" I say, when Jake comes to the door.

"He really had a great time today," my aunt tells me, as I give him a hug.

"You did?" I ask Jake. "What did you do?"

"Mom, it was awesome!" Jake starts, so excited, he can barely get the words out. "Sean's friend Luke had his party at Jumpers, and it was so fun! I got on this slide thing that was so high! And then we had cake and candy, and jumped in all of these huge jump houses! It was awesome!"

"There was a lot of candy," my aunt winks at me.

"Jake! Come here and see this!" His cousin Sean calls him back in to look at something on TV.

"So, is it true?" Clara asks, when Jake goes back inside.

I lean against the doorframe. "About tonight?"

"Your mom told me about it. Are you nervous?" My aunt's smiling and I can tell she's happy for me.

I smile back. "I am a little, if I'm being honest, but I'm excited."

"What are you going to wear?" Clara asks suddenly. "Jeanette may have something. Do you want to take a look?"

Jeanette is Clara's daughter, and although we're about the same size, we have very different tastes.

"Oh that's okay," I say politely. I look down at my feet, still humbled by Liz's stunt today. "I have something. I'm borrowing a dress from Liz."

My aunt can tell by my face that something's wrong, but she doesn't ask. Knowing Liz herself, she's probably guessed what happened today.

"Great," she finally says. "What color is it?"

"Purple," I say, looking at her unable to keep from smiling.

"You're kidding?" she says with a knowing smile. "How perfect!"

"It's better than perfect. It's stunning."

"Well, you better take some pictures!"

"We will, and thanks for today. Sounds like it was a hit."

"They did have a good time."

"Jake?" I call over my aunt's shoulder. "Ready to go, buddy?"

"Coming mom!"

I hear him say goodbye to his cousin and then he comes to the door. My aunt and I say our goodbyes, and I make Jake thank her for today.

"How about a snack?" I ask, as he hurdles his way into the backseat – way too hyper for me.

"A snack sounds good!" he says. "Where are we going?"

"I'm thinking of maybe a pretzel at the ball field. What do you say?"

It's a nice day out, and football will be in full swing at the ballpark. Jake loves football. It's in his blood.

"Awesome!" Jake shouts from the back seat.

I promised I would let him play in a few years. I just can't stomach the thought of him on that field at his age. It's too dangerous.

We pay our dollar at the gate and Jake takes off toward the concession stand.

"Hiya, Jake!" says Mr. Crowley from behind the counter. "How ya doing, sport?"

"I'm good Mr. Crowley. How are you?" Jake asks, pulling up on his tiptoes, eyeing the candy bars on the counter display.

"I'm good son. Where's your momma?"

"Right here Mr. Crowley," I say, as I walk up. "It's good to see you again!"

Mr. Crowley lives in Bristol, but he's from Delia and is a big supporter of the high school Booster Club. He used to be at nearly every game, but I haven't seen him around in ages.

"Good to see you too, sweetheart! What'll you have?" Mr. Crowley has a nice smile.

"Two pretzels, I think?" I look down at Jake as he wistfully looks again at the candy on the counter. I shake my head "no" and he smiles. "Two pretzels," I say, answering my own question, "and two bottled waters."

"Comin' right up!" Mr. Crowley turns to get our order, and I turn to look out at the field.

This place brings back so many memories, ones that I'm always hesitant to dredge up, but I'm better about that now. It took me a couple of years, but the old saying is true: *Time heals all wounds.*

"Here ya go little lady! Ya'll enjoy the game!" Mr. Crowley hands both pretzels over to me, and I give Jake his, while grabbing the waters from the counter.

"See you later Mr. Crowley," I call back, as I chase after Jake who's already running to the bleachers.

Jake and I sit and enjoy our afternoon snack. Jake's enthralled with the game, asking questions every now and then about different plays. Sometimes I know the answers, and sometimes I don't, but Jake doesn't seem to mind. I'm happy to see the pretzel and water are doing the trick on his sugar rush from earlier.

I watch the game a bit, but mostly, I'm nostalgic. I look at the Junior Varsity cheerleaders on the sidelines and remember how it wasn't so long ago that I was wearing that outfit, freezing my butt off at the games. I never really liked being a cheerleader, but I liked the camaraderie. At the time, I thought we would all be friends forever. I was wrong.

Some of the girls are still here in Delia, and most of them are married now, or on their way to being married.

It's not like we meant to grow apart, but when you have to drop your future plans to start raising a baby at eighteen, it changes things, including your friendships.

I don't regret my path because it brought me to Jake, but I do miss some of my friends every once in a while.

Not a lot of people around here go to college. Most think of high school as their "glory days". Some would even give anything to go back.

I liked high school, but you couldn't pay me enough to do it all again. I'd rather believe my "glory days" are yet to come.

The final whistle after the fourth quarter pulls me from my train of thought. There's another game after this one, that I'm sure Jake would love to stay for, but I have to get going, if I'm going to make it to Sydney's by four.

"Ready baby?"

"Sure mom." I was right. Jake looks a little disappointed, but I know how to cheer him up.

"Guess what?" I ask him, as we walk back toward my car. "Grandma called and told me what you guys are doing tonight."

Jake's eyes get big. "What did she say?"

"Well, she told me she wanted me to keep it a surprise, so never mind." I love to tease him.

"Mom!" Jake's hanging from my arm now. "*Please* tell me!"

"Okay fine, but it's not that big of deal." I open the back door for Jake to get in.

"Mom!" he yells from the backseat.

"She just said it was..." I pause to sit in the front seat and then turn quickly to face Jake "...MOVIE NIGHT!!"

"Yes! Yes! *Yes*!!" Jake starts kicking his feet and raising his hands in the air.

He loves movie night with my mom. She makes super buttery popcorn, just like at the movies, and she even has these plastic red and white stripped containers that look like old-school popcorn boxes. She also puts up blankets over the windows to make it really dark in the living room, and she makes a huge palette on the floor with pillows and blankets to pile on.

Her television isn't anything special, but she always knows what movies to rent – thanks to a little help from me – and she and Jake will stay up and watch movies all night until he passes out. I'm not sure why he loves it so much, but he does. I remember loving it too when I was young, so I guess he gets it honest.

By the time we get back to the apartment, it's a little after three. I take a quick shower, while Jake packs up his stuff for tonight.

I don't bother with hair and make-up. I just throw on some sweats and sneakers to wear over to Sydney's house. As I pack my make-up and hair essentials, the idea of tonight really starts to kick in. My adrenaline is running high, and I can't stop smiling.

"Jake, are you ready?" I call to him, barely able to contain my excitement at this point.

Jake comes bustling out of his room, pulling on his hoodie as he walks.

"Ready!" He looks me up and down. "Mom, you're not going to the party like that, are you?"

I narrow my eyes at him. "No, Mr. Smarty Pants. I'm getting dressed at Sydney's, thank you very much."

Jake laughs. "Just making sure."

I put my arm around him and hustle him to the door, locking it behind me.

When we get to my mom's house, she's on the front porch, snapping green beans, but she looks like she's about to pack it up.

"I should've had your mom bring you by earlier, so I could put you to work!" my mom says to Jake, as we walk up.

Jake smiles and makes his way inside. I stop to grab one of her buckets and help her bring things in the house.

"So, tonight's the night, huh?" My mom playfully nudges my back as I walk ahead of her into the house.

"I guess so," I say, my excitement and anxiety threatening to take over at any minute.

"Don't be nervous now," my mom says, as if it were that easy. "Just be yourself. He'll love you."

I smile as I walk into the garage where we drop off the buckets of green beans and then head back into the house. Jake has already taken up residency at the kitchen table with his art supplies. I say goodbye to him and make my way back to the front door.

"I hate to drop him off and run, but I don't want to be late, as usual," I tell my mom.

She just smiles and follows me out. "You have fun now, and don't let Sydney get you gals into any trouble."

I smile back at her and walk toward my car. I turn once to see her watching me. I wave goodbye, and she stays on the porch until I drive away.

CHAPTER 5

I kissed Jake what probably felt to him like a hundred times before I left. Part of me is still feeling guilty for leaving him again and the other part was just nerves, trying to cling to something that makes me feel grounded.

I try to take some deep breaths on my way to Sydney's house, hoping to be feeling a little better by the time I get there.

As I pull in the driveway, I'm shocked to find I'm the first to arrive. I walk in the front door and see Sydney is already in full party mode, music blaring in the house and a glass of red wine in her hand.

"Hi Shelia!" I have to yell my greeting to Sydney's mom over the loud music.

Sydney still lives at home with her parents and probably will, until she gets married. That's what most girls do around here. Sydney dropped out of college about two months ago and came home. She's been in school for over three years, but claims she wasn't even close to graduating.

She's been working at the courthouse on and off since high school, and now it's permanent for her. But her main job these days is looking for a husband, preferably a rich one.

"Hi Sam!" Shelia yells back, moving her oversized hips to the music as she puts some appetizers on a plate in the kitchen.

Shelia is the ideal mom. Not that I have a thing against my own, but Shelia is one of those people that is born to be a mom. Her kids have never had to do a thing for themselves, which obviously has its disadvantages, but all three of them seem to have turned out okay.

Sydney notices my entrance then and goes to turn down the music a bit.

"I'm so excited you're here!" she squeals, coming over and nearly choking me with her hug.

Right about then, Liz and Rose walk in together, both carrying duffle bags and dressed almost exactly like me — sweats and sneakers, zero make-up and partially wet hair up on their heads.

After everyone gets the "hellos" out of the way, Shelia asks, "Who's first?"

Shelia is a hairdresser, and despite being from a small town, she manages to create fairly modern up-dos. Most of the hairdressers in this town think an up-do means prom hair, circa 1965.

"Me!" Sydney screams. "Me first!"

"Alright, hunny. Get in the chair."

Sydney sits down as the rest of us help ourselves to her bottle of wine.

"Are you guys nervous?" Rose asks. She obviously is, but it's coming off as excited. Mine is more like panic.

"Not too bad," Liz says.

Of course, Liz isn't nervous. No big surprise there.

"I'm a little nervous," Sydney speaks up, as her mom puts rollers in her hair. "I really like Scott, and I get butterflies whenever I see him."

We all "awww" appropriately at that sentiment. It's really cute, and very unlike Sydney to say something like that. She doesn't normally get all mushy over guys.

Everyone looks at me then, including Shelia, awaiting my response. I decide to be honest.

"I'm terrified, of course!"

I let out a huge gust of air that I feel like I've been holding since Sydney told us the news yesterday. It's good to get that off my chest.

"I know you are, Sam! You've been waiting for this for how long? A thousand years?" Shelia trills from her perch at Sydney's side.

I narrow my eyes at Sydney's sweet mother, briefly reconsidering my admiration of her earlier.

"T-Technically, only a few years," I stammer.

I've been crazy about Ethan for a long time, but the possibility of meeting him would have never crossed my mind until they started shooting his new show here in Delia. I will admit that the increased odds for meeting him haven't really changed the way I feel about him. I was as crazy for him in the beginning as I am for him now.

"Sam," Rose starts, "have you thought about what you'll do after tonight?"

"What do you mean?" I ask, as I take a sip of my wine.

"Well, you've been waiting all this time to meet him. If you finally get to meet him tonight, what happens then?"

I stare at Rose for a moment. She's stumped me. I've honestly never thought of anything past meeting him. Again, I have of course fantasized about an extravagant wedding at The Plaza in New York, with a honeymoon in Fiji. But as far as reality is concerned, I've never gotten past the "meet cute".

"I have no idea," I say finally, finishing off my glass of wine. "Probably move on to my next victim," I tease.

"Who's next?" Shelia calls, as Sydney gets up – her thick, blonde hair full of hot rollers – to get herself some more wine.

"I'll go!" Rose says as she makes her way to the chair.

"I'm going straight tonight, Shelia," Liz says. "I think it would be the best look for my dress, don't you guys?"

I smile. We all know she's only asking our opinion to be nice. Her mind is already made, so we know not to argue.

"I think that sounds perfect!" Sydney says excitedly.

"What about you, Sam?" Shelia asks, as she starts getting Rose in curlers. "Up or down?"

Thinking about hair styles makes me realize I haven't even tried on the dress. What if it doesn't fit? What if it doesn't look as good as I hoped? I suddenly can't picture myself in it, like I did in the store.

Liz pipes up. "The dress has a bare back, so I'm going with down...unless you disagree."

Once again, she added the end only to be nice, but I do agree that down would probably be best.

"How about partially up?" I ask Shelia, looking to Liz. She smiles in confirmation.

"I think that would look great!" Shelia says. "I already have something in mind!"

I get into Shelia's chair after Rose, and Shelia puts several rollers in my normally board-straight hair.

"I love your hair, Sam," she says, as she places the rollers precariously throughout my hair. "It's so healthy, and a gorgeous color. Don't ever let anyone tell you differently." Once she's finished, she puts a hair net over it to keep everything in place.

By the time I'm done, it's Sydney's turn to get her actual hairdo started. Liz, Rose and I sit at the kitchen table and snack on the appetizers Sydney's mom put out. I think again about how nice it is spending time with the girls. I find myself completely at ease after only a half hour in their company. I'm hoping that will last me through the rest of the evening.

We all watch as Shelia puts Sydney's hair in a beautiful up-do with soft tendrils hanging down around the sides and in the back. It makes Sydney look older than she is, which she always appreciates, but I also think it will look perfect with her petal pink dress.

Shelia gets to work on Rose next.

"So, you guys have to get me up to speed, in case anyone asks any questions tonight," Liz says.

She's never caught up with the show. She claims she never has much time to watch TV.

Sydney rolls her eyes, like this is blasphemy. "How much have you missed?"

Sydney is by far the biggest fan of the actual show. She never misses an episode and has seen most of them several times. I wouldn't be surprised if the filming is one of the reasons she dropped out of college.

"Um, I don't think I've seen any of season two yet," Liz admits.

Sydney nearly comes out of her chair at the table. "Liz! They are on episode *nine*! How are we supposed to get you up to speed after you've missed so much?" she whines, and Liz smiles at her.

Sydney starts giving Liz the play-by-play of the entire second season, and I look over at Rose. She and Shelia are having a full on conversation about the trouble they have with the men in their life. They are chatting with love though, as I know both of them are in awesome marriages.

Shelia actually married her high school sweetheart, which makes me think for a moment what would have happened if I would have married mine.

Luke wanted to go into the military after high school, and he was a lot like Liz. Once he made up his mind, there was no changing it.

He said it would be the best thing for us, and the only way he could provide for his family. Luke was a football player, not a bookworm, so he was probably right. However, I knew he was just trying to run away, and I was angry that I couldn't talk him out of it. I basically told him not to bother coming back. I haven't seen or heard much from him since. I guess I was right about the running away part.

Luke's parents still live in town, and they see Jake from time to time. I know they talk to Luke and send pictures, which is fine with me. I told them, in the politest way possible, that I want nothing to do with their son. They never say a thing about him to me, and I know it's better that way.

Luke hasn't been home since he left. He's never even met Jake, but Jake knows who he is from the pictures his grandparents show him, and the stories I tell. For now, Jake doesn't seem too upset about not having a man in his life. I do worry some about the pre-teen years, but I guess we'll just cross that bridge when we come to it.

I will admit I think about Luke at times, wondering where he's sleeping at night in the dessert or worried that he may get hurt – not because I still have feelings for him, but he is Jake's father. I hope Jake can meet him someday.

"You ready?" Shelia calls to me, after she's done with Rose's hair.

I take an appraising look at Rose's do as I walk over to the chair. It's completely different from Sydney's, but just as pretty. It's all up, but a little looser than Sydney's – just a bunch of red curls sitting atop Rose's head, and it suits her perfectly.

"I love it!" I tell Rose, as she walks by.

"Thanks!" she says and walks over to sit with the other two at the table.

I see Liz has gotten the straight iron out and is running it down her short black locks. Her hair is already board-straight like mine, but the iron does give it a silky sheen.

I sit down in the chair and Shelia starts in immediately. "So, half up, right?"

I take a few minutes to try and explain the dress to Shelia, but Sydney goes and grabs it from the door it was hanging on to show her mom.

"Oooo la la!" Shelia fans herself with her comb when she sees the dress. "You're going to look irresistible, Sam!"

I smile. *That's exactly what I'm going for.*

I sit and listen to Sydney and her mom prattle on about the dresses, while Shelia works to get my hair up. She's moving so fast, having been a hairdresser all of her life; it's like second nature to her now. She has it up and done in less than thirty minutes, which is good because we now have exactly twenty minutes before the limo arrives. Luckily we all did our make-up at the kitchen table while waiting for each other's hair to get done.

"Dresses!" Sydney shouts, as I look at my hair in the mirror. Shelia pulled up just the sides of my hair with a few curls arranged unkempt on the back of my head. She left a couple of loose tendrils to frame my face, and the rest falls into soft, dark-brown waves down my back. I love it.

We all rush up and move toward Sydney's room for changing. I'm the last to put my dress on, afraid I may start sweating from nerves and mess it up.

When we're all finally dressed and accessorized, we stop and stand side by side in front of Sydney's very own three-way mirror. Sydney still has a three way mirror in her room from her pageant days, which ended up coming in rather handy this evening.

We all smile as we take turns looking at each other.

I think Sydney looks gorgeous, as usual. Her body fits perfectly in her dress and the accessories ended up coming together very well.

Rose and Liz look great too. Rose looks beautiful and very unlike the everyday Sheriff's assistant we're all used to hanging out with. Liz looks severe in her black dress and jet black hair hanging crisp at her shoulders. She chose heavy rhinestone jewelry that only Liz can pull off.

I'm afraid to look, but when I finally find my own eyes in the mirror, I'm shocked.

"Wow," Liz says quietly, as she catches me staring at myself.

I see the other girls smiling at me too from the corner of my eye, but I can't look at them. I'm temporarily stunned.

The dress fits me perfectly. The deep purple satin and chiffon flows over my body like water running over smooth rock. Lucky for me, my skin looks flawless tonight, and my red lips bring color to my normally pale face. The smoky eyeliner – courtesy of Sydney – makes my blue eyes come to life, and my long dark waves are cascading gently down my back. I feel elegant and for the first time ever, I feel like I could give Liz's confidence a run for its money.

A car horn pulls us all from our trance.

"He's here! Let's go ladies!" Sydney shouts.

We all run into the living room, our excitement fueling us now.

Sydney has several mink stoles, satin trenches and muffs for us to choose from, all collected through her years of pageantry. We each grab something from the pile Shelia's created on the couch.

I decide on a simple black satin trench coat that buttons down the front. It probably won't be the warmest coat ever, but my adrenaline is doing an excellent job of keeping me warm at the moment.

We all say our "good byes" and "thank yous" to Shelia as we head for the car.

"Pictures!" Shelia suddenly yells as we were making our way into the shiny, black stretch limo currently parked on the street in front of Sydney's house.

We all stop, as someone gets out of the passenger's side of the limo. I can only assume it's Scott, and my suspicions are confirmed when he goes directly to Sydney and plants a kiss on her full, powder pink lips.

Sydney's grinning from ear to ear when Scott finally releases her, and I can instantly tell she must really like him. She would normally never stand for any man smearing her lipstick like that.

"I didn't think you were coming!" she says excitedly to Scott. "What a great surprise!"

"I was able to sneak away," he says, stealing another kiss, "but I probably won't be able to see you home. I hope that's okay."

Sydney looks disappointed at the possibility of losing time with him, but she quickly starts smiling again. We're all excited for tonight.

"Say *cheese!*" Shelia yells as we all crowd into each other for the picture. Scott moves aside to let us girls have our photo op. "Now I want to get a shot of you guys inside the car, okay?"

We all shuffle into the limo, and as we take our seats, Shelia leans in and gets a picture of us.

"Have a great time girls!" she says as Scott closes the car door.

"This.Is.*Incredible!*" Sydney squeals once we start moving.

Scott is riding in the passenger's seat upfront, but he lets the partition down so he can chat with us – and probably so he can gawk at Sydney.

"Scott, thank you *so* much for this!" Sydney tells him.

"You ladies look very nice," Scott says from the front seat, with a very charming smile, and eyes only for Sydney.

He isn't the typical, devastatingly handsome type that Sydney normally prefers, but he's still a very nice looking man. He must be at least six feet, with light brown shaggy hair that hangs in his blue eyes. He looks very uncomfortable in his tux, which makes me like him instantly.

"Oh my God! I forgot to introduce you!" I smile at Sydney because she looks genuinely mortified at her social blunder. "Scott, this is Liz, Rose and Sam," she says, gesturing at each of us in turn. "Ladies, this is Scott."

"It's very nice to meet you," Scott says, oozing southern charm. There's nothing better than a southern gentleman, if you ask me.

"Nice to meet you," Liz says, used to introductions.

She's probably the only one of us who has ever been in a limo before, but she doesn't say a word. I can tell she's excited about tonight too.

Rose and I just smile at Scott, both probably too nervous and overwhelmed still by all of this. I know I am.

Scott turns to chat with the driver for a bit, and we all start giving each other smiles and wide-eyed stares, privately sharing the awesomeness of the situation.

"So, Sam," Sydney looks at me like she has the most important news ever, "you look absolutely fabulous, by the way!"

"Thanks," I say blushing.

"But I wanted to ask," she continues, with a wave of her hand. "Do you know what you plan to say to him when you meet him, other than your crazy nice-to-meet-you speech?"

I narrow my eyes at Sydney, but we're both still smiling. "No," I admit truthfully, "I have no idea."

Sydney looks appalled. "You're kidding, right? I mean, this is a once in a lifetime opportunity, Sam! You have to be prepared!"

"Agreed," Liz chimes in. "You should profess your love to him immediately, so he can take you in his arms and you guys can elope in Vegas."

"I don't think so," I say to Liz, smiling, but eager to end the conversation.

"Who are we talking about?" someone asks from the front seat, and I'm startled by the deep voice.

I had no idea Scott was listening. My back was to the partition, so he could have been listening the entire time. How embarrassing!

"Ooooo," Sydney is eager to tell the story, and it all spills out before anyone can stop her, "Sam is in love with Ethan Grant from

Stephen's Room! We're trying to make sure she knows exactly what to say when she meets him."

I suddenly feel the need to explain myself to Scott. "They're just joking around," I say, with as much nonchalance as I can manage. "I do like him, but it's just a little celebrity crush, you know?"

Scott winks at me. "Sure thing," he says. He's very laid back, another characteristic I like about him. "You guys are fangirls. I get it."

We all chuckle a little at his remark. It's true, even if some of us are a little old for that sort of thing.

Atlanta is about an hour away, so we have plenty of time to chat and keep our excitement up before we get to the event. Plus, Scott was kind enough to provide a bottle of chilled champagne in the back for us. That effectively helps take the edge off, but when Scott announces we're minutes away from the venue, my stomach immediately starts turning into knots. I'm hoping I can keep my champagne down. I certainly don't want to ruin this dress.

"It's time to reapply!" Sydney calls out, as she grabs her lipstick from her small pink clutch that matches her dress perfectly.

On cue, each of us grab our bags as well and do the same.

"You ladies ready for some fun?" Scott asks from the front seat.

The limo is moving slowly now, but I can't really see any traffic around us. I turn to look through the partition out the front window, and that's when I see it.

"Are we walking down a red carpet?" My voice is shaking. The other girls seem excited by the idea. I suddenly feel like vomiting is imminent.

"Star treatment!" Scott says with excitement. He thinks he's doing us a favor. Little does he know I have on five-inch heels.

"How exciting! I had no idea!" Sydney is beside herself. She's probably been waiting for this her entire life.

The limo finally pulls up to the walkway, and Scott gets out to open the door. Liz is the first one out, and I see all of the flashes go off. Liz does look like she could be someone important. I'm eager to see the reaction to Rose. She's the next one out of the limo.

To my surprise, there are just as many flashes for Rose. I turn and motion for Sydney to go. She eagerly accepts, and I look quickly back around at the driver, wondering if I can bribe him to take me to some bar close by where I can sit this out.

Liz pokes her head back in the car. "Get out of the car, Sam," she says in her serious lawyer voice.

She's smiling, but something about the tone of her voice tells me I should probably listen to her. I close my eyes and say a quick prayer before I finally put my foot onto the pavement. Scott's there to help me out, and the cameras start going crazy again. The strange part is that they don't stop until we get to the door.

"Good grief at the cameras!" Rose says when we finally enter the conference center. "I thought I may go blind!"

We're all smiling again from the sheer adrenaline of the situation. "I know!" I agree. "I thought it would stop once they figured out we were 'nobodies'."

Sydney walks up behind me with Scott on her arm. "Silly girls," she says, like she does this sort of thing all of the time. "You wouldn't be here if you were a 'nobody'." Then she winks at me.

Ugh. Why don't I have just an ounce of that confidence?

"Follow me ladies," Scott says, with just as much confidence, although, he *does* do this sort of thing all of the time. "And you will need these." Scott reaches into his coat pocket and holds out four badges on strings. "You don't have to wear them, but make sure to keep them on you at all times. There's a lot of security and they may be doing random checks."

We each take our badges and hold them with death grips as we follow Scott to the right and up an incredibly long escalator that leads to a huge lobby area. There's security at the bottom of the escalator, as well as the top.

The lobby area is blocked off by large black partitions at the top of the stairs, and there's a small entrance in the middle, where we have to show our badges one more time.

As we walk into the lobby, we're all a little breathless. To say that this is the most exhilarating thing I've ever done would be an understatement.

The lobby is gorgeous, filled with buffet tables beautifully catered and draped in platinum bunting. There are waiters in tails carrying champagne flutes around for the guests, and there are four bars open in each corner. The room is lit mainly by candles and dim lighting from the chandeliers – just beautiful.

"This way, ladies." Scott grabs Sydney's hand and leads the way.

We follow him to one of the bars in the far left corner. There are only a couple of people in line, so we chat a bit while we wait our turn.

"Trent, these ladies are my personal guests tonight," Scott says to the bartender as we approach. "Take care of them for me, okay?"

Trent – one of many gorgeous people in this place – smiles and nods. "You got it, Scott," he says, with a lovely British accent. Wow. Even better.

"I have to go check on some things, okay?" Scott says to Sydney before he leaves. "I'll find you later." He leans over and gives her a very tender kiss. Liz, Rose and I roll our eyes in unison.

While Sydney and her puppy dog eyes watch Scott leave, I push my way up to the bar. "Vodka Cranberry," I say, hoping liquor is the answer I need.

"Going for the hard stuff tonight Sam?" Liz asks with a smile.

"Might as well," I reply. I'm going to need it if I have any chance of getting up the nerve to even be in the same room as my celebrity crush.

We all get our drinks and turn toward the crowd. "What now?" Rose asks, appropriately. I shrug, scanning the room for any sign of him. So far, no luck.

"I think we should mingle." Sydney says. "I see James Royce not even twenty feet away! I'm going to talk to him." And like that, she's gone.

Liz, Rose and I stay put and watch her walk up to him like she's just as important.

"How does she do that?" Rose looks exasperated, and I share her feelings. "He's one of the biggest directors on the YA Network!"

"She's Sydney." Liz offers.

I watch Sydney work her magic for a moment before turning to Liz with a challenging smile.

"So Liz," I start, honestly trying to make some conversation to keep my mind off the fact that he's definitely not here yet. "See anything you like?"

Liz answers my challenge with a devious grin. "Not yet, but I'm sure I can find something by the end of the night."

I've known Liz for over four years now, and I'm not sure if she's ever been on a date since she's lived in Delia. She's completely tight lipped about her love life, and nobody dares question her about it. She's made a few comments to us girls about a couple of men from her past, but best I can tell she's currently single. With Liz, you just never know.

"Umm, Sam?" Rose is suddenly tugging painfully on my arm. "He's here."

"What?" I say quietly as I scan the crowd. Unable to find him, I look at Rose, trying to follow her line of sight.

As I'm still trying to zero in, Sydney comes bustling over to us, acting like a thirteen year old at a Justin Beiber concert.

"He's here!" she nearly shouts.

We're still standing in close proximity to pretty Trent at the bar. I look over to see if he heard her, but he's flirting with some blonde who looks like someone famous, but I can't take the time to be sure. I'm too interested in finding *him*.

"Where?" I say flustered because everyone is seeing him now but me.

"Right there!" Sydney starts pointing furiously, and I quickly grab at her arm trying to make her stop.

Finally, I see him – all 6'2" inches of him. There's no denying the fact that the man is beautiful. He has on a black tux with a straight black tie and white shirt. His typically shaggy brown hair is perfectly coifed for this formal event, and I can see his light green eyes shining from across the room. We watch as he starts talking to some dark haired man who currently has his back to us.

"Are you going to talk to him?" Sydney asks, looking at me like she knows I've already lost my nerve.

"I'm going to have to work up to that." I say, voice shaking, but unable to peel my eyes away.

Suddenly, Scott shows up behind Sydney, out of nowhere.

"Ladies…" he says, scaring Rose and me who are still transfixed on a certain celebrity in the room. "How are we doing?"

"We just noticed that Ethan's here!" Sydney tells him. "I'm trying to get Sam to go talk to him!"

"Do you want me to introduce you?" Scott asks.

"Yes! Let Scott do the introduction!" Sydney begs.

The other two look at Sydney, and then at me. They can tell I'm not ready, and besides, that isn't how it's supposed to happen. I'm supposed to introduce myself. Of course, that's in "Fantasyland" where I apparently have oodles more confidence than I do in reality.

"Not right now," I say, feeling the sweat start to pool up under my arms. "Maybe later on?"

I'm so embarrassed. It's one thing for my close girlfriends to know about my obsession, but Scott is a stranger — a stranger who deals with celebrities all the time. He probably thinks I'm a complete nut case.

"Okay then," he says, seemingly not even noticing my panic, "I'll see you guys in a few minutes when we get ushered into the ballroom. Enjoy your drinks!" Scott gives Sydney another kiss before disappearing into the crowd.

I make my way over to a high top table near where we're standing. I put my purse and drink down on the table, and place both hands on the table's edge. I close my eyes and take a deep breath. I feel woozy, but I'm going to get a grip on myself if it kills me.

"Are you okay?" Rose is always worried.

I open my eyes slowly and look up at her. "I feel stupid, Rose."

"Why do you feel stupid?" Liz asks, her voice reeking with authority.

"This crush? This obsession? It makes me feel ridiculous!" I try to explain, but I don't want to get too upset and ruin my make-up.

We still have the whole night ahead of us, and the only thing I could fit in my small purse besides my cell phone, ID and money was a tube of red lipstick.

"Look at me," Liz commands. "You are not ridiculous. I don't think you're obsession — if you want to call it that — is crazy at all."

"You don't?" I look up at her, eager to believe.

"No. No, I don't," she says, her voice very calm, almost hypnotic. "Maybe it's not typical, but that doesn't make it wrong, Sam." She pauses looking over at the object of my affection for a moment before turning back to me. "Who cares if you lust over some guy you've never met? Millions of girls in America are doing the same thing right now."

I look down at my hands still gripping the sides of the table. She's lumping me in with the rest of the crazy fangirl population — the kind that scream and cry when they see their favorite celebrity in concert or at some cheesy autograph session at the mall.

As if sensing where my thoughts were heading, Liz goes on.

"But you know why you're different than the rest of them?"

"No," I answer honestly, now staring at the swirly pattern on the carpet.

Liz startles me by lifting my chin, forcing me to face her. "Because you're beautiful," she says. "You have poise and intelligence. You're an excellent mother and a genuinely wonderful person to know."

Liz is not helping keep my make-up intact with her sappy speech. Plus, it's very unlike her.

"And most importantly," she continues on. "You have tonight.

Sydney's right. This is a once in a lifetime opportunity, and you shouldn't waste it."

Well, she can win over a crowd, that's for sure. Both Rose and Sydney's eyes are misty, as well as mine. Liz is good.

"You're right," I say, with some conviction now. "I'm talking to him tonight, no matter what."

Sydney puts her arm around my waist. "He didn't bring a date tonight, so you could potentially do more than *talk* with him, huh?" she says with a wink.

I laugh and push her playfully away from me. I grab my drink as the light blinks above us; I assume signaling us to move into the ballroom.

"You never know," I say with a smirk on my face. "You just never know."

CHAPTER 6

Scott is at Sydney's side shortly after the first signal, letting us know the show is about to start.

"Come on," he says. "I'll show you to your table."

Scott leads the way, and I suddenly feel woozy again. I close my eyes briefly, trying to will away the unwelcome dizziness, when all of a sudden I hear a voice come over what sounds like a loud speaker. Strange.

"Mr. Spovak," it pages. "Please come to the lobby. Mr. Spovak, to the lobby."

"Who's Mr. Spovak, I wonder." I say to Rose as the voice cuts off and we walk into the ballroom. "Is a celebrity lost or something?"

The name sounds vaguely familiar, but my TV watching has decreased dramatically over the past few years.

"Mr. Spovak?" Rose asks, barely paying attention to me as she looks excitedly around at all of the famous faces.

"You didn't hear that page?" I ask, still trying to place where I know the name from.

Rose turns to laugh at something Liz is saying, and then turns back to me. "I must not have been paying attention," she says. "Liz and I were gawking at the two guys over there from that show, *L.A. Lawyers*! This is so exciting!"

I have no idea who Rose is referring to, so I just smile at her as we walk to our table. I'm happy to see her having such a good time.

As we get closer to the table, I notice a man at the podium on stage. He requests that a Mr. Spovak go to the lobby again, and a tall man comes rushing past us out the front doors of the ballroom.

"That was Chuck Spovak!" Sydney squeals as he hurries by. "Scott just told me they found his cell phone out front."

I smile at Sydney. I still have no idea who this guy is, but I'm glad to make sense of it all and glad my woozy feeling has finally passed.

I lost sight of Ethan after my near breakdown in the lobby, but that's okay. I'll find him again, and I *will* talk to him tonight. I have drink in hand, and there's wine on the tables. I should be full of confidence by the time this thing is over.

We sit down at our round table, and I'm ashamed I don't recognize anyone sitting with us. They're apparently famous because Sydney is salivating, but I have no idea who they are. It seems I need to brush up on my Hollywood education.

I'm really not much of a TV watcher any more. Jake and work take up most of my time these days, but I do like the occasional movie and I watch a few TV shows – nothing on a regular basis, except the obvious, of course.

That's what happens when you're a single parent. The only time I have to watch TV is at night after Jake goes to bed, and I'm normally so tired by then, I can barely keep my eyes open to watch my favorites.

I can always watch Ethan though. I have no problem staying awake for him.

As Rose and Liz become involved in conversations with two of the people sitting at our table – Rose informed me earlier that they are actors in one of the night time police/investigator dramas – I take a moment to scan the room again hoping I can find him.

Suddenly, Scott pops up behind me. He leans down and whispers in my ear, "Two tables up and to the left."

"Thanks," I mouth to him as he walks away. I'm really starting to like Scott.

And there he is, smiling broadly, looking like a million bucks. Now that I know where he's seated I'm wondering how I'll keep my eyes off of him all night. It will be hard not to look. He's less than twenty yards away.

Stop acting like a freak! I tell myself. *He's just a person too!*

I look at my friends, occupying our table guests and think for a second how crazy I really am about this guy. I'm having ridiculous fantasies, about some guy I've never even met! He could be a complete asshole — and he probably is, since most people do think of him that way. What am I thinking?! He's just a guy — a beautiful, god-like creature with emerald green eyes, but at the end of the day, just a guy!

The two second conversation in my head seems to do the trick for temporarily talking me off the ledge. As I grab for the bottle of wine to fill my glass, like everyone else has already done, I vow that after tonight, this is definitely over. I'm done worshipping the untouchable.

There is obviously some void I'm not filling in my life to make me sink to this level of immaturity, and I plan to fix it. A.S.A.P.

Rose looks over at me then and smiles. "That's Guy Rivers!" she says, pointing to some blonde man at the table across from us, like I should know who he is.

I just smile and give a look like I can't believe it either, then I take a big gulp of wine — not a very classy move, but who do I have to impress?

"Are you okay?" Rose asks. "You look a little frazzled."

"Totally fine," I say, taking another unladylike gulp of wine.

The lights dim then, and the MC for the evening — another celebrity that everyone is ogling over, but only looks vaguely familiar to me — comes to the podium to start the event. Rose turns her attention from me to the stage.

Thank you celebrity I don't recognize! You just saved me!

I gladly watch the presentation – and pick at my dinner – while my friends continue to flirt with the celebrities at our table. Maybe it's the alcohol – or possibly the adorable videos of some baby pandas in China – but by the end of the evening, I'm so sold on the foundation that I make a mental note to look them up online when I get home so I can get involved.

"Time to reapply!" a rather loopy Sydney says, after we finish our dessert.

She grabs her bag and I go to grab mine so I can recharge my lips as well. That's when I notice my bag is missing.

Even with all of the wine, I start to completely freak out. I instantly have that empty stomach feeling you get when something like this happens. I have no idea where I left it, and unfortunately, my slightly sloshed friends aren't much help.

"Did you have it when you came in?" Liz asks.

I try to think. I honestly can't remember. The last time I remember having it was in the limo when I reapplied with the rest of the girls before we got here. I may have left it in the car.

"Sydney, where's Scott?" I ask hurriedly. Even though it's a small bag with very little inside, I feel naked without it. "I think I may have left my bag in the car."

"I think you brought it in Sam," Rose speaks up. "I think I remember seeing you with it inside."

"Either way, I should probably check both," I say, getting ready to move as soon as Sydney hears back from Scott.

Sydney looks up at me after a couple of minutes. "I texted him," she says. "He's on his way over."

Scott is there in a flash. "What's going on?" he asks, seeming genuinely concerned.

"I think I may have left my purse in the limo," I tell him, "but I'm not sure. Is there any way to check?"

Scott stops to think for a second, "Let's see," he pauses and looks at his watch. "Trevor should actually be out front by now waiting. I can call him, if you'd like."

"It's okay," I say, already getting up. "I'll just go down there. I want to look around in here as well. I'm not sure where I could have left it."

"Just let me call security." Scott obviously doesn't want me to go through any trouble, but I actually feel like I could use the break.

"It's okay, really," I assure him. "I'll talk to one of them outside. I'm sure I'll find it."

Scott smiles and nods, already busy again, paying attention now to whoever is talking into the small earpiece in his ear.

Honestly, I'm not sure why anyone at this party would want my five year old cell phone, ID, Mary Kay lipstick and $40. I'm sure most people here would probably throw it in the trash before they would take it home.

"Do you want me to come with you?" Liz asks, grabbing my arm as I walk from the table.

"No, I'm fine," I say. "I'll be back soon."

The truth is I'm not fine.

Ethan left almost a half hour ago. I watched him stand up from his table and walk quietly out the door, taking my once in a lifetime opportunity with him. Rose and Liz saw it too, and they both gave me the I'm-so-sorry-girlfriend face, but they quickly resumed their conversations with their new celebrity table buddies. I think Liz is hitting it off with the tall, dark and handsome one.

I start walking quickly to the doors, suddenly needing to get out of the room. I make it through one set of double doors and go directly through the lobby and down the escalators, not even stopping to chat with security about my lost purse. I feel sure I left it in the limo for some reason, but my head is swimming from the wine. Maybe I just need some fresh air.

I get downstairs and walk outside into the November evening. It's freezing — an unwelcome and rather sobering experience.

I quickly walk back inside, cursing myself for not remembering it's November before I walked outside in a sleeveless satin gown. How stupid. I should have gotten my coat from coat check before coming downstairs.

That's when I realize my purse is not in the car. I checked my coat and put the ticket inside my purse, so it has to be inside. I smile, mainly relieved I don't have to go back into the cold again, and I start my walk/run back to the escalators. I'm definitely starting to feel my five-inch heels.

I finally get back to the escalators, eager to get back upstairs, but I'm stopped by security.

Oh no. My badge. It's in my elusive purse.

I try frantically to explain the situation to the security guard, but he keeps giving me a you-have-to-be-kidding-me look. I'm screwed.

"Didn't you see me just come down the stairs?" I ask. *You were standing right here!*

"I didn't see a thing," he says calmly to me, like that's some protocol way to handle crazy people.

"Scott..." I pause because I have no idea what his last name is, "Umm...Scott with WWF, he invited us. If you could just call him, he could clear this up." At this point, I'm begging.

"Miss, unless you have a pass, I cannot let you in. Those are the rules."

I can tell the guard is losing patience, and I'm not sure how much more of my sob story he'll take.

I don't know if it's the alcohol or me finally releasing the stress of my adrenaline high, but I suddenly start crying. "Please," I beg again. "I lost my purse, and my badge was in there. Has someone turned a purse in tonight? If so, my ID would be in there, and we could verify everything."

The not-so-nice guard radios another not-so-nice guard, who let him know that nothing has been turned in tonight, which roughly translates into "you're shit out of luck".

"I am sorry Miss," the guard says, with barely a touch of feeling there. "The show's almost over anyway. You don't have long to wait."

I can't imagine how I appear to him now. Obviously not a

celebrity, he probably thinks I'm just your average mooch that he runs in to all the time at functions like this. The sad part is that he isn't far off, but I do think I look respectable enough in my new dress. It's inexcusable for him not to let me back in. Wait until I tell Liz about this!

I step away from him, feeling utterly defeated. I have no idea what to do. I have no cell phone, and it's unlikely my friends will come looking for me any time soon. I'll just have to sit down here and wait for the event to end. Hopefully, Scott can get my coat back.

"Where's the restroom?" I ask the guard as I walk away.

"Down the hall there, on your right." He points in the direction, eyeing me suspiciously.

Maybe he thinks I'm trying to lure him away from his post so I can sneak upstairs. It's not a bad idea, but I'm not cunning enough for that, and I've had way too many glasses of wine.

I sigh and make my way to the ladies room. It's a big bathroom, and I take up residence at the nearest sink.

Thankfully my face is still in pretty good shape, even after the short crying stint with the security guard. I could use a little more lipstick, but other than that, I'm not a total disaster. The wine and adrenaline are actually giving my cheeks some great color.

I'm about to turn and leave, when out of nowhere I hear a muffled "Help!", as someone bursts into the door of the ladies room.

Surprisingly, the cry for help doesn't startle me as much as the actual voice. It's a man's voice. In the ladies room. This should be interesting.

The figure is a blur in my mirror as he runs past. I turn around only to catch a glimpse of a suit jacket flying into a stall and locking the door. Shortly after the door lock clicks, a crazed looking young girl flies into the restroom.

"Hi!" she says, frantically looking around and immediately bends over and starts looking under stalls.

"Hi," I repeat, a lot less enthusiastic, but I feel obligated to help whoever is in the stall. "I assume you're looking for someone?"

I have no idea who has come into the bathroom, but I'm smart enough to deduct it's a celebrity and he's being chased. I regularly stalk a film set. I've seen it all.

"Did you see him?" The girl takes a break from bending over and checking in stalls to turn her crazy eyes on me.

"No one in here in but me. Sorry, hun." I frown at her, feigning disappointed. "Maybe the men's room?"

"Crap!" she yells, and flies out of the bathroom, her jean jacket and all of her badly permed hair chasing wildly behind her. Oddly enough, she reminds me of a good friend from middle school, which makes me smile.

I wait a few seconds for my mystery guest to come out, but he seems to be making double sure he isn't going to run into his "fan" again.

"I think you're good." I try to sound as calm as possible. For all he knows, I may react exactly like that girl when I see him. Lucky for him, the odds are in his favor, considering I'm not as hip to Hollywood as most.

Finally, I hear him jump down off the toilet seat he's been perched on and then click open the lock. I keep my post at the sink, waiting for him to reveal himself, thinking mournfully about how badly my feet are killing me.

"Thanks for that," he says, before he makes it completely out of the stall, and I don't have to see him to know who's behind the door. I would recognize that voice from anywhere.

When he fully emerges, I see he looks absolutely terrified. It's adorable and endearing and my heart immediately starts racing.

"No problem," I say, trying to act casual, praying I'm pulling it off.

He pauses and eyes me up and down. It should probably make me uncomfortable, but instead I feel my body heat up as his green eyes appraise me.

"Well, I better head back up," he says, after clearing his throat.

He suddenly looks embarrassed and extremely awkward, like he just realized he was standing in a ladies room.

I'm not sure where this next hit of confidence comes from, but I decide to go with it.

"Could I ask a favor?" I say, stopping him as he walks out the door.

He turns back to me. "I guess I owe you that." His smile is electrifying.

"Please don't think I'm crazy, but I've lost my purse," I tell him, and it all starts coming out in a rush. I want to make sure he believes me, since I had such bad luck with the security guard, but I probably sound like an idiot. "And I can't find it, and my badge is inside, and the security guard won't let me back upstairs, and I don't have my cell, so I can't call my friends, and--"

"I can get you back up there," he says, thankfully interrupting me.

"You believe me?" I'm not sure why I ask him this. It probably does little for my defense, but I'm still feeling pretty defeated by the rent-a-cop.

Ethan continues to smile, which is making me feel all warm and toasty on the inside. "I remember seeing you earlier."

He saw me? Wait. What?

"Oh." I have no other response, so I just smile too, once again, probably looking like a total idiot.

"Shall we?" Ethan hangs his elbow out for me to grab onto, and I start to wonder if I'm dreaming.

I continue to smile, as he walks slowly out of the bathroom, checking both ways. Once he's convinced the road is clear, we make our way toward the escalators.

"I feel like I've seen you before," he says casually, as we walk. "I know that sounds like a terrible line, but I'm being honest. Have we met before?"

The only time I've ever seen him is on set, but I'm positive he's never seen me.

I'm also fairly confident it's too soon to tell him I'm somewhat of a stalker, so I decide to go with a lie.

"No. I'm pretty sure we've never met before," I say. It's not a *total* lie.

I can't help but look a little smug as we approach the security guard at the bottom of the escalators. *You gonna turn me away now?* I ask him with my eyes. He doesn't seem amused.

Ethan shows no badge of any kind, or identification at all for that matter. He acts like he doesn't even see the guard standing there.

"You do look familiar though. I'll figure it out," Ethan continues, as we step onto the escalator.

I notice his eyes are fierce, like he's daring me to refute him. It's obviously not just rumors. The guy is intense. I find it a little frightening, and completely sexy.

"That's a great dress," he adds, as we approach the top of the escalators.

"Thanks."

I'm not about to tell him it's borrowed. This is turning into a

Cinderella evening for sure.

"So what were you doing downstairs?" I ask, eager to keep up conversation.

"Just needed a break," he says without looking at me. Then, he slides his arm out from mine and reaches for something in his front pants pocket. It's lip balm. I look away as he applies it, afraid of getting too wrapped up in his lips.

He smiles and offers me some when he's done.

I'm tempted, but only because I want my lips to be where his were.

"No thanks." I smile, once again not wanting to give in to my "crazy".

"I guess we should get back inside," I add, as we approach the doors. I don't want to leave him, of course, but he doesn't seem overly interested in conversation.

He nods in agreement, but his face is torn. He doesn't say anything further, so I walk ahead of him, and I'm about to reach the door, when he suddenly grabs my elbow.

"Wait," he says, and I turn back to him. "Actually, do you want to have a drink?"

"Sure." I answer too quickly, but I'm obviously elated by the thought of spending more time with him, even though so far he doesn't seem like "Mr. Personality".

"I wouldn't normally do something like this," he says, leading me toward our earlier bartender, Trent. "It's been a crazy week, and I could use the company, if you don't mind. You're not in the business, are you?"

I shake my head, assuming he means the entertainment industry.

"No. I'm here as a guest of a friend," I tell him. "He's with the WWF."

"That's good. Even better."

I'm surprised to see Ethan's eyeing me in a very speculative way. I guess he's still trying to work out where he remembers seeing me before. I kind of hope it's not on set. When I'm stalking, out in my regular clothes, in my town, with my friends, it doesn't seem as bad. But here, in this setting, with him, in this dress, it feels different. I'm embarrassed by my little obsession, like I probably should have been all along.

"What would you like?" he asks as we approach the bar, but Trent answers before I can.

"Vodka Cranberry," he says in his delicious accent, but it's rather flat. Honestly, he looks kind of irritated.

Ethan turns his eyes back to me for confirmation, and I nod and smile.

When we get our drinks — Ethan ordered Crown Royal on the rocks — we head over to the same table the girls and I were perched at earlier.

"Did you ask security if anyone turned your purse in?" Ethan asks, taking down nearly half of his drink in one shot.

Ethan is definitely very serious. I feel the sudden urge to tickle him or something to loosen him up.

"Yes," I say with a sigh. "They said they haven't seen anything."

"That's too bad," Ethan replies, seeming interested in our conversation but far away at the same time. "Did you need to use a phone or something?"

I smile because it's very nice of him to ask. I actually do want to check on Jake. I was just going to use a friend's phone in the limo.

"That would be great," I say, and he hands me his phone from his inside jacket pocket. It smells like him.

"Thanks," I say again while dialing, and then I manage a discreet sniff of his phone as I pull it to my ear. Crazy? Yes, but so worth it.

I already know my mom won't answer, because she won't recognize the number. When her voicemail picks up, I leave a quick message.

"Hey mom, it's me. I just wanted to check on you guys and let you know that I lost my purse and my cell. If you need me, just call one of the girls. Love you."

I quickly hang up and return his phone. He smiles at me, and at first I thought he wasn't going to ask. I was wrong.

"You still have to check in with your parents?" He's smiling, but I can tell he's genuinely curious.

"Yes," I say with the straightest possible face, "but they're letting me stay out past curfew tonight...special occasion and all."

"Good to know," he says with a wry smile. "Seriously, is everything okay?"

I look at him for a moment, trying to figure out if he's really interested, or just harassing me. Either way, I decide I don't mind.

"I have a son," I tell him, always happy to brag about Jake. "He's staying with my mom tonight, and I wanted to let her know about my phone." I could have dreamed it, but I swear he just took a quick look at my left ring finger.

"How old is he?"

"Eight." I sit there, waiting for him to do the math, although he has no idea how old I am, and I'm sure I could pass for at least thirty in this get-up.

"Please don't take this the wrong way, but you do not look old enough to have an eight year old."

"I guess I'm not really, but I have one," I say smiling. Okay, so maybe I don't look thirty. Of course I don't take offense to this.

"What's his name?"

"Jake."

"I like it," he says, right before we hear a roar of laughter coming from the ballroom. It's a harsh reminder for me that other people exist on the planet other than him and me at the moment.

"Should we go back inside?" I ask, still not wanting to leave, but also not foolish enough to think this won't eventually have to end anyway.

I can see Ethan doesn't want to go back, but I'm certain it's not for the same reasons I don't want to go.

"I guess," he says, chugging the rest of his drink. I leave mine on the table. I've had enough for tonight, and no amount of alcohol can take away the pain these shoes are inflicting, so why bother?

"Excuse me? Miss?" Trent calls out to me as Ethan and I start making our way to the ballroom.

I look at Ethan before walking back over to the bar. When I get there, Trent hands me my purse. I'm shocked and very relieved.

"Thank you!" I exclaim, wanting to throw my arms around him but I refrain.

Trent leans across the bar toward me, and speaks quietly. "You left it on the table there, and I planned to use it to chat with you later in the evening. Please don't think ill of me?"

Needless to say, I'm floored by the gesture. And as I look into his handsome face, I know it would probably take a lot for me to get upset with Trent, even if he hadn't just presented me with my lost purse.

"I'm flattered," is all I can get out, and I can feel the blush in my cheeks.

"Well," Trent starts, leaning back over to his side of the bar and casting a sideways glance at Ethan, "it appears I am too late any way."

I look at Ethan then back at Trent and shrug. He's absolutely right. As beautiful as Trent is, he's still no match for Ethan, at least not for me.

"Sincerely, thank you," I tell him.

"My pleasure," he says with a wink, and I stroll gleefully back over to Ethan.

"You got your purse back," Ethan says, as he opens the doors to the ballroom and gestures for me to enter first.

"I did," I say smiling widely now.

"Let me guess," he says, with a pensive look on his face, "he picked it up after you left it somewhere, planning to use it to introduce himself later?"

I snap my head in Ethan's direction, shocked he guessed the details of our conversation. I don't think there's any way he could have overheard us.

"How did you know that?" I can see my table now, and you better believe my friends' eyes are glued to me and my escort coming down the aisle. As a matter of fact, I notice quite a few people have turned in our direction.

Ethan laughs at my question. "Just a hunch," he says smiling.

"What?" I tease. "Are you stereotyping my sweet Trent?"

I'm flirting with Ethan, which will probably be something I'm going to regret later.

We're at my table before he can answer. Ethan pulls out my chair, and I sit down. All of the non-celebrities at my table are staring, mouths wide open in shock.

He leans down before he leaves to whisper something in my ear. I cannot begin to describe what it feels like to have his face that close to mine, his breath on my neck.

"I wasn't stereotyping," he says, his hands still resting on the back of my chair. "I would have done the same thing."

And with that, he's gone.

It's a good thing that my friends are as paralyzed from the situation as I am because I can't speak.

I watch as Ethan goes back to his table for a minute, but he doesn't sit down. I continue watching him from the corner of my eye, hoping I'm not being too obvious. He says something quickly to the man who's been seated next to him at the table, and then they both walk out the door, not even a last look in my direction.

"No.Fucking.Way." Sydney's the first to come out of the trance.

CHAPTER 7

Sydney's statement is followed by several "Oh my Gods!" and hand flutters over the next few minutes. The celebrities at our table have all but been forgotten. We are sixteen again, and the quarterback of the football team just asked me to prom.

"Holy shit! I can't believe it!" Sydney is wasted. "We have to leave now, so I can get every detail in the limo. It's way too loud in here."

"Let's go," I suggest, gladly getting up and making my way toward the door.

I notice my feet are almost numb at this point from the pain my shoes have been inflicting. It's an improvement for now, but will probably suck tomorrow.

Nobody asks me any more questions as we make our way to the coat check and then downstairs to the lobby. Instead, they keep looking at me like I'm some magical being that may disappear at any moment. I guess they're all waiting for the privacy of the limo to hear the story. With so much build-up, I hope they won't be disappointed.

Sydney texted Scott before we left the ballroom, so when we reach the lobby, he's waiting for us to say goodbye. Rose, Liz and I each give Scott a quick hug and express our sincerest thanks for the invitations. Then we watch as Scott and Sydney say their mushy and rather wet farewells before we're on our way.

"Okay," Sydney says excitedly as she plops down in the same seat in the limo she had earlier, "start from the top!"

I sit back, and eagerly kick off my shoes, happy to relive every detail. I start at the unpleasant security guard, through to the moment in the bathroom where I first saw him. It doesn't take long to tell my story because no one interrupts — all three of them are hanging on my every word. Liz is the first to speak after I finish.

"And what did he say to you at the table before he left?" she asks, and I squirm, even though I knew it was coming.

"He said 'It was nice to meet you'," I tell them, but I'm a terrible liar.

Surprisingly, no one decides to press me on that, and I couldn't be more grateful. I'm having a hard time wrapping my head around the last line he dropped on me. I'm not ready to open it up for discussion.

"But wait," Liz starts again, holding up a wobbly finger, looking like she's been partaking quite a bit in the refreshments tonight as well. "He doesn't even know your name?"

I shake my head, and Liz looks disappointed.

"Aww, Liz," I say, patting her arm. "What does it matter? What did you think would happen?"

"I thought you would fall madly in love and get married, of course!" she says smiling. "Oh, and have pretty babies."

All of us are laughing now.

"I'm not disappointed at all guys. He was really nice," I say, feeling a smile stretch across my face as I start to remember his. But I'm not being totally honest. I'm a little disappointed, but I think that's to be expected and understood. No need to dwell.

"I'm glad you *finally* got a chance to meet him," Rose offers, "and he wasn't the jerk everyone thinks he is."

"He wasn't a jerk at all," I say, feeling very defensive now that I've officially met him. "He was intense, but not rude. I thought he was actually quite the gentleman. He opened doors for me, offered his arm as we walked, and even pulled out my chair."

"Sounds like a keeper to me!" Rose is always the cheerful one.

I look over at Sydney. She's yet to say a word. She's looking quizzically at me, and I know what's coming, but I'm going to let her take her time stewing.

"I can't believe you didn't even tell him your name!" she finally says. "How many times have you gone over that ridiculous speech in your head? It's only like four lines, and you couldn't make it happen?"

I smile as she nears irate, which is more like a cute and fuzzy bunny yelling at you — not very threatening at all.

"How is he going to find you?" Sydney's whining now. "If you didn't give him your number, and he doesn't even know your name, how will he find you to see you again?"

I stare blankly at her. Was she not listening to the story? Did I give the wrong impression?

"Sydney, I don't think he wants to find me again," I say. I seem to be much more sober than the rest of them.

"Bull shit! That's impossible!" Sydney interjects, and I have to stifle a giggle.

Hearing profanity coming from something that looks so pure and innocent is always fun. And her vocabulary is all the more colorful when she drinks.

"Thank you sweetheart," I say, flattered, "but I'm pretty sure that was the first and last time I'll ever speak to him, and that's okay." I add the last part in hopes that I can make myself believe it too.

"Where's your fight?!" Sydney asks with some authority which momentarily catches me off guard. "You've been in love with this guy for years, and you're just going to give up like that? Where are your *balls*?" She forms her tiny right hand into a cup for emphasis. I have to laugh. We all do.

"Sydney, this will all make more sense in the morning when your head is clearer," I assure her. "He's famous, lives in Hollywood for the most part, and dates models. It's not going to happen, okay? I never expected it to, so I'm not disappointed. I just wanted to meet him."

I look down at my hands, clasped in my lap, and remember for a moment his perfect face when he came out of the bathroom stall. He seemed so scared and vulnerable...and quite adorable, really. I can't help but smile at the memory.

"I don't know why he became such an obsession," I tell them. "I mean you hear people say crazy things about celebrities all the time like 'I feel like we have so much in common' or 'I feel like we were meant to be together'. I always thought those people were freaks...until Ethan."

I see Liz and Rose are looking at me now with sad eyes. Sydney still looks bothered.

"It's not like I've ever felt we were meant to be together or anything," I say, trying to make light of my recent unintended confessional. "I've had my fantasies of course, but I'm not completely delusional. The truth is I'm smart enough to know that my obsession with Ethan is probably just filling some other gaping hole in my life that I don't know how to fix. I'm focusing on the unattainable instead of one of my multiple real life issues, and I understand that."

I look down at my hands once again, hanging my head in shame. "He's probably no different from my other long list of ridiculous infatuations over the years, but when they announced *Stephen's Room* was filming in Delia, I thought it was fate. I've let things like that convince me it's more than just some silly fangirl thing, so I can keep holding on."

I look back up to see my friends all giving me sad eyes now. "But after tonight," I say, trying to end on a positive note, "I think I can put this behind me. My plan was to meet him, and mission accomplished."

I'm kind of dumbfounded to see Sydney is actually crying. "Does that mean you're not set stalking with us anymore?" she asks.

I laugh and move over to put my arms around her. "Of course I will still stalk with you! Maybe not when Ethan's there," I add. "I didn't tell him I did that, and after tonight, I think it would be a little embarrassing."

"I understand." Sydney's voice is thick with her tears.

"Well, I really had a lot of fun tonight gals," Liz says, and I let out a long sigh – grateful for the subject change, and to have the attention off me for the first time this evening.

"Me too!" Rose adds with a yawn. "But it's way past my bed time."

"I'll second that," Liz says, as she catches on to the contagious yawn.

I stay next to Sydney, who eventually falls asleep on my shoulder before we get back to her house.

When we finally arrive, I decide to go in to change back to my sweats. I hate to take off the dress in a way, but I gladly give the horrible shoes back to Liz. I pull my hair down and into a ponytail, say my good byes and head to my car to make my way home.

In the car, I start thinking about Cinderella again. Maybe it *was* a mistake to not have been a little more forward with Ethan tonight. Maybe I should have given him something to remember me by.

I'm not sure what the girls thought about my speech, but I know the way I feel about him, especially after tonight. It's much more than just fangirl lust. I can't make any sense of it, but I like him. It's not the characters he plays, and certainly not the person the tabloids make him out to be. There's just something about him.

I know one thing is for sure; Cinderella deserves a little more credit. The whole glass slipper thing was actually a damn good idea.

❦❧

I didn't wash my face last night, which was a mistake. I was just too tired, but now I'm kind of disgusted by the colorful stains on my pillow case, and the mascara running down my face, nearly to my mouth.

I call my mom shortly after I get up, eager to see Jake. It's early, and my son likes to sleep, so she tells me to take my time.

I decide to make some coffee and watch a little TV. I rarely have days anymore where I can just sit and flip through channels, so I take advantage. I sip my warm coffee and watch the end of some sappy movie on the Hallmark channel, feeling very content.

After that, I make my way to my bathroom to get cleaned up. I make a mental note to change my pillowcases before heading to my mom's. Gross.

The shower is extra hot, just the way I like it. I close my eyes and let the water beat down on my shoulders to try to relax, but all I can think about is Ethan.

Ethan, Ethan, Ethan, Ethan.

Frankly, it scares me because I always thought that meeting him would help take him off my mind, but of course, it's the exact opposite. Why did I ever think otherwise?

It's that line he laid on me before he left last night: "I would have done the same thing." I'm trying hard not to read too much into it, but it's difficult.

I finish up my shower and start getting ready, doing whatever I can to think about something, *anything* other than him. But as I pull out my lip balm, I realize there's no hope.

On the way to my mom's house, I try to think of something fun to do with Jake today, still feeling a little guilty about the lack of time I've spent with him lately. This seems to work to take my mind off Ethan, if only for a while.

Maybe I can take Jake to JJ's Crab Shack for lunch. It's a fun atmosphere, and they have a small arcade with skee-ball and air hockey. Jake loves it.

I pull into my mom's driveway around ten. Jake's sitting on the porch swing waiting for me. When he sees me pull up, he rushes to meet me at the bottom of the porch steps. There's nothing in this world that can compete with one of his hugs.

"I missed you!" he says, as he hugs my neck.

"I missed you too, sweet angel."

"Did you have fun?" he asks, already letting go of me — a little prematurely for my tastes — and walking toward the door.

"Yes, I had a really great time," I say, thinking again about last night.

I realize I've hardly been able to stop thinking about it since we left Atlanta.

"Did you meet any one famous?" he asks, excitedly turning toward me to see my face.

We're inside the house now, and my mom's looking at me too, eagerly awaiting my answer.

"I sure did." My voice is shaking. "I got to meet Ethan." I half smile, and Jake looks at me confused.

"Is that a bad thing?" he asks, one eyebrow cocked. I see my mother is waiting for an explanation as well.

"No," I say, trying to shake off my regrets from last night. "It was great!" I try to put on a genuine smile for Jake, but I know I'm not fooling my mom.

"Was he nice?" Jake's more excited now, completely falling for my fake smile.

"He was very nice."

"Will I get to meet him now?"

"What do you mean buddy?"

"Well, since you guys are friends now. Will I get to meet him?"

Oh no. I kneel down in front of him and try to explain.

"Well, actually, just because I met him, doesn't mean we're friends," I tell him as my mom walks back into the kitchen. "He has a very different life than we do. He has so many friends and meets so many people. He probably won't even remember meeting me."

I try not to look sad, but it's hard to keep the disappointment off my face. Jake laughs, which startles me.

"What was that for?" I ask, smiling at him.

"You're crazy mom," he says, recovering now from his laughing fit. He puts his little hand in mine. "How could anyone forget meeting *you*?"

I'm stunned, and I look up to see my mom standing in the doorway to the kitchen, a tear already running down her face.

"Thanks, my sweet angel. I'm sure you're right." I say, when I'm finally able to get something out. I wipe the tears from my eyes. "Why don't you go play for a bit, while I talk to Grandma, okay?"

"Okay mom."

I watch Jake go upstairs to his room – probably planning to have a race with his matchbox cars – before following my mom into the kitchen.

"That boy," my mom says, wiping the tears from her eyes with a dishcloth.

"I know," I reply, trying to keep my tears down for now. "He never ceases to amaze me."

"So," my mom turns to me, sucking up the last of the tears, "how was it?"

"It was..." I have to pause, not even sure how to describe the evening. "It was incredible mom. It really was."

My mom turns away from me then, and goes back to cutting up potatoes, I assume for lunch. "Which part, the event or the meeting?"

"Both," I shoot back. I knew how she would feel about this. "He was really nice, and the event was a lot of fun."

"Tell me about the meeting," she says, acting like she's being forced to ask the question.

"Look, mom." I don't want to get into it with her. "I know what you're thinking. I am a little down about it today, but it's over okay? It's done. I met him. I had my time, and now it's back to reality."

My mom turns her face to me again, looking a little sad. "I just don't want you to get your hopes up, hun. I don't want you to get hurt."

"I know." I look down at the table and start studying the grains in the wood. "I'm fine."

My mom puts down her knife and comes to sit with me at the table. "Listen to me," she says, in her best motherly voice. I look up at her. "I have supported this crazy thing you have for this man and I'll admit, I think it is a little unnatural, but I love you, so I support you." My mom sighs. "It's just that, well now that you've met him — which is what you told me was your only intention — I just want to see you let this go."

I look at her in disbelief. Of course that's all I ever told her, but did she really think meeting him would be enough? Apparently, my look says it all.

"It's not over, is it?" My mother looks defeated. She sits back in her chair in a huff.

"No," I answer honestly, the tears starting again now. "I'm afraid not."

"Oh, hunny." My mom takes me in her arms, and I cry into her shoulder for a minute or so, trying to get a hold of myself.

I finally sit back up and wipe my face with my sleeve. "I will get over this though mom." I want to believe it. I have to. "I know it's irrational and most importantly, it's never going to happen. I just need a little bit of time."

"Okay baby girl." My mom lovingly pats my knee before heading back to her cutting board. "Do you want to tell me how it went?" she says, as she starts chopping again. "I would still like to hear about it."

I proceed to fill my mom in on the details of last night. I find telling the story makes me feel a little better, rather than worse like I thought it would.

"So, he was nice?" she asks.

"Yes," I say defensively. "I don't know what everyone's always going on about. I thought he was the perfect gentleman."

As I recall the story to my mom, I feel like last night went the way it should have. I was a "nobody" in a pretty dress, who met a very famous celebrity. We talked. He left. And I'll probably never see him again. That's the way it normally works with these types of encounters.

The only thing that keeps sticking and rolling around in my head are his last words to me, which I decide to leave out when retelling the story to my mom, just like I left them out when I told the story to my friends last night. I'm keeping those words to myself, for now. I don't want to say them out loud. I don't want them to seem silly or inconsequential, as I know they will once I get them out of my head. I want to keep them tucked away tightly, preserved forever exactly as they are – perfect.

CHAPTER 8

"Did you see?" Sydney asks me excitedly over the phone. "I saw the cables today on the corner by the courthouse. I didn't think they'd be back before the holidays! I'm so excited!"

For the second season of the show, they've built several new sets in studio, so the filming isn't taking place in Delia quite as often now. And it's nearing Christmas, so production will be taking a hiatus soon.

"I hadn't noticed," I lie. I noticed the cables yesterday morning when I came to work.

"Okay," Sydney says, obviously annoyed by my lack of enthusiasm.

"Sorry Sydney." I sigh, feeling bad. "I'm just busy today. Can I call you back a little later?"

"Sure, okay. Call me later!"

She sounds better, so I guess my apology worked.

"Will do. Bye." I hang up, and lay my head on my desk.

It's been almost three weeks since the Atlanta trip, and I'm doing much better. I think. The days have been kind of a blur.

I know I'm getting better at accepting the fact that the fundraiser was my first and last chance with Ethan. I'm getting better with admitting to myself that it went very well, considering. I'm even getting better with the idea of getting back to set stalking, whether Ethan is there or not.

The girls have convinced me that Ethan probably won't recognize me in street clothes, and he never gets close enough to see anyone anyway. Plus, it will give me a chance to keep admiring him from afar, which I'm not sure is a good idea. I promised myself I would give up my crush and find the real root of my needing to obsess over such an unattainable object, but I'm not doing a very good job so far.

"Lunch?" Rose interrupts my sulking.

I slowly lift my head, but don't turn to look at her. "I brought mine today."

Rose comes to sit on my desk, so she can look at my face. "You're lying," she says, arms crossed, waiting for an answer.

"Yea, so?" I admit.

"It's not like any one is here yet. I drive by the trailer lot on my way in. There aren't even trailers here yet."

I silently curse myself for being so transparent.

"I'm nervous," I finally say, grabbing my stomach to try and stop it from doing somersaults.

"You never saw him out and about before, so what are the odds you would see him now?"

Rose is right. Ethan only comes out of his trailer for filming, and I can avoid that easily enough. Of course, I'm not being completely honest with her though. It's not just the nerves that are bothering me.

"I know," I say with a sigh. "Let's go to lunch."

"Great!" Rose is glad she won the battle. "You choose."

"Let's do Mexican," I suggest. Drowning my sorrows in cheese dip seems like a good plan.

❧❧

"You're not just nervous about possibly seeing him again, are you?" Rose asks, as we munch on chips at the restaurant.

"No," I reluctantly confess to my friend. If any one's going to be understanding and supportive, it's Rose. "That's not everything."

"You're worried about him not recognizing you, right?"

Once again, I make a mental note to stop wearing my emotions on my sleeve.

"Yes," I say, looking down at the table, feeling ashamed.

"Don't worry," Rose says in a cheerful voice. "One of two things will happen," she assures me. "One, he will not recognize you — if he even sees you — and things will go back to how they've always been. Or two, he will recognize you, you guys will get married and live happily ever after."

I look up and laugh at my friend. "Thanks Rose."

"You're welcome. And don't worry so much." She looks at me like that's going to be impossible. She knows me too well. "Stalking wouldn't be the same without you, so promise me you'll go?"

"I promise," I say, reluctantly giving in, but Rose is right.

One of two things will happen, but I'm thinking it will probably be the one where he doesn't recognize me and everything goes back to normal. It is the least desirable of the two, but it's the right one. That's for sure.

On a whim, I decide to tell my best friend the truth about what Ethan said to me before he left that night at the fundraiser. The shock on her face makes me giggle.

"Okay, first," she starts, holding up her index finger, "how dare you keep that from me for this long?"

"I'm sorry," I say smiling. "I honestly wasn't sure what to think about it, and I just didn't want to get my hopes up."

Rose stares unbelievingly at me. "Why not?" she asks. "That line is something to get pretty freaking excited about, Sam. Ethan Grant basically said you're hot! Hello?"

I roll my eyes. "Maybe so, but I'm certain I'm not the first girl that he's ever dropped a line on." Rose goes to interrupt, but I stop her. "And it's not like anything will ever come of it any way. He doesn't even know my name."

Rose stares at me a moment longer, then sighs. "I guess you're right," she admits, "but holy crap, Sam. If Ethan Grant said something like that to me...I could live happily off that for the rest of my life!"

We both laugh for a moment, which is a nice change from my incessant need to pout for the last three weeks.

"So, enough about that!" I say, eager to talk about something else, anything else. "How's Danny? Did you tell him about your promotion?"

"I haven't told him yet. It hasn't been confirmed." Rose tries to play it down, but I can tell she's proud of herself for this one. She's been waiting for this for two years, and she and Danny could really use the extra money.

"You'll get it," I assure her. "You're a shoe in!"

"I hope so," she says, grinning ear to ear. Rose is the perfect employee. There's no way she's getting passed up this time.

When we finally get our lunch – this restaurant is notorious for taking forever to bring your food; hence its appeal while lunching during the work day – we eat and chat more about work, Danny and a little about Jake. Right before we're about to get up to pay, Rose touches my arm from across the table.

"Sam, I just want you to know something."

"What's up?" I ask. She seems so serious, which puts me immediately on edge.

"I haven't said anything since Atlanta, but I want you to know how I feel."

Not this again. I don't need anyone else telling me to get over it, or that I'm crazy, chasing a pipe dream, whatever the case may be. I go to stop her, but she interrupts me.

"Just let me get this out," she says, "I just want you to know that I don't think you're crazy." I wasn't expecting that, so I lean back in my booth, eager to hear more. "I've known you a long time, almost all my life, and I've never seen you so goo-goo over a guy, not even Jake's dad."

"You're a good friend Rose," I say, needing to stop this conversation, but Rose isn't having it.

"I'm not done."

I sigh. "Go on."

"I'm not trying to upset you, Sam. I just want to tell you that I don't think you should give up on Ethan. I don't care what the circumstances are, or if you don't really know him. I think you should follow your heart, and not let other people convince you otherwise."

Rose is the first person to ever say this to me. It's what I've wanted to hear for so long – a confirmation of what I feel and what I want – but no one has ever said it. Not until now. A lone tear starts rolling down my face.

"Oh stop that!" Rose says, noticing the tear. "I didn't mean to make you sad!" She hands me her napkin.

"I'm sorry." I wipe my face and look at my friend. "Thank you so much Rose." That's all I can manage. I hope she recognizes the sincerity in my voice.

"You're welcome," she says quietly, her shaky voice telling me she knows what it meant to me. "Go for it girl," she adds with a wink.

❧

The end of the week came quickly. Every day, we watched as more and more filming paraphernalia started to litter the square. The cast trailers arrived yesterday, and I've already been informed by Sydney, Rose and Liz that Ethan is definitely filming tomorrow.

"Liz spoke to John," Rose explains at lunch. "He told her that he's talked to Lamont and Ethan's definitely coming."

"Gotcha," is my short reply to Rose.

John is the owner of a chic little coffee shop in the square, La Tazzina. Of course everyone in town mangles the name, but John doesn't seem to mind.

He's made friends with a ton of the film crew needing caffeine injections and he's also made friends with Ethan's bodyguard, Lamont. It seems John and Lamont have similar music tastes, so they're always emailing about bands, concert info, etc. back and forth. Apparently, Lamont mentioned to John he'd be in town tomorrow, which can only mean Ethan will be here.

I find I'm the perfect mixture of anxiety and excitement. That's normally how I feel when I think I may have a chance to see Ethan though, so it's nothing new.

"I told you not to worry." Rose gives me a look. "You are coming, right?"

"I told you I would."

I've actually been trying to think of a way out for the last couple of days, but nothing has presented itself.

"Good," Rose says, and I'm glad she seems to be satisfied with my lackluster smile. "Sydney is bringing some cookies that Shelia made. I'm sure they're delicious."

"Sounds good," I say, picking at my sandwich now, getting more anxious by the minute.

Rose ignores it. "Liz is also bringing something, or I should say someone."

This gets my attention.

"Someone?"

"Yes!" Rose is excited now. "His name is Bill, and he's not a fan of the show, but he agreed to come with her."

"And who is this *Bill*, and why haven't I heard of him?"

"Don't feel bad. I only heard about this last night," Rose explains. "Liz called and asked about the plans for tomorrow, and she told me she was bringing a friend. I of course asked who it was, and she told me *his* name. I didn't ask questions. Hopefully, we'll find out more tomorrow."

Rose lives for romance, so it's no wonder she's salivating over the idea of Liz actually dating someone.

"Bill, huh?" I ask, trying to figure out where he could have come from. "I wonder if he's a friend from home."

"No idea," Rose says. "But I hope it's more of a date and not some friend thing. Liz could use a date."

I nod my head in agreement, but I'm not confident it will be a date.

Liz has some secrets. That's for sure. And one of them is definitely about a guy.

Based on comments she's made in the past, it seems someone broke her heart to pieces in that department, and I don't think any of us will ever know the details. For something to upset Liz like that, I'm not sure I want to know about it.

Rose and I finish up lunch and the rest of the afternoon passes pretty quickly. I leave the office and head to my mom's to get Jake. He always rides the bus there so he doesn't have to stay in the after school program.

Jake greets me on the porch, with a sad face.

"Hi mom."

His shoulders are slouched like he's just lost his best friend. It isn't until I get closer that I notice his black eye.

"Jake?" I start to panic. "What happened?" I rush to him and examine his eye.

"I got into a fight," he says, hanging his head.

I barely notice my mom walk out the front door. "Did you see the shiner?" she asks.

I nod, without taking my eyes off of Jake and the huge bruise covering his left eye.

"You got into a fight?" I ask him. This is not like Jake at all.

"It wasn't my fault mom," his words start spilling out so fast, I can hardly keep up. "I was telling Sean that you met Ethan and you were friends now and then Johnny said that wasn't that big of a deal because everyone's met him, and I told him that you got to meet him at a special party that weekend when you went to Atlanta, you know? And he said no one would ever want to be friends with you, so I hit him, and then he hit me back, then the teacher came, and I got in-school suspension for three days."

Jake's crying now, but I'm not sure what it's about. Either he's reliving the fight, or he's upset that he has to miss school for three days. It's probably a little of both.

I wait a minute before I speak, trying to allow all of this information to sink in. First, my son got into a fight, which is completely out of character, but he was defending my honor, which is *very* like him. Next, he's telling people I'm friends with Ethan Grant, which is not true, and I thought I'd explained that to him. I feel bad for not doing a better job.

"Jake," I say, trying to remain calm, "the first thing I have to ask is why you thought it would ever be okay to hit someone?"

"I wasn't just going to let him talk bad about you mom!" Jake's still a little hyped up from his experience, it seems.

I pull him over to the porch swing and sit him down next to me. My mom takes the plastic chair by the door and listens in.

"Jake, sometimes people are going to say things you don't like. It's not a reason for violence. There is never a reason to act like that."

Jake's crying still. "I know mom. I just hate that kid."

"You do *not* hate him Jake. You don't hate anyone." I thought I'd taught my child better than this.

"Well," Jake starts, looking up at me with his big blue eyes, "I don't like him very much."

The truth is, I know this Johnny kid, and I don't like him either. He's a trouble maker and a smart ass, and his parents aren't much better. He probably deserved what Jake gave him and then some, but I have to be the bigger person here.

"Has Johnny said other stuff to you Jake? Was this just the straw that broke the camel's back?" Not that it makes a difference, but

I'm trying to talk him down.

"He's never nice to me," Jake explains. "He's never nice to anyone. He makes fun of kids all the time. I hate---" he starts, and then looks at me, "I just don't like him some times."

"Well, you know you'll have to be punished for this."

"Mom!"

"Jake, I appreciate that you were trying to stick up for me, but you cannot just haul off and hit people and not expect to face some repercussions. I'm sorry." I try to keep my authoritative face on, but it's hard. I'm such a sucker for my child's tears.

"I know," he grumbles, staring at his feet.

"I'll think about your punishment tonight and let you know what I decide," I tell him. "Go inside. I'll be there in a minute."

Jake gets up and sulks into the house, giving me a glance over his shoulder as he opens the door.

I feel terrible for him, but what else can I do? I can't allow him to think it's okay to hit people, but more importantly, I have to clear up this Ethan-and-I-are-friends thing.

"Can you believe that?" my mom says, wrapping her sweater tighter around her.

I put my head in my hands. "No, I sure can't."

Just then I have a bizarre shooting pain in my side that nearly takes my breath away. I rub at it and try to calm myself down.

"Are you okay?" my mom asks, as I continue to rub at my side. The pain is gone now.

"I just think this thing with Jake is upsetting me more than it probably should," I admit.

"Careful, hun. You'll be old before your time." My mom smiles and comes to sit by me on the swing. "He's growing up so strong Sam, even without Luke in the picture. He has his dad's fire, you know."

"Yes, I see it every day," I say, staring out into the front yard. I know it's selfish, but I don't like to think about my son belonging to anyone other than me.

"How will you punish him?"

"I have no idea. Any suggestions?"

"Well, he loves his cars. You could take that away for a while."

"That's a good one," I agree.

"And Maybe TV?" she adds. "He watches too much for my tastes anyway."

"Also good," I say, but in all actuality, Jake watches very little compared to most kids his age. He does love it though.

"Honestly, hun," my mom continues, "I don't think you need to be too strict. Jake's a good boy. He knows what he did was wrong. You just need to talk to him. I think he'll understand. I think he's most upset about disappointing you."

I let out a small laugh. "I don't know why that kid loves me so much."

"It's easier than you think," my mom says. Then she kisses me on the forehead and leaves me alone on the porch.

I sit there for a while, breathing in the cold air, lost in thought. I have so many things to get my head around. I don't need my eight year old getting in fights suddenly added to the mix. My mom is right though, as usual. Talking to Jake will be the best bet. I'll have to give him a little punishing, but he's a smart kid.

I mainly need to clear up this crazy idea of Ethan and I being friends. I laugh because the thought brings Ethan back to the front of my mind. It doesn't take much.

I start picturing his eyes, and how much prettier they are up close.

No photo shoot could ever correctly capture the color or the depth. I start thinking about the way his mouth turned up on one side when he smiled at me that night. I can still picture the way his arm felt in mine when we walked up the escalator or the way his phone smelled like him when he let me use it. I think about all of these things over and over, but they only make me sad. I'll never be able to experience them again.

Where's the justice in that?

I know it's crazy, but I've finally found a guy I feel connected to, and he's one hundred percent out of my reach.

With that in mind, I go inside, prepared to dish out some damn punishment.

CHAPTER 9

My mom agreed to watch Jake after school today. I don't know what I would do without her.

I dropped Jake off this morning and on my way to work, I noticed they'd already set lights up in the square and were preparing — I found out later — to start filming this afternoon.

My boss agreed to let me off early, and Rose talked hers into an early day as well. It's been a slow week, so he's probably excited about saving some dollars on payroll.

Finally it's time to go, and we see Liz in the lobby of the courthouse on our way out. She's preparing to leave, but says she'll be back in a couple of hours.

"Off to get *Bill*, is it?" I tease.

"Yes. I should have known Rose would snitch," she says giving a mischievous grin to Rose and me. "He's meeting me at my house in about an hour, so as soon as he gets there, I'll head back up."

"Make sure to shower afterward!" I shout at her as she walks to her car. She throws her middle finger up behind her back, but doesn't turn around.

"I can't wait to meet him!" I say excitedly to Rose, as we giggle about the possibilities.

"You ready?" Rose asks. "Sydney's already out there. She's been camped out since noon."

I'm not ready, but I'm excited about seeing Ethan again in person, even if it's from afar.

"Let's go!" I say to Rose, as we walk out the courthouse doors and onto the square.

Rose, Sydney and I watch throughout the afternoon, but Ethan never shows. We do find out they'll be filming another scene this evening in front of the courthouse, so hopefully, he'll show up then.

They're actually planning to stop traffic in the square tonight, which they've yet to do for the show. Most of the time, they let traffic move through while they're shooting, but they are already setting up road blocks in certain areas and eventually, the square will be closed down.

At around six P.M., it starts to get chilly. The weather's been pretty warm this week, but of course Mother Nature chooses tonight to start acting like December.

"Where's Liz?" Sydney asks, her hands wrapped tightly around her hot chocolate.

Rose and I exchange a conspiratorial glance.

"Still with Bill, I presume," I tell her.

And as if on cue, Liz comes walking around the corner with what one would only describe as a Demi-God here on earth holding her hand. All three of us are rendered speechless.

"Ladies, this is Bill." Liz introduces her new beau to us, as we all try to casually pick our jaws up off the pavement.

"Good Lord!" Sydney exclaims, as subtle as always.

Bill doesn't seem the slightest bit embarrassed. He reaches his hand out to her. "I'm Bill. Nice to meet you."

"Sydney," she says, openly gawking at him as she shakes his hand.

"Hi Bill," I finally manage. "I'm Sam. Pleasure to meet you."

"Great to meet you too," he says. His voice is husky and deep, like you just want to crawl into his arms knowing you'll be safe there forever.

He's tall, well over six feet, with salt and pepper hair and hazel eyes. He has a perfectly chiseled jaw line, broad shoulders, but not too broad, long legs and a killer smile. All I can think is *Way to go Liz!*

"I'm Rose," Rose says, extending a shaky hand to Bill.

"Good to meet you Rose." Bill seems to radiate confidence, making him even more attractive.

He pulls out the two folded chairs he had slung over his shoulder and opens them up for him and Liz. Liz sits next to me, putting Bill at the end of our semi-circle.

"Seen anything good yet?" Liz asks me.

I was about to say *I'm looking at it* as I gawk at Bill, but I wise up.

"Jayce and Miranda had a scene this afternoon. It was on the rooftop there," I tell her, as I point to the location.

"Any sightings yet?"

I obviously know who she's referring to. "Not yet. I hear he's shooting tonight."

"Great!" she says, rubbing her hands together. "I can't wait!"

I cock my eyebrow at her, but she just smiles and turns to Bill. They enter into a conversation that looks very private, so I turn away.

Around seven, they start setting up cameras in front of the court house. Luckily, the spot we chose will work out for this shoot as well, so we stay where we are. You're only allowed so close to the set, but from here, we have a completely unobstructed view.

It's about thirty minutes later, when I finally see him.

They drive the cast and crew around in these un-marked white vans. We see one pull up on the corner, and then we hear a few girls scream. I look over to the van, and sure enough, Ethan's inside. He's smiling his half smile, but he never rolls his window down or says a word.

One of the other actors from the show, Vick, who happens to be the fan favorite, is in the front seat. He has his window completely down, and is talking and allowing a few fans to shake his hand. People love him because they feel like he's the most appreciative of his fans. Maybe that's true, but I think he just has a more outgoing personality than the others. Perhaps I'm a little biased.

The van eventually pulls up next to the director's tent which is now set up in front of the court house, about thirty yards from where we're sitting.

I take a moment to study my obsession, as he starts to get out of the van.

As always, my insides feel warm the minute I see him. He's wearing black jeans, a black t-shirt and a brown hoodie. His hands are in his pockets the moment he steps out of the van, and he slumps his shoulders to brace against the cold on the way to the tent. He doesn't look my way, or up at the crowd one time.

"He's here!" Sydney is squealing at me as Ethan walks into the tent, but I can't pay attention to her. I'm suddenly shaking with panic. All I can think of is that I can't let him see me. What if he *does* remember me? I'll be mortified!

I feel pretty positive that he won't recognize or remember me. He probably forgot about that night immediately after it happened, but I don't want to take the chance. I feel pathetic. I don't want him to see me like this. I don't want him to see me in my element, being a fangirl, being a stalker. My stubborn pride doesn't want him to know that I like him this much. I don't want him to know how I feel. For all he knows, it was over that night for me as well.

"I have to go," I say urgently to Liz as I get up and start folding my chair.

"What?" Liz gets up too, trying to stop me.

"Where are you going?" Rose asks me, now perched on the edge of her seat, ready to pounce.

I shake Liz off. "I have to go. I shouldn't be here."

I start putting my chair back in its bag, when my phone vibrates in my pocket. I put my chair down to take a look. It's a text message.

Leaving so soon?

It's from a number I don't recognize. I look around at my friends, scowling in confusion.

"What is it?" Rose asks, standing now, seeming worried about my expression.

I look first to Bill, thinking he would have the only number not plugged into my phone, but he's looking at me too, waiting for me to explain.

"Did one of you just text me?" I finally ask, holding up my phone for proof of the message.

Everyone looks at me, like I'm crazy, except for one — except for Liz. Liz is looking toward the director's tent.

I turn and follow her gaze, and I can't believe my eyes. Ethan's standing outside the tent, in a heavy winter coat now, seemingly staring straight at me. It's hard to tell from this distance.

I look away immediately and back down at my phone.

Please Sam, don't faint, I tell myself. I feel like it. My head is all swimmy. I feel myself pale, but I never pass out. *Thank you, God.*

My phone vibrates again, but before I look at the message, I sling my eyes slowly back toward Ethan. He holds up his phone, as if indicating I should answer. This is not happening. There's no way this is happening.

I look back at my phone and see that I have a new text.

I knew I recognized you. Want to talk?

I look over at Liz then, my eyes blinking rapidly. Is she in on this?

"Okay," she starts, "I had to go over to your mom's house on my way home today because I left my thermos there a while ago and I wanted to bring coffee tonight." She grabs my shoulders, and turns me toward her, but I think it's probably more of an effort to keep me standing. "Your mom mentioned someone named Ethan has been calling her house, trying to get your number, but she didn't want to give it to him. She thought it was a joke."

I start shaking my head, refusing to believe this impossible turn of events.

"I'm not lying," Liz confirms. "She told me he somehow convinced her, though she didn't go into details about that part. She said she didn't like it, but she gave him your cell, hoping it would be harmless," Liz says smiling.

"Why didn't she tell me about this?" I manage to choke out. My mouth is the Sahara all of a sudden.

"She said she didn't want to scare you," Liz explains. "She thought he was a crazy person at first, and then when she found out it was him...well, she knows what people say about him, and she *is* your mother."

I sneak a look over my shoulder to where Ethan's standing. He's still there, hands in his pockets, staring in my direction. I turn back to Liz, and cross my arms across my chest. I have goose bumps all over, but not from the cold.

"What made her decide to give my number to him again?" I ask, barely remembering Liz speaking a moment ago. Seeing Ethan staring at me seems to have rendered me incapable of coherent thought.

"She didn't tell me," Liz says, looking like she would like to know the answer to that one too. "She just said she finally gave in, and hoped for the best. I guess she did a good thing." Liz is smiling from ear to ear. I've never seen her look quite so happy.

"Sam!" Sydney yells from behind my back. I turn to her. "Are you going to leave Ethan Grant hanging or what?! Answer that damn text!" She stomps her tiny foot on the pavement.

A few other bystanders have unfortunately been listening to our private conversation and are now staring at me.

I sit down in Liz's chair to answer the text.

Sure.

I press "Send" and look up to gauge his reaction to my message.
He gets it quickly, and then looks at me and flashes a killer smile.
Oh God.

I watch as he puts his head down to send another text, which I eagerly await, along with the rest of my party who's now hanging over me waiting for my phone to vibrate. The only one still sitting is Bill, who seems perfectly happy — and absolutely gorgeous — watching this unfold from his chair.

About to start. Can I call you after?

My hands are shaking uncontrollably. I can barely type.

Sure.

A little unoriginal, but I don't think anything more can be expected of me at this moment.
I watch him again, as he texts back.

Can't wait.

The fainting spell comes over me once more.
"Does that say 'Can't wait'?" Sydney squeals. "Oh.My.God!" Sydney sits down in her chair immediately and starts pressing buttons on her phone. She's a much more proficient texter than me, so I'm sure she's spreading this news. I grab her arm.
"What are you doing?" I ask, still trying to find where all of my saliva has disappeared to.
"Just texting Scott," she says, snatching her arm from me. "Don't worry. I'm not stupid."
Since I took her seat, Liz picks my chair up off the ground and unfolds it on the other side of Bill. I look at Rose, and she honestly

looks as spell bound as I do. Liz is talking animatedly to Bill, and from the few words I pick up on, she's giving him a dissertation of my long-standing obsession with Ethan.

"I can't believe that just happened," Rose says.

I'm listening to her, but my eyes are trained on Ethan now as he's filming.

"Me neither," I say, trying in vain to pull my eyes away.

It takes a little over an hour for Ethan to film his scene. My girlfriends and I naturally spend that hour analyzing every word in each of his texts. Bill smiles at us and doesn't seem to mind.

Ethan jumps back in the van after his scene, as usual, but his co-star, Vick, comes over to visit the crowd.

I could care less, but Sydney jumps at having her photo taken with him for probably the tenth time.

My heart sinks a little as I watch Ethan drive away without one look in my direction, but then my phone rings, not even thirty seconds after he leaves.

"Hello?" I say, barely able to hold the phone to my ear, because of nerves and also because Liz and Rose are jumping with excitement while holding my arms.

"Hi," he says. His voice sounds cautious.

I wait for him to say something else, but he doesn't, so I break the silence. "How did you get my number?"

Liz already gave me the rundown, but I have no idea what else to say to him.

"It wasn't easy," he says, and I can tell he's smiling on the other end. "Do you have time for something to eat?"

I don't think there's any way I can eat, and it's kind of late for dinner, but I'm not about to pass up this opportunity.

"Sure," I say shyly. It appears that's going to be the favorite word in my vocabulary this evening.

"It will have to be in my trailer, if that's okay." I can tell now he's already getting out of the van. His trailer is walking distance from where we are. "I have to head back to Atlanta later tonight."

"Okay," I say nervously, so it sounds more like a question.

Ethan laughs. "Do you know where my trailer is?"

"I know where the trailers are," I admit, "but I don't know which one is yours."

"My friend will be out front. He's a pretty big guy. You can't miss him."

I smile. I know what Lamont looks like, but I'm not sure if I should admit that or not. "Okay. When should I come over?"

"Come over?" I hear Sydney repeat behind me. Talking to Ethan, I had forgotten again that anyone else was around.

"Give me about twenty minutes, okay?" Now he sounds like he's taking his clothes off, which makes me sweat a little.

"Okay," I say.

"See you soon," he says, and hangs up.

I put the phone down at my side and look at my friends.

"So?" Sydney is the impatient one, of course.

"He said..." I'm almost afraid to say it out loud, like it will wake me from this impossible dream. "He said he wants me to have dinner with him, in his trailer."

All three girls look at each other and then start screaming and hugging before they turn their excitement on me.

"I knew it!" Rose says. "I knew this would happen for you."

"Thanks Rose," I say smiling, still unable to completely grasp what just happened. "I need to call mom, let her know what's going on.

She's not going to believe this."

As I start telling my mom the story, I can see that I was right. My mom is floored, but she doesn't act that way, only I can tell.

"It's about time that man came around," she says. "Bout time he made a good decision."

"I love you mom, and I'll try not to be too late," I tell her. I don't even bother bringing up what Liz told me earlier. I will deal with her deceit later on.

"Don't you worry about us," she says casually, but I know she's beaming on the other end. "I'll let you be the one to tell Jake about this though, okay?"

"Yes, please." I don't want him running off to his friends about this one. That's for sure.

"Be careful, hun. I'll see you in the morning."

"Love you, mom."

"Love you too."

I hang up, and turn again to the girls.

"All set!" I say. My voice is about 10 octaves higher than normal.

I can't hold the grins or the shakes back any more. I'm beside myself with excitement.

We're all laughing and smiling, when Sydney suddenly gives me a disapproving look.

"Look at your face!" she whines. "That's unacceptable! Come here to me."

She waves me over, and sits me down. She then unloads a huge bag from her even bigger purse and opens it up. It's full of make-up.

While Sydney starts to touch me up, Rose and Liz stand next to me to chat. Bill has Liz in his arms, still looking completely content.

"You know you have to call us tonight," Liz says, smiling into Bill's chest.

"Absolutely!" Rose agrees. "I better get a phone call. I don't care what time it is!"

"There," Sydney says, putting the final touches on my lips. "You can thank me later."

She hands me her mirror, and I'm glad to see it isn't too bad. It's more than I usually do, but that wouldn't take much. I make a mental note to dab a little at the eye shadow and lipstick on my walk over.

"How long did he say again?" Liz asks, looking at her watch.

"Twenty minutes," I say, looking at my own watch for confirmation. "Has it been that long?"

I haven't even been paying attention to the time.

"It's been about eighteen minutes since his call," Rose says. Leave it to Rose. "You should probably make your way over."

We're all frigid from standing out in the cold, but no one seems to mind, especially me.

Everyone starts packing up their stuff, and I join in.

"Rose, will you take this?" I ask, handing her my chair.

"Sure," she says, and gives me a smile. "Is it too corny to say good luck?"

I smile back. "I probably need it, so no. I think it's appropriate."

"You need zero luck," Liz says, hugging me. "Have fun."

I wave at them over my shoulder, as I walk away.

"Phone calls!" I hear Sydney yell, and I smile.

I thought I'd be shaking like crazy walking to his trailer, but I feel a sudden calm rush over me as I leave the girls. Perhaps I'm playing games with myself again, but the feeling makes me think this is meant to be.

As I get closer to the trailers, I realize Ethan was right. You can't miss Lamont. I knew what he looked like, but even if I didn't I would've noticed him immediately. He looks pretty intimidating, but John from the coffee shop swears he's a teddy bear.

"Evening," Lamont says as I approach. He has the deepest voice I've ever heard.

"Hi," is all I can say, rather sheepishly, I might add. I feel guilty, like I'm doing something bad. It makes Lamont smile.

"He's waiting for you," he says, and holds open the door.

I walk in, and Ethan is resting on one of the couches on the side of the trailer, watching TV. He turns it off when he sees me and smiles.

"Welcome, Samantha," he says, as he stands up to greet me, looking as beautiful as ever. He's now dressed in a gray V-neck t-shirt and dark jeans.

It's strange to hear him say my full name, which always sounds a little odd to me. Of course, Ethan can call me whatever he wants.

"Thanks," I say, after taking quick inventory of his space. "You can call me Sam, if you'd like."

I never told him my name the night we met, so I can only assume my mom filled him in.

I notice his trailer is small, but nice and tidy. There's nothing too extravagant. There's a tiny kitchen in the front with a small fridge, a sink and a microwave. Then there's a couch on either side with a small television mounted in the corner near the kitchen. There's a short hallway to my left that leads to a closed door. I assume it's his bedroom.

"Does everyone call you Sam?" he asks, and I notice for the first time the smell of Italian food.

"Most everyone," I say nodding. "Why?"

"I think I like Samantha better."

"You have an issue with the name Sam?" I'm confused by this conversation.

"Not at all," he says smiling. "I just want to stand out from the crowd."

"Are you being serious?" I giggle.

"Can't have you forgetting about me," he says, still smiling, which is making me feel faint again. "Lasagna?" he asks, pointing to the kitchen counter, where I now see a pan of lasagna still steaming.

"Sounds great," I say smiling too, trying to recover from Ethan's obvious flirting. It's more than my brain can handle at the moment.

He gets up to walk toward the kitchen, and I'm bathed in his scent quickly in such close quarters. I can tell he just showered, as his hair is still a little wet. And he smells clean, like soap and fabric softener.

"Take a seat," he says, when he gets to the kitchen.

"You need some help?" I ask, noticing him preparing our plates.

He turns and smiles at me before returning back to his preparations. "I'm good. Make yourself comfortable."

Ethan seems different tonight than when I met him at the fundraiser. He seems happier, more relaxed. Perhaps he's more comfortable away from his Hollywood life. From the little I know about him, that would make sense.

I put my purse down on the couch next to me and pull my jacket and scarf off as I sit down. I now hate that I didn't choose a better outfit for stalking tonight. I'm not normally a very fancy person, but I can do better than this. Unfortunately, I just went with my usual jeans, t-shirt, hoodie and my favorite pair of beat-up navy blue Converse. Oh well.

Ethan's trailer is very modest, but I suppose he probably isn't in it very much.

I read an article recently about how some celebrities have crazy requests when it comes to trailers – Italian leather furniture, solid gold toilet seats. It doesn't surprise me that Ethan isn't like that. The simplicity of his trailer makes me like him even more.

Ethan brings a TV tray to me with a paper plate on it that has a square serving of lasagna and a small salad on the side. I also have a plastic silverware set wrapped with a napkin, salt and pepper included in the mix. Definitely not very fancy, but it's perfect for me.

"What can I get you to drink?" he asks, after setting his own tray next to mine in front of the couch. "Beer? Wine? Water? Coke? Vodka Cranberry?"

I'm not sure alcohol is the best idea, even though it may be nice for my nerves, and I like how he's proving to me he remembers my drink from the night at the fundraiser. I smile at him.

"Coke would be great," I say, deciding to play it safe. Ethan grabs a Coke for himself as well.

He sits next to me, placing my drink on my tray, and then turns the television to some random music channel. His scent is really strong now, and I can't help but breathe it in. It's so homey and pleasant.

We eat for a while without talking, just looking at each other periodically and smiling. I get the feeling he feels kind of nervous about this too, which helps me relax a little.

"Thanks for coming," he says, finally breaking our silence as we chew. "I was afraid I might scare you off with the text message."

The irony makes me laugh. I'm the scary one here, not him.

"What's so funny?" he asks.

"Nothing," I say, not wanting to state the obvious.

"Tell me," he says, his green eyes locking with mine. I'm suddenly defenseless.

"It's just that, I'm the stalker here. Not you," I reluctantly admit. I look down at my lasagna, hoping he won't kick me out or something.

Instead, he laughs. "True enough, I guess. But you're not the average stalker. You're not very scary."

"I could be scary," I say, pretending to be defensive and feeling very glad he hasn't seemed to clue in yet to my hopeless devotion.

"No," he says, looking at me like he's trying to get inside my head. "I don't think so."

"Thanks, I guess?" I say laughing.

I'm having a great time already, and I'm much more comfortable than I thought I would be. When I'm around him, I feel at ease. Worshiping him from afar seems to be the nerve wrecking part. It's hard to believe he's better up close.

He laughs too. "How's the food?" he asks. "I'm sorry it's not more."

"I think it's great," I say, after finishing my bite. "We have food, drinks, silverware, and music." I gesture to the television with my fork. "What more do we need?"

Ethan smiles again. "I'm totally content," he says, taking another bite of his dinner.

"Me too," I say in a small voice, seeming to lose my cool a little each time he looks into my eyes. Thankfully, I'm able to regroup quickly. "So, you never told me how you got my number."

"From your mom. She's a tough one to crack."

"Yes, she is." I try to act surprised by the info, even though Liz already told me the story. "I can't believe she gave some stranger my number. I'll have to talk to her about this."

Ethan feigns offended. "I am *not* a stranger. We've met before."

"Okay fine," I concede. "But my mom couldn't have known it was you."

"She didn't believe me the first few hundred times I called," he admits, "but she finally came around, just today, as a matter of fact. I'd planned to call you after my shoot, but then I saw you leaving."

My heart starts pounding thinking about the fact that he's obviously been trying to get in touch with me since my trip to Atlanta. All this time I thought that was the last time I would ever see him, and now I'm sitting next to him, eating dinner. I don't know whether I want to hug my mom or shoot her.

"How did you know I was going to be at the filming?"

Ethan hesitates for a second before answering. "Your mom told me."

It seems like this is a lie, but I don't push.

"If you don't mind me asking, what did you say to my mom to finally get her to give in?"

The woman is hard as nails, so this question's been plaguing me since Liz told me the story. Plus, my mom isn't really Ethan's biggest fan.

"Nothing special," he says, taking his final bite of lasagna, but he's obviously lying again. I decide to push a little this time.

"Tell me," I say, trying his eye trick from earlier when he looks over at me.

He hesitates for a moment, then smiles.

"I didn't tell her anything," he says. "I went to see her."

I choke on my most recent bite of salad. Ethan pats my back. "You okay?" he asks.

"You--" I cough again, trying to dislodge the lettuce from my throat. "You went to my mother's house?" I gasp.

Ethan suddenly looks nervous, like he's done something wrong. "I'm sorry," he says. "She wouldn't give it to me over the phone, but I thought if I went by, I could convince her."

All I can think about is that my mom saw Ethan today, in the flesh, and didn't mention a word to me. I spoke to her after work for Christ's sake!

"What time were you there?" I ask, finally recovering from my embarrassing choking fit.

"This afternoon," he says, still looking scared he may have upset me. "It was maybe around lunchtime?"

I can't believe she kept this from me! I'll deal with her later.

I finally get my food down, and smile at Ethan. I feel embarrassed about my overreaction.

"You just showed up at my mom's house? How did you know where she lived?"

"I have connections," Ethan says smiling, now that he sees I'm calming down a bit. "I called first to tell her I was coming by, but she didn't believe me. Surprise, surprise."

"What did she do when she saw you?" I try to imagine my mother's shock. She doesn't like to be proven wrong.

Ethan seems lost in thought for a moment. "The odd thing was she didn't seem very surprised when I got there. I mean all those times, rejecting my requests, acting like she didn't believe me, and then she seemed like she expected me to show up all along. It was weird."

I smile to myself. That would be about right. She probably just wanted him to prove it in person. She knew the truth all along.

"And?" I ask, wanting more. "Please continue."

"Well," Ethan pushes his tray away so he can angle himself toward me, "I got there, and she met me on the porch. She said she wanted to make sure my intentions were honorable."

I must be fourteen shades of red, based on the smile that spreads across Ethan's face.

"It's okay," he assures me. "I kind of expected that. She had been tough over the phone."

"I'm horrified," I say, putting my head in my hands.

His touch makes me jump, as he pulls my hands from my face. I look up at him.

"It's perfectly fine," he says, smiling into my eyes again. "My intentions are very honorable."

There goes the embarrassing blush again. I feel like a thirteen year old — like this is the first boy I've ever had a crush on. It's ridiculous, and I need to get a handle on it quickly.

"Well then," I say, releasing myself from his trance inducing gaze, "that's good to know." I take a nervous sip of Coke, hoping I'm not blowing this because I'm acting like a pre-teen.

"She was also interested in why I wanted to see you again," he adds.

I look at him, a bit curious about that one myself.

"What did you tell her?" I ask, when he doesn't continue.

Ethan stands up then, seeming a little uncomfortable, and takes our plates to his tiny kitchen. He has his back to me when he finally answers.

"I told her I didn't know."

This should probably upset me, but it doesn't.

First, we don't know each other, so it makes perfect sense. But also, it doesn't upset me because I would have answered the same way. It's what I always say when asked why I'm so in to him. I can never describe it accurately out loud. There's just something about him.

"You didn't know," I repeat, and try to sound like I understand.

"It's the truth," he says, turning to me now. "I've seen you before, watching me. It should probably freak me out, but it doesn't. I like it."

I want to crawl under the table out of embarrassment, but then I catch Ethan's blush.

"Are you blushing?" I giggle, suddenly feeling so very giddy.

"No," he says, turning to the plates again to avoid me.

I get up and walk over to him to take a look for myself.

"You *are* blushing," I accuse him, and his answering grin is magnificent. "I thought you said my mom told you where I was tonight?" I tease.

"Fine. You got me." He sighs, still smiling. "I've noticed you on the set before. I made the connection a couple of days after the fundraiser. Do you think I'm creepy now?"

I laugh. Once again, he seems to be thinking about this in a very backwards way.

"Let me get this straight," I say, walking back over to the couch, and Ethan follows.

"I'm the one who sits in a folding chair for hours, in the dead of winter, just waiting to catch a glimpse of you, and you're the creepy one?"

"I like you," Ethan says bluntly, ignoring my question, as we sit and face each other on the couch. "I'd like to see you again."

"That would be nice," I say smiling, surprised and very excited by this admission. Then I wonder if his confession may mean he has to call it a night. "Do you need me to go?"

"No," he answers quickly. "I mean, no. Please don't go yet. I just wanted to put that out there. I can be kind of blunt some times." He looks apologetic.

"It's okay." I smile, happy I don't have to leave.

"Can I ask a question," he starts, looking hesitant, "and it may seem kind of odd, but I would like to know, especially in your case?"

"Shoot," I say. His face has me curious.

"What's the appeal?" he asks, gesturing to his perfect chest, "Why me?"

I'm not sure if I can answer. There are so many things, but I'm not sure if I'm ready to go there yet — to unleash my feelings on him. It's hard to pinpoint just one thing anyway. I like it all.

"Um," I'm so nervous to answer this, so I go with honesty, "I'm not totally sure. For me, it's probably a million different things."

Ethan smiles. "Can you give me at least one?"

"Well," I decide to go with the first thing that brought me to him, "I think you're an incredible actor. I saw you for the first time in *Jimmy's Story*, and I thought you were amazing."

"Thank you," he says sincerely. "That means a lot."

"You're welcome." I hope he'll be satisfied with one. Of course, he is not.

"Anything else?"

I want to tell him how beautiful I think he is, after staring at him in a semi-snug t-shirt and jeans all night, but I decide not to go there.

"I like your honesty," I blurt out finally.

Ethan raises his eyebrows. "My honesty?"

"When you do interviews," I try to explain, "I always get the feeling you're being really honest. I can see it in your eyes." He doesn't say anything to that one, so I continue. "I also like the way you take your work so seriously. I know some people feel like you're...unapproachable, but I've always assumed it's because all of these people are trying to bother you while you work, and you don't want the distractions."

He laughs. "You're the first person to ever say anything like that to me. I've managed to convince everyone, but you it seems, that I am a complete ass."

"Do you think I'm nuts yet?" I feel worried I may have overdone it.

"On the contrary," he says. "I already think you may know me better than most of my friends, which is pretty scary."

"I've wanted to know you for a long time." *Uh oh.* Now it seems it's my turn for blunt. "I know a lot of people obsess over celebrities, but I promise it's not like that for me. Or maybe it is."

I close my eyes briefly and shake my head, trying to gather my thoughts. "What I'm trying to say is that it's never been about anything crazy, like getting a lock of your hair or a napkin you wiped your mouth on. I just wanted to meet you."

I look down, feeling embarrassed about what just came out of my enormous mouth, but when I finally look back up at him, I'm surprised by what I see.

He isn't looking at me like I'm crazy. He's looking at me in awe, like I'm some fabled creature. It's the most amazing feeling, but I barely have time to register the emotion. The next thing I know, his lips are on mine, and he's kissing me.

I thought if I ever had the pleasure of kissing Ethan, I would somehow screw it up because my nerves would certainly get the best of me. I was wrong.

The second his lips touch mine, my body responds immediately, and my nervousness is forgotten.

All of my senses move to focus on him and only him. As I close my eyes, all I can see is a reflection of his beautiful green eyes behind my lids. His mouth on mine is all I can taste. The sound of his soft moans is all I can hear. His freshly showered body is all I can smell. His hand, softly caressing my cheek, is all I can feel. I'm enveloped by him, and I never want out of this pleasure-filled cocoon.

When he finally breaks away, we're both breathless.

"I guess I said something right?" I joke, as I try and catch my breath.

Ethan laughs, with his trembling hand still on my cheek.

"You didn't have to say anything at all," he says softly. "I don't know what it is about you, Samantha. I know this may be hard to believe, due to my profession and all, but I don't normally do this. I promise I'm not some Casanova that lures girls to his trailer with lasagna. I just wanted to talk to you. That kiss wasn't part of the plan."

"Plans change," I say smiling, as Ethan continues to look at me with wonder in his sparkling green eyes.

"So it seems," he breathes, and puts his forehead on mine.

Wow. Ethan is certainly intense. In all things, it seems.

He kisses the tip of my nose, and I rise to meet his lips, eager for another turn. Ethan doesn't seem to mind, and we launch in to a second kiss that rivals the first. I stretch my arms around his neck, running my fingers through his still damp hair, as he wraps his arms tightly around my waist, slowly curling his fingers up and down my back.

I break away this time, and a look of disappointment instantly appears on Ethan's face.

"I have to go," I admit.

It's the last thing I want to do, but I know it's the right thing. This is moving a little fast. I need to get my head around it.

"I know," he says sadly, still holding me close to him. "You have to get home to Jake."

"Yes," I lie, but it's a sure fire way to get me out of this trailer. I don't want to push my luck tonight. It would be near impossible for this evening to get any better.

Ethan moves his arms from around my waist, and takes my hands in his.

"When can I see you again?" he asks, face still flush from our unexpected make-out session.

"When do you want to see me again?" I ask, smiling as I feel the thirteen year old resurface.

"Tomorrow?" he asks.

"Sure." I can't believe this is really happening to me. "What time?"

I've been away from Jake all day today, so I really need to get in some quality time tomorrow. I hope Ethan will understand.

"Do you have plans?" he asks, obviously reading the indecision on my face.

"No, it's just that I haven't seen my son all day. I hate to abandon him again tomorrow."

"Bring him along," he offers. "Would you mind? I have tickets to the Hawks game. Box seats. Does he like basketball?"

"He loves it," I say, floored by the gesture.

Ethan looks elated. "It's settled then. I'll be back in Atlanta tomorrow, so do you mind if I have a car come and pick you up? Say around four? We could do dinner before we go."

"Sounds perfect," I agree.

He leans down to kiss me again. It's soft and sweet and doesn't last nearly long enough. Then he gets up and grabs his phone. "I'll get your address tomorrow," he tells me.

"Who are you calling?" I ask, as he dials.

"Lamont," he says. "I wanted to see if he would walk you back to your car."

"Oh, thanks for that." I start thinking about Lamont then, hoping he hasn't been standing outside all this time.

Ethan's conversation is quick. "He'll be here in a few minutes," he says, coming to sit by me again. He leans back into the couch, and I'm glad to see he seems very at ease around me now, and happy.

"I'm so used to seeing your serious face on TV and on set. It's nice to see you smile," I comment.

He reaches up to touch my face, and then smiles hugely, showing all of his teeth, mocking me. It's playful and adorable, and I love it. "I do like smiling," he says, "believe it or not."

I grab the hand that's still caressing my face and hold it in my own. "I had a great time tonight," I say. "Thanks for inviting me."

"Thanks for accepting," he says, and then someone knocks at his trailer door.

Ethan takes his hand from mine and gets up to open it. I start putting my jacket back on, preparing for the cold walk to my car.

Lamont barely fits in the doorframe, but he manages to squeeze himself inside. It makes the trailer look that much smaller with him in it.

"Thanks for doing this," I tell him.

"My pleasure," he says with a smile, his white teeth shining brilliantly against his dark skin.

"Don't get any ideas," Ethan teases him.

"You know me, man. I'll have her eatin' outta my hands two steps from the trailer."

"I don't doubt that," Ethan says smiling, and then he turns to me.

"Tomorrow?" he asks me.

Lamont walks back out the door and pushes it closed; obviously, letting us say our good-byes.

"Tomorrow," I repeat, hoping he'll kiss me again.

Lucky for me, my wish comes true.

Ethan puts his hands on either side of my face this time, and pulls me to him. I'm sure kissing Ethan is something I'll never get used to. It seems different every time, and every time, more exciting than the last.

Once again, the kiss isn't long enough for me, but I'll let the thought of getting to see him again tomorrow hold me over.

"You have my number now," he says, opening the door. "Please call me when you get in, okay?"

"I only live a few blocks from here," I tell him, elated by the idea of him caring about me.

"No matter," he says. "Call me, please?"

"Okay," I agree, as I walk toward Lamont who's waiting a few steps from the trailer. I look at Ethan for the last time tonight over my shoulder. He winks at me, and then closes his door.

"What have you done to him?" Lamont's deep voice startles me.

"What do you mean?"

Lamont laughs and I swear he could cause an earthquake with a good solid chuckle.

"He's up in the clouds," Lamont jokes.

"How do you know it's because of me?" I ask, trying to pry. We'll be at my car in no time.

"Trust me. I know," Lamont says, smiling.

I smile too. I gave up on not getting too excited about this evening the minute I walked into Ethan's trailer. I don't care if I ever speak to him again after tonight. I hope I will, but even if I don't I won't have any regrets. Tonight was perfection.

"I didn't do anything to him," I say finally. "We ate dinner and talked. That's it."

"Just don't break his heart, okay?" Lamont's face is serious, as we approach my car.

I stare at Lamont, completely taken aback.

"Wouldn't you think I'd be the more logical victim here?" I say shyly.

I mean, Ethan's a celebrity. He's dated supermodels. If anyone is going to get hurt, it will most likely be me.

"No," Lamont says, as I unlock my car door. "Ethan's not as tough as most people think. He's got a good heart."

It sounds like a threat, so I nod and smile and leave it alone.

"Thanks for the escort," I say, as I sit down in the driver's seat. Lamont reaches to close my door for me.

"He likes you," he says smiling.

"I really like him too," I admit. There's something about Lamont, like you can open your soul to him with no judgments.

"I know," he says, smiling again. "Have a good night."

"Thanks again," I say, as he shuts my door. I roll down my window, mad at myself for not asking sooner. "Do you want me to drive you back over?"

"No," he answers, already several feet away. "I'm good."

It's freezing out, but I'm sure it takes a lot for a guy as big as Lamont to feel cold. Plus, he's bundled pretty well. I watch his large frame round the corner before I back out of the deserted square and head home.

It's early enough for me to pick up Jake, but I call my mom and find out he's already asleep. I decide to let him rest and tell my mom I'll be over first thing in the morning to get him.

I decide to text Ethan when I get home instead of call. Apparently that wasn't good enough for him.

"Hello?" I answer on the first ring since the phone is already in my hand.

"I wanted to hear your voice," he says, then pauses. "Am I creeping you out yet?"

"No," I laugh, "surprisingly, not."

"Good." He's laughing as well. "Sweet dreams, Samantha."

"Sweet dreams."

I plop down on my bed, kick off my shoes and crawl in. I don't even bother putting on pajamas. I'm suddenly exhausted from tonight.

I cuddle into my pillows, knowing I'll be asleep within seconds, sure to have sweet dreams indeed.

CHAPTER 10

I wake up to the sun shining brightly in my bedroom window, matching my happy mood.

From this view, I can pretend it's springtime. There's a light breeze blowing the tops of the trees, and the sun seems to be warming the rooftops across the way, but I know it's probably blisteringly cold out there.

With that thought, I pull the covers up around my neck and snuggle back into my pillow. It's seven A.M. – a little too early to go get Jake, who I'm anxious to see.

As soon as Jake leaves my mind, I instantly go back to last night. *Did that really happen? Could it be true?*

I try hard to remind myself it wasn't a dream, but back in the comfortable normalcy of my apartment, it sure seems that way.

My phone vibrates on the nightstand, which pulls me from my day dreaming about kissing Ethan.

I have twelve text messages: six from Sydney, three from Rose, two from Liz and one from an unknown number I'm coming to recognize very well. With a grin that threatens to split my face in two, I decide to read that one first.

Good morning. I hope you have a wonderful day. See you tonight.

So, it wasn't a dream. I text him back, short and sweet.

Same to you. See you tonight.

I close my eyes briefly, once again letting my mind drift to his soft lips before I read my other messages.
They are all along the same lines...

Call me as soon as you get up!

Sydney, being the most persistent of course...

CALL ME NOW!!!!

I notice that all of them sent at least one text last night and then one this morning, or five in Sydney's case. I can't believe she's up this early.
I type a message to each of them, telling them to meet me at Ken's Diner for breakfast in thirty minutes. "Be there, or be square." I type, laughing at myself and my joyful mood.
I jump up after that and get in the shower thinking about Ethan the entire time. I think about the way his eyes smoldered after we kissed, his beautiful smile and the way it felt when he gently held my hand or touched my face. I think about how tender, but

passionate his kisses were, and it brings goose bumps to my skin, even in my hot shower.

I dress quickly, skipping the primping, and head to Ken's Diner to meet the girls by eight.

All of them already texted me back confirming they would be there.

I decide to call my mom on the short drive over, just to let her know my plans.

"So, how did it go?" she asks.

"It went well," I say, "but I'll be having a discussion with you later on about this." I try to sound angry, but there's no way I could be upset with anyone today.

My mom laughs, probably at my attempt at an angry voice. "Yes dear. Whatever you say," she playfully mocks me. "I'll see you later on."

"Love you, mom."

"Love you too, hun."

The girls all beat me to the restaurant. Sydney's wearing a baseball cap and it appears as if she hasn't even showered, which is completely out of character for her. She must have been extremely anxious for this story. I'm glad it probably won't disappoint this time.

"Sydney, did you take a shower?" I ask, as we sit down in a booth in the restaurant.

"Of course not!" she says with a disgusted look on her face like she's still working to try and deal with the fact. "I didn't have time to get ready with a shower, and I wasn't about to miss this!"

Liz looks gorgeous, even in sweats. She has a glow about her that tells me she had a good night as well, but I don't ask any questions.

We all know better. Liz will talk, but only on her terms.

We all order coffee and our standard selections when the waitress comes by, and as soon as the waitress leaves, I'm accosted.

"Start from the top," Rose begs. "We want to hear every detail."

I smile and start with me walking into his trailer. I describe what he was wearing per Sydney's request, and then give a few details about his trailer.

"I'm so glad he's not pretentious. I like him even more now," Liz says.

"I know!" I agree. "I was happy about that too."

"Go on!" Sydney whines. "What was for dinner?"

I tell them about the lasagna and what a gentleman he was, fixing my plate.

I realize, as I'm retelling the story, that there wasn't much conversation involved last night, but I use as much detail as I can while we all eat our grease-filled breakfasts.

Then Sydney interrupts. "So, what did you tell him when he asked 'why him'?"

"Well, I told him I loved him as an actor," I say. "You guys remember *Jimmy's Story*, right?"

Rose grabs her chest. "Oh, the one where he plays the troubled teen? Incredible. I love that movie."

"That's the one." I smile. "I told him I thought he was amazing, and he said that meant a lot to him."

I'm smiling ear to ear now, realizing I get to relive our kiss yet again.

"Go on," Liz prods.

I tell them about how he made me give him more reasons, then how I blurted out the part about wanting to meet him.

Sydney looks at me with wide eyes. She would never be that forward with a guy, especially not so soon, but before she can reprimand me, I interrupt her.

"Then he kissed me," I say, and the crowd goes wild.

"What?!" Sydney screams, causing everyone in the small diner to turn toward our table. "He did *what*?!"

"He kissed me," I repeat in a hushed tone so our new eavesdroppers won't overhear.

Rose is shaking the booth as she hugs me. Liz just has a look of "I told you so" on her face and Sydney's still in shock, but smiling now.

"I *need* details," Sydney says slowly to me. "Good kisser? Soft kisser? Nice lips? Tell me everything."

"I don't really want to share those details, if that's okay," I say shyly.

"Fine," Sydney huffs, crossing her arms across her chest, but still smiling at me.

"He invited Jake and me to a basketball game with him tonight," I add.

Sydney starts blinking rapidly. "I don't think I can take much more!" she says, patting her cheeks on either side, looking every bit like a blonde Scarlett O'Hara.

"He invited Jake?" Rose asks with a huge smile, knowing how very happy this must make me.

"He did." I return her smile. "I wouldn't normally want Jake involved in something like this so soon, but I think this situation is a bit different."

"I should say so." Liz smiles at me.

"He's sending a car for us. We're having dinner then going to the game," I tell them.

"Well, look at you, superstar," Liz says. "You deserve this, you know," she adds.

I look at my friends and think again about how lucky I am to have them.

Rose and I have been friends nearly our whole lives. We went to elementary school together and have been pretty much inseparable since third grade. We've been accused more than once of sharing the same brain.

The other two came along later – after high school – but I'm beginning to feel the same for them as I do for Rose.

They're the sweetest and most loyal people I've ever known. All three were there for me when my dad died, and I'm confident they'll be there for me for the many other hard times I may experience in life, just like I'll be there for them.

My train of thought brings a tear to my eye. Rose notices.

"Oh no!" she cries. "Why are you crying again?" She starts patting my arm. "You're always crying!" she laughs.

"I just feel so lucky to have you guys," I say, sappily, and they all laugh then.

"We're lucky to have you too," Liz says, winking at me from across the table.

"And you're *very* lucky to have Ethan," Sydney says which prompts a roar of laughter from everyone at the table, including me.

"Thanks for believing in me and not thinking I'm crazy," I tell them.

"Who says we don't think you're crazy?" Liz asks, sipping her coffee.

I smile at her. "I never thought I would ever have an opportunity to meet him, let alone have dinner with him."

"And *kiss* him!" Sydney interjects.

"And kiss him," I say smiling. "I never thought it would happen. I hoped it might, but I never thought it would."

"We did," Rose confesses. "We knew the minute he got one good look at you he would be smitten." She looks smug.

Liz laughs again. "Definitely," she agrees. "And it seems we were right."

"I love you ladies." I'm feeling all kinds of emotional this morning. My mom's going to have a field day with me.

"We love you too," Liz says. "Now stop blubbering and eat your pancakes."

❧

Mom's waiting for me on the front porch with Jake when I pull up.

"Morning!" she yells. "How was breakfast?"

"Good," I say, smiling. "Ken says hello."

The owner of the diner has been sweet on my mom for decades. She'll have nothing to do with him, of course, but I know she's flattered by the thought.

"Huh," she laughs. "That one's still after me, I see. Well, too bad. He's too old."

"So, mom?" I ask as we walk inside. "You want to tell me why in the world you would keep something from me like Ethan Grant calling this house?"

Jake turns to me with wide eyes.

"He called here?" he asks with wonder.

I smile at him and then kneel to the ground in the living room so we're at eye level.

"Your eye looks much better today," I tell him.

"It feels fine," Jake says, hastily brushing my fingers from his face. "Now tell me about Ethan!"

"I have some good news, buddy." I laugh at Jake staring open-mouthed at me, waiting for me to continue. "I met Ethan again last night, and he invited us to a basketball game with him."

"No way!" Jake screams. I notice my mom put her hands over her mouth, covering up her smile. "Did he really, mom?"

"He did," I happily confirm. "He wants us to have dinner with him and then we have box seats at the Hawks game!"

I can't hide my excitement, though I could care less about basketball and more about the opportunity to see Ethan again.

"He invited *both* of you out?" My mom's smiling, obviously warming more to Ethan by the second.

"He did," I confirm again.

I share a look with my mom that explains to her exactly how I feel, and although I can see the apprehension in her face, I know she's genuinely happy for me.

"How fun will *that* be?" my mom asks Jake.

"It will be awesome!" Jake squeals. "I can't wait to tell my friends! Can I call Sean mom?" Jake is anxious to get the gossip started.

"Why don't you wait until tomorrow?" I suggest. "That way, you can tell him all about the night and how much fun you had."

I don't want Jake rushing to the phone to call his friend and brag just yet.

Even though I got my wonderful text from Ethan this morning, it still feels too much like "Fantasyland". I'm still not one hundred percent convinced that tonight will actually come to fruition.

"Okay," he agrees, looking defeated.

I smile reassuringly. "You can call him first thing in the morning. I promise."

"So what time are we leaving?" Jake is smiling again now.

"He's sending a car at four to pick us up." I know Jake will be over the moon about this. I'm getting increasingly nervous now about that car ever showing up.

"A car?!" he shouts. "Like a limo?!"

"I'm not sure buddy. He just said 'a car'."

Jake throws himself theatrically down on the couch. "I can't believe this!"

"I'm glad you're happy. I'm sure we'll have a great time."

"What's he like mom?" he asks, sitting back up to face me. "What's Ethan like?"

I notice my mom waiting to hear the answer to this question as well.

"He's very nice, buddy." I'm not sure what to say. I'm honestly still not quite sure myself what Ethan is like, other than a very good kisser. "He let me eat dinner with him last night, and he was a gentleman. He made my plate, and even had his bodyguard walk me to my car afterward."

That last part was for my mom's benefit, but Jake seemed just as impressed.

"Wow," Jake says in awe. "I can't believe my mom is really friends with Ethan Grant."

I smile, thinking about our kiss again. My mom catches on to my blush.

"Why don't you go out back and play a while," my mom suggests. "No TV, remember?"

Jake would normally be upset about this, but instead, he runs happily out back, jazzed by the recent news.

"So, a basketball game, huh?" My mom's smiling at me.

"Can you believe it?" I throw myself into a chair at the kitchen table. "I'm still wondering when I'll wake up."

"He must have called here a million times. I thought he was a lunatic at first."

"Yes, please do explain this further," I prod. I'm eager to see why she felt she should keep this from me.

My mom's making cookies. I smelled them when I came in. She pauses from placing spoonfuls of the latest batch on her cookie sheet to face me.

"The first time he called was the day after you went to that party," she admits, and my mouth hits the floor.

"What?" I finally manage to get out.

"I'm not gonna lie. I thought it was a joke at first," she says, turning back to her cookies, "but after the first couple of times, I started thinking he may be for real."

"How? What did he say?"

"He told me lots of stuff, but it wasn't what he said that made me think he was the real deal."

I pause, waiting for her to continue but I can't keep my mouth shut for long. "Elaborate, please?"

"I just got this feeling. I knew in my heart that it was him. I knew it had to be."

"What do you mean?"

My mom turns to face me again. "Because I've never seen you want anything more in your whole life. I knew this would happen for you."

I laugh. "Why? Because I always get everything I want?" The sarcasm is thick. I can't help myself.

"No," she says calmly, "because you *deserve* to be happy."

Tears threaten my eyes again, but I manage to choke them back. "Thanks, momma."

"You're welcome, hun." She's back to her cookies now. "And I think Ethan will make you very happy."

"Just one question though." One thing is still bugging me. "Why string him along for so long if you knew it was really him? And why not tell me?"

My mom chuckles. "I'd think that would be obvious."

"Not really," I confess.

I was miserable after our trip to Atlanta, and you'd think she would have at least told me he called to ease my suffering.

"For starters," she says, pointing her tablespoon in the air for emphasis, "I didn't want you to get your hopes up, just in case. And second, I needed him to work for it."

"Mother!" I'm horrified. "What do you mean you 'needed him to work for it'?"

She turns to me and gives me her are-you-serious look.

"I just told you, hun, I've never seen you want something so badly. Maybe I thought it was kind of crazy at first, but that doesn't mean I'm not always looking out for you. I'm not going to let some boy come in and break my little girls heart!" The tough Southern woman is coming out. It's my favorite persona. "Besides, that boy could've gotten your number if he wanted. He didn't have to go through me."

"I hadn't thought about that," I ponder. "Why did he try so hard with you?"

"I'm not sure," she admits. "But I figured he just wanted to get on my good side, prove to me he was good enough. So, I made him work for it."

I smile at her. "Thanks mom. I appreciate you watching my back."

"I didn't know the first thing about that man, but you can bet your bottom dollar I got to know him pretty well over these past few weeks on the phone." She turns to look at me again. "And you have my blessing."

I'm stunned again. "What? Like you had deep conversations with him?" I nearly yell. "About what?"

"That's between him and me," she says firmly. "If he wants to share it with you, he can, but I'd rather not."

I lay my head on the table. I can only imagine the Hell my mom must have put him through, but the encouraging thought is that he kept calling back.

"You know what's crazy?" my mom asks.

"You?" I respond.

"Besides that," she laughs, as she puts her cookies in the oven and comes to sit with me at the table. "On the phone, he seemed just as crazy to talk to you again as you have been to meet him all this time. I mean, this kid barely knows you, and here he is calling me nearly every day, practically on hands and knees for your phone number, when he could surely get it himself. I've never seen anything like it. There's only one way to explain it."

"What's that?" I ask smiling.

I like what my mom just said. I like the thought of him wanting me as much as I want him.

"Fate," she answers, confidently. "As crazy as I thought you were for obsessing over another movie star, it seems God had a plan for you guys all along."

I'm not sure about all that, but I don't dispute it. It sounds like a good plan to me.

"I'm scared," I admit to her.

"I know," she says, rubbing my hand on the table, "and you should be. But you can't let that hold you back from living life."

"You're right," I sigh, as my mom's words awaken some long suppressed feelings of regret. "I just don't know what to expect from being with him. His life is very different, and this is moving kind of fast."

"Just take it one day at a time. You'll be fine," she assures me, her hand patting my face. "Mother always knows best."

CHAPTER 11

I breathe a sigh of relief when a huge black car with tinted windows pulls up outside my apartment at four on the dot.

"Ready?" I ask Jake, when I probably should be asking myself this question.

"Let's go!" Jake yells, as he runs out the front door.

I take one last glance in the mirror. I put on a little more make-up than normal, per Sydney's suggestion, but it's still modest. I went with my favorite dark jeans, brown boots, a long, tan, scoop-neck sweater and a fun necklace I picked up at a flea market several years ago. I didn't want to be too dressy, but I didn't want to wear my usual t-shirt/sneaker combo either. Jake gave me his approval, so I guess that's good enough.

Throwing on my coat, I follow after Jake to the car parked out front. To my surprise, Lamont gets out of the driver's seat and comes to open our doors. It isn't a limo, but it's still pretty impressive. I know very little about cars, but I recognize the Cadillac symbol on the hood of the huge SUV. It's sleek, all black, with extremely dark tinted windows.

"You're his driver too?" I tease him.

"I offered," he says with a smile.

"We really appreciate it," I tell him, as he helps buckle Jake into the backseat, before opening the front door for me.

"It's no problem at all." Lamont has such a friendly disposition.

Jake seems a little apprehensive, I'm sure caused by the sheer size of Lamont, and probably by his deep voice as well.

"Jake, this is Lamont," I tell him, turning around in my seat once Lamont gets in. "He's Ethan's friend."

"Nice to meet you," Jake says quietly, as he extends a nervous hand to Lamont.

"It's great to meet you too Jake," Lamont smiles widely and shakes Jake's hand. "Where'd you get the shiner?"

"Got into a fight," Jake sticks his little chest out like he's proud, but I give him a look that makes him cower back into the seat. "Got in trouble too," Jake adds, looking at me.

"Sorry to hear about that — the fight and the punishment," Lamont says, looking at me with a smile. "How about some TV?"

Jake looks at me for approval and I nod. I decide not to enforce the "no TV" rule for the car ride.

"That'd be awesome!" Jake tells Lamont.

Lamont presses a few buttons on an extremely complicated looking touch-screen computer on the dash, and within a few seconds, I hear "Sponge Bob Squarepants" coming from the backseat — not my favorite, but it's a special occasion, I guess.

"All set now? Ready to hit the road?" Lamont turns to ask Jake, once he gets the television going.

"Ready!" Jake says, seemingly encouraged by Lamont's smiling face, and more likely his ability to choose good television programming, at least in my son's opinion.

"Let's go then!" Lamont pulls out of my complex, and we head for the highway.

"So, tell me about yourself, Samantha. Are you from Delia?"

I suddenly realize why Lamont offered to pick us up.

"You're feeling me out, aren't you?" I decide to call him on it.

"Maybe a little," he admits, smiling. "It's not that I don't like you or don't trust you. I'm just nosey like that." He winks at me, and I smile.

"I understand," I say. "You're looking out for him. It's okay with me. I'm sure he comes across some not-so-savory people every once in a while."

"You could say that." We exchange smiles again, before he starts back. "So, you're from Delia then?"

"Born and raised," I say with pride. "I grew up not far from where I live now. My mom actually still lives in the house where I grew up. And you can all me Sam, if you'd like," I add at the end.

"Okay, *Sam*." Lamont smiles at me again. "Any brothers or sisters?"

"Nope. Just me. I always wanted a sibling, but enjoyed being the one and only at the same time."

I see Lamont take a quick look in the backseat, perhaps to rethink a question about Jake. I'm relieved.

"Where do you work?" he asks instead.

"I work for the city at the courthouse. I'm not crazy about it," I admit. "I'm a glorified secretary, but the benefits are good and I like the hours. It allows me to spend time with Jake."

"Did you go to college?" Lamont asks, and I know this question is probably based on what I told him I did for a living. I try not to be offended.

"No," I say, before taking a quick glance over my shoulder to the back seat. "I never did."

Luckily, Jake seems oblivious to the conversation, as he watches the small television hanging from the ceiling in front of him.

Lamont gives me an apologetic look, and I smile. I know he doesn't mean any harm. I'm just a little sensitive when it comes to Jake.

"I went to FSU," he says. "Played ball for four years. Could have gone pro, but Ethan asked me if I'd help him. This job is much better."

"FSU?" I ask, trying to get the conversation off me for a bit. "Florida State in Jacksonville?"

"That's the one," he says. "I grew up in Maryland with Ethan. I was looking to get out of the cold. I chose the warmest place that offered me a scholarship."

"You've known Ethan a while then?" I'm always eager to hear more about Ethan.

"Nearly all my life," he admits. "We grew up together, but didn't become friends until middle school. He saved me from getting my butt kicked one time."

I stare at him, obvious shock on my face. "Ethan helped *you* in a fight?"

Lamont smiles. "I haven't always looked like this."

"I see." Lamont is so easy to talk to. "And you've been protecting *him* ever since I take it?"

"Something like that," he says. "I don't think Ethan ever thought he'd be where he is now. It scares him. I think he needed a friend more than anything."

"Well, you're a good friend," I say to him again, repeating my words from last night.

"I guess," he laughs. "Ethan's pretty easy to like."

I like how it seems Lamont's trying to sell me on Ethan. It makes me feel as if maybe Lamont likes me a little, which can only be a good thing.

"Yes, he is easy to like," I agree. "So why do you think he has such a bad reputation?"

Lamont pauses to think for a moment.

"Maybe because Ethan doesn't really care what people think," he finally says. "He's not out to impress everyone, and he's a very private person. Some people just misinterpret his serious side."

"Believe it or not, I never thought he was a bad person," I admit, truthfully. "There was always something there, when I saw him in interviews or on screen, which felt so raw and honest. It's what I've liked most about him all of these years."

"All of these years?" Lamont teases. "Maybe I do need to do a more thorough interview to make certain you're not one of the crazy ones. Tell me more about your family."

We smile at each other then and continue our small talk all the way to Ethan's place.

Lamont eventually stopped the drilling. I guess after a while he was satisfied that I wasn't a complete loon, so he decided to back off. When we pull into Ethan's apartment building, it's a little after five.

The building has a security gate with a guard outside, and Lamont explains that a lot of celebrities in Atlanta have taken up residency here. Apparently, the security is excellent.

The building is your typical Atlanta high-rise — modern architecture covered in mirrored glass and steel. We park in the garage underneath the building and Lamont comes around to open our doors again after we find a spot.

As we walk through the lobby, I see the building is very contemporary inside and out.

I'm not much for modern style, but the lobby is exquisite — all white, with white walls, white tile floors, white countertops, white everywhere.

The floors are dotted with shaggy white rugs, and the lights are white paper chandeliers hanging over the white couches in the waiting area. Even the front desk workers are wearing all white. As a mom, all I can think about is how I'd hate to be the one in charge of keeping this place clean.

One side of the room is entirely windows, which provides a view of the pool and hot-tub just outside among the trees. The trees are lit with white lights, of course, woven meticulously throughout the branches. It's really beautiful.

I take a quick look down at Jake, wondering how he's doing, how he's taking all of this in. I'm happy to see he looks excited, perhaps to see Ethan. I'll have to admit, I am too.

"Shall we?" Lamont asks, gesturing toward the elevators.

I smile and follow him to an elevator on the far left. It's separate from the others, and when we get in, I see why. Lamont has to slip a key card into a slot to make the doors close. Then he presses the button for the thirty-fifth floor.

"Is that the top?" Jake asks excitedly.

"Yep," Lamont answers with a smile.

"Awesome!" Jake says before turning to look out the back of the elevator, which is all glass, so you can see the Atlanta skyline on your way up.

"Aren't you impressed, Sam?" Lamont teases me, as I watch Jake having so much fun already.

I look up at him and smile. "I promise I'm not some gold digging groupie."

Lamont laughs. "Just testing you."

I punch him lightly in the arm. Lamont must have a million friends. The process is effortless.

We arrive at Ethan's floor in no time. As we get off the elevator, I notice there aren't a lot of apartments on his floor. From what I can tell, it looks like two apartments total.

Lamont leads us to the door on the far left, and Ethan opens it before we can even knock.

"I heard the elevator," he explains with a shrug to Lamont, who has his fist raised still prepared to knock.

They smile at each other, before Ethan notices Jake and me.

"Hi," he breathes when he sees me, and my heart nearly flutters out of my chest.

"Hi," I say, aware that I'm blushing, but I don't really care. Jake pulls on my hand. "This is Jake," I say, putting my arm around my son.

"It's very nice to meet you Jake," Ethan says, and Jake grins widely. "Why don't you guys come in?"

Jake and I follow Lamont inside.

"Would you like something to drink?" Ethan offers, as I look around his place.

"I'm okay," I reply. "Jake?" Jake shakes his head. He's acting a little shy, which is unusual.

Ethan's apartment is a little flashier than his trailer, but it still isn't over the top.

The front door leads directly into the living area. There are two pretty plush leather couches with a coffee table in the middle. He has a very large television, which I caught Jake eyeing the minute we walked in.

There's a kitchen to our left, and then the back of the room is a wall of windows, just like in the lobby. The pool downstairs was lovely, but I like the view from this window much better. It's an incredible view of the city.

Jake and I sit down on one couch, and Lamont goes to sit on the other. Ethan plops himself down casually on the coffee table in front of Jake and me, and I notice for the first time what he's wearing — faded jeans, a gray t-shirt and a dark green, V-neck sweater. His shaggy brown hair is tousled just the way I like it, and the sweater makes his sparkling green eyes look amazing.

"I hope Lamont didn't harass you too much on the ride up?" Ethan asks.

I can hardly take my eyes off of him, even though I know I need to be careful today with Jake in tow.

"He was pretty gentle," I say, smiling over at Lamont.

"She's being nice," Lamont says. "I grilled her pretty good."

"And? Your conclusion?" Ethan smiles at him. Their chumminess is very endearing.

"She's okay in my book." Lamont winks at me.

"Good." Ethan looks over at me then, his eyes are soft. "Glad to hear it."

"Ethan?" Jake breaks our deep stare. "Could we turn on your TV?"

"Sorry," I say, as I gape at my child. "He's been on punishment, without television." I point to my own eye and Ethan nods in understanding. "I guess he's having withdrawals. And your TV *is* rather large," I add with a smile.

I can't stop smiling. Ethan looks incredible, and just being near him again makes every cell in my body pulse with excitement. I never knew I could feel this way about anyone.

"It's not a problem at all." Ethan grabs for the remote. "What shall we watch?" he asks, moving to sit beside Jake.

"Um," Jake puts his tiny finger on his chin, deep in thought, "how about some sports? Can you find some sports somewhere?"

Ethan smiles at him. "I'm sure I can."

"A man after my own heart!" Lamont says, and I'm in heaven.

"So, do you like Japanese food?" Ethan asks me, after he finds ESPN for Jake.

"Sure," I say. I don't have much experience with sushi, if that's what he's referring to, but I'm sure I can feel my way through.

"There's a great place down the street that I thought we could try – one of those places that cooks in front of you. I thought Jake may like it."

"Sounds great!" Jake says, but I'm pretty sure he would agree with anything Ethan has to say after their TV bonding moment.

"Sounds fun," I tell Ethan, feeling warm inside at the thought of him taking Jake into consideration this evening.

"I made reservations for six o'clock, if that's okay. It's a little early, but I thought you guys might want to do a little sight-seeing before the game. Do you get to Atlanta much?" he asks.

"Honestly, no," I admit. "I know it's only an hour away, but it may as well be in another state. We don't have a lot of reasons to visit."

"Until now," Ethan corrects with a smile.

"Until now," I agree.

God, his smile is out of this world.

Ethan and Lamont monopolize the conversation until it's finally time to go. Ethan would look at me periodically out of the corner of his eye, and I wonder if he thought I wasn't having a good time, since I didn't participate much in the conversation. Little does he know, I could sit on his couch and listen to his voice all night and be perfectly happy.

"Time to go," Lamont says, glancing at his watch.

"Ready to try some foreign food?" Ethan asks Jake, as he turns off the television.

"Ready!" Jake eagerly replies.

I go to put my jacket back on, and like a true gentleman, Ethan moves behind me to help.

"Thanks," I say, turning to him as I button my jacket and fold my scarf around my neck.

"Welcome," he says with a huge smile.

Our eyes linger on each other a little longer than necessary, and Jake starts to get impatient.

"Mom! Let's go!" he says, tugging at my hand.

"Sorry bud." I reluctantly peel my eyes away from Ethan. "Let's roll!"

☙❧

The Japanese place was incredible. It was small, kind of a hole in the wall, which I think everyone knows are the best places to eat. And Ethan didn't just make a reservation. He reserved the entire restaurant.

We all stuffed ourselves with teriyaki chicken, grilled shrimp, fried rice and some red sauce that I couldn't seem to get enough of.

Dinner took longer than expected, so we agreed to skip the sightseeing. We decided to walk to the MARTA station and catch a train to the arena.

I keep worrying Ethan may get recognized and some riot will ensue. I have no idea how that works outside of his filming stints in Delia, but I've seen pictures of him getting mobbed leaving the movies with Lamont, and once coming out of a grocery store in Buckhead.

Tonight, he put the hood up on his jacket after we left the restaurant and has managed so far to go completely unnoticed. I think having Jake and I with him may be throwing people off as well, even though Lamont sure causes some stares.

We get to the arena and use a special entrance to access the private suite. I'm not surprised to find out we're the only ones in this particular suite tonight. Ethan has once again rigged the situation for privacy. I'm starting to grasp how lonely life must be for him.

"So," I say when we sit down, "you like your privacy, huh?" Lamont took Jake to get a snack, and this is the first moment we've had alone.

"I do," he says, putting his hand on my leg and leaning forward to steal a kiss. "It's good to see you."

"It's good to see you too." I'm embarrassed that my voice is shaking a little.

"Do you want something?" Ethan asks as he gets up to make himself a drink at the full bar inside the suite.

I'm not sure if I'll ever get used to the excitement of being with him, let alone all of these extra perks.

"Gotta beer?" I ask.

"Coming right up."

He hands me my beer and sits back down on the barstool beside mine.

"I was worried someone may recognize you on our way here," I confess. "Do you worry about that a lot? I mean, don't you feel isolated, having to rent out entire restaurants just to have a nice meal?"

"Well," he smiles, "it's actually not as bad in Atlanta as it is in L.A. or New York, but it still happens from time to time." He grabs my hand. "And I don't normally rent out entire restaurants. I just didn't want to have to deal with any craziness tonight. I'm used to it, but I would rather avoid it with Jake around. The paparazzi can be ruthless sometimes."

I'm relieved to hear him say that because that's my concern too.

"Thank you for taking him into consideration so much tonight," I smile. "He's having a blast."

"He's a great kid. I like him a lot."

As if he heard us talking about him, Jake comes running into the box.

"Mom, this is so cool!" he squeals. "I got this huge slushie and some candy, and then Lamont said he could take me down to the court a little later on to watch some of the game. Isn't that awesome?!"

"I'm sure the sugar will only add to the fun." Lamont winks at me.

"That's great, angel." I look up at Lamont. "Are you sure you don't mind babysitting?"

"I am NOT a baby!" Jake yells back at me from the front of the suite.

"I don't mind at all," Lamont says in earnest. "I have a little nephew that I don't get to see much anymore. I'm making up for lost time."

"Gotcha," I say smiling. "Thank you."

Lamont and Jake move to the seats in front of the suite to watch the action, which leaves Ethan and I alone again. I've noticed Ethan has been very hands off tonight, which I appreciate while Jake is around.

"So, do you live in Atlanta full time?" I ask him.

"Pretty much," he says, and I like the way he gives me one hundred percent of his attention when we talk. It's so different from the first night I met him. "I'm in New York and L.A. a lot for work, but most of my time is spent here for the show."

"Don't you miss your family?" I ask, with honest curiosity.

I don't know much about his family, and he never really speaks about them in interviews.

Unfortunately, Ethan's face completely changes with my question. It's the blank mask everyone is accustomed to from him, more like the Ethan I met at the fundraiser. I realize this is not only his "work face", but it must also be the face he wears when he's trying hard not to expose his true feelings or the one he wears to hide his pain. It's amazing how such a simple gesture can explain so much about someone.

"Honestly," he starts, "I'm not very close with my family any more. We've drifted apart over the years, so I don't see them often."

"I'm very sorry," I offer. I don't know what else to say.

"It's okay," he says, smiling down at me. I see he's back to his less guarded expression, and I start to feel a little better.

"Could I ask you another one then?"

"Sure."

"What made you want to be an actor?"

I know it's probably a question he's been asked before, but I like the idea of hearing things from his own lips.

"Good question," he says, taking another sip of his beer. "I actually used to be really shy and awkward, and to get me to come out of my skin a little, a friend suggested an acting class. Surprisingly, for everyone who knew me, I liked it."

He turns toward me and his knee touches mine. I'm not sure if he notices, but I seem to be hyper-sensitive to the slightest touch from him.

"I kept taking classes, and eventually, I was recruited for a role in my first TV show," he continues.

"'Edinborough'," I recall, naming his first show. "I used to watch every Friday night with my mom, but I didn't know you were in it until well after the show ended. You only did two episodes, right?"

"Yep. I was a long, lost cousin of Damian's," he laughs. "I was only fifteen, and scared to death, but I made it through."

"Do you still love it?" I ask.

"Yes and no," he admits, and I love how honest he's being with me. "I'll confess that sometimes it feels more like a job than it used to. I didn't use to have all of the criticism and invasions of privacy. I led a pretty normal life. I'm a very private person."

He pauses and gives me a sad smile. "I know the paparazzi are a part of the celebrity lifestyle, but I just can't get used to people needing to be so involved in my personal affairs. I'm really not that interesting."

I laugh, thinking about how much more interesting his life is than mine.

"I'm sure it's a pain," I agree, "but why don't you give in every once in a while? It might stop people from saying such rotten things about you."

"Because I could care less what people think."

I can see he's getting defensive, and I wish immediately that I could take back my previous statement.

"It's not worth it to me," he continues. "I want people to watch my shows or see my movies because they appreciate me as an actor, not because of who I'm dating or because they feel bad for me because I don't have the perfect family life."

Okay, he's very defensive. It's obviously a touchy subject.

"I'm sorry," I say, and he seems to soften a bit. "That wasn't fair. I have no idea what it's like. I'm sure it's awful." I grab his hand under the bar. "I just never liked hearing such negative things about you. I knew they were lies, and I guess I always wished you would prove them wrong, just once."

He squeezes my hand and then studies my face.

"Where did you come from?" he asks in a whisper.

His green eyes are intense, and I suddenly realize I'm not breathing.

I break the stare, trying hard to maintain my composure, but wishing I could kiss him right now more than anything.

"One more question?" I ask him, finishing off my beer.

"Anything."

"You asked me last night what was so great about you. Remember?"

"Yes," he says smiling.

"Well, I'd like to ask you the same question...about me?"

I'm not sure if I really want to know this, but I honestly can't come up with anything. I have to know that it's more than just him having fun for a while with some infatuated fangirl.

"Another good question," he says, looking a little uncomfortable.

I try to wait for him to continue, but my nerves don't allow it. "If I'm just a fun time for you while you're in Atlanta, or just some company so you don't have to eat alone, I would like to know now."

I can't believe I just said that. I look down quickly, shocked by my boldness.

It's just that this is moving too fast for him to have any real feelings invested, I'm sure. My feelings are a plenty – irrational and naïve maybe, but in abundance to say the least.

"Could I get back to you on that?" he says, as Jake starts walking toward us from the seats.

"Lamont said we can go downstairs now. Is that okay mom?" Jake asks hurriedly, the excitement and sugar combination is evident.

"If Lamont doesn't mind, it's fine with me."

"Great!" he grabs Lamont's hand and they head quickly out the door.

I'm nervous as I watch him go. It's such a big place, and I barely know Lamont. I'm not questioning the fact that he's one of the nicest people on the planet, but I have no idea if he's capable of taking care of my child. What if he lets go of his hand? What if Jake gets lost? I find myself suddenly panicked.

"Will he be okay with Lamont?" I ask Ethan, hoping I don't offend him again.

"Are you kidding?" he says, smiling at me. "Lamont would probably die before he let anything happen to him."

That makes me feel a little better, but I still get up to look over the edge of the suite to see if I can tell where they will turn up around the court below.

I hear Ethan get up, and he comes to stand beside me. "They're going right over there," he says pointing to the right, "behind that goal. They should be there in a few minutes."

"Thanks," I say, hanging my head, still unable to look into his eyes since he is yet to answer my last question.

"I lied when I first met you," he suddenly blurts, which successfully gets my attention.

"What do you mean?"

"When we first met, I played it cool and told you I thought you looked familiar." He pauses, looking sheepish. "I knew exactly who you were."

Ethan's face is guilty, but not ashamed. I'm shocked but obviously eager for the rest.

He leads me back to the barstools and sits me down, but he remains standing.

"I don't know where to start. I'm not overly excited to tell you this." He starts slowly pacing in front of me. "I planned to tell you eventually, but I know you'll probably never want to see me again, and I just---" He stops when I grab his arm to stop the insane pacing.

"Just spit it out Ethan. I can take it," I assure him, although I'm making no promises.

"Okay." He lets out a big gust of air and comes to sit next to me at the bar. "I knew who you were at the WWF fundraiser. I knew who you were. I knew your name. I even knew where you lived."

"I'm sorry?"

Surely I'm not hearing him correctly.

He clasps his hands behind his neck and closes his eyes. "The first time I ever noticed you was about three months ago while I was filming."

He pulls his hands to his lap and looks down at his feet.

"You were wearing this white sundress, looking like an angel, and you were watching us film at the river that day. Do you remember it?" he asks, looking up at me now.

"I do," I answer in a small voice.

I have no idea how to feel about this, so I just go with shock. The horrible part is I remember that day well. It was the first time we all noticed Ethan glance at the crowd. It was like a small miracle in our group, but we were so far away from the set that day that there would have been no way to tell where his eyes were focused.

Ethan continues. "I saw you that day, and I was..." he pauses, trying to find the right words, "instantly attracted. However, I don't normally make it my business to mingle with fans, as I'm sure you've noticed. No offense but in my personal experience, they can be a little...shallow."

I nod and he continues. "Do you remember anything else about that day?" he asks.

"Yes," I answer, and I do remember that day for more than his first glance at the crowd. "It was the day that Snow Stevens visited the set."

Snow was a reporter for a local network, and he was a scumbag. Everyone hated him, but he was famous for digging up impossible dirt on celebrities and politicians, so he kept his job. Losers like him are the reason I hardly ever watch the news.

"Exactly," Ethan says smiling.

"That was the day I punched Snow Stevens in the mouth," I say, laughing.

I can't believe Ethan knows about it, even though I was on every news channel in town, plus I think a couple of major networks may have picked it up. There were set stalkers all over that day, so there were cameras all around. People were sending me pictures of the assault at different angles for weeks afterward.

The best part? I got off scot-free.

Snow was technically trespassing on private property without permission and the owner happens to be my boss. I tried to tell Snow to leave but he refused, not before making several rude comments and calling me some rather unpleasant names. My boss pressed charges against Snow — seriously, everyone hated him – and my punch was deemed "self-defense".

"And why exactly did you punch him?" Ethan asks, smiling widely now.

"For saying nasty things about you," I admit, feeling so embarrassed.

"Needless to say," Ethan continues, "I had to meet you."

"How did you know the truth though?" I ask, surprised.

Most people know I hit Snow because he was making rude comments, but I never confessed to anyone exactly who he was talking about. People may have made assumptions, but only my closest stalking buddies know the truth.

"Snow Stevens," he says laughing. "I saw him at a bar a few days later in Atlanta. He came up to me and basically started cussing me out for causing him to lose his job. Luckily, Lamont was with me. When Lamont showed back up from the bathroom, it cut Snow's rant short, but I heard enough. Lamont also told him that if he ever came after you, he would lose more than his job."

My heart starts pounding. "Lamont wasn't the one who...?" I start, unable to finish my question.

Snow was killed in a bar a couple of weeks after our little altercation. It seems he stepped over the line one to many times. They never caught the person who did it, but most people conspired it was a "government job".

"No!" Ethan says quickly. "It wasn't Lamont. I promise."

"Okay," I breathe. *Whew.* "Then why wait all this time to talk to me?"

"Well, it's not that easy for me," he says. "It's not very easy for me to trust people."

I nod in understanding, and then a thought occurs to me. "You said you knew where I lived?"

Ethan looks uncomfortable again. "I did some research, just in case. Goes back to that whole can't-trust-people thing."

I nod again and smile, but I have to pry. "That still doesn't explain the waiting."

"Honestly?"

"That would be nice."

"I found out you had a son," he says, and then hurries to finish, probably seeing the disappointment on my face. "It didn't turn me off or anything. I was just reluctant to bring you into my world, with a child to worry about."

"Oh," I say, still trying to digest all of this new information. "And how did you get my mom's number?" I ask.

"This one is pretty bad," he says, hanging his head, but I smile. He's so adorable. How could I be upset with him?

"Go ahead," I push.

"Well, I offered you my phone that night at the fundraiser, and I saved your mom's number."

I start thinking about that night again – me losing my purse with my ticket inside, helping him from a crazy fan. "You didn't plan all of that, did you?"

"No," Ethan answers quickly again. "It was total fate that brought us together that night. I'm not that good."

I smile at him for using the same word as mom used earlier to describe our meeting. *Fate.*

"Good," I say. "That would have definitely been a little scary."

Ethan laughs at me. "I just told you that I have basically been stalking your house and sneaking glances of you while I'm on set. Plus, you already know about me calling your poor mother a million times to beg for your number, and all you're worried about is the possibility of a little arranged meeting?"

"Pre-meditation is characteristic of a serial killer," I say, still smiling.

"I'll keep that in mind."

"One last question..." I start, "why call my mom for my number? Couldn't you have gotten it through other avenues?"

"Well..." Ethan looks at me, like he's not sure how much to reveal. Then he sighs, resigned. "I guess I don't have much to lose at this point."

"Not much," I confirm, with a laugh.

"The truth is I probably never would have spoken to you if I hadn't met you at the fundraiser that night. I can be a horribly shy person in certain situations – not a complete dick, like everyone thinks."

"I never thought you were a dick."

"I know." God, I love his smile. "So I thought when I met you, it must be fate, right? But I still couldn't muster up the courage to call you. I thought maybe if I could win your mom over, then she would help me, but your mom ended up being a lot tougher than I expected."

"I'm so sorry." I smile back at him.

He thought he would need my mom to help win me over?

Hilarious!

"That probably was not your best route," I say, but all of a sudden the obvious occurs to me, and I start cracking up.

"What is it?" I can see Ethan is confused by my roar of laughter.

"I just thought of something," I manage to get out between giggles. "We're *both* stalkers!"

Ethan starts laughing too, and then the next thing I know, my face is in his hands and he's kissing me again.

It's a little more passionate and reckless than the kiss last night, but I'm not complaining.

"But I'm worse, I think," he says, as he holds my face close to his and continues to place tiny kisses on my nose, my cheek, my chin. "I'm the creepy one. Not you."

"I don't think you're creepy," I whisper. "I think you're incredible." His kisses are like truth serum. "You're everything I thought you would be and more."

"I could say the same thing about you," he whispers, before he kisses me again – this time soft and sweet, but just as pleasurable.

When he finally lets me go, Ethan pulls me off my barstool and over toward the edge of the suite. He then finds Jake and Lamont in the crowd below and points them out to me. Jake now has an inflatable basketball in his hands and is twirling it in excitement as he and Lamont watch the game from what has to be some of the best seats in the house.

"This has been an amazing night," I say to Ethan. "Jake won't forget it any time soon."

"I'm glad you had a good time," he says. "And you're sure you're not upset with me? I promise it's you. You bring out very strange behavior in me."

"How could I be mad at you?" I assure him, smiling. I'm just as guilty. "You bring out the crazy in me too. I haven't been this infatuated with anyone since Justin Timberlake and N'Sync," I tease.

Ethan laughs. "Me and Justin, huh?"

I lean into him as he wraps his arms around my waist from behind and nuzzles into my neck.

"Well, I'll always have a special place in my heart for Justin, but I'm pretty much over him now."

"Good to know," he says, as he starts kissing my neck.

I turn to face him, eager to feel his lips on mine and he willingly obliges. He hugs me close, before finally breaking free.

"How about we go watch some basketball?" he suggests with a smile. "It looks like Lamont's having all the fun."

CHAPTER 12

The girls and I always do lunch on Sunday after church. Normally Jake comes along, but I let mom take him home with her this time because I knew there would be questions about last night.

Ethan touched my hand a few times last night in front of Jake, and of course we shared some intense eye contact, but I know Jake suspects nothing other than friendship at this point, and that's the way I want to keep it for now. I feel like this whole thing with Ethan is moving fast for *me*, so I can only assume it would be a roller coaster ride for Jake.

Plus, even though it is *Ethan Grant*, I have to be careful. I have to be a responsible parent. I've never believed in having man after man come in and out of my son's life, and I won't start now.

"So, let me get this straight," Sydney says slowly as she sips her sweet tea, "*he* was stalking *you?*"

I nod my head slowly, as I stuff a bite of salad in my mouth.

Sydney puts her tea down and dramatically throws her hands up in the air. "Un-freaking-believable."

"I thought the same thing," I admit, after finishing my bite. "I probably should have been scared, and I would have been under regular circumstances, but it was like I understood, you know?"

My girlfriends are smiling at each other, adding to my giddiness.

"This is so incredible, Sam. You do realize that, right?" Rose says, smiling.

Rose is the most excited about my seemingly impossible romance with Ethan.

"You are dating Ethan Grant!" she adds, which is followed by several twelve-year-old-girl-like squeals from each of us.

I'm dating Ethan Grant. Yep. That's going to take some getting used to.

"I'm having a hard time with it myself," I admit. "I never expected this. I just wanted to meet him, and say the lines I had been rehearsing in my head for months. I never even told him my name the first night we met in Atlanta." A contented sigh escapes me. "Things never happen like you plan."

"That's right," Liz agrees. "Sometimes things turn out even better."

"You just never know," Sydney adds with a smile.

❧

Work has been brutal this morning. After Friday and Saturday night in "Dreamland", then church on Sunday followed by lunch with my girls, it ended up being a pretty perfect weekend. I have zero desire to get back to the grind.

Ethan texted me this morning, which is quickly becoming a ritual. I miss hearing his voice, but he had to travel to New York yesterday for some press junket. He's coming back today and said he'd call me later tonight. I can hardly wait.

As I sit at my desk, staring out one of the windows across the way – and avoiding work at all costs – I try to let this past weekend sink in a little.

I can't think about Ethan without smiling. It's laughable how wrong the media has him pegged. From what I can tell, he's nearly perfect – generous and caring, with a huge heart.

I will have to admit though that perfection scares me a little. I keep waiting for the other shoe to drop.

"You want to go to lunch today?" I hear, and turn to find Rose with a stack of folders in her arms. She looks upset.

"What's wrong?" I immediately ask.

"I don't think I'm getting my promotion," she says, head hanging low.

"What?"

I'll be outraged if Rose doesn't get this. Her boss, Tom the Sheriff, is a total jerk, yes, but there's no way anyone can deny Rose deserves the job.

"I heard Tom and Gina talking in his office this morning. I think she might get it."

"No way!"

Gina is a new employee. She's nice enough, but she's only been here for a few months. Rose has been here for nearly six years!

"She'd probably be a better candidate than me. She has sales experience, so she's good with people." Rose looks utterly defeated, and I hate it. For someone so beautiful, the woman has zero self-confidence.

"Rose," I say, standing up and grabbing her shoulders, "you listen to me. That's *your* job. You deserve it. You can do it, and everyone knows it. You have to fight for it!"

"You're right," she says, picking up her head and putting her load of files on my desk. "I'm going to talk to Tom right now."

"Go!" I say, giving her a light shove, "And don't come back here without that promotion."

Rose leaves me, and I pretend to work some more while I wait for her to return. To my surprise, she's back about twenty minutes later, and her face is as white as a ghost.

"Rose? Are you okay?" I ask, as she stands staring blankly at the wall of my cubicle.

"I quit."

Okay. I didn't expect that.

"You what?" I ask, trying to hide my shock. She looks like she's about to lose it.

"I quit," she says again, now looking at me with tears pooling in her eyes.

"Um, okay," I say, grabbing my purse and jacket and ushering her out the door. "Let's get out of here for a minute."

When we get outside, Rose is still in a semi-catatonic state.

"Rose?" I say, grabbing her face so she'll look at me. "Rose, you need to pull it together and tell me what happened."

She plops down on the courthouse steps. She doesn't have her jacket and it's freezing out, but she hardly seems to notice. "Danny left me."

Okay. Definitely didn't expect *that.*

"Oh, Rose." I sit down next to her and pull her close to me. "What are you talking about? How come you didn't tell me?"

"You've been so happy with all of the excitement this weekend. I didn't want to spoil it."

Rose is crying now, and my guilt is overwhelming. I've been focusing on nothing but myself for the past twenty six years. I'm a horrible friend.

"Are you kidding me?" I ask in disbelief. "You were going through this, and you didn't say anything to me?"

"He just left this weekend."

I sigh and hug her even closer.

"I knew you seemed a little off yesterday at church. What happened?" I have to ask, but Rose is crying hard now, so she can't even answer.

"Come on," I say, pulling her from the cold stone steps in front of the courthouse. "Let's go to my car."

I hold Rose as we walk to my car. I get her inside, start the car and turn the heat on full blast. I'm freezing, even with my jacket on, but Rose still doesn't seem to notice the cold.

"He didn't want to have kids," she mumbles. "That should have been a sign. He wanted to have them before we got married, but he changed his mind a couple of years ago."

"Rose, tell me what happened, and start from the top."

It's official. I want to kill Danny.

"He told me he wasn't in love with me anymore," Rose says, turning her soaking wet eyes on me. "After all of these years, he just fell out of love with me."

I'm tearing up now, just trying to imagine what my poor friend has been going through.

"I'm so sorry Rose." I push a stray piece of her gorgeous red hair behind her ear. "We'll get through this, okay?"

"Okay," she says, sobbing again.

"Are you sure you want to quit your job?" I ask, sorry to bring up the subject, but we need to make this right sooner rather than later if she's going to keep it.

"You know what?" Suddenly, Rose is staring resolutely out my front windshield toward the square. "I think I do."

"What about your house, Rose?" I ask.

There are so many things to consider, and I'm so worried about my friend. There's no way she can afford the house on her salary. Danny's the bread winner, and that isn't saying much.

"I'll have to sell it," she says, drying up a bit now. "I don't want to live there anymore." She looks over at me. "I was thinking I could maybe get an apartment in your complex?"

"That would be great!" I exclaim. "I would love that more than anything in this whole world." I grab her hand. "I'm so sorry, Rose."

"It's okay."

"No, it's not." I sigh, feeling horrible. "I'm selfish, and I'm really sorry. You should have told me you guys were having problems."

"That's just it," she says, wiping more tears from her face with her sweater sleeve. "I didn't think we were having problems. This came completely out of left field for me."

"Do you think there's someone else?"

It's the first thing that came to mind, and knowing the depth of Rose's insecurities, I know she's thought of it already too.

"That's my guess." She lets out a tired laugh. "It doesn't matter now. It's over."

We sit for a moment in silence – Rose staring at the square, me holding her hand.

"So, what now?" I ask.

I glance at the clock on my dashboard, and if I want to keep *my* job, I better get back.

"Well," Rose starts, pulling down the visor to check her face in the mirror, "now I go pack my desk and tell Tom he can fuck himself on my way out."

Wow. Now that's not something that would normally come out of sweet little Rose's mouth.

"I think I might like this new Rose," I admit with a smile.

She closes the visor and turns to me. "Me too."

���

On the way to get Jake from my mom's house, Ethan calls.

"Hi beautiful," he says, and my pulse speeds up, as usual, from only hearing his voice.

"Hi," I breathe. "How was New York?"

"It was work," is all he says. I can tell he doesn't want to elaborate, so I don't press.

"And back to work tonight then?" I ask him.

"I have to be at the studio at nine. We're filming some night scenes."

"Exciting stuff!" I say, but I honestly want to see him so badly it hurts.

"So, I told Vick about you yesterday at the junket."

"You did?" I didn't even think he and his co-star were very close. "What did he say?" I ask, hesitantly.

"He said he thought I was kind of creepy."

"You told him about the stalking?" I smile.

I'm sitting in my mom's driveway now, and I know Jake will be out in a second, but I selfishly don't want to get off the phone with Ethan.

"I did," he says laughing. "I told him about your stalking tendencies too, but it seems I'm still the creepy one. I told you so."

"You must not have told him about everything then. What about my knowing more about your life than you do from the internet? What about that?"

"You never told me about any internet research," he says, and I wince, but I can tell he's smiling. "You *are* creepy."

For a moment, I'm surprised. I thought I told him everything. I thought he knew me better than anyone. I have to check myself every once in a while. We only truly met for the first time a month ago, and we've missed a lot of time in between.

"Whatever. We both know the truth," I say smiling, as Jake comes running out to the car. "I think someone might want to say hello to you."

"Jake?" Ethan seems eager to talk to him. "Put him on."

"It's Ethan," I say to Jake, as he reaches my driver's side window. I step out of the car and give Jake a hug. "Do you want to say hi?"

"Yea!" Jake rips the phone from my hand. "Hi Ethan!"

I can't hear the other end, but Jake seems to be doing most of the talking.

"I had so much fun at the game!" Jake continues. "And Lamont is so cool! And the basketball players were like so huge! And I totally want to be a basketball player when I grow up!"

I smile as I listen to Jake relive the evening...*again.*

"When are we going to see you guys again?" Jake asks, and I'm glad. I was wondering the same thing.

"Really? Where?" he adds, and I look confusingly at Jake, before I hear a car driving up the long dirt drive leading to my mom's house.

My heart instantly speeds, like it knows who's in that car before I do.

"They're here!" Jake screams as he runs to meet the black SUV that's now coming toward us.

"Who's that?" I barely hear my mom yell from the porch.

I turn to her and smile, hoping that will answer the question.

Ethan gets out of the car first, followed by Lamont. He walks slowly over to me, looking embarrassed. He must have thought this would be too much. I run to him, and throw my arms around his neck letting him know this is more than okay. This is wonderful.

"I missed you," he whispers in my ear, as he holds me.

"You said you have a night shoot?" I question as I pull away, without completely letting go. It feels so good to see him.

"I have a couple of hours," he says smiling. He looks over at Jake then, who is high fiving Lamont. "Hi, Jake," Ethan says, and to my surprise, Jake runs over and hugs Ethan around the waist.

"Hi Ethan!" Jakes says, excitedly.

Ethan doesn't say anything, but I can tell from his face how much it means to him. I, of course, want to start bawling at the gesture, but I hold it together.

"What's for dinner?" Lamont asks, pulling a giggling Jake up over his shoulder, as we walk toward the house.

"And how are you, Mrs. Harper?" Ethan walks up to my mom and gives her a hug.

"I'm doing very well, Ethan," she says, a huge smile on her face. "And how many times do I have to tell you to call me May?"

Ethan smiles at her, and it seems to me they're having a private conversation with their eyes. I know now my mom and Ethan must have had some intense conversations. She doesn't let just anyone call her by her first name.

"Now come on in here," my mom continues. "Ya'll are gonna catch your death out in this weather."

We all sit in my mom's living room, while she starts dinner. It smells like country fried steak and gravy – probably with mashed potatoes, green beans and biscuits. That's the typical menu when she makes her famous steaks. This meal is my mom's specialty, which means she's trying to impress. The thought makes me smile.

I'm sitting on the couch with Ethan beside me. He hasn't let go of my hand since he got here, which suits me just fine. Jake doesn't seem to notice or care, but I'll be prepared for questions later, in case they come up.

Lamont's in the recliner and Jake's bouncing around all three of us. He's basically playing "Show and Tell" with all of his toys, performing for the guests.

"Somethin' smells good," Lamont says, as he inhales deeply. "Mind if I catch the news?"

He grabs for the TV remote, but Jake stops his hand.

"I'm not allowed to watch TV," he tells Lamont with a long face.

"And why's that?" Lamont asks, sitting up and putting his huge hands on his hips.

"I got in a fight," Jake looks over at me out of the side of his eye. "Remember?"

"I do remember you telling me about that." Lamont points to Jake's left eye, still showing signs from the scuffle last week.

Jake nods. "Mom took away TV for a week."

"I should have done more than that, but he was defending my honor." I smile at Jake. "I'm hoping he now understands that you can't just hit someone every time they say something you don't like."

"Yes ma'am," Jake says, hanging his head.

"Hey Jake?" Ethan gets his attention. "Tell us what happened."

"I don't think we want to relive that," I interject, but Jake eagerly starts the story.

"Well, there's this mean kid named Johnny at school, and he heard me telling my cousin, Sean, that you and momma were friends, and he said it was nothing big because you had lots of friends. Then he said no one would want to be friends with my momma, and so I hit him. Then he hit me back, and we both got in trouble."

My head is in my hands. I'm completely embarrassed.

I dare to look up, only to find Lamont and Ethan both looking at me and smiling.

"Your mom's right Jake," Lamont says. "You should always try and avoid a fight."

"I know," Jake says. "I promised her I wouldn't do it again. I just got real mad."

"It's okay," Ethan says. "We all make mistakes." Ethan lets go of my hand and scoots forward on the couch toward Jake. "This Johnny kid goes to school with you?"

"Yep," Jake confirms. "And he's on my soccer team."

"You play soccer? That's awesome!" Lamont says, slapping Jake a high five.

"When are your games?" Ethan asks.

Ethan looks like he has a plan. I furrow my brow.

"His last game is tonight, at 6:30. Why?" I ask, leaning up toward Ethan, but he's still looking intently at Jake.

"Will Johnny be at your game?" he asks Jake, and Jake reluctantly nods yes. "Well, I think I'd like to go to that game." Ethan adds.

"Really?" Jake's eyes light up like it's Christmas come early. "You'll go to my game?"

Lamont and Ethan start exchanging conspiratorial looks. I should be upset about this. I'm not sure it's sending a good message to Jake, but I'm so touched by the gesture, I nearly want to cry again.

"We probably can't stay for the whole game, but we could watch a little," Ethan tells Jake. "I think all Johnny needs is a little proof that you and I are friends, and maybe that will settle your differences."

"I can't believe this!" Jake screams. "This is so awesome! Can I call Sean, Mom? Can I? He's never gonna believe this!"

"Yeah baby. You can call Sean."

Jake takes off up the stairs as quick as lightening.

"Are you sure about this?" I ask Ethan, still having to force my tears to stay put.

"I'm positive," he says, grabbing my hand again. "I have a problem with bullies."

"Absolutely," Lamont says grinning, as he gets up to go harass my mom in the kitchen.

"This means a lot to Jake, and to me," I tell Ethan after Lamont leaves. "And did I mention that I'm so glad you're here?" A tear manages to escape my eye.

"Why are you upset?" Ethan's smiling, as he wipes the stray tear from my face.

"I'm not upset," I say, drying it up quickly. "I'm happy, really happy."

Ethan keeps smiling, as he kisses me gently on the lips.

❧

After three plates of food, Lamont is finally full, and we decide to leave for the soccer game.

My mom asked to stay home this time, probably excited she doesn't have to sit through another game with me.

I drive separately, since Ethan and Lamont will have to leave before the game's over to get back to Atlanta. Ethan rides with me, and Jake rides with Lamont, of course. They're becoming fast friends.

"Thank you again for doing this," I tell Ethan in the car ride over, "but are you sure you want to? There could be photos taken."

Ethan laughs. "Haven't you seen?"

"Seen what?" I say, curious.

"You were front page news yesterday, mostly online. You really looked beautiful Saturday night." Ethan's smiling. I am not.

"What?" I nearly scream. "I was on the internet?"

I glance over and see Ethan looks confused. "How could you have missed it? I mean, did you really think we would get through the basketball game without a few photos being taken?"

I can't believe Ethan's so calm about this. How can he be so calm about this?

"There are pictures of you and me – and Jake even – online?" I say the words slowly, still trying to wrap my head around this new information.

"Yes," Ethan says, looking worried now. "It's okay. They're good pictures."

"I don't care if they're good or not!" Does he think I'm that vain? "I feel so, so..." I can't think of the word.

"Violated." Ethan says in a quiet voice, staring out my front windshield.

I sigh. Once again, I'm thinking only of myself, of my problems.

"Yes," I say, feeling miserable. "Violated. How you must feel every day."

Ethan looks over at me. "I'm used to it," he says, "but I thought you knew this would happen. I thought you knew to expect this."

"I guess I just didn't think about it. I'm new to all of this."

Wow. Random pictures of me and my son online. This will definitely be hard to get used to.

"I know," he says. "I'm sorry for dropping it on you like that. I'd planned to talk to you about it later on, give you some pointers, tell you some things you can expect, but I thought you'd already seen the photos."

"I can't believe no one's called me about it."

I realize suddenly I haven't heard from a single person, and I'm sure someone would have seen it.

"Well, there were a few out Saturday night and yesterday. The majority of them just came out this afternoon. Your friends may not have had a chance to see."

I pull into a spot at Jake's school, and Lamont pulls in next to me. Jake is out of the car in no time, running over to us.

"Don't worry about it." Ethan smiles, but there's still worry in his eyes. "We'll talk about it later. It's not that bad." The way I handled the news obviously didn't please him.

"Ready mom?" Jake's opening my door, rushing me out of the car, Lamont's hand in his.

I quickly pull myself together. I hate to leave our conversation this way, but I do need to put some thought into this. I'm definitely not going to like this particular aspect of dating a celebrity.

"Let's go," I say, stepping out of the car, with Ethan right behind me.

Jake grabs Ethan's hand now, so he has Lamont on one side and

Ethan on the other. I'm still not sure how I feel about it – Jake's clearly showing off — but I decide to let it go. My mind's a little pre-occupied at the moment.

"Hi Sean!" Jake yells, as he lets go of Ethan and Lamont's hands to run to his friend.

"Hiya Jake!" Sean looks up to see Jake's escorts and his face suddenly pales. "You weren't joking," he says slowly.

"Nope." Jake's grinning hugely. "Wanna meet them?"

Ethan and Lamont start toward the field and they're soon rushed by thirty, eight year olds. Even the little kids know who Ethan is, due to the fact that our small town kind of revolves around the taping of his TV show these days.

Lamont starts picking some of the kids up and flying them around the field like airplanes. Ethan's kneeling down talking with some of them, but then some mom's and their teenage daughters make it to the field, obviously anxious for the rare opportunity to meet him. He signs a few autographs and takes some pictures.

Most of the kids want their photos taken with Lamont. They probably think he's some kind of real life giant.

I decided to take a seat on the bench and watch the chaos. I notice "mean Johnny" is standing away from it all, obviously too cool to be a part of the action. However, he's not doing a very good job of hiding the shocked – and very annoyed – look on his eight-year old face. Mission accomplished, I guess. It still feels kind of wrong, but at least Jake doesn't seem to be rubbing it in. As a matter of fact, I don't even think he's noticed Johnny at all. Jake's genuinely excited to be around Ethan and Lamont. Who would blame him?

Ethan seems calm and collected, but I can tell he's uncomfortable. This is more like the Ethan I remember from the first night we met at the fundraiser. I can't believe he actually gets away with spending so little time with his fans. His success is a true testament to his acting ability because he stinks at marketing himself.

I see Ethan look up and wink at me every once and a while and I wink back, but I'm still feeling very anxious about the conversation in the car.

Eventually, the coach gets irritated and clears every one off the field so they can start the game. Lamont and Ethan take that as their cue to head back to Atlanta.

"Can we have a minute?" Ethan asks Lamont, as we walk toward the gate to the parking lot.

"Sure man."

Lamont turns back toward the field to watch some of the game, and Ethan and I walk the short distance to the car in silence. He opens the passenger door of the big black SUV for me, and I get in. He slides into the driver's seat a few seconds later.

"We better hurry," I advise him. "I'm sure the town has been alerted that you're here. People will start showing up soon in buses."

"You're upset about the photos," he says, staring out the front windshield and ignoring my comment.

I hate the tension between us, but I'm definitely freaked out about all of this.

"Yes," I admit, honestly.

"Is it too much for you?" he asks, his voice soft.

"What are you thinking?"

I look at him, and grab one of his hands from the steering wheel. Does he think I want to stop seeing him because of this?

"Look, Samantha," he starts, still not looking at me, "I know this is hard for you, and if you want out, then please tell me."

I don't answer right away. I have to compose my thoughts for a moment so they come out right. I can't believe he thinks I want to end this.

"Wild horses couldn't pull me away," I finally say to him, putting my hand on his cheek to turn his face to me. "It just scared me, Ethan, that's all. We joke about who's the worst of us, as far as stalkers go," I continue, my voice shaking now, "but it's me Ethan. I win."

His laugh sounds tired. "Why would you say that?"

I'm not sure I can or should say this right now, but I have to convince him I want to stay.

"Because I fell in love with someone I'd never even met," I blurt, before I can stop myself. "This is not some celebrity crush, Ethan. Not for me. It never has been." I refuse to break eye contact with him at this point, afraid he may go running. "I love you like I've never loved another man before in my life. Now, you tell me. Who's the crazy one?"

Ethan looks away from me again, out the driver's side window. I sit back in my seat, still holding tight to his hand, but realizing quickly that I went way over the line.

"Ethan, I..." I want to take back everything I just said. It's too soon. I'm such an idiot.

Ethan looks over at me and releases my hand, but only to pull me toward him. His lips are hungry, unrestrained against mine. All the walls are down.

I put my arms around his neck, as his hands start moving up and down my back, clenching handfuls of my sweater. Eventually, I move my hands to either side of his face – touching, caressing, running my fingers through the sides of his hair.

Ethan's the first to break away, which I don't like, but I'm sure he has to go. He says nothing, just stares into my eyes. His face is sad.

"I better go," I say finally, never eager to leave him, especially not now. Something about that kiss didn't feel right.

"Okay." His voice is low. "I'll call you tomorrow."

"I can hardly wait," I say, trying to reassure him.

I reach over to kiss him one last time. He obliges, and puts his hand behind my head, pulling me closer, prolonging our kiss.

"Bye, Samantha," he says, breaking away again sooner than I'd like.

"Bye," I tell him, as I open the car door. It's hard to let him go after that, but I don't have a choice.

As I walk back toward the field, I feel something change inside of me. I know that things will never be the same between Ethan and me after that. Is it crazy that I told him I loved him after three days? Probably. Do I care? Not at all.

The fact that he didn't say it back should probably bother me a little, but it doesn't. I'm used to my infatuation with Ethan being one-sided.

"He's ready," I tell Lamont, when I find him on the bench, cheering on Jake. He looks disappointed he has to go.

"It's a good game," he says, getting up from the bench.

I smile at Lamont. "I'll bet."

"I'll see you guys again soon," he says, giving me a huge bear hug.

"Tell Jake I said bye?"

"Will do," I assure him.

I try to be a good mom and watch Jake's game after that, but as usual I can't get my mind off of Ethan.

I pull my phone out of my jacket pocket. I'm still curious to know why no one's called me yet about the pictures, but the blank screen on my cell phone explains everything. My phone's dead. I smile then, thinking about the sure to be full voicemail box I'll have at home and work.

CHAPTER 13

"You have to be kidding me!" Sydney squeals over lunch on Tuesday. "You're so famous now!"

"I actually feel pretty violated, like I'm a victim of identity theft or something," I admit.

It's a dirty feeling, having your life documented without your permission.

"Whatever." Sydney rolls her eyes at me. "I'm going to have to give you some pointers on Hollywood."

Liz laughs out loud. "What do *you* know about it?"

"I know plenty," Sydney says, with some attitude. "She's going to embarrass herself if she doesn't get some advice. There will be cameras around her constantly now, and she needs to be prepared."

"Ethan actually said he would give me some pointers," I tell Sydney. "And don't worry. I'll make sure to never leave the house without lipstick on."

"Good." Sydney looks genuinely relieved.

"How did Ethan feel about the pictures?" Rose asks. "Was he upset?"

"Ethan's used to it," I say, as I play with the straw in my glass of water. "Mostly, he was upset that I was upset."

"Does he think it scared you off?" I can tell Rose is concerned, and frankly, so am I.

"I tried to convince him otherwise," I tell her. "But I haven't spoken to him since last night, and I wasn't one hundred percent comfortable with the way we left things."

I normally get a text from Ethan in the mornings, but I didn't even get that today. I'm becoming more and more worried now that I definitely said too much, and once again, ended things too soon with my big mouth. I am starting to think our kiss last night may have been a kiss goodbye.

"What's the matter?" Rose asks, placing her hand on my arm.

I pause, not sure I want to admit my enormous blunder.

"I may have told Ethan that I was in love with him last night." I close my eyes so I won't have to see the judgment.

"You did what?!" Sydney is appalled, of course. "You've technically known him for what? Like a *week*! What were you thinking?!"

"Sydney, be quiet," Liz says, brushing Sydney's comment away with her hand as she looks at me. "Sam, why did you think you had to tell him that?"

"I was just trying to convince him that I didn't want out," I try to explain. "He thought I was really upset about the pictures, and he thought I wouldn't want to see him anymore, which is ludicrous!" I slump back in my seat in the booth. "I just wanted him to know that there was nothing that could make me want to stop seeing him, but I think I said too much."

Liz and Rose look at each other and then at me. I get the sneaky suspicion they agree I may have said too much, but they're being nice.

"What happened after you spilled your guts?" Liz asks.

"He kissed me."

Liz and Rose exchange looks again, smiling this time.

"That's not so bad," Rose says, in her usual optimistic tone.

"What if it was a kiss goodbye?" I ask, hesitant to bring up my thoughts from earlier, but I want to put it out there. Maybe I'm nuts to think that.

"It most definitely was." Sydney isn't helping.

"Sydney, enough," Liz says, still looking at me. Sydney gives Liz her best "eat shit" look and then gets up to go to the restroom.

Liz leans in toward me. "Sam, I'm not sure I agree with pouring your heart out to a man so soon, but so far, there's not a lot of convention in your relationship with Ethan."

I smile. "I guess not."

"And," Liz continues, holding up her pointer finger, "we are talking about a guy that crazy stalked *and* psycho called your mom's house for your number for almost a month. I'm thinking he may have pretty serious feelings for you too, even if they haven't reached the *love* level quite yet."

"Totally agree," Rose adds. "I don't think that was a last kiss. I think he was probably just overwhelmed and not sure what to do."

"Exactly," Liz agrees.

"What did I miss?" Sydney asks, now back from the bathroom.

"The dessert menu," Liz tells her, holding up the menu that the waiter just dropped by the table. "I'm going with the key lime pie," she says, and gives me a wink.

I smile a tentative smile at her. I feel a little better about things, but I know I have to talk to Ethan. That's the only way I'll be one hundred percent sure that I didn't just ruin the best thing that's ever happened to me.

∂∽∾

Ethan hasn't called or texted me the entire week. I've thought about calling him, but I'm stubborn, and I just can't make myself do it.

While getting our coffee this morning, John proceeds to tell us that the cast will be here on Monday for filming. The store owners get letters alerting them to when the filming will be taking place. John's always nice enough to share his with us.

Unfortunately, John doesn't have any insight into which members of the cast will be here, so I'm not sure if Ethan will be here or not. At this point, I don't think it matters. I'm not planning on watching the filming either way.

"He may not be here," Rose suggests, as we sip our lattes in a booth inside the coffee shop. It's a cold day, and the coffee is the perfect fix.

"I don't care if he's here or not," I tell her with the voice of calm indifference I've adopted ever since I realized it's over between Ethan and me.

Rose rolls her eyes. "I sure do wish you would snap out of this."

"What do you mean?" I ask, pretending to not care while idly playing with the seam in my coffee cup.

"Look at me," Rose demands. I look up and see Rose's face is filled with concern. "This is not healthy, Sam. You said yourself you never though it would last, so what's with the depression?"

"But I never thought I would have it in the first place," I try to explain, letting a little emotion creep out. "Then I had a taste, and it was magical. But I ruined it." I quickly slide back into the indifferent voice. "It's my fault, Rose. It's my fault I lost him."

"You're being ridiculous!" Rose raises her voice, which startles me, since it's a rare occurrence. "Just because you told someone how you feel, and he may or may not have felt the same way, you think that is grounds for self-loathing? That's insane!"

"I am not self-loathing," I tell her, but that's exactly what I'm doing, of course.

"Yes, you are." Rose calls my bluff. "I think it's time you get over yourself."

I stare at my friend in disbelief. Rose is the understanding one. She's the one who always offers a shoulder to cry on. Who is this person sitting in front of me?

"I'm sorry? What?" I ask her in a tiny voice, wanting her to repeat herself so I can make sure some alien hasn't invaded my best friend's body.

"I didn't mean that," says the Rose I know. I sigh in relief. "It's just that I hate seeing you like this. You've been moping around for a week, and it's not worth it. You told him how you feel, and if he doesn't feel the same way, then screw him. He's the one losing out here. Not you."

"You're going to make me cry," I tell her. "Again."

Then we both laugh.

"I'm sorry, Rose," I admit. "I hate being this way. I was just so happy to finally have the chance to be with him, and everything was going so well, until I said the fatal words. I just wish I would have waited. Maybe things would be different."

"Whether you said those words now, or a year from now, it doesn't matter. And technically, you still don't know how he feels."

I roll my eyes at my friend. "I think he's made that pretty obvious."

"Sam," Rose starts, her eyes soft and sincere, "he could be scared. It wouldn't be unheard of, you know? The guy's a pretty private person. Maybe he feels the same way, but just isn't ready for it."

"Then he's a coward," I say, but without the extra aggression I was hoping for.

I don't think Ethan is a coward. I just think he doesn't feel as strongly for me as I do for him, and why should he? What makes me so special? Ethan confirmed it. I'm not special, not very special at all.

"I know you don't believe that," Rose says, once again calling my bluff.

"You're right," I sigh. "I just wish he would have called either way. I can take rejection. I just can't take this silence."

"Maybe he'll call," Rose says, her standard optimism ringing through.

"Maybe." I nod, but I know the truth. He won't be calling, and that's that. I need to learn to start living with that fact and move on.

"We better get going," Rose says, looking at her watch. "I don't want to be late for my interview."

We get up then, say our goodbyes to John, and leave the coffee shop.

Rose and I are silent on our short walk back toward the courthouse. I know she's probably thinking about her interview, going over things she needs to say or do.

Me on the other hand? I start thinking about Jake.

Even if no one else on earth thinks I'm special, Jake does. No matter how many mistakes I make, he still thinks I hung the moon.

That thought makes me smile, and I know this will be the beginning of the end of my depression. Rose is right. It is time I get over myself.

"Good luck, Rose," I tell her as she gets in her car.

She has an interview today for a waitressing job at a restaurant in Bristol. It's nothing special, but she seems excited for the change.

"Thanks, hun." She smiles back. "I'll call you later."

I walk back into the courthouse with a good feeling — not great, but good.

∽∾

My weekend was literally a blur. I can't remember much about it at all. I swear I have no idea where my time goes.

All I know is that Monday came quick, and it's hard to resist watching the filming. It's even harder to resist possibly seeing him again, even though I decided I was over him.

"You sure you're not coming?" Sydney asks me, as we sit by our cars after work.

"No, I don't think I should," I tell her. "I think it's best for me to stay away."

"But we don't even know if he's here. Please, come," Rose pleads.

"I'm honestly not in the mood," I lie. "I feel a headache coming on, so I think I'm just going to go pick up Jake and call it a night."

"Okay," Rose sighs. "Tell Jake we love him."

"I will."

"Coward," Sydney says, as she hugs me goodbye.

I let go of her to look at her face, but she's smiling.

"I am not a coward," I tell her.

"Yeah, you keep telling yourself that, okay?" Sydney's still smiling, but she's not kidding with me. I don't mind.

Part of me wants to deck her, but the other part knows she's right. I'm definitely being a coward.

I eventually get in my car and start toward my mom's house. I start regretting not staying with my friends. I actually like to watch the filming. I've grown to love it. It's exciting and something different to do in a town that rarely offers much variety.

Besides, no one has heard whether or not Ethan will be here tonight. If anything, we got the impression that he's definitely not filming tonight, but no one could confirm it. I even persuaded John into asking Lamont if he would be here, but Lamont never responded.

When I'm within minutes of my mom's house my phone rings.

"Sam?" my mom's voice sounds excited on the other end.

"Hey mom. I'm almost there," I assure her.

"Oh good," she says. "I'm thinking pork chops tonight. How does that sound?"

"Sure." There's something she's not telling me. I can feel it. "Is everything okay mom?"

"Everything's fine, hun," she says, but her voice is not very reassuring.

"Mom, is Jake okay?" I'm getting nervous now. My car starts picking up speed as I drive the final mile to her house.

"Jake's fine," she says, sounding exasperated now. "Just wanted to see where you were, for dinner and all."

Now I'm confused. "Well, I'm almost there. Be there in about two minutes."

"Sounds good! See you then!" she says, and hangs up.

That was weird.

As I pull into my mom's driveway, the weirdness starts making perfect sense. Someone's waiting for me on the front porch, and it isn't my son, as I expected.

I sit in my car for a moment, trying to catch my breath. Ethan's sitting on the porch swing in a black leather jacket. Why does he have to be so gorgeous?

We're staring at each other. He's on the swing, and I'm still shaking like a leaf in my car. I finally decide I'm as under control as I'm going to get and open my car door.

"Hi, Samantha," he says in a quiet voice, as I walk slowly toward the porch.

I don't reply. I just walk up the porch steps and turn to face him.

"Can we talk?" he asks, standing up and walking toward me.

"Don't you have some filming to do?" I ask, backing away, trying painfully to keep my senses in check.

"No, I don't actually," he says, stopping in his tracks. "I'm here to see you."

"Ethan..." I have to look down. It hurts to even say his name. "I think you should probably just go."

"Just hear me out, okay?" he pleads, coming closer now. "I want to explain myself, and then if you are still angry with me, I promise I'll go. I'll never bother you again."

I look up and stare into my favorite green eyes for a moment. "Fine," I say, giving in. "But it's freezing out here. Let's go inside."

I lead the way into my mother's house. She's busy in the kitchen, humming like it's any other day. I frown in her direction from the living room. I'll deal with her later.

"Hi mom!" Jake comes running from the kitchen as we walk in.

"Hey baby," I say, hugging him. "Did you have a good day?"

"It was okay. How about you?" he asks, looking up at me, then Ethan.

"It was okay," I tell him, and grab his hands. "I'm going to go talk with Ethan in the den for a minute. I'll be back soon."

"No problem," Jake says, and then runs back to the kitchen with my mom.

I turn to Ethan and motion for him to follow me back to the den.

The farmhouse has a living room in the front of the house, then a smaller den in the back. The den always reminds me of my dad because it's where he spent most of his down time, relaxing in his recliner and reading. The recliner's still there, along with a small loveseat, but the rest of the room has inadvertently been turned into a playroom for Jake.

I take a seat in the recliner, and Ethan removes his jacket before taking a seat on the side of the loveseat closest to me. I get up then to shut the door and sit back down, waiting for him to start. I have nothing left to say at this point.

"I just want to start by saying that I'm sorry." He looks incredibly nervous, which I don't take as a good sign.

"Okay," I say, trying to keep stone-faced, but on the inside, I'm dying to jump into his arms.

"I don't have any good excuses for you, Samantha," he tells me, hanging his head. "There was no reason for me not to call you last week."

"Thanks. That clears things up," I mumble, more confused now than ever.

Ethan looks up at me. His eyes are sad and vulnerable.

"I'm scared, Samantha," he admits, his voice breaking, and I take a deep breath before I speak. I can't cry. Not yet.

"Me too, Ethan," I finally manage, "but I don't think that's a reason not to try."

I feel so disappointed. I can't believe he's giving up, just like that.

"I told you," he says, half smiling. "I don't have any good reasons."

I don't take the smile well. I don't think this is very funny at all.

"Well, good excuse or not, it didn't stop you from using it," I say, starting to feel my heart breaking all over again.

I can't look at him now. I said I could take rejection, but I'm not sure I can, not from him.

"Samantha," he whispers, "I have so few people in my life — so few I really care about. And I'm okay with that. I'm used to it."

"And you want things to stay that way," I add, and Ethan quickly gets off the loveseat and moves to kneel in front of me.

"No," he says, grabbing my hands. "No, I don't want things to stay this way."

His touch and his words are a shock. "I don't understand, Ethan."

I'm crying now, which never takes much for me. I knew I wouldn't be able to keep the tears down for long.

"Samantha," he starts again, "I've spent the majority of my life alone, and I don't mind it. I've actually grown to like it, but that's because I didn't know what I was missing."

I watch cautiously as he takes one of his hands away from mine and places it gently on my face.

"I thought I could go back to my lonely life and be content," he continues, "but I can't. Not now."

"What are you saying?" A headache is still simmering in the back of my head, and his words are jumbling together. I can't trust my ears.

"If I'm too late," he says, grabbing both my hands again and staring at them, "if I'm too late, or if you're too angry, then tell me. I just had to try."

I grab his chin so he'll look at me. "Are you saying you want to give this another chance?" I ask quietly, tentatively. I don't want to get my hopes up.

"If you'll have me," he confirms, and all of the anger I had inside vanishes in an instant.

In most cases, I wouldn't have given in so easily, but with Ethan, I'm defenseless.

"It's hard," he continues, after seeing me smile. "The idea of being close to someone is so scary. And even scarier is the thought of that person being close to me, but I can't think of any one I would rather take that risk with than you. I'm ready for this, Samantha. I'm ready for you."

I don't say a word. The tears are falling steadily now. I release my hands from his and throw my arms around his neck, hugging him fiercely.

Ethan pulls me close, and buries his face in my hair, instantly removing any lingering hurt or indecision.

"I love you too," he whispers in my ear, and I pull him closer to me, silently vowing I will never let him go again.

CHAPTER 14

I knew things would never be the same between Ethan and me after that night at Jake's soccer game, and I was right. But instead of getting worse, they've only gotten better – much, much better.

The paparazzi and the invasion of privacy still terrify me, but I try to stuff that deep inside, letting my love for Ethan erase my doubts.

I see pictures online regularly, and still get calls from friends and family who have no idea what's going on.

Unfortunately, there are also the various articles and comments about me and my family out there. Even though I have nothing to hide, it's hard to see all of your personal business hung out to dry like that.

Ethan calls me every day. I find I can hardly remember anything that happens day-to-day that doesn't involve him. I'm officially hooked.

He finally gave me the pointers he mentioned about how to deal with our sudden media attention, and I feel a little better. It's just one disadvantage of being with Ethan, and it seems to be the only disadvantage I can find for now, so I'll learn to live with it.

It's been two weeks since our talk at my mother's house, and I'm sorry to say, I've seen very little of Ethan.

He's been busy filming, but he's made a couple of short trips to Delia to see me, and I met him halfway one night for dinner. Other than that, most of our time together has been on the phone, but we planned a real date the last time we talked and today is the day.

Ethan invited Jake to come along, but I really wanted some time alone with Ethan. Jake actually asked to spend the night with Sean. I'm thinking a new video game may be involved.

"What are the plans for tonight?" I ask Jake as we pull out of our apartment complex, heading to my Aunt Clara's house.

"I think Sean's girlfriend has some Christmas play at her school, and we have to go." Jake doesn't seem too thrilled.

"Girlfriend?" I smile at Jake in the rearview mirror. "Since when does Sean have a girlfriend?"

"He met her at church about a month ago. She goes to some private school."

Jake seems kind of grossed out by the whole girlfriend idea, which makes part of me kind of happy, but I know it will only be a matter of time.

"That could be fun," I say optimistically, trying to change his mind about tonight.

"I guess," he says sullenly.

"What about after that? You get to play video games all night, right? Bummer," I tease.

Jake smiles up at me. "And Aunt Clara said we could order pizza for dinner!"

"Sounds delicious," I say. My kid is a sucker for pepperoni.

"What are you and Ethan doing tonight?" Jake asks me innocently.

"I'm not sure, exactly. Ethan didn't say."

"It's a surprise?" Jake's also a sucker for surprises.

"I guess." I laugh. "I don't think he has anything special planned. Maybe we'll just decide when I get there."

When we finally get to my Aunt Clara's, Jake and I say our goodbyes and I'm on my way.

Ethan asked me to meet him at his place tonight at seven. A glance at my watch and realize I'll probably be a little early, but I don't mind. I'm sure I can find something to entertain me when I get to Atlanta.

☙◦❧

Just as I'd thought, I get into the city almost forty five minutes early. There are several quaint looking shops around Ethan's building, so I decide to waste some time in one or two before I go to meet him.

I luck into a parking spot on the street in front of a promising antique store.

"Welcome," an older lady says from behind the counter as I walk in.

The shop is bigger than it looks from the outside, and I can see I'm the only customer at the moment.

"Let me know if you need help finding anything," she adds.

"Thanks," I say before I start making my way through the aisles.

I'm in the store maybe fifteen minutes, and toward the back, when I start hearing this strange clicking noise. I heard the bell on the front door ring a while ago, so I know I'm no longer the lone customer, but I didn't pay much attention to who came in.

Click. Click. Click. Click.

The clicks are fast and barely audible, but they're making me edgy for some reason.

I look over my shoulder, trying to see someone else in the store, but I can only see the lady at the cash register. She's studying something intently on the counter in front of her.

Click. Click. Click. Click.

I hear them again, and they're closer now. I look behind me once more, and catch someone ducking behind one of the tables full of old dishes.

I start quickly making my way toward the front of the store, and I can hear footsteps behind me. The clicking sound is getting much louder as well. I quickly realize it's a camera, and someone is taking pictures – a lot of pictures.

The cashier won't even look at me as I pass; making me think she probably had something to do with all of this.

As I exit the store, I'm shocked to find two more people outside by my car, cameras in hand, apparently waiting for me to leave.

"Samantha! Look over here!" they start yelling at me, as I try frantically now to get to my car.

I try to think about what Ethan told me to do in these circumstances, but I can't seem to recall a single detail. I'm scared, and they keep yelling at me.

"Samantha, are you going to Ethan's now?" one of the photographers asks, and I also hear "Are you and Ethan living together?" and "Where's Jake?".

I finally get to the driver's side without uttering a word and peel away from the shop, nearly side-swiping a car on the way out of my parallel spot. My hands are shaking and I'm fighting tears. I didn't want them to take my picture, but I couldn't stop them. I was completely powerless, and it's an awful feeling.

Ethan's apartment is just a few blocks away, and I didn't waste much time in the store, so I'm still about twenty minutes early. I don't care. I need to see him. I need someone to tell me everything's going to be all right.

I check in with security and make my way to the parking deck, following the same path that I remember from my last visit with Lamont.

Ethan actually meets me in the lobby. Security must have called him to tell him I was here. Needless to say, he isn't pleased to see my fragile state.

"What happened?" he asks, pulling me close to him, before leading me to the elevators. He seems even more upset than I am.

"Paparazzi," I get out between shakes.

It seems silly that someone doing something as trivial as taking my picture can affect me like this.

I feel Ethan relax a little, when we get in the elevator. He squeezes me tightly, before punching in a short code on a keypad in the elevator – not a card, like Lamont used.

"You're going to be fine," he promises. "I've got you now. You're going to be okay."

I catch a glimpse of myself in the mirrored doors of the elevator and see that I'm crying. Ethan puts both arms around me and pulls me into his chest.

"I'm so sorry I wasn't there," he says quietly.

I don't say anything. I just take comfort in being with him for the moment, safe in his arms, away from those horrible people.

Ethan holds me the entire ride up, and I never release my tight grip around his waist.

Once inside his apartment, he sits me down on his couch and then sits down beside me, pulling me close.

"Do you need anything?"

"I'm fine," I mumble into his chest. "It was just kind of scary."

Ethan starts rubbing my arm. "It's okay," he says, soothing me. "You're with me now. It's going to be fine."

After a couple of minutes in Ethan's arms, my tears stop, and I start feeling much better.

"I'm so sorry, Samantha," he says quietly, and I look up to see his tormented face. "I hate that this is happening to you. I'd do anything to make it go away."

I pull away from him and straighten up. I have to make him feel better. He can't beat himself up about this. It's not his fault. And I won't let this upset my much anticipated evening alone with him.

"I'm fine, really," I try and reassure him. "It was just unexpected, and I got a little spooked. This is not your fault."

"I know how scary it can be," Ethan says, still clearly upset, "especially when you're not used to it."

I take his hands in mine. "Ethan, do not beat yourself up about this, okay? This is what it's like for you, and I want to be a part of your life. I'll learn to deal with it. Maybe I'll take some Tae Kwon Do or something. I may need some ninja skills to defend myself."

"You just might," he agrees with a chuckle and kisses me tenderly on the forehead. I'm glad to see my joke worked to lighten the mood.

"How about a drink?" I ask as I pull off my coat.

Ethan smiles and nods before taking my coat from me. He lays it across the other couch and starts into the kitchen.

"Beer?" he turns to ask.

"Perfect."

Ethan's reassuring smile is making me feel much better, and I'm relieved at how quickly I seemed to put this experience behind me. It makes me feel more positive about my future with Ethan.

"What's on the agenda for tonight?" I question, excitedly.

"Well," he laughs from the kitchen, "luckily I planned a night in this evening. It's a good thing, I guess. After what just happened, you would probably be reluctant to go out again."

Ethan walks leisurely back over to the couch, and I take my beer from him and take a swig.

"Yea, at least until I get my ninja skills." I smile up at him.

"Right. We'll sign you up right away," he says, moving back in next to me.

I cuddle up to him and think about how much I love his smile.

"Dinner will be here in about thirty minutes," he adds, glancing at his watch.

"What's for dinner?" I take another sip of my beer. I don't recognize the label on the bottle. German maybe? But it tastes great.

"It's a surprise," he says with another smile. "Do you want to sit on the balcony?"

I look at him and cock an eyebrow. "A little cold out, isn't it?"

"Not on *my* balcony."

He stands and flashes me a very sexy and rather wicked grin. I take his offered hand and jump up to follow him outside.

Before he opens the sliding doors that lead to the outside, he presses a few buttons on a complicated looking keypad on the wall to the left.

I jump as a long sheet of glass comes down from the ceiling's edge and eventually fits itself into the solid concrete railing below.

"It's mirrored and tempered glass," he explains. "No harmful rays, and we can see out, but no one can see in. Complete privacy." He grins. "And warm."

He presses another button and two fireplaces come to life in each corner of the wide balcony. They're sunk into the walls, so I didn't even notice they were there.

He then opens the doors and gestures for me to lead the way. It's still a little chilly, but Ethan assures me the fireplaces will do the trick soon enough.

Ethan takes a seat on something the size of a double bed with the top half raised to a reclined sitting position. I move in next to him, and we both lay back, sides touching, in the cushy pillows, stretching our legs out in front of us. Ethan looks over at me, and I smile, hopefully letting him know how happy I am to be near him again.

"I spend quite a bit of time out here," he says, taking in the beautiful skyline in front of us. "It was one of the reasons I bought the place."

"Quite a selling feature," I agree.

The banister is solid concrete, but it's low enough that it doesn't obstruct the view, even when we're basically lying down. You still have a clear view of the skyline, and since most of the ceiling is glass as well, you might as well be sitting outside. It's gorgeous.

"May I ask a question?" Ethan says, breaking me away from my gazing.

"Of course."

"What are your plans for Christmas?"

"Well," I pause. I haven't really thought about it. "I assume I'll be at my mom's."

"Would you like to come to L.A. with me?" Ethan asks. "I have business for a few days before and after Christmas, but I thought if you and Jake would like to come, we could just extend the stay through New Year's."

I'm floored by the gesture, but as much as I would love to spend time with him, I don't feel right leaving my mom.

"I don't think I can," I tell him, and Ethan looks disappointed. "My dad passed away a little over a year ago," I quickly explain. "The holidays have been really hard for my mom. I don't think I could leave her alone at Christmas."

Ethan reaches over to touch my cheek. "I'm sorry to hear about your dad."

"Thanks," I say, relishing in his gentle touch. "I miss him very much. So does Jake." A little ache for my sweet daddy ripples through my heart. "He and Jake were pretty close. It was his first real experience with loss."

"Loss is hard for everyone," Ethan says, "especially for some one young, like Jake."

I sit my beer down on the small table next to me, and turn on my side to face him. "When my dad died, people kept telling me things like 'time heals all wounds', and I hated it. I didn't want to hear stuff like that. I just wanted my dad back. But they were right. I'll never forget him, but it gets a little easier to bear every day."

Ethan leans over to kiss me. I put my hand on his cheek, so excited to feel his warm skin on mine again.

"It's good to see you," he says. "I'm sorry you had to drive all the way here though, and I'm still sorry about what you had to go through earlier. Do you want to tell me about it?"

"No," I say quickly. "It was my idea to drive to you, for starters, and second, I do not want to talk about my impromptu photo session this evening ever again, okay? Let's just forget about it." I reach to kiss his lips once more. "It's good to see you too," I whisper, and he pulls me close.

I relax in his arms for a few minutes, before I hear a buzzer go off. "What was that?" I ask, confused.

"Dinner," he says, with a playful grin. "That's my doorbell. It rings out here too — sound proof glass." He winks and taps the sliding glass doors, before walking inside.

I suddenly feel a little uncomfortable, thinking about how much this place probably costs. I've never really thought about the fact that Ethan has money, and it still doesn't matter to me in the least. It's just one more thing to get used to, I guess.

"I hope you're ready for this," Ethan says, as he rolls a cart out onto the porch. "We are going five-star this evening."

I smile, as I get up and walk over to him. The cart is draped in an ivory linen table cloth. On top, there are several dishes, each with a shiny silver cover, formal silverware placement, three different crystal glasses for each place setting, and a simple blue vase holding three red roses in the center. It's elegant for sure. I can't wait to see what's inside!

I realize how hungry I am, as I inhale the delicious-smelling aromas, but the most prominent...wait...it can't be. "Do I smell French fries?"

"I told you," Ethan says, as he uncovers the two largest dishes simultaneously, "five-star, all the way."

I look at the two plates and smile — cheeseburgers and fries. *Perfect.*

"I am very impressed," I tease.

"I thought you might be."

Ethan proceeds to set the table, before going inside for another beer for each of us.

After he has uncovered everything but two dishes on the cart — which I suspect are dessert — and placed them on the table, we sit down to eat.

"This looks incredible," I say, as I look down at my first-class cheeseburger.

"There's this diner in town that has the most amazing hamburgers. I called in a favor." Ethan takes a bite and gestures with his chin for me to try mine. "Dig in," he says with a mouth full of food. He's in a very playful mood, and I love it.

"So..." I start, as I take my first bite, but I have to pause and comment on the burger. "Oh my God. This *is* incredible."

"I told you," Ethan says, tucking a French fry in his mouth.

"So," I start again, after I get my bite down, "tell me about yourself."

Ethan laughs. "Don't you already know most everything?"

I blush. "I know a lot," I say, smiling, "but there has to be a few things about you I don't know."

"Let's see..." Ethan looks up at the glass ceiling to think. "I don't know what all you know," he continues, "so I'll just start from the top."

He finishes chewing before he starts again.

"I was actually a really shy kid. I didn't have a ton of friends. My father desperately wanted me to play sports, but I just wasn't into it, and was never really great at anything anyway. I've always loved music; Led Zeppelin is my favorite band of all time. I have every album. I play piano and guitar, but neither very well. I didn't have a serious girlfriend until after high school, and even then, it didn't last very long. I think the longest relationship I've ever been in was about three months." Ethan looks over at me. "Sorry. I probably could have left out that last part."

I smile. "Well, that depends on why they were so short."

"Oh," Ethan says, taking a sip of beer, "that's easy. I made bad choices." He winks at me.

"So *you* did the breaking up?"

"Most of the time. Yes," he confirms before sticking another fry in his mouth. "The truth is I never wanted to pick any one I thought I could be with for a while. You could say I was only looking for short term."

Well, that doesn't give me a huge swirl of confidence. Is he telling me I'm short term?

"Okay," I say, before taking another bite of burger, failing miserably at trying to hide my concern.

Ethan laughs, which catches me off guard. "Samantha, the last girlfriend I had was over two years ago. I had given up."

I look over at him and stop chewing for a minute, lost in his eyes. I hurry to finish my bite, as it seems he's waiting for me to speak.

"Let me guess," I say, swallowing the last of it. "Until you met me?"

"Exactly," Ethan says with a boyish grin. "I realize that's a horrible line, but it's true."

"It was pretty bad." I smile, before taking another sip of beer to wash down my last hurried bite. "You really expect me to believe that one? You *are* an actor, you know."

Ethan's answering smile is radiant. "Believe me when I tell you that I'm more myself with you than I am with anyone else. You've brought out things in me that *I've* never even seen before."

"That's good. I like it that way."

"So do I. It's one of the many advantages of being with you."

Once again I'm lost in Ethan's eyes, but this time I sense a longing there that I'm not sure I'm ready for. Will he want me to stay the night? Is it too soon to for that?

I'm not ashamed to admit my sexual fantasies about Ethan are abundant, but believe it or not, this is the first time I've ever considered it as a real possibility. It's been a long time for me, and I have no idea what kind of history Ethan has with women, but it wouldn't take much to make me feel like a total amateur.

I've never been one to rush into the physical part of a relationship. Of course it *was* high school, but I dated Jake's dad, Luke, for two years before we ever even tried. And Jake was the product of our first time; so needless to say, I still get a little paranoid when it comes to sex. I've only been with Luke and one other miscellaneous boyfriend over the past eight years.

Suddenly my heart is racing so fast, I fear my anxiety may overwhelm me. But as I continue to stare into Ethan's eyes, I feel my breathing slow. There's just something about Ethan. I feel so comfortable and at ease around him.

"I find it hard to believe you were a shy child," I say, finding my smile again.

"Believe it," he says, taking another bite of his burger.

I'm glad to see my brief moment of panic and insecurity must have gone unnoticed. Ethan looks as calm and relaxed as ever.

But as I look down at my plate, I realize now that I've contemplated the possibility of being intimate with Ethan, I can't think of anything else. And I certainly can't eat another bite.

"Tell me more," I say, in a hopeless attempt to change the direction of my wayward thoughts. "Tell me a funny story about your childhood."

Ethan licks some ketchup from his bottom lip, and I shift slightly in my seat. *Oh goodness.*

"Well," he says, still smiling, "there was this one time that I stuck an electrical cord in my mouth and it shocked me. I had to be revived."

"What?" I start giggling. "How old were you?"

"I think I was like three or four. I have the scar to prove it."

He pulls out his bottom lip and leans toward me to show me the small raised scar on the far left side. The proximity of him and his perfect lips does nothing to help slow the weakening of my resolve. "That was super smart," I tease him.

"I was a toddler," he says, in a very pouty and adorable way. "Cut me some slack."

Ethan puts his napkin on his plate, clearly done with his dinner. Mine is less than half eaten, but I'm done as well, so I copy him.

"What about you?" he asks, leaning back in his chair. "I know nothing about your childhood at all, so spill it."

I laugh. I guess my personal info isn't quite as readily available, at least not for now.

"I was far from quiet and shy," I admit. "I was prom queen." I glance up at him to check his face. He's smiling, so I continue. "I was head cheerleader. People expected a lot out of me. I was dating the captain of the football team. I was on top of the world. Then I got pregnant."

I feel my face turn sad, but not because of Jake. I'm sad because it always sounds like Jake is an excuse to hold me back, and I've used it for many years.

"How old were you?"

"I got pregnant with Jake at seventeen."

"That's too bad," Ethan says quietly, but it sounds more like a question.

I give him a look, and he starts again quickly.

"I mean, Jake is an awesome kid, and I'm sure you have no regrets, but I think anything unplanned that is that huge, especially at seventeen, well, I just can't even imagine."

"It wasn't easy," I admit with a nervous laugh, but the nerves have nothing to do with this conversation. I can't seem to stop looking at Ethan's perfect mouth.

"I finished my senior year," I tell him, "but Luke and I — Jake's father — we never got married. I just couldn't do it. It wasn't exactly how I pictured my wedding day, and I didn't think having a child together all of a sudden made us suitable as husband and wife."

"Is Luke still in the picture?"

"Not really. He's in the military. He joined right after Jake was born and I haven't seen him since — another reason why I'm glad I never married him."

"You didn't love him?" Ethan looks uncomfortable, anxious for my answer. It makes me laugh.

"I have no idea," I giggle. "I think I loved him, but either way, it wasn't enough."

I look down at my unfinished burger. I haven't talked about this in a long time, and it's harder than I thought it would be. "There would have been so much resentment between us," I add.

"Do you still have feelings for him?"

"No," I assure him. "I'm really not sure if I ever loved him. I was seventeen."

Ethan smiles, seeming relieved. "I think you're an amazing mom."

"Thank you." I smile back. "That means a lot to me. It hasn't always been easy, but you're right. I have no regrets. It has definitely changed me. I'm not the same person I used to be, but I think most of the time, that's a good thing."

"Well, I don't how you used to be, but I like the twenty first century version quite a bit."

"Thanks." I laugh. "That's enough about me. Tell me more about you."

"More about *me*? Honestly, I don't think I could tell you much that you haven't already read or seen on TV."

"Nonsense," I scoff. "There has to be something. Tell me one thing that no one else knows. What's your biggest secret?"

Ethan looks up at me through those beautiful lashes, his eyes intense, but he's still smiling. "No running to the press, okay?"

I make the gesture of crossing my heart with my right hand, before Ethan leans toward me and grabs that same hand in his.

"I'm hopelessly in love with you," he whispers, bringing his free hand up to touch my cheek, as his crystal green eyes lock onto mine. The longing there this time is unmistakable, and my inexperience surfaces once again, making me a little anxious. But I simply can't resist him any longer.

I stand up slowly, never taking my eyes off Ethan's, and move to his lap, straddling him in his chair. I put my hands behind his neck, and he places his gently at my lower back.

Ethan looks confused, just sitting there, waiting for my next move, but I like that he's not pushing this. He's letting me make the decisions. He's letting me be in control.

I don't kiss him immediately, although I'm dying for a taste. I just stare into his mesmerizing eyes for a little longer, running my fingers slowly through his silky hair, mainly trying to memorize this moment so I can hopefully recall it every night in my dreams.

When I finally lean down to kiss him, Ethan's rigid at first, hesitant, which does nothing for my self-confidence, but after a few seconds, he pulls me closer and begins kissing me back in earnest.

"Samantha, you feel so good," he whispers against my mouth, as his hands roam freely over my body, pressing me against him, and it's like I've been waiting for this moment my entire life.

I move my mouth from his lips, only to kiss his cheek, his chin, all along his chiseled jaw — once again, trying to memorize every feature, how he feels against my lips, how he smells, how he *tastes*. I place my lips under his ear and gently move them down his neck. He grabs at my waist and I hear a soft moan that makes me smile, my confidence now back in excess.

"What are you trying to do to me?" he growls, as I unbutton the first few buttons of his shirt and slip my hand inside. I smile again. Maybe I'm not so bad at this after all.

I quickly move back to his perfect lips, never wanting to leave them for too long, as I let my hand roam around under his shirt, on his bare chest, down his side, around to his back, which arches in response to my touch.

"Samantha." He says my name again, but this time it's a whimper, as I start moving slowly up and down, against him.

He fists a hand in the back of my hair and I close my eyes, as his lips start moving persistently down my neck. "I love you, Ethan," I breathe, and when his mouth moves back to mine, I kiss him, hard, nibbling a little on his bottom lip. Ethan's reaction startles me.

"That's it," he says, as he puts his hands under me and stands up with surprising grace.

I lock my legs and arms around him, and look at his face to see if I did something wrong, but his smile is wide, and his eyes are liquid green and bright with excitement. He moves toward the glass door and halfway frees a hand to open it.

"Where are you taking me?" I whisper into his neck, and I feel him tremble against me.

I love the affect I'm having on him. I'm not usually this bold, but his reaction to me is very encouraging.

He doesn't answer me, and the next thing I know, I'm sitting on the edge of his bed. Ethan's standing in front of me, his hands on either side of my face.

"Are you sure?" he says, his voice husky and delicious.

I stand up and start undoing the remaining buttons of his shirt.

"Positive," I whisper. *I've never wanted anything more.*

Ethan keeps my face in his hands and kisses me softly, as I finish unbuttoning his shirt. Once I'm done, I rain kisses across his beautiful, bare chest, as I push his shirt slowly off his shoulders. It falls to the floor, and Ethan's arms are quickly around me, pulling me into him. His mouth is back on mine briefly before he moves to pull my sweater over my head, and I lift my arms willingly, eager to feel his warm skin on mine.

We are fully undressed in no time, and we both take a moment to study each other with carnal appreciation. I watch as Ethan drinks me in, and with a just a look, he makes all my insecurities disappear. I can't believe how gorgeous he is. Every inch of him is perfection, inside and out.

"You're so beautiful," he says quietly, placing a warm hand gently on my face, before guiding me slowly down onto the bed.

He starts kissing me again, tenderly, lovingly, as I put my arms around him, pulling him against me, wanting him close, *needing* him close.

"Thank you for loving me," he whispers onto my shoulder, causing my body to tremble with need.

"My pleasure," I breathe, and I can feel his smile against my skin.

"*Pleasure,*" he repeats, drawing the word out in a soft purr against my neck, as we both surrender ourselves to the impending bliss.

❧

I always thought Ethan seemed too good to be true, and it turns out, I was right.

It feels like my heart may beat out of my chest, as I lie next to him, nuzzled into the crook of his neck, trying to catch my breath. We're still on top of the covers. We never even bothered to pull them down.

Eventually, everything starts to slow back to its normal pace. Ethan eases me off his chest and we both turn on our sides to face each other.

"Hi beautiful," he whispers.

"Hi," I breathe. I'm sure the smile on my face is permanent at this point.

He kisses me again, and now that I know where that can lead, my body starts tingling, yearning for what comes next.

"Do you want to know another secret?" Ethan asks, as he pushes a piece of hair from my face.

I shiver, which he mistakes for a chill. He pulls the blanket up from the end of his bed to cover us both.

"Please," I say, as I snuggle into the soft blanket.

Ethan sighs, and his face falls. "I don't think I like being an actor anymore. I used to love it...I think. I honestly don't know that I've ever loved it."

I put my hand on his cheek. He seems sad and I can't have it, not after the experience we just had. But he's entrusting me with something important, and I have to be there for him.

"Tell me," I encourage him to continue.

Ethan sighs again. "I just want to walk through a mall. I want to go to a movie with my girlfriend." He puts his hand on my cheek now. "I want to be with you without worrying about cameras attacking us every time we leave the house. It comes with the job, and that's the price you pay, but what if you don't even like the job? Then all of the hassle seems like exactly that — a hassle."

Ok. This conversation needs to take a turn.

"Ethan, I think you may just be a little burnt out. That's all."

"I think it's more than burn out," he says quickly. "I'm miserable."

"But on set, it seems like you love it. You take your job so seriously." I don't know how someone could put so much into something they hated.

"Because it's all I have." He sits up, and rubs at his forehead.

"You have me," I say quietly, sitting up next to him.

"Yes," he says, looking over at me. "And that scares me. I'm so afraid something will happen to you, or that it will get too crazy for you and you'll leave."

"Ethan..." I marvel at how confident he can be at times, and how

utterly insecure he can be at others. "I'm not going anywhere."
Ethan gives me a weak smile. "I'm sorry. That was kind of heavy
and ruined the moment, didn't it?"
"I don't think anything could have ruined that moment," I tease.
Ethan pushes me playfully back down on the bed and hovers over
me. "Ready for round two?"
I reach up to kiss him, giving him my answer.

⋆⁓⋆

I ended up staying the night at Ethan's, although we didn't get
much sleep.
It's early morning now, and I'm sitting on Ethan's kitchen counter,
in my undies and his blue, button down shirt from yesterday,
loving the smell of him all over me. Ethan is making us coffee in
nothing but a pair of worn, heather gray sweatpants. What an
outstanding view.
"How do you like your coffee?" he asks, as he gets two mugs from
the cabinet and places them on the counter.
"Less coffee, more cream and sugar."
Ethan looks at me sideways. "But you're plenty sweet, my love."
"And you're plenty sappy, my love," I tease.
"You're awfully chipper this morning." Ethan moves in between
my legs and I lock them, along with my arms, tightly around him.
"I wonder why?" I say softly.
"I bet I'm happier," he says, before placing a soft kiss on my chest.
"I'd take that bet."
"Equally happy then?" he says, raising his head to look at me.
"Equally happy," I agree.
Ethan finishes the coffee and we start making our way to the huge

bed/chair on the patio again to watch the sun come up. I sip my coffee and almost feel for a moment that I'm a different person. I feel like a princess, living a life of luxury. I don't feel like the twenty-six year old, single mother, working for a little more than minimum wage woman that I am.

You're living the fantasy, Sam. It's a sobering thought.

"What are you thinking?" Ethan asks, setting his coffee on the table next to him and grabbing my free hand.

I sit my coffee down as well and roll to my side to face him. "I was thinking I feel a little outside of realty at the moment."

"Yes, you are rather dreamlike," he teases, caressing my face.

"Oh hush." I giggle. "You're the dreamy one. You're *Ethan Grant!*" I do my best excited fangirl impersonation.

"Not around you," he says quietly. "I'm just Ethan when I'm with you. I'm the person I want to be."

I snuggle into his chest then, and close my eyes.

"I don't want to leave," I whine.

Ethan laughs and his chest shakes under me. "I don't want you to either."

"I have to go get Jake though."

The thought of Jake makes me feel a little better about leaving. I just wish Ethan could come with me. He has to be in New York again next week, then L.A. for Christmas.

"I guess it will be a while before I see you again, right?" I try not to sound as miserable about it as I feel.

Ethan sighs. "It will be a couple of weeks, but I'll call you every day — maybe even two or three times a day, if that's okay with you."

I raise my head to look up at him. "Four or five times?" I smile.

"I didn't want to push it, but that's exactly what I had in mind."

Part of me hates how desperate I am for him, but I'm comforted by the fact that he seems to feel the same about me.

We sit on the patio for just a few minutes more before I have to get dressed. I promised Jake I would pick him up early today and we would go to breakfast before church. I definitely need confession after last night. *Forgive me father, for I have sinned...a lot.*

Ethan asks to walk me to my car, afraid of a repeat of last night in front of the antique store. He told me he normally doesn't have much to worry about at his place, but he doesn't want to take any chances.

We say our goodbyes at my car, and I have to try very hard not to cry, knowing I won't see him again for another two weeks.

"Be careful driving home, okay?"

Ethan has me pinned against my car, one hand on the driver's side window, the other on the side of my neck. He's kissing me sweetly, all over my face, which isn't making my leaving easier at all.

"Okay," I say, my voice shaking, just like the rest of me – now an immediate reaction to him touching me in any way.

Ethan looks up at me and smiles. "Are you sure you're okay to drive? You didn't get much sleep last night." He cocks one perfect eyebrow.

I narrow my eyes at him. "And whose fault was that?"

"Mine," he says, kissing me again on my neck this time. "All mine."

"I have to get going." I shudder. "You're driving me crazy."

Ethan finally releases me and opens my door. "Call me when you get home?"

"I will." I can hardly take my eyes off of him as I sit down in the driver's seat.

"I love you," he says, leaning down so our eyes are level.

"I love you," I repeat, trying even harder now to hold back the tears.

Ethan shuts my door and I put the car in reverse to pull away from him. Leaving him is painful. The more time I spend with him, the more attached I become. I think it may be reaching an unhealthy level. I laugh to myself. As if it wasn't unhealthy before?

I check my rearview and see Ethan still standing next to my parking spot, his hands in his jean pockets, watching me drive away. As soon as I pull out of his parking deck, I lose the battle with my tears.

CHAPTER 15

I pull into my apartment complex around eight thirty. I made really good time, but now I only have about thirty minutes to get ready before I need to leave to get Jake for breakfast.

I jump out of my car and start making my way to the stairs. I try and go through my seemingly never-ending mental to-do list as I walk. Ugh. Back to reality.

I made a few calls on my way home. Jake was first, assuring him breakfast and church were still on this morning.

Sydney and Rose both called me this morning, wanting to do lunch today after church, and obviously wanting to hear the details from last night. I agreed to lunch with them, but refused to divulge anything over the phone.

Then I called my mom, making sure she would be fine to take Jake after church while I ate with the girls. I frown as I walk into my apartment, remembering my conversation with her.

"Leaving him again so soon?" my mom said jokingly, but I know her well enough to know there was some truth behind it.

"It's just lunch mom," I said defensively. "And Ethan is out of town for the next two weeks, so Jake and I will have plenty of time together."

"I was just teasing you."

Of course she was, but only after she found out I wouldn't be seeing Ethan for two weeks.

"You know that I never mind keeping my grandson," she adds. "How about dinner tonight?"

"Are you cooking?"

"Pork chops, mashed potatoes, black eyed peas and cornbread. You interested?"

"I wouldn't miss it," I assured her before hanging up.

As I look at myself now in my bathroom mirror, a wide smile spreads across my face remembering the last call I received before I got home. It was a little unexpected. Ethan called me.

"Yes, I miss you already," he said, before I even had a chance to say hello.

"I miss you too," I told him, with a huge grin.

"I just realized that I am not okay with having to wait until I return from New York to see you again."

"Okay," I said, smiling even wider now. "What do you have in mind?"

"Well, if I told you I want to see you again tomorrow tonight, would I run the risk of you getting sick of me?"

That one made me laugh. "Um, I'm not sure how many times we have to go over this, but if I saw you every second of every day, it still wouldn't be enough."

"It seems once again, we're on the same page then," Ethan said. "So, how about I come to you this time?"

"Sounds good," I agreed. "You want to come to my place?"

"Yes, and I'll even cook for you."

"Wow. You cook too?"

"Only one thing, really, and I'm not very good," he said, "but I have another request."

"What's that?"

"I want to meet your friends, officially," he said. "Would they be willing to come over?"

I laughed again. "I think maybe they would."

I'm pretty sure my friends would cancel their own weddings for this opportunity.

"Great!" Ethan was excited. "I'll be at your house late afternoon, if that works for you. Will I get to see Jake?"

Ethan just saying Jake's name makes my heart swell.

"I'm sure I can arrange that," I told him. "Jake will be excited to see you."

"I can't wait," Ethan said. "I'll see you tomorrow then."

"See you then."

"And Samantha?"

"Yes?"

"I just wanted you to know that last night was one of the best nights of my life."

"Mine too," I managed to get out, before my eyes started filling up with tears, once again.

"I love you, and I'll see you tomorrow night."

"I love you too," I said, before hanging up.

I just can't believe this is happening to me.

As I finish getting ready, eager now to see Jake, I still can't stop smiling. My life seems like it's been an emotional roller coaster over the past few weeks, but I sure am enjoying the ride.

I manage to get ready in record time and make it to my Aunt's a little after nine.

"Hi mom!" Jakes says, running out to meet me when I arrive.

"Hey sweet angel. I missed you."

It's true. I always feel like a little piece of me is missing when we aren't together.

"Are we going to Ken's?"

"Yep."

"Just me and you?"

"Yep."

"Great!"

I give my thanks to Clara before we leave, and shortly after, Jake and I pull up to a crowded Ken's. We luck into a booth, recently unoccupied.

"So, did you have fun last night?" I ask him, as I sip my second cup of coffee today. The lack of sleep is bound to catch up to me eventually.

"I did!" Jake says excitedly. "Sean has the coolest video games. We played all night!"

I feel a slight twinge of guilt, not being able to afford any gaming systems for Jake. However, I never wanted him to be that kid that never sees the light of day because he can't leave his Xbox.

"What did you and Ethan do last night?" he asks, and his eyes light up.

It seems Ethan already has him wrapped around his finger. I know the feeling.

I try to prevent my face turning red again, but I feel the heat rise despite my efforts.

"We just had some dinner. It was nice," I tell him, but I suddenly remember my unpleasant experience last night before meeting Ethan though, and I want to talk to Jake about it. "Jake sweetie, I want to talk to you about something."

"Are you and Ethan getting married?" Jake asks excitedly, and I nearly spit coffee all over our table.

"Why would you think that?" I ask, after I quit choking.

"I don't know," Jake says nonchalantly. "I thought you really liked him."

"I do buddy, but that doesn't mean we're getting married." Jake looks confused, so I quickly continue. "When people like each other, they date for a little while, to make sure they're compatible. Then, if they love each other, and feel like they make a good fit, they get married."

"You and Ethan aren't a good fit?" Jake looks depressed now. I have no idea what's going on in that beautiful little head.

"I don't know that yet, buddy." I watch as his frown becomes even deeper. "But I really do like him, a lot," I add. "Jake, are you sad?"

"I like Ethan," he says.

"Me too, but Jake, why would you want me to marry him? It's not because he's famous or has money, or anything like that, is it?" I don't think Jake would go there, but he seems to be in to proving something lately, with the soccer game and his fight at school.

"No mom," Jake says, crossing his arms, obviously offended. "I don't care if Ethan is famous. It's cool, but that's not why."

I laugh at how cute he looks when he's angry. "Why then?"

Jake softens with my laughter. "Because I want you to be happy, mom. You're happy when you're with him. I thought if you married him, then you would be happy forever."

"Thanks buddy," I say, fighting back tears big time.

"You should be happy mom."

"I am happy baby." I reach across the table and grab his little hands that are still crossed across his chest. "You make me happier than anything or anyone else in the world. All I need is you."

Jake rolls his eyes. "Okay mom," he says laughing. "Whatever."

I let go of his hands and playfully smack his cheek from across the booth. "When did you get to be such a smart-aleck?"

Jake just smiles. "So, if you're not marrying Ethan, what did you want to talk to me about?"

Our orders arrive then, and Jake starts munching on his hash browns.

"I had a little run in last night with the paparazzi," I tell him. "I was at a store near where Ethan lives and they were following me, taking pictures, asking very personal questions. It was kind of scary."

Jake stops eating. "I'm sorry mom. Does Ethan know? I bet he's mad."

"He does know, and he was mad, but that's what I wanted to talk to you about. This is what life will be like while I'm with Ethan, and it will probably happen more than once." Jake starts in on his hash browns again, seeming completely unfazed. "It could happen to you buddy, while you're at school, or while you're out with Ethan and me. It may be kind of scary."

"Okay," Jake says, acting like it's no big deal, but I know he hasn't experienced it, so he doesn't really understand.

"I guess I just want to make sure you're okay with that," I add. "This may change our lives a little bit."

"Mom," Jake puts his fork on his plate and looks up at me, "I'm a big boy. I can handle it, okay?"

I smile. "Okay, Mr. Big Britches. I hear ya."

"I'm sorry you got scared," he says.

"It's okay. It will just take some getting used to."

Jake and me finish our breakfast with some more chit chat about Sean's video games and then make our way to church.

"Hey girlfriend!" Sydney shouts at me across the parking lot, as she comes running over to meet Jake and I.

"Morning!" I say waving to her.

I kiss Jake goodbye before he leaves me to go to his class, and Sydney grabs me around the arm and escorts me into the sanctuary.

"So, how was last night?" she asks as soon as Jake is out of earshot, wagging her perfectly shaped eyebrows at me.

"Fine," I say smirking.

"Ugh!" She drops my arm. "You're no fun! You're so private! I hate it!"

I smile at her, as Rose comes walking over from the lobby.

"Morning ladies," Rose says cheerfully.

"Don't even try it," Sydney tells Rose, a disgusted look on her face. "She's not budging."

Rose smiles at us both. "Come on. Liz and Bill are saving us seats."

Church goes by in a rush, probably because I spend most of the sermon daydreaming about last night. It feels rather blasphemous, but I can't help it.

As the sermon comes to a close, I start thinking about the words "I love you". Ethan loves me. He's told me so, more than once now. I haven't said those words to another man since Jake's father, and

I'm not sure it was sincere then. We were so young.

But when Ethan tells me he loves me, and I repeat the words to him, it's like no other words in the English language matter.

Those are the only words I understand, and I only want to hear those three words...over and over again. My heart stutters and jumps whenever his soft voice repeats them to me.

"Chinese food for lunch?" Liz asks, as she kisses Bill goodbye.

I guess he's letting us have a girl's lunch, but Liz doesn't seem too happy he's leaving.

"Sounds good to me," I say. I'm still kind of full from breakfast, but I can order some soup or something.

I take Jake by my mom's after church and then make my way to the restaurant. My mom hasn't been to church since my dad died. She hasn't lost her faith completely, but she says she's still arguing with God a little.

We have to wait a few minutes for a table at the Chinese place. "You can start any minute now," Sydney says, still trying desperately to pull something out of me.

I smile at her. "What exactly do you want to know?"

Sydney rolls her eyes. "You're not going to tell us anyway. I don't know why I bother."

I put my arm around her. "We had dinner. It was very classy – cheeseburgers and fries."

"Seriously?" Sydney looks appalled. "What was he thinking?"

"I thought it was perfect," I say smiling.

"Of course you did." Sydney looks as if she feels sorry for me. "All of that fame and fortune, and he serves his date a cheeseburger?"

"It was a really good burger." I happily defend Ethan's choice.

We finally get seated, and Sydney takes the seat beside me,

obviously determined.

"So, what is everyone doing for Christmas?" Liz asks, before Sydney can start in again. I smile as I watch Sydney give Liz an evil glare.

"I'm staying here," I say. "Mom has a hard time during the holidays." Everyone gives me an understanding look. "Ethan did ask Jake and me to go to L.A. with him though."

I add the last, mainly for Sydney's benefit, but also because I like talking about Ethan as much as possible.

"For the holidays?" Rose asks. "Now I'm curious about what happened last night too."

Sydney points her finger at Rose and nods her head before looking back at me.

"I hated to decline, but I just can't leave momma at Christmas," I say, skipping right past the elephant in the room for now.

"Can't you take her along?" Liz asks. I hadn't thought of that, but Ethan didn't mention it, and I would never ask.

"I think she likes being at home," I say instead.

"Just knock it off!" Sydney says finally, tossing her menu back on the table. "We know you spent the night with him, so spill it!"

I smile. These are my best friends. It's not like they're crazy reporters or anything.

"I did," I confirm, taking a sip of my water. "And?" I ask defiantly.

Sydney backs down, a total weakling, as soon as I cut my eyes at her. "I have to know," she begs desperately, unleashing her fully perfected puppy dog look at me. Liz laughs out loud.

Thankfully, I'm saved temporarily by the waiter coming to take our orders, but it doesn't take long for Sydney to start back up, as soon as he leaves.

"So?" She still has the puppy dog look going on. "Please?"

"Fine!" I say, exasperated. "I spent the night there. Is that a crime?" I'm trying to act mad at her, but I can't hide my smile.

"No! It's wonderful! How was it?" Sydney asks excitedly, now that she thinks I'm about to open up. Little does she know...

"Sydney, I will not discuss this with you, or anyone else for that matter." I pat her arm. "I love you, but you'll just have to use your imagination."

Sydney looks sad but resigned. "Fine," she says quietly. "A girl can dream."

"Maybe I'll tell you all about it one of these days. You never know."

Sydney looks at me and smiles. "You never know."

We eat our lunches then and chat a little about Ethan and me.

I decide to tell them about my scary camera experience, and they all look as terrified as I felt last night.

"That's not going to be any fun," Liz says.

"No, it's not," I agree. "However, it's the only disadvantage I can find so far, so I'll learn to live with it." I'm ready to change the subject. "So Liz, it's your turn."

"I'm sorry?" She looks appropriately abashed.

"I want to hear more about Bill." I let his name roll of my tongue in a seductive way. Everyone laughs.

"You know better," Liz says, looking at me, raising her eyebrows in defiance.

"Come on Liz. I'm not asking about your sex life. I just want to know what's going on with you two. Where did he come from? Which *GQ* shoot did you snag him from?"

"Very funny," she says snidely, but she's eager to talk about him. I can tell. "He's an old friend, and we reconnected when I went home a few weeks ago. Things are going well, but nothing too serious...yet."

"*Yet?*" I repeat. "Mmm hmm."

She tosses her napkin at me. "Stop it. You're more likely to be married before me, so I don't want to hear it."

"What?" Sydney nearly chokes on her noodles. "Did I miss something?"

"No!" I exclaim. "None of that. Not quite." The other girls giggle along with me. "But I do have to extend an invite, if you guys are interested."

"Another party?" Sydney asks excitedly.

"No." I smile at her. "Ethan wants to meet you guys, officially. He's coming to my place tomorrow night and cooking dinner. He wanted me to invite you."

I look around at all of their shocked faces. Sydney's is by far the most amusing.

"Shut. Up." Sydney says, dropping her fork onto her plate.

"Seriously?" Rose is all smiles.

She's obviously happy that Ethan's making a gesture like this, and I love her so much for it.

"Yes." I nod at her, smiling.

"I can make that happen," Liz says, seeming uninterested, but smiling at me like Rose.

"I am *so* there!" Sydney finally says.

"Great! Then I'll see you guys tomorrow night!" I say, and the thought of my friends and Ethan together makes me smile.

"Oh no," Sydney says sadly, hanging her head, interrupting my moment of joy.

"Sydney? What's wrong?" I ask concerned.

I look to Rose and Liz, but they shrug, just as confused as I am. Sydney looks like she may start crying. I reach to put my arm around her shoulder.

"It's just that..." she starts "I haven't been shopping in days. What am I going to wear?"

We all start cracking up, including Sydney, and I'm smiling widely now at the light mood and the anticipation of seeing Ethan again tomorrow, as we finish our Sunday lunch.

CHAPTER 16

I am so glad Jake and Ethan spent some time together today. Jake was so happy to see him, and reflecting back on it now, it makes me want to tear up a bit when I think about how great Ethan is with him.

Unfortunately, Jake hasn't had a lot of men in his life he can look up too. My dad was the only one, and now that he's gone, I do worry about Jake not having a positive male influence.

Ethan is slowly beginning to erase that worry. Whether Ethan and I stay together or not, I have a feeling he would never do anything to hurt Jake. He seems to really enjoy my son's company. Who wouldn't?

And now, after a wonderful afternoon with my two favorite men, Jake is safe and happy at my mom's house, while I sit on the couch and admire my view, thinking about how incredibly lucky I am.

Ethan looks more beautiful than ever tonight. I'm not sure why. Maybe it's because he's wearing green again, which is definitely his best color. It brings out his eyes.

I watch him as he cooks in my tiny kitchen, and I smile as I realize that Ethan looks just as comfortable here as he does at his own place.

Then he catches me staring for the hundredth time tonight.

"Are you checking me out?" he asks smiling.

"Why, yes I am."

"My view's not so bad either." He winks.

I smile at him as I get up to make my way to the kitchen. "Are you sure you don't need any help?" I ask.

As I get closer, Ethan stops his current task of cutting veggies and wraps his arms around me.

"I've got it," he says before placing his warm lips on my neck.

Ethan smiles at my brief shiver before continuing. "I've made this dish several times," he tells me. "It's the meal I usually make when I need to impress someone, and it's really the only semi-fancy thing I know how to cook. Other than this, I'm only good for peanut butter and jelly and canned soup."

"I hope you realize you do not have to impress my friends," I assure him, smiling. "And I can think of a few other things you're good for," I tease as I place my lips on his neck this time.

Instead of shivering like me, I hear one of his soft moans and the sound is electrifying. My lips involuntarily move to his mouth, as if they have a mind of their own.

Ethan willingly complies. He pushes me against the countertop, as our kiss grows more intense, and places his hands on either side of my face. I move my hands up the back of his button down shirt, unable to resist the feel of his bare skin. Ethan moans again before relaxing into me.

"I've missed you so much," he whispers into my ear, as I continue to rub his back.

"I was with you just yesterday morning," I murmur, smiling, as I bury my face into his neck. He smells incredible.

Ethan moves his lips back to mine, but unfortunately, our make out session is short lived, interrupted by the doorbell.

Ethan breaks away and sighs. "I forgot we were expecting company for a minute there."

"Later," I say, and kiss him one last time before going to answer the door.

I pull at my sweater making sure everything is back in place before opening the door. It's Rose.

"Hey lady!" Rose says as she gives me a hug. "I brought a pie."

"Apple?" I ask, which is Rose's specialty.

"Of course." She winks. "Just came out of the oven."

"Hi Rose." Ethan waves at her from the kitchen.

"Hi!" Rose is trying to act cool, but I can tell she's nervous.

"Let me take your coat," I say, hoping to distract her.

I can see she's having a hard time taking her eyes off Ethan. I understand. It's hard for me to get used to the idea of him standing in my apartment as well.

I go to take Rose's coat back to my room, and Ethan winks at me as I pass. I smile and wonder if my desire for him will eventually simmer or if it will always burn red hot like it does now. I'm betting on the latter.

I decide to check my face in the bathroom after I put Rose's coat away — I want to make sure lipstick isn't smeared all over my face from my earlier tryst with Ethan — and by the time I return to the living room, I see Sydney and Liz have arrived.

Rose and Sydney are sitting on the couch, looking a little uncomfortable, while Liz is in the kitchen, chatting with Ethan.

I quickly grab Liz and Sydney's purses and coats and take them to my room. When I return, I decide to go see what the conversation is about on the couch.

"Hi ladies," I say as I approach. "What's going on?"

They look at each other before looking at me. "Nothing," Rose says smiling, but I can tell something's up.

I put my hands on my hips. "What's the matter?" I ask, and Sydney pulls me down to sit between them on the couch.

"We apologize if we're freaking out a little because *Ethan Grant* is in your kitchen!" Sydney explains in a harsh whisper.

I smile at both of them. "Now Sydney, it's not like you to be so star struck. What's up?" I tease.

Sydney glares at me. "Don't act like you're one hundred percent okay with this either. I mean, I know you're making out with him and stuff, but Ethan Grant is in your kitchen, Sam. Ethan.Freaking.Grant."

Rose laughs. "It *is* a little hard to believe."

"I know," I agree with them both. "And you're right, Sydney, I'm still adjusting, but he's amazing you guys. You'll see."

"I can't believe this was his idea," Rose says, smiling at me.

"It absolutely was," I confess. "He said he wanted to meet my friends. I guess he was tired of just hearing me talking about you all the time."

"Or maybe he loves you, and wants to meet the important people in your life," Rose adds, and I smile.

"Maybe that too."

"What's going on in there?" Liz pipes up from the kitchen.

"Just catching up," I turn to tell her, still smiling.

I decide to leave Rose and Sydney to their fangirling in the living room, while I go to join Liz and Ethan in the kitchen.

"What's going on in *here*?" I ask. Ethan looks up at me and smiles.

"I was just complimenting Ethan on his skills in the kitchen, but I now understand they don't extend much beyond the dish we will be experiencing this evening," Liz explains.

"Sorry to disappoint," Ethan says, and out of the corner of my eye, I notice the two in the living room turn to face the kitchen at the sound of his voice.

Liz and I watch as Ethan puts the remaining veggies into his sauce pot and then turns to us.

"All done for now," he says. "Things will have to simmer for about a half hour, and then we can eat."

"Anyone want some wine?" I ask. I decide it may help take the edge off a bit before we go sit in the living room together.

Everyone agrees to the wine, so I make my way to the cabinet to grab the glasses.

"Nervous?" I whisper in Ethan's ear as I pass him in my small kitchen.

"Maybe a little," he whispers in my ear as well, but adds a small kiss to my earlobe, and I briefly close my eyes.

I open them and turn to see Liz smile at me before she rolls her eyes and heads to the living room with the others.

Ethan opens the bottle of wine for us, and I pour everyone a glass. We then carry the glasses to the living room and pass them out among my friends.

Sydney is staring at Ethan in a way that makes me nervous, but Ethan's knowing smile tells me he's use to it. Luckily, Liz has been calm from the start, and Rose seems to be relaxing a bit now as well.

"Sydney?" I decide to break her trance, as Ethan and I sit — him on the chair and me on my coffee table. "Did you officially meet Ethan when you came in?"

"No," she says, still staring, eyes wide, as she offers her hand to him. "I'm Sydney."

Ethan shakes her hand smiling. "Nice to meet you Sydney," he says, and then frowns. "Are you okay?"

This successfully breaks Sydney's stare and makes everyone else laugh.

"Oh my god," she says. "I'm so sorry. This is just a little surreal," Sydney admits.

Ethan smiles at her again before looking directly at me. "I feel the same way."

"Ugh. You guys are gross," Sydney says, but I look over to see her smiling, and I'm glad to see her snark is back.

"Honestly," Ethan continues, "this situation is a little intimidating for me. I've been kind of nervous about it."

Rose laughs. "Why would you be intimidated by meeting us?"

"Well, you're like the judge and jury, right? Getting your approval is an important step, is it not?"

We all collectively laugh. The fact that he feels he needs my friends' approval is adorable, but the fact that he actually thinks there's a question there is even better.

"I approve!" Sydney raises her hand, and Ethan smiles at her.

"I second that," Rose says, raising her hand as well.

Everyone looks to Liz. "I'm going to have to wait to see how dinner turns out." I glare lovingly at her. "I'm just being honest," she continues with a smile.

"See," I look at Ethan, "you have already won them over, without even trying."

"I wish your mom would have been that easy," Ethan says with a laugh. All of the girls start laughing as well.

"I've been friends with Sam forever," Rose says, "and I'm still kissing Mrs. Harper's behind."

"Yep," Sydney agrees. "Good luck with that one. We're kittens compared to her."

"I'm hoping that's the case," Ethan admits.

"So, Ethan," Liz starts, "everything we know about you is from the internet. What is the one thing you would want us to know that we can't find online?"

I'm envious of Liz's poise. Great question.

Ethan looks at me and smiles before he answers, probably remembering my similar question from last night.

"Well, I'm not really sure what all is out there, but I guess if I had to pick one thing I would want a person to know about me, it would be..." he pauses, a pensive look on his face, as my friends all sit eagerly on the edge of their seat waiting for his answer, "I guess it would have to be that I hate beets."

Sydney rolls her eyes, obviously now over her earlier stage fright for the most part. Rose and Liz both laugh and I finally relax. I never questioned whether or not my friends would love Ethan, so I'm not surprised to find this setting pretty close to perfect — Ethan, my friends, and a lot of laughter? Add Jake in the mix and it would be my idea of heaven.

Ethan continues to make my friends swoon over him until the buzzer finally goes off, letting us know the food is ready. We're each on our second glass of wine at this point, and I for one am thankful that we finally get to eat.

The sound of the buzzer sets everyone in motion. I get up to set the table, and Rose and Liz follow. Ethan gets up to put the final preparations on his meal. If it tastes half as good as it smells we're in for a treat.

"Sydney?" Liz calls to her as we start putting out the plates and silverware. "I assume you feel you are the most helpful by sitting on the couch and looking pretty?"

Sydney turns to eye Liz, flashing her best beauty queen smile. "*That* and I'm here for direction if needed."

My small breakfast table is really only meant for four, but I pull the chair from my desk so we can all sit together. It's close, but comfortable, as we all sit and start passing around the food.

"This smells heavenly," Rose says as she passes the sauce to Liz.

"I hope you like it." Ethan smiles at her. "It's one of my grandmother's old recipes."

As we all start to dig in, everyone is silent for a moment. I'm not sure if it's the fact that I'm starving or if Ethan is really this great of a cook, but the meal is amazing.

"What's in this sauce?" Liz asks as she finishes a bite. "And where did you find shrimp this fresh in Delia?"

Ethan laughs. "The shrimp is from a market in Atlanta, actually, and the sauce? It's a secret, of course."

"Right!" Sydney exclaims, as if a light just went off. "You're real last name is Gravago. You're Italian!"

"You got it," Ethan confirms. "But unfortunately, this is the only recipe I've attempted. I'm honestly not crazy about cooking."

"We feel very privileged then," says my sweet Rose.

"And good for you then that Sam loves to cook, and she's great at it," says Liz. I roll my eyes, but she continues. "Her veal picatta is out of this world. I'm sure your Italian roots would approve."

I look over to see Ethan smiling.

"Next time, maybe I'll cook for everyone," I tell him.

"I can't wait," he says, "but if you think your veal picatta will even compare to my grandmother's, you have another thing coming."

"Burn!" Sydney teases, and I smack Ethan playfully on the arm.

We all laugh, and the happy conversation continues through dinner and Rose's apple pie.

"I'm so stuffed," Sydney says, now leaning back into my couch. "I can't believe I ate that much."

I smile at her. Sydney ate maybe three or four bites of Ethan's pasta dish, which means she must have loved it, because I don't think I've ever seen her eat that much in one sitting. Then she had one bite of Rose's pie from Liz's plate.

"I'm stuffed as well, and actually pretty beat," Rose says. "I think I may head out."

"I'm going to do the same," says Liz. "Sydney, roll your fat rear end off the couch and let's go."

Sydney looks legitimately offended, but Liz just smiles at her as she goes to grab everyone's coats and purses from my room.

"Thanks for having us." Rose gives me a hug at the door. "I had a great time," she says, looking at me then Ethan.

"I did as well," Ethan says, as Liz returns with everyone's things.

We all take a moment to give hugs and say our goodbyes. No one hugs Ethan, of course, which I find kind of funny.

I thought they'd mellowed a bit throughout the night, but I guess they're still a little star struck. I, on the other hand, can't wait to get my arms around him.

"Did you have a good time?" I ask, after everyone leaves and Ethan and I are snuggled into each other on my couch.

"I had a great time," he says. "Thanks for doing that."

"My pleasure," I tell him. "I know the girls enjoyed it."

We relax into each other on the couch and spend a few minutes in comfortable silence. Ethan is running his fingers soothingly up and down my back, and I feel totally content.

"May I ask a question?" Ethan breaks the silence.

"Sure."

"I think I missed a private joke tonight."

I raise my head to look at him. "What do you mean?"

"If you don't want to tell me, I understand." He smiles at me. "I'm just curious."

Now I'm curious too. "What private joke?"

"Rose said something tonight, and when she said it, you all looked at each other and smiled."

I instantly know what he's talking about. "'You never know'?"

He nods in confirmation.

I laugh. "It's kind of silly, really."

"It's okay," Ethan says. "You don't have to tell me."

"No, I don't mind. It's just not a big deal."

Ethan looks at me with interest, so I continue.

"It is just something that Rose says...a lot." I smile at him. "Liz started teasing her about it, and then we all kind of slowly picked up the phrase. At first, it was mocking, but then we started analyzing it over several bottles of red wine one night and realized it was a really hopeful and optimistic thing to say, especially coupled with Rose — the unrelenting optimist."

"I like Rose," Ethan says smiling.

"Me too."

"So, 'you never know' equals 'hope'?" he asks.

"Something like that."

"That's nice."

I nod and smile at him.

"You have really great friends, Samantha."

I nod again. "I'm very lucky."

"Do you really think they liked me?"

I'm shocked to find genuine concern on his face, and I laugh out loud. "Are you seriously worried about whether or not they approve of you?"

"Of course," he says, looking a little disappointed that I'm not taking this seriously. "At the end of the day, I'm just a regular guy, you know. And what's so wrong with a guy wanting to make sure his girlfriend's friends like him? Isn't that pretty typical?"

I sit up so I can explain.

"Ethan," I start, smiling widely, "for starters, I could care less if my friends approve of you. No one could change my mind about you."

Ethan starts to interject, but I stop him with my finger to his lips.

"I'm not done," I say before he kisses my finger then smiles at me. "And second, even taking the celebrity out of it, you are so far from typical that it's not even funny."

"What does that mean?" Ethan asks, looking down at our interlocked fingers.

I lift his chin so he'll look at me. "I find you rather remarkable," I confess. "And I know for a fact that my friends do as well."

"You think so?" He really was seeking their approval tonight, and the look on his face is so innocent and adorable that I can no longer resist the temptation.

I grin wickedly as I grab the back of his head with both hands and pull his face to mine. Our foreheads touch for a moment and I wait and let the anticipation of kissing his perfect lips slowly simmer. Just as I feel I can't wait any longer, Ethan's lips are on mine – the need is obviously mutual.

Ethan pulls me swiftly around onto his lap, never breaking our kiss, and I groan softly into his mouth as he starts to run his hands slowly up the front of my sweater.

Our kiss is long and passionate, as he caresses every inch of me under my sweater before finally pulling it over my head. Once again compelled by the need for his skin on mine, I nearly rip the buttons off his shirt as I try to remove it.

Ethan smiles as he lifts me up off the couch, but we don't get far. He lays me gently on the floor, and hovers over me — one hand on the floor by my head, the other behind my knee, pulling my leg up around his waist. I reach up to kiss him once again, but Ethan pulls away after a moment. His beautiful face is flush with excitement and his emerald eyes are blazing.

He looks down at his own hand that is now on my thigh and follows it with his eyes as it begins moving slowly up my leg, to my hip and up my side. He pushes my arm up above my head before locking his fingers into mine. His eyes move slowly back to me, and the heat between the two of us makes me gasp.

His lips are quickly on mine again, and I slide my hands down his sides now, over his tight stomach, moving toward his waist. I unbutton his jeans, but before I can pull them down, Ethan sits up and finishes undressing me, smiling widely the entire time.

I help remove the last of Ethan's clothes and then take a moment to admire the gorgeousness in front of me. Ethan's face is serious now, filled with longing and I'm in a trance, locked in his beautiful, hungry eyes as he leans against the couch and pulls me once again back into his lap. A loud, passionate cry escapes my lips, as I move on top of him. I bring my trembling hands to his beautiful face and stare in awe. Ethan is the perfect combination of strong and vulnerable when we make love...as if I needed another reason to love him.

My breathing picks up as Ethan's soft lips start to move from my mouth to my cheek, then down my neck, and suddenly, my thought from earlier crosses my mind once again. I laugh silently to myself because not only am I sure my desire for him will never wane, I know now that it will continue to burn flaming hot, for as long as he'll have me. The passion and incessant need I have for him grow every time we're together. I just hope he feels the same.

As if he could sense my brief moment of insecurity, Ethan whispers breathlessly in my ear. "I love you, Samantha."

"I love you too," I whisper back.

Forever, I add in my head, as I move his sweet lips back to mine.

❧◦❧

The next morning, I wake up to the most beautiful sight, and it's not out my window. It's lying next to me.

Ethan and I are lying on our sides, facing each other. Our legs are tangled together, and he's holding my hand. His lips are hard to resist this close to mine, but I decide not to wake him.

Instead, I smile as I gaze at him, sleeping peacefully beside me. His hair is an adorable mess after all of the love-making last night, and there's a slight smile on his face, even as he sleeps.

After a few minutes, I can no longer resist. I slowly move my face closer to his and kiss him softly on the cheek.

He opens one eye then the other before grinning widely at me.

"Good morning, sunshine," he says sleepily.

"Morning." I smile back at him.

"Have you been watching me sleep?"

"Guilty."

"Creeper."

"Guilty."

"I love you."

Ethan winks at me, and suddenly I think I may explode with happiness. I'm just not worthy.

"I love you too," I tell him with a wink of my own.

"That was incredibly sexy."

"What?"

"You winked at me."

"I was just returning the gesture," I say. "I think yours was sexier."

"No way."

"It totally was."

"There is no way I'm sexier than you." Ethan rolls on top of me, and I giggle. "No one is sexier than you," he whispers as he caresses my face, and I sigh. My love for this man is barely containable.

"What's wrong?" he asks, his face is concerned.

"Nothing," I assure him. "Nothing at all."

Ethan wipes a tear from my eye and smiles as he shows it to me on his finger. I blush, completely unaware and completely embarrassed. Ugh. Me and my crying.

"Sorry," I say sheepishly. "It doesn't take much, if you haven't already noticed."

Ethan smiles at me. "Just one of many things to love about you."

He leans down to kiss another tear from my cheek. "Are these tears of happiness?" he asks.

He's smiling, but there's still concern in his voice. I place my hands on his face, eager to comfort him.

"They are most definitely tears of happiness," I tell him. "I'm just...amazed sometimes."

"Amazed?"

"By you," I confess. "I keep wondering when I'm going to wake up and find out this is all a dream."

Ethan smiles and rolls his eyes at me. "You and your backwards thinking," he chides. "The truth is that you're the dream," he says softly, "and I'm never waking up."

I shake my head in wonder as I reach to run my fingers along his cheek and his perfectly chiseled jaw. He closes his eyes as I touch him, and when they open, I recognize a now familiar look that makes me tingle in all the right places.

"I think it's time for round..." Ethan cocks an eyebrow, his eyes smoldering.

I smile up at him, and pull his face to mine. "Who knows?" I whisper onto his lips.

"Who cares?" he replies before his lips meet mine, and our blissful dream continues.

CHAPTER 17

Ethan works a ton, but he managed some time off for the holidays. He stood by his offer to take me to L.A. with him, but it didn't feel right. I couldn't leave my mom. Christmas is too hard for her without dad.

We tried to see each other again before he left, but he had to cancel our plans twice due to work. It was disappointing, but I've come to the realization that life with Ethan is going to be different. I'll just have to get used to these ups and downs.

Ethan called me every day that he was in L.A., most of the time, more than once. I always got the impression he was surrounded by total chaos, and he seemed relieved to talk to me.

Ethan is back in Atlanta now for New Year's Eve, and as promised, he's taking Jake and me downtown to watch the Peach drop and see the fireworks.

I love how Ethan always wants Jake to come along with us. Even though alone time with Ethan would be nice, I like how he seems to realize Jake is, and will always be, a permanent part of the picture.

"Have I told you how amazing I think your kid is?" Ethan tells me, as we snuggle while waiting for the New Year's countdown to begin.

Jake and Sean are laughing and playing with their glow-in-the-dark necklaces, acting like they can't feel the cold at all.

Their excitement is contagious, and I can't help but to smile while watching them.

"He's pretty incredible," I agree.

"Like his mother," Ethan whispers before leaning down and stealing a quick kiss.

Although the selfish part of me hates Ethan's unyielding restraint when Jake is around, the fact that he respects my child so much only makes me love him more.

But because I'm feeling selfish at the moment, and because I haven't seen Ethan in a while, I grab the back of his neck and make the kiss a little longer than Ethan usually allows. I also suck a bit on his bottom lip before pulling away, which I've found out drives him crazy.

"That's not fair," he growls breathlessly, which makes me smile.

"I'm cruel like that," I tease.

Ethan chuckles and then presses his lips on my neck, right beneath my ear, but not before running the tip of his tongue over my earlobe which makes me noticeably shiver.

"Two can play that game," he whispers, a mischievous smile on his face, his green eyes on fire.

He has my engine revved, no doubt about it, but mostly, I just can't believe how much I love him and he loves me. I smile as I reach up and touch his beautiful face. He grabs my hand and holds it to his cheek.

"I know. I love you too," he whispers, as the countdown to the New

Year finally begins.

༨༧

It's late January now, and my birthday is fast approaching. I haven't seen Ethan since New Year's Eve, and I've been missing him terribly.

"I can only imagine what your man is doing for you," Rose says as we eat our salads for lunch. "He's sure to overshadow us all."

"He's taking me away for the weekend, but he won't tell me where, of course. He told me to pack for cold weather, so at least I don't have to worry about bathing suits."

"What?! When did you find out about this?" Rose feigns offended. "And why didn't you tell me?"

"Last week," I admit laughing. "And I didn't tell you because it's no big deal."

"Right." Rose shrugs. "Your ridiculously hot, rich actor boyfriend is taking you on some surprise, sure to be wonderfully romantic, location for your birthday weekend, but that's no big deal. Sure. Happens all the time."

"Seriously, I don't really know anything, so there was nothing to tell," I tell her. "And I've been swamped with work. Forgive me?" I flash my most playfully pathetic face at her.

She rolls her eyes at me. "Fine," she scoffs. "But when I get invited to dinner at the White House or tea at Buckingham Palace, you'll be the last to know."

"I understand," I say, smiling.

Truth be told, I'm way too much of a planner to be taking a trip where I know nothing about the destination. I'm all for surprises, but this is playing a little too much to my hopelessly neurotic side.

"Just go with it," Rose says, as if she could read my mind...and she probably can. "You know it will be a beautiful place, but I'll have to say, it's too bad it won't be warm." She shivers. "Warm would be a nice change of pace."

"Good point," I agree. It's been a cold winter here. "But honestly, I could just use the vacation," I admit.

"Exactly! And I'm sure this vacation will be one to remember," Rose says, as she finishes her salad.

I take the last bites of my own salad and notice Rose staring out the window in seemingly deep thought.

"Wanna talk about it?" I ask her.

She looks back over at me before responding. "Not really," she says. "Same stuff, different day."

"I'm really sorry, Rose. I hate seeing you go through this."

Things with Danny are getting worse and worse, and even though Rose is trying hard to be strong, I know she's dying inside. I hate Danny for that.

This situation will harden my sweet, innocent Rose, and that is an unforgivable crime against humanity, as far as I'm concerned.

"It's just so hard." She sighs. "When you decide you're going to be with someone forever, you don't expect that promise to be one-sided, or at least I hoped it wasn't. I just feel like an idiot."

I grab her hand on the table. "You are not an idiot, and you know that," I assure her. "Danny's the idiot here. You did everything right."

"Did I?" Rose asks. "Maybe I could have been better. Maybe I could have been a better wife."

"Rose, I will not have this," I tell her with a stern look. "You will not take this out on yourself. Do you understand?"

Rose smiles at me. "Yes ma'am."

I smile back. "I'm not trying to be your mother. But I will not allow you to doubt what a wonderful, amazing, beautiful, kind person you are. Sometimes things don't work out. End of story. We will get through this together."

"I know." She sighs again. "Have I told you that I love you yet today?"

"I love you too," I tell her. "And I will always be here for you. Always. You can live your life without him, Rose. You *are* strong enough."

"Thanks Sam. I don't know what I'd do without you."

"I don't either," I tease, and we both laugh through our tears.

୨ৎ

Finally, my birthday weekend is here. I'm more nervous than ever and feeling horribly unprepared.

I've spent the entire week trying to get ahead at work, since no one is available to do my job while I'm out. It will only be a couple of days, but we've been busy lately with a new project, and I've been covered in paperwork.

Mom's keeping Jake on Friday night, and then Clara agreed to keep him on Saturday so mom could have a break. At least I don't have to worry about Jake. He's very excited about all of the sleepovers.

As I'm about to make a few calls for work, my cell rings. I see it's Ethan, so I get up and start walking outside to talk to him. I know just the sound of his voice will help me relax.

"Hello, my love," he says when I answer.

"Hi there." I smile, already feeling better.

"Are you having a bad day?" he asks.

"Why would you think that?"

"You told me you were busy this week at work, and we're leaving tomorrow. I just assumed."

I sigh. "You assumed correctly."

"I didn't mean for this trip to stress you out. We can cancel if you want."

"No!" I nearly yell. "I mean, I have a lot to do, but it's been a while now since I've seen you. Do you know how incredible a weekend alone with you sounds?"

"My thoughts exactly," he agrees.

I can tell he's smiling on the other end, and I can hear the relief in his voice. He talks a big game, but it would break his heart if I said I wanted to cancel this trip. He's been so excited about it.

"I will get everything done, and tomorrow, I promise to be better," I assure him.

"Not possible," Ethan teases. "It's absolutely not possible for you to get any better."

I'm grinning now from ear-to-ear.

"I'm not sure if I can wait until tomorrow to see you," I confess.

"Funny you should say that," he says.

I look up from the front steps on the courthouse to find the love of my life pulling into a parking spot across the street.

I hang up and slip my phone into my pants pocket. I'm smiling wide as I start walking quickly toward him, trying hard not to sprint.

He jumps out of the driver's side and waves to me, a huge smile on his face.

I give up on my restraint and run into his arms. He lifts me off the ground as he hugs me.

"I couldn't wait either," he says into my ear, and every worry instantly melts away. Ethan is comfort food for my soul.

I kiss him, and then notice Lamont standing by the car. "Hi Lamont. I didn't see you there."

"Imagine that," Lamont says, and winks at me.

"Jake texted Lamont and wanted to know when he could come hang out again," Ethan explains. "So, I thought I'd bring him with me on my little road trip. Hope that's okay. Does Jake have plans tonight?"

I laugh, as I look at Lamont. "Jake has your cell number? That was probably a mistake."

Lamont just smiles his friendly smile back at me. "Nah. I gave it to him at the soccer game. Told him to call or text any time he wanted."

"That was very nice of you," I say. "I hope he's not abusing that privilege."

"This is actually the first time he's ever used it," Lamont says. "No worries."

"Well, lucky for you guys, Jake has no plans tonight," I tell them. "I need to finish packing, but you're both welcome to hang out at my place as long as you'd like."

"Is Jake at school now?" Ethan asks.

"Yep. He'll be getting on the bus to my mom's in about thirty minutes though. Did you want to meet him there?"

Ethan looks at Lamont, and Lamont nods his head. "How about we pick him up from school? Can we do that?"

I smile at both of them. Jake will love this.

"Sure. That will be a nice surprise," I say. "I'll call the school to let them know."

Ethan pulls me close, and Lamont starts walking back to the passenger's side of the car.

"See you later Sam," Lamont says.

"See you later." I wave, before he gets back into the car.

"I suppose you'll be working late?" Ethan asks me.

I cuddle into his chest. Sometimes, I feel like I just can't get close enough to him.

"Actually, I came in early, so I'm doing pretty well. Just go to my mom's if you want, and I'll meet you guys there in probably about an hour or so."

"I can hardly wait," Ethan says, and kisses me gently on the lips.

I give him quick directions to the school, which isn't too far from the square, and Ethan and Lamont are on their way.

As I'm walking back inside the courthouse, I notice some paparazzi on the sidewalk in front of the nail salon. Seems Ethan was followed.

I roll my eyes, imagining the shots that will pop up tonight or tomorrow of our moment in the square just then.

This kind of attention is hard to take in, but I just keep reminding myself that it's for Ethan, and when I think of it like that, it seems like a small sacrifice to make.

❧❦

I end up staying at work a little over an hour more. I finally just give up, realizing I'm never going to get caught up, so what's the point? Plus, worst case scenario, I get fired, and I'm honestly not sure if that would be such a bad thing.

But most importantly, the thought of Ethan being within twenty minutes of me is making concentrating on anything else really hard.

I pull into my mom's driveway and even though it's a beautiful sight, I'm a little surprised to find Ethan sitting on the front porch swing alone.

I get out of my car and start walking toward him, but as I get closer, I realize he doesn't look happy. My first thoughts are of Jake.

"Where's Jake?" I'm officially panicking, my eyes darting from Ethan to the front door. "Is he okay?"

Ethan stands and walks down the steps to meet me. "He's totally fine," he quickly assures me, taking me in his arms. "He's fine."

I reluctantly pull away from Ethan. "Well, then what's going on?"

Ethan sighs and leads me back up on the porch and into the swing. He sits down beside me before he begins.

"There was a little incident at Jake's school," he says, and I realize then that Ethan looks awful.

"He got into another fight?" I ask. It's all I can think of, but it doesn't explain why Ethan looks like he just lost his best friend.

"Not exactly," Ethan says, and I reach to touch his cheek. He seems to soften a bit at my touch, but his eyes are still sad. "I had no idea, Samantha. I'm so sorry it happened, but I hate most that it happened to Jake."

Then it clicks for me. "You were followed by paparazzi today," I say, and Ethan nods as I confirm his thoughts. "I saw them on the square after you left."

Ethan hangs his head. "I swear I had no idea," he says. "Lamont and I are normally hyper-aware of it, but today, it was just a last minute trip. I didn't even think about being followed. I especially didn't think the vultures would come to Jake's school."

"They must have heard me give you directions in the square," I realize, but Ethan's beating himself up so badly that I start to worry again about Jake. "You're sure Jake's okay?"

Ethan won't look at me. "He's acting like it was nothing, but I know it had to scare him a little."

I turn to look at Ethan and take his face in both of my hands so he'll look at me.

"If Jake's okay, I'm okay," I assure him. "Just tell me what happened."

Ethan pulls my hands from his face and stands up. He starts pacing in front of me. I can't believe he's taking this so hard.

I feel guilty for a moment, wondering if I should be more upset.

"Well," he starts, "Lamont and I parked and started inside the school. I didn't notice them when we got there, but they were there when we came out with Jake."

Ethan comes to sit back down beside me. He takes my hands in his. "I swear no one touched him," he says fiercely. "I would never let that happen, and neither would Lamont. These guys were relentless though and they got close. It was chaos for a minute, but Lamont picked Jake up and got us both to the car."

I squeeze Ethan's hand. "I'm glad you're okay."

"Don't do that," Ethan tells me quietly. "Please don't worry about me like you worry about Jake. I could have cared less about myself in that situation."

"I know," I assure him. "And that's one of the many reasons I love you."

Ethan looks up at me then, and I see the first glimpse of hope in his eyes since I arrived.

"You're not upset with me?" he asks. I notice now that his hands are trembling, and I don't think it's from the cold.

I cannot deny that this incident scares me to death. It ended up fine, but it could have been worse, much worse.

"It's not your fault," I tell Ethan. "This is not your fault."

And that's why I can't be mad with him. He didn't ask for this. It just comes with the job.

"I know this scares you," he says. "You have no idea how guilty I feel for knowing I put you and Jake through this just so I can have you in my life. I want you to be okay with it, but I will have to understand, if you're not."

I laugh at him. I can't help it.

"Ethan, I know you feel bad, and it is scary," I admit. "But it seems like such a small price to pay when I think about the fact that I get to be with you." I reach up to try and smooth his furrowed brow with my fingertips. "I know some of these guys can be ruthless, but on a whole, they're not trying to hurt anyone. And Jake is a strong boy. If he says he's fine, he probably is."

Ethan brushes a stray piece of hair behind my ear. "What did I do to deserve you?" he whispers.

"I have no idea, but it must have been something really good." I have to at least attempt to lighten his mood. I'm glad to see him smile after that one.

"I'm just so sorry, Samantha. I've hated the spotlight for years, and now subjecting you and Jake to it? It seems criminal."

"Nothing is perfect, Ethan," I tell him. *Except for you*, I think to myself. "If we didn't have a couple of unwanted elements, the universe would be out of balance because every other thing about you, about us, is so amazing."

Ethan leans down and kisses me, which I will have to say I've been waiting anxiously for since I pulled up in the driveway.

"What happened to the guys?" I ask him after I have my momentary feel of his lips. "Where did the paparazzi go?"

Ethan smiles a devious smile. "It seems they're not allowed on school grounds. Lamont helped the security guards restrain them while the principal called the cops. Guess these guys were new to the business."

"Nice." I smile, and squeeze Ethan's hand once more for reassurance. "So, should we go inside?"

Ethan pulls me up off the swing and into his arms. "You're sure you're not mad with me?"

I look into his extraordinary eyes. Why do men always get blessed with the best eye lashes?

"Ethan, I'll probably never get used to this part of it, but I will never blame it on you. It is not your fault," I tell him again. "And I completely trust you with Jake. I know you'll keep him safe, and that's all that matters."

"Thank you." Ethan sighs. "That means a lot."

"You're welcome." I smile and then kiss his perfect lips one more time. "Now, let's go inside and enjoy the start of what is sure to be one of the best birthdays I've ever had."

CHAPTER 18

Ethan and Lamont only stayed for about an hour after I got to my mom's last night. I'm still not sure if Ethan ever fully believed me when I told him I wasn't upset with him. He kept giving me sad smiles all night, and despite me rolling my eyes at this gesture toward the end of the evening, he kept doing it.

I made sure to tell him again before he left that I wasn't angry, but his parting smile was still not quite right. I guess I'll have to spend the weekend proving to him that I'm not upset. That thought makes me smile.

Ethan wanted to pick me up this morning, but I insisted on driving to his place to meet him. He lives closer to the airport, so it just makes more sense. It's like he's been a celebrity so long now that practicality eludes him.

As I pack the last few remaining items into my suitcase, I'm starting to get nervous again about the trip. I have no idea why I'm getting butterflies at this point. It's probably the fact that I have no idea where I'm going. And it's hard to believe I actually get an entire weekend alone with Ethan. We barely get any time together, so an entire weekend seems like an eternity.

Plus, I never like leaving Jake. This will only be the second time since he was born that I've left him for more than one night.

Jake went ahead and spent the night at my mom's last night, so I wouldn't have to worry about getting him to school this morning. Everyone thought it would be better and give me more time to pack. I was against the idea because I wanted to say goodbye to him in person before I left, but Jake was the main one that insisted.

"Why can't we just say goodbye tonight mom? What's the big deal?" he asked me last night.

It broke my heart, but I didn't let him know it. My little angel is getting so big. It's hard to watch. I'm so proud of the man he's becoming, but sometimes, I just want my baby back.

I thought about calling him this morning, but then I realized that Jake was right. I told him goodbye last night, and that was enough. It's time for me to start trying to cut the cord with Jake. He will always be my number one, but he needs his independence now. And honestly, so do I.

With that thought, I roll my suitcase into the living room by the door, and do one last sweep of the apartment to make sure I didn't leave anything on or plugged in. After deciding everything is in order, I make my way downstairs and into my car.

As I'm about to drive away, I feel my phone vibrate in my pocket. I'm surprised to see who's calling.

"Hi mom. Is everything okay?" I think briefly I may have forgotten something for Jake.

"Yes, baby. Everything's fine," she tells me. "Someone decided he wanted to tell you goodbye this morning after all."

I can't hold back the tears while she hands the phone to Jake. "Hey, mommy," he says. "I'm going to miss you."

I don't want Jake to know I'm upset, so I do my best to pull it together. "I'm so glad you called, sweet angel. I'm going to miss you too."

Jake sighs. "Stop crying mom. I'm going to be fine."

"I know," I laugh. "Pretty soon you won't need your old mom anymore at all."

"That's not true, mom," Jake says. "Just have fun, okay? I'll see you on Sunday."

"Thanks buddy. You have fun too, and be good."

"Yes ma'am. Love you, mom."

"I love you baby. I'll see you again soon."

I hang up, and while I'm drying my tears, I take a minute to realize how very lucky I am – as a parent and as a girlfriend.

Ethan.

The sudden thought of him makes me wish I had a racecar or a private jet. My Toyota just isn't going to get me to him fast enough. After my call with Jake, I feel more relaxed and prepared for the weekend. I guess it was the thought of leaving him that was bothering me the most.

I decide to spend the majority of the drive daydreaming about where Ethan is taking me. He said to pack for cold weather, so I'm imagining fireplaces and hot tubs. I could have a good time with Ethan anywhere, so thinking about being in his arms, nestled in front of a cozy fire, is like a slice of heaven.

My cell ringing again brings me back to reality. I initially think it may be work, but when I finally look at my phone, I'm excited to see I'm wrong.

"Good morning." I smile at my unusually high-pitched, cheerful voice.

"Good morning indeed," Ethan replies. "I assume you're close by now?"

I look at an upcoming highway sign to get my bearings. "Probably about fifteen minutes away," I tell him.

"It will be the longest fifteen minutes of my life," he says, and I smile.

"Well, let's stay on the phone until I get there. It will make the time pass by faster."

"Sounds like a plan. Are you excited?"

"Yes," I admit. "I have to say I'm a little anxious because I don't know where we're going, but I was having fun dreaming up some possible scenarios on my drive this morning."

Ethan laughs. "Oh you were? And do I get to hear about these 'possible scenarios' of yours?"

"Let's just say most of them involved you, me, some blankets and a cozy fireplace."

"Are we clothed?"

"Nope."

"Well then, you were dead on."

We keep up our playful banter until I pull into Ethan's place.

"I'll be there in a second," I tell him as I pass through the gate.

"I'm coming to meet you at your car, so I can help with your luggage."

"I only have one bag. I can manage."

"Okay fine. I'm just eager to see you," he playfully confesses.

I tell him where I'm parked in the lot, and he's at my car before I even open my door. He must have been waiting in the lobby this whole time, excited to see me. The thought makes me smile.

When I finally get out, he takes me immediately into his arms.

"I missed you," he says, hugging me close. He smells divine.

"I just saw you last night," I tell him, but I've missed him too.

Ethan smiles down at me. "Do you know how excited I am for this trip? Just the two of us? No interruptions? No work?"

"Sounds fabulous," I agree.

Ethan gets my suitcase out of the backseat. "I can't believe you packed so lightly," he says, as we walk toward the entrance of his building.

"I know. I'm kind of regretting not packing a couple more outfits now. Perhaps I packed too little?"

"I doubt it," he says, a lethal smile on his lips as we approach the elevator. "This weekend, clothing is optional."

☙❧

Once we make it up to Ethan's apartment, we have a little less than an hour before we have to leave for the airport. I'm surprised to find Lamont waiting for us when we arrive.

"What are you doing here so early?" I ask Lamont as I sit down on the couch. Ethan leaves to make me some coffee.

"Just making sure you guys make it to the airport okay," he says. "How's the little man doing?"

"He's fine," I say smiling. "He called this morning to say goodbye. I cried, of course."

Lamont smiles too. "That's to be expected, I guess."

"Have you ever left him for a weekend before?" Ethan asks as he sits down beside me with my coffee.

"No," I admit. "I've never left him for longer than twenty four hours, really. It's scary, but honestly, it's more me than him. That kid is growing up much faster than I'd like."

"He's a good kid," Lamont says, "and I'm sure he's in good hands."

"I do think he likes my mom better than me sometimes," I confess.

"I doubt that," Ethan says, chiming in.

Something in his voice compels me to look at him, and for a moment I'm lost. He's absolutely radiant. He's casual today — wearing a dark blue sweater, dark jeans and boots — but Ethan's "casual" still makes him look like a runway model. And his brilliant green eyes are shining. I know it's because he's excited about this trip, which is making me excited too.

The three of us spend the rest of the hour chit chatting about anything and everything until finally Lamont gets the call that the car is waiting downstairs.

Ethan only has one bag as well, so he takes his and Lamont takes mine, as we head to the elevator.

We walk back through the lobby and into the parking garage where a long black limo is waiting for us. Ethan gestures for me to get in first, then he and Lamont follow.

Ethan and Lamont chat for a bit about his work schedule next week. Then Lamont says he needs to make a call. He tells Ethan he wants to call to let the pilot know we're on our way.

"Pilot?" I whisper to Ethan as Lamont makes his call. "You have to make special arrangements with the pilot when you fly?"

This seems a little over the top to me. I mean, Ethan is a celebrity, but he's not the President for goodness sake.

"This time we do," Ethan says, smiling. "I'm rolling out the red carpet for you this weekend. Five-star, all the way."

"You didn't have to do that," I tell him, blushing. "We could have stayed in your apartment for all I care. I just want to spend some time with you."

"I'm not trying to impress you," he says. "I just think you deserve it."

I grab his hand. "I don't deserve you," I tell him.

"I think you have that backwards madam, yet again."

"Well, we can agree to disagree on that one."

Ethan leans down and gives me a quick kiss on the cheek. "You're going to love it," he whispers. "I promise."

"Looks like everything is good to go," Lamont says once he finishes his call. "And don't worry," he says to me, smiling. "I promise I'm not crashing your weekend."

I smile back. "I didn't think you were. I know you just want to make sure Ethan gets safely on the plane."

"You *and* Ethan," he corrects me. "I want to make sure you *both* get safely on the plane."

"Oh, well I feel very special," I tease.

"I actually asked Lamont to go with us," Ethan says, "but he thought we would be okay without him. He does have a friend where we're going that we can call if needed. I hope you'll feel safe."

I roll my eyes at him. "Ethan, please tell me you are not still upset about yesterday."

"Maybe a little," he says with an adorably guilty face. "I just want to make sure this weekend is perfect."

"You'll be there," I tell him. "It *will* be perfect."

I'm happy to see that Ethan seems to be all smiles this morning. He puts his hand on my cheek. It's such a sweet gesture, and I get lost momentarily in those beautiful eyes.

"Almost there," Lamont says, breaking up our intimate staring contest.

I look out the window to see the airport fast approaching.

Honestly, I'm not surprised when we don't pull up to baggage claim and ticketing like the rest of the population. Everything with Ethan has been a little unexpected, so why should things change now?

Instead, we pull into what looks like an underground parking garage. After the driver speaks to the person at the gate, we pass by several rows of cars and continue on into a long tunnel. As we come out of the tunnel, the next thing I see is a row of huge hangers and a few smaller planes already on the tarmac. The limo pulls into one of the hangers on the left, and inside is a small jet plane.

"Is that what we're riding in?" I ask, completely shocked.

A private jet? Seriously?

"Yep," Ethan says, smiling at me as the limo pulls to a stop.

Lamont opens the door and gets out. I watch him walk over to speak to a couple of crew members, and I suddenly feel a headache coming on. I will not have that this weekend, so I quickly grab my purse and pull out two Ibuprofen.

"Are you okay?" Ethan asks.

"I just feel like I may be getting a headache, so I'm going to nip that in the bud right now." I open one of the bottles of water in the limo to help get the pills down.

"You've been too stressed," Ethan says. He looks ashamed and very worried. "It's my fault. I should have given you more time to prepare for this trip. I was being selfish. I just wanted to spend time with you."

"Ethan, please stop worrying," I say, quickly cutting him off. "I'm fine. I may have been a little stressed, but I don't feel that way now. I assure you, I'm perfectly happy."

I'm hoping that's the last of the headaches for the weekend. I know it's probably stress, excitement and anxiety all rolled into one. Life with Ethan is definitely going to take some getting used to for this small town girl.

"You're okay?" Ethan asks again, as he pushes my hair from my face. "You're sure you're okay with this?"

I smile and take his hands into mine. "I'm more than okay with this," I assure him. "I've been looking so forward to it."

"Me too," Ethan says in a whisper. "Me too."

"You love birds ready?" Lamont's head suddenly pops into the limo.

Ethan gets out of the car first and I follow closely behind.

"Good morning Mr. Grant," says one of the men standing outside, as we step toward the plane. "My name is Harold, and I'll be your steward for the flight. May I direct you to your seats?"

"Thank you, Harold," Ethan says in his professional voice.

He already has my hand in his, and he squeezes it as he looks back at me. I assume he's making sure I'm still okay, so I just nod my head and smile. Ethan smiles back and we make our way inside the plane.

I have to contain my gasp as we enter. The plane is small, but the inside is absolutely beautiful — leather seats, mahogany everywhere, crystal glasses and china on a small table on the side of the plane between two of the comfiest looking chairs I've ever seen.

Harold offers to take my purse and both of our coats before asking what we would like to drink. Ethan orders a Bloody Mary, so I decide to follow suit.

"It's vacation, right?" he asks smiling at me as we take our seats.

"Yes it is," I agree, with a smile of my own.

"Well, I just spoke to the captain," Lamont says, as he makes his way over to us. "I threatened his life if anything happened to the two of you, so I think my work here is done."

"Thank you, man." Ethan gets up to hug his friend, and I get up to do the same.

"You guys have an awesome time, and please call Derek if you need anything," Lamont tells us.

"You bet," Ethan nods. "See you in a couple of days. Be good."

Lamont gives Ethan a mischievous grin, and I chuckle at Ethan using the same "Be good" line that I used earlier with Jake.

After Lamont leaves, the captain shows up to speak with us briefly. He's very polite and actually very handsome. There's just something about a man in uniform.

Not long after we speak with the captain, we're headed for the runway and on our way to some unknown destination...well, unknown to me at least.

Ethan and I enjoy our drinks and some catching up after we get in the air. It's an absolutely beautiful day, perfect for flying.

"So, don't you think you can tell me where we're going now?" I ask after a while, growing more and more impatient by the moment, even though I'm definitely starting to feel that second Bloody Mary.

"Not a chance," Ethan says, glancing up at me.

We moved from our cushy seats to an even cushier couch once we were allowed to remove our seat belts. I'm curled up on the end, and Ethan's lying with his head in my lap. I'm enjoying running my fingers through his silky hair, nearly as much as the view. Ethan has his eyes closed, smiling. It's nice to see him so relaxed.

"Please?" I beg. "Pretty please?"

"I will not fall for your tricks, woman."

I move my fingers from his hair to run them across his pouty lips. "Please?" I whisper.

His eyes slowly open and he looks up at me. "You're pure evil," he teases.

"You're easy to coerce," I tell him smiling.

"You haven't won yet," he says, as he kisses my fingers that were grazing his lips.

"Why won't you tell me?" I whine. "I'm dying to know."

Ethan looks at his watch. "And know you shall, in approximately one more hour."

I look at my watch too. It seems like we've only been in the air a few minutes, so I'm surprised to see almost two hours have passed.

"You know," I start, "I'm going to start guessing if you don't tell."

"Okay," Ethan laughs. "But I don't have to tell you if you guess correctly."

"Come on!" I whine again. "I'll just keep begging and harassing until you give in. I'm extremely competitive and I have loads of patience."

Ethan sits up and turns to face me. "Then it seems I'm going to have to figure out a way to keep your mind occupied until we get there."

The look in his eyes makes me quiver, as I watch them stare longingly at my lips.

The next thing I know, Ethan is lifting me off the couch and carrying me toward the back of the plane.

I noticed the door there earlier, but I didn't think this plane would be large enough for a bedroom, and when Ethan puts me down and turns the light on, I realize I was right. It's a bathroom.

"I apologize," he says quietly. "But it's the only place we're guaranteed some privacy."

I smile at him and look quickly around. It's small, but not as small as the bathrooms on a commercial plane. I hop up onto the sink and put my legs around his waist. Ethan's smile is blinding when he realizes I'm willing to comply with his naughty plans.

"I'm sorry to be forward," he says, "but it's been a while, and I've missed you."

"I've missed you too," I say as I reach up to kiss his perfect lips.

As we start kissing, the passion and burning need for each other are quickly evident. Clothing is removed lightning fast, and before I know it Ethan's bare chest is pressed against mine. I moan softly as he buries his face into my neck, his breath warm against my skin. Pure bliss.

As we make love, I realize how complete I feel when I'm with Ethan – a feeling I haven't experienced in a very long time. And when he wraps his strong arms around me and holds me close, I know without a doubt I will never feel as comfortable, as safe, and as *right*, as I feel when I'm with him.

CHAPTER 19

Our bathroom-of-an-airplane love-making session was over in no time, but honestly, it was as passionate and intimate as ever. Ethan just keeps getting better and better. I smile, thinking about what the next time will be like.

Now, as I sit back on the couch with him, cuddled in his arms, I feel happy. It's been so long since I've been in this place. Honestly, I'm not sure I ever have.

"Tell me what you're thinking," Ethan demands, but his voice is far from stern. It's lush and husky, as it always seems to be after we make love.

"Why?" I ask, wondering what my expression must look like.

Ethan reaches to touch my cheek. "You're face just looks so...so..."

"Happy? Blissful? Totally content?" I ask. I'm all of those things and more.

"Beautiful," Ethan says. "All I can think of is *beautiful*."

I raise my head off Ethan's chest so I can look at him. I'm not sure if it's his words or his face that leaves me speechless, but I can't utter a sound.

Harold comes in then, which I'm kind of thankful for. I feel like I may start crying again.

"We're approaching our destination," Harold tells us. "May I get you anything before we begin our descent?"

"I'm fine," Ethan says, getting off the couch to go sit back in the chairs for the landing.

"I'm fine as well. Thank you," I say, as I follow Ethan to the seats.

Harold smiles at me as he walks back toward his seat in the front of the plane, and I feel my cheeks blaze red. I've just become a member of the "Mile High Club", and Harold was all but witness to it.

"Don't worry. I'm sure we're not the first," Ethan says to me smiling, confirming the fact that my cheeks look as hot as they feel. "Harold has probably seen much worse."

I smile, as I take my seat across from him. It seems Harold placed some small bowls of snack mix and water on the table in our absence, so I grab a bowl and help myself.

Ethan was successful in making me forget all about our destination for a while, but now that I'm sitting next to a window, I have to sneak a quick peek.

I let out an audible gasp and put a hand over my mouth. The scene is breathtaking.

"You like it?" Ethan says smiling.

"It's...it's..." Once again, I find myself at a loss for words, and almost at the brink of tears.

"It's incredible," I finally manage.

It seems it's a beautiful day in...wherever the heck we are, and as we begin to slowly drop from the clouds, I can't see anything but rolling landscapes and snow-capped mountains.

For a girl who's never been more than a state away from her

hometown, I may as well be on a different planet.

"Vermont," Ethan finally says.

"What?" I'm still in awe of the scenery out my window.

"I'm taking you to Vermont," Ethan tells me. "I used to come here when I was younger to ski, and I still love it. I know you will too."

"You mean *snow skiing*?" I look at him in shock. "Ethan, I can't snow ski."

I suddenly remember reading something about Ethan liking to ski and snowboard, and I guess the cold weather trip should have made things click for me, but either way, I feel incredibly nervous about this. There's not a lot places to practice this sport in the south. I don't think they even sell snow skis in the sporting goods store in Delia.

"Have you ever tried it?" Ethan smiles, obviously mocking my anxiety.

"No, but I'm not sure I'm cut out for it. I mean, I'm more of a warm weather sport kind of gal."

"Trust me, you'll love it. You just need a good teacher, and lucky for you, I'm excellent."

I smile at him. "*Excellent*"? I repeat. He's got that right.

Ethan flashes a brilliant smile at me, and I sigh.

"Fine," I concede. "I'll give it a shot, but if I run into a tree or fall off a cliff, please make sure to take care of Jake, okay?"

Ethan leans in close to me, as close as his seatbelt will allow. "I would never let anything happen to you," he says, his face serious before he begins smiling again. "And worst case scenario? You don't like it. Then we'll just have to spend all of our time in the house. That wouldn't be awful."

There's a small table between us, but I lean toward him as well. I can get close enough to reach his lips, which will have to do for now.

"That sounds more like it," I tell him, and we kiss until I feel the wheels touchdown on the runway.

The plane lands and eventually pulls into a hanger, similar to the one we departed from in Atlanta.

Also like in Atlanta, another limo is waiting for us when we get off the plane. Ethan wasn't lying when he said we were going first class this weekend.

I get in the limo as Ethan stops to speak quickly to the driver.

"Are you ready?" he asks, moving to sit beside me. His face is beaming with excitement.

"Absolutely," I assure him, and the limo pulls out of the hanger.

Ethan has to return a few calls and emails for work, but he's still the most relaxed I've ever seen him, and I'm starting to get there. I'm definitely happy to be with him.

While Ethan works, I admire the view out the limo's window. Everything is covered in snow here. And even though I'm not really one for cold weather, the snow is so beautiful. I love the way it makes everything seem so clean and new.

I watch as the flakes fall and melt when they hit the street. Then I smile, as I notice all of the cars on the road and people walking around outside. We close down the entire town of Delia with even a threat of snow in the weather report.

"Are you enjoying the view?" Ethan startles me.

"It is lovely," I admit.

Ethan reaches up to stroke my cheek. "I'm already having the time of my life," he whispers.

"Me too," I tell him. "I'm happy to be with you."

Ethan sighs and kisses me softly. "We're almost there," he says, as he moves his hand from my cheek to my knee. "Are you ready for this?"

"Absolutely," I say excitedly. "So ready."

I resume my sight-seeing and a few minutes later, we finally pull into the resort.

It doesn't look like a main entrance. There's a small sign at the beginning of the drive, but it's covered in snow, so I can't read it. The drive way is lined with huge trees on either side, and I can't see the end. We drive for a few minutes before I can finally make out the resort in the distance.

"Wow," I say, mouth agape. "I've never seen anything like it."

The place is huge, and appears to be a small village all by itself. The main building is what Buckingham Palace would look like if it were refashioned for the snowy hills of Vermont.

Ethan laughs at my gawking. "That's actually not where we're staying." I look at him confused, so he continues. "Our place is another five miles or so past the main building."

I'm giddy with excitement. I like the sound of "our place" a little more than I probably should.

Because of the weather and terrain, it takes about twenty minutes to get to where we'll be staying. When we pull up and get out of the limo, I can hardly believe my eyes.

Once again, poor Ethan chose what is probably the most private and secluded place the resort has to offer, but this time, I don't mind.

"Unbelievable," is all I can think to say. And this house is exactly that.

Ethan grabs my hand and leads me to the door. As we walk, I can't decide which I'm more in awe of, the house or the spectacular view surrounding us.

The house is stunning, nestled in a bunch of huge trees like the ones that lined the drive as we entered the resort. But behind the house, the view is absolutely breathtaking. In the distance, there's nothing but mountains with snowy slopes, winding like mazes through the trees.

Ethan walks slowly to the door, seemingly admiring the view like me. The door is unlocked, so we walk right in. Ethan turns and smiles at me.

"What do you think?" he asks.

"Give me a second," I plead. I have to take a moment to get my head around this place.

For starters, this has to be the most beautiful home I've ever seen in my life. Even the entryway is impressive, but as Ethan continues walking, it's like every room was created to rival the next.

The house has a very modern look to it on the inside, but the fall colors and relaxing décor give it an undeniable homey feel. One part of me doesn't want to touch anything, but on the other hand, the overstuffed couch just makes me want to fall right in.

We stroll through what Ethan calls a "gathering room" while the limo driver brings in our things.

"May I get you anything else, sir?" the driver asks before leaving.

"I think we're all set," Ethan tells him. "Thank you."

"Absolutely, sir," the driver says, and gives Ethan his card. "Please call if you need anything."

"Thank you," I tell him, and then with a smile, he starts back out the front door.

And at last, Ethan and I are alone.

"So, do you want a tour?" Ethan asks me.

"Sure," I say. "This house is beyond amazing."

"You haven't seen anything yet."

Ethan's smile is exhilarating, as he leads me back toward the entryway, where we both kick off our shoes, and then head down a short stair case.

"I want to show you the bottom floor first," he says.

I follow along, smiling. There are no words to explain my state of mind at the moment. If I were any happier, I would burst.

"So, this is the living room," he says, as we enter the downstairs.

This room is huge with a full bar on one side and a comfy-looking, green, u-shaped couch that faces a ridiculously large television that's mounted on the wall.

"Then this way should be the guest room," Ethan says as he leads me down a hall to the left.

The guest bedroom is bigger than two of my bedrooms put together.

"If this is the guest bedroom, then the master bedroom must be fabulous," I remark.

"I thought we'd check that out last."

Ethan winks, and my heart nearly stops beating.

"There's another bedroom over here," Ethan says, leading me back through the living room and down another hall on the right.

This bedroom is adorable — the embodiment of a child's fantasy get-away, complete with built-in bunk beds on both sides of the room, another oversized television and some built-in shelves and cabinets full of toys and various board games.

"Monopoly later?" Ethan asks, as we look around the room.

"I'm not sure we should do that," I say.

"And why is that?"

"Because I will dominate you."

Ethan's smile is sinful. "I kind of like the sound of that."

I walk over to kiss him, and as we kiss, all I can think about is how I have two more days of nothing but me, Ethan and Ethan's lips. *Heaven.*

"We'll check out the outside later, if that's okay with you," Ethan says. "We don't have our shoes."

I smile at him, still breathless from our kiss. "Fine by me."

All I can think about is seeing the master bedroom at the moment.

"Ready to see the upstairs?" Ethan asks, smiling back at me.

"Yes, please." *Finally!*

We head back upstairs and walk through the kitchen and dining area. "Are you hungry?" Ethan asks as he opens up the refrigerator. "I asked them to stock it for the weekend, so we should be all set."

"No, I'm fine."

Ethan closes the refrigerator and walks slowly toward me. He puts his arms around my waist and nuzzles his face into my neck.

"Ready to see *our* bedroom then?" he breathes.

I shiver, which Ethan correctly takes as a "yes".

He kisses my neck softly before leading me into the master bedroom. My smile widens immediately.

This room is definitely the best part of the house. As if the flawless décor and breathtaking view from the floor-to-ceiling windows aren't enough, there's a fireplace in front of the bed with a chilled bottle of champagne, and a very inviting palette on the floor created from large feathery pillows and cozy warm blankets.

"I called ahead, before we got on the plane in Atlanta," Ethan says, as I stare at the impossible scene in front of me. "I really liked your scenario this morning. Thought we could see how it plays out in real life."

I smile up at him as he places a gentle hand on my face. "I'm so happy right now," he whispers.

"So am I," I tell him. "I definitely don't think I'll be forgetting this birthday anytime soon."

"I'll make sure of that," he says before leaning down and pressing his lips against mine.

We kiss lovingly for a moment before Ethan slowly moves his hand from my face, down my neck, to my shoulders, my arm and then around my waist. He slides his other arm around me, and I grab his upper arms to steady myself as he pulls me toward him with a force that makes desire course through my body like wildfire.

I continue to hold on to those powerful arms as he walks me backward toward our charming love nest in front of the fire, never once breaking our kiss.

Before we sink into the pillows, Ethan takes off his sweater and t-shirt, and then helps me with mine. He puts his hands on either side of my face afterward, pulling my mouth immediately back to his, as I run my hands over his smooth, bare chest. I feel goose bumps rise in the wake of my touch, and I revel in his response to me. It's invigorating, empowering and oh so sexy.

My eager hands move slowly along his sides, over his perfectly tight tummy, and down to the waistband of his jeans. He pulls away and smiles, as I gladly help him out of his jeans and he helps me out of mine.

"I've missed you so much," he breathes, before we lower ourselves slowly down to the floor.

The pillows and blankets prove to be as plush as they appear, and Ethan and I spend what feels like hours enjoying our long-awaited reunion – kissing, caressing, loving. There's no rush this time around. We have all the time in the world. No words are spoken. No words are needed.

At some point we manage to lose the rest of our clothes, but I barely notice because I'm lost in Ethan once again — the delicious scent of him, his lips, soft and warm on mine and the quiet sounds he makes when I kiss him in certain places.

I'm amazed at how our bodies seem to be in complete harmony, totally in sync – every movement continuously threatening to ignite the burning heat that's building inside of me.

So many times I find myself on the brink, fighting the urge to give in to the overwhelming sensations, but it's as if my body won't allow it. My body needs more. *I* need more. I'll never get enough of him.

"Samantha," Ethan eventually whispers in my ear, finally breaking the long silence between us, as well as my resolve.

I feel him tremble against me, and I cry out as the simmering heat turns quickly to scorching flames.

Neither of us move when it's over. We just stare into each other's eyes as we both try to catch our breath.

Eventually, I manage to place an unsteady hand on Ethan's cheek. I love touching his face, and not just because it's one of the most beautiful things I've ever seen. It's also the way he reacts whenever I touch him there, like I'm the only source of happiness he has in this world.

He closes his eyes, and relaxes into me as I caress his cheek with my trembling fingers.

He places his forehead on my chest for a moment and I move my hand to the back of his neck, running my fingers through his cool, damp hair.

"I wish I could explain how I feel right now," he whispers against my chest.

"I think I understand," I whisper back, as I reach to kiss the top of his head.

Ethan rises to look at me. "I know you do." He's caressing my face now with a trembling hand of his own. "That's the best part."

I lean up to kiss him, and as we kiss Ethan rolls over, pulling me with him, so I'm now sprawled across his chest. His rapid heartbeat matches mine.

"How about we vow to never let each other go this entire weekend?" he says to me, in that same gruff, sexy voice I'm starting to learn and love. His arms are wound tightly around me.

"I have no problem with that," I happily agree.

I cuddle into his chest and we lay there for a while longer, tangled up in one another, basking in the afterglow. But embarrassingly enough, it's my stomach that eventually breaks our peaceful silence.

"Hungry?" Ethan giggles.

"I guess so," I say. "How about we go check out that fridge again?"

Ethan hops up and heads for the bathroom. He returns with two very plush, beige-colored robes.

"One for me and one for you," he says, as he hands me mine.

"Very nice."

I stand up to slip it on. It's comfy, floor length and fabulous.

Ethan puts his on as well, and we make our way to the kitchen, hand in hand.

The kitchen is enormous, large enough to fit a long island in the middle and a table to seat twelve. The house is full of windows, and the kitchen is no exception. It truly is breathtaking.

Ethan picks me up and places me on the island, while he pokes around in the fridge. "Sandwiches?" he asks, as he turns to me with a loaf of bread.

"Perfect," I say, hopping off the island. "But why don't you let me make them. I'm feeling a little inadequate."

Ethan laughs. "Why would you be feeling inadequate?"

"I haven't used my mom skills yet today," I smile. "I'm not feeling useful."

I turn to find Ethan grinning widely at me. "I think you've made yourself very useful today."

"Stop being naughty." I smack him playfully on the arm, feeling so very in love at the moment. "And go find me some plates."

CHAPTER 20

Ethan watched dutifully as I made our turkey sandwiches on rye, and now we're sitting next to each other on top of the huge, twelve-person table enjoying our feast and the beautiful view.

"I love all of the windows," I remark, as we watch the sun begin to set behind the mountains.

"Definitely," Ethan agrees. "But I think the view inside is much better."

I look over at him and he's staring at me, one eyebrow up.

"You are so corny," I giggle, still feeling high from our earlier tryst in the pillows.

Ethan smiles as he takes another bite of his sandwich. "Corny maybe, but honest nonetheless."

"I don't mind corny," I confess. "I don't mind it at all."

We both finish our sandwiches and Ethan goes to grab the champagne that we neglected earlier from the bedroom.

He opens the bottle over the sink, pours us each a glass, then comes back to join me on the table.

"Why are we sitting on top of the table again?" I ask.

"Seemed like a good idea," Ethan says casually. "It's fun to break the rules some times, don't you think?"

"I'm not much of a rule breaker," I admit. "Minus my teen pregnancy, I'm a pretty good girl."

"Really?" Ethan acts surprised, but I know he's not. I kind of radiate "wholesome".

"So, tell me. What's the craziest thing you've ever done?" he asks.

I think for a moment. "Honestly? Probably...on the plane today..." I trail off, feeling shy for some reason.

Ethan smiles. "That's a good one. I've never done that either."

"So, what about you?" I ask. He's not going to get out of this one. "What's the craziest thing you've ever done?"

"Me?" Ethan points to his superb chest. "I'm actually a pretty boring person."

"No way," I tease. "You had to have encountered some crazy stuff in Hollywood, or what about when you filmed that movie in Italy with that bad boy actor? What's his name again?"

"Royce Hammond?" Ethan laughs. "He's not as bad as everyone thinks."

"Really?"

I'm shocked. I've read some pretty raunchy stuff about him.

"Stupid media," I mutter.

"Exactly," Ethan says, smiling. "And I was just your average tourist in Italy, when we weren't filming. Nothing crazy."

"Wait!" I say, suddenly remembering something I read about him. "Didn't you steal a car once?"

"Ok. That's kind of scary." Ethan laughs again. "Exactly how much *do* you know about me?"

"Sorry." I wince. *How embarrassing!*

"Why? I love it." He smiles at me. "I'm flattered, really."

"No you're not." I smile back at him. "You think it's creepy. I know."

"We've already been over this," he reminds me. "Or did you forget? We already established that I'm a stalker too, and if I could be a creeper and look things up about you on the internet, I would."

"Well, since you can't, and I'm convinced there are still maybe one or two things about you I don't know," I grin "how about we each get five questions?"

"This sounds like fun," Ethan says, grinning widely now. "More champagne first?" he asks, looking down at my half full glass. "Or do you want something else?"

"Sorry," I admit. "I'm not a huge fan of champagne."

"Don't be sorry. I'm honestly not a huge fan either."

"Do we have any beer?"

"That's my girl." Ethan winks at me and then goes to get us both a beer.

He returns with our drinks and we both sit crossed legged, facing each other on the table.

"Okay, who goes first?" Ethan asks.

"I'll go." I'm eager to learn as much about him as possible. "First question...You said you're questioning your career path, but I know you love it. I want to know, what do you love most about acting?"

"Starting kind of deep, I see." Ethan smiles and takes a swig of his beer. "Honestly, I'm not questioning my career path so much because I don't enjoy what I do," he tells me. "I'm just not crazy about everything that comes along with it. But to answer your question, what do I love most? I love the ability to live outside of reality, if only for a little while. Life is tough, and acting can be a great escape. I'm not sure if that's a good or bad thing, but it's the truth, at least for me."

"That's a good answer," I tell him, "and completely understandable. I think everyone can appreciate a break from reality every once in a while."

"My turn," Ethan says, smiling, which makes me kind of nervous. "Number one, what's your favorite color?"

I roll my eyes. "You only have five questions, and this is what you choose?"

"This will tell me more about you than you think." Ethan laughs. "And besides, I can't look up your bio online, remember? I need to know all of the details, big and small."

"Okay, well then it would have to be...*green.*" I answer, smiling, as I look into his eyes.

Ethan smiles too. "Your turn."

"Okay, let me think."

It's embarrassing, but I do know quite a bit about him from the internet. It's harder than I thought it would be to think of questions.

"Alright, number two...If you could visit anywhere in the world, where would it be?"

"Good one," Ethan observes. "There are a million places I would like to go, but the first one that pops into my mind for obvious reasons would be Switzerland. I do love to ski, and I would like to try out the slopes there."

"That sounds fun," I say, still unsure about the whole skiing thing.

"Of course, if you decide you hate skiing, then I would choose some place different," Ethan adds.

"That's very considerate."

"Wherever you are is where I wanna be," he says, and leans forward to kiss me.

"Cheeseball," I tease.

"My turn," he says, smiling lovingly at me. "Number two...What's your five year plan?"

"What is this?" I snort. "A job interview?"

"You obviously don't like the way I play this game." He narrows his beautiful eyes at me.

"I just don't think you're trying very hard."

"Okay. How about...do you think you will ever have more kids?" Ethan corrects.

"Okay then." I nod, a little surprised by the question, but I decide to go with it. "I would love to have more, if the situation was right."

"If the situation was right?"

"You know, it might be nice to be married first this time." I laugh.

"Gotcha." Ethan laughs too. "I'll keep that in mind."

What? I can't even think about the possibility of marrying Ethan right now, so I continue to talk out of nervousness.

"I would probably be a better mom to the second one," I admit. "I was a child raising a child with Jake. And there was a lot to sacrifice, having a baby so young."

"Like what? Like college?"

"College is one, I guess. I would still love to go. I've found a love for cooking in recent years, and I wouldn't mind going to school to learn more about it."

"And I love to eat, so we make an excellent pair."

"Good to know." I can't stop smiling at him.

"Do you regret not going to college?"

"Is this your fourth question?"

"Yes." Ethan grins. "I'm skipping your turn."

"Fine," I lightheartedly concede. "I think 'regret' is a tough word. I can't say that I regret it because the only way I probably could have gone would be if I didn't have Jake. Obviously, I have no regrets there."

"Obviously. Jake's the best."

"Yes, he is," I agree. "But I will say that I do sometimes regret using Jake as an excuse for not going. Looking back now, I think I could have made it happen. It would have been hard, but I could've done it."

"You did the best you could." Ethan grabs my hand. "That's all you can do."

"I'm not so sure about that sometimes," I say. "As horrible as it is to admit, I felt sorry for myself for a long time, and sometimes still do. Jake is the best thing that ever happened to me, but he was definitely unexpected."

"So, you went down another road." Ethan shrugs. "And that road led you here. Don't you like it here?" he asks, taking my hand and putting it over his heart.

"I love it here," I say in earnest. "Thank you for that reminder."

"My pleasure," he says. "Now it's your turn."

"Okay, this is number four, I think?" I ask, and Ethan nods in confirmation. "If you don't want to answer this, I understand, but I've been wondering why you're not close to your family."

Ethan's smile fades as he looks away from me toward the window, and I can see the tension build in his shoulders. I instantly regret asking.

"I'm sorry," I say quickly, wishing so badly I wouldn't have asked.

"I don't mean to pry. It's just surprising to me. That's all."

"What's surprising?" he asks, still not looking at me.

"I think you're so wonderful," I tell him in a rush, trying to correct my mistake. "You're amazing with me, with Jake, with everyone you know. So it surprises me that you don't get along with your own family."

Ethan sits staring out the window, drinking his beer, refusing to look back at me. I feel like crying for sure this time.

What have I done?

Here we are having this perfect weekend, and I decide to bring up what is obviously a totally painful subject to discuss? *Way to go Sam!*

I glance in the window so I can at least see Ethan's reflection. Then I realize why he isn't looking at me.

I reach up to wipe a tear from his face, hoping he isn't so angry he'll push my hand away. Instead, he does the opposite and grabs my hand, pressing it to his cheek. I sigh with relief.

"I'm so sorry," I say quietly. "I'm such an idiot for bringing that up."

Ethan doesn't say a word. His eyes are closed, and he's taking deep breaths, as he pulls my hand from his face and holds it in his lap.

"This is not an easy subject for me, and you have me feeling a little vulnerable at the moment," he says, as he turns back to me with a sad smile that nearly breaks my heart in a million pieces. "So, can I just say that my family...they are not the best of people. I always felt like an outsider, so I got out as soon as I could and never looked back." He looks at our hands in his lap. "I believe in the power of choice, Samantha. You can choose to be whoever you want to be. I chose to be nothing like them."

Even though Ethan doesn't seem to be angry with me, I still feel awful. "I'm so sorry Ethan. I should never have asked that."

"Please don't be sorry...well, maybe a little for threatening my manhood by making me cry," he says, flashing me a more genuine smile this time. "But seriously, I want you to know everything about me. That part is just a little difficult and kind of embarrassing, really."

"Hey," I put my free hand under his chin, so he'll look up at me, "we're all ashamed of our family at one time or another. It is nothing to be embarrassed about," I tell him. "And please know that I only asked you that question because I find it so hard to believe that there are people out there that don't know what an incredible person you are. I mean, I guess I thought if anyone was going to love you more than I do, it would be your family."

"Yea, not the case here," Ethan says, looking out the window again before looking back at me. "Looks like you may be the only one," he adds, quietly.

I smile at him. "That's not true, and you know it," I say. "But you know what? In a selfish way, I wouldn't mind that at all. Then I could have you all to myself."

"I'm yours," he says, his face sincere. "For as long as you'll have me, I'm yours."

"I hope forever works for you," I tell him, and I'm happy to see him smile again. "I want to go ahead and ask my last question, okay?"

"Are you going to make me cry again?" he teases.

"I'll try not to."

"Fine." Ethan sighs, with a smile. "Go ahead."

"Well, I wanted to know, and it may sound silly, but I was just wondering..." I'm afraid to ask this, and I'm not sure why. Nothing could be as bad as the last question.

"You can ask me anything," Ethan says, squeezing my hand that he's still holding in his lap.

I look into his heartfelt eyes and suddenly find the strength. "I wanted to know why...I want to know why you love me."

"Seriously?" Ethan looks legitimately surprised, which I'm not sure how to take.

I feel a little silly, so I try to explain. "It's just that I've never felt this way about someone before, and I'm not afraid to admit that. This is all so new to me, and I'm absolutely thrilled by the fact that you seem to feel the same way. So, forgive me for my indulgence, but I just want to hear you say it."

Ethan laughs, which gives me hope that he's feeling better now about my earlier blunder. I'm so relieved.

"Well, when you put it that way..." Ethan starts. "But this is definitely a first for me too, so it's kind of hard to put into words."

"Do you feel like this is all moving too fast?" I ask.

"No," Ethan answers quickly, which makes me feel better. "I mean, from the outside, it may appear so, but on the inside, this just feels...*right*, and I hope you agree."

"I do," I assure him. "One hundred percent."

"So, do you still want to know why I love you?"

"Please. I know it seems incredibly self-fulfilling, but I would really like to hear it."

"I don't mind telling you at all," he says. "I just hope it comes out right."

"I'm sure I won't be disappointed."

"Okay, let's see..." Ethan looks down and starts playing with my fingers as he speaks. "At first, the egotistical side of me kind of liked that you were a fan, and of course you're absolutely beautiful." He smirks. "I don't have many fans that will punch reporters for me."

I smile, but stay quiet. I will never live down the Snow incident.

"But then I met you at the fundraiser," he continues, looking up at me now, "and when I found out that bartender planned to hit on you, I was jealous. It's ridiculous, I know, but I think that was confirmation for me. I barely knew you, but I had feelings enough to get jealous of some random guy hitting on you?"

"He was no match for you," I remind him.

"I remember how stunning you looked in that dress," he says smiling. "I can't believe I didn't have to fight every guy in that place for you."

I laugh. "Okay, that's enough of that."

"It's true," he says. His eyes are soft, laced with sincerity. "That night I got to see past the pretty fangirl. You were amazing, the way you helped me with that crazy person in the bathroom. And when you speak about Jake? You should see the love in your eyes." He pauses before starting again. "That alone would have been enough to make me fall madly in love with you, but then you had to go and do the unthinkable."

"And what was that?" I ask softly.

"You went and loved me back," he says, staring into my eyes, and I smile through my tears. "I think that's my favorite part," Ethan reaches up to touch my wet face. "I just love that you love me."

Ethan leans toward me and when his sweet lips touch mine this time, there's nothing sexual about it. I love him and he loves me, and there's proof of that in this kiss. It's like we're exchanging bits of our soul.

We're both breathless when it's over, and all smiles, as we let that surreal moment sink in.

"Wow," Ethan finally says.

"Exactly."

I reach to touch his face again, this time trying to make sure he's real, and he is. His skin is warm against my hand. I'm the luckiest girl in the world.

"So, you have one more question," I remind him.

Ethan gives me a playful grin. "I think I may save my last one for a rainy day," he says, before leaning in to kiss me again.

This kiss is a little different than its most recent predecessor. I can feel a familiar heat begin to rise up inside of me, as Ethan begins pulling away the sides of my robe and slowly moves his hands up my legs.

"What should we do now?" he whispers as we kiss.

"Hot tub?" I suggest, which comes out as more of a whimper, as his hands reach my inner thighs.

"Or this table..." Ethan's voice is deep and confident, as he gently lays me down on the table and presses himself against me.

"Yes," I say, my mind and body suddenly consumed by him. "Yes," I say again, the only word I can seem to manage.

CHAPTER 21

I wake up feeling very out of sorts. It's still dark outside, and my body feels a little sore, but with good reason. I think Ethan and I managed to christen every room in this house last night.

It takes a minute to figure out where I am, but what I'm more concerned with is that Ethan is nowhere near me.

Surprisingly, I'm in some makeshift pajamas – Ethan's boxer shorts and his gray t-shirt – which I have zero recollection of putting on, but that's okay. The shirt smells fabulous.

When I open the door to the bedroom, I hear music, but it sounds far away. I follow the sound, walking through the kitchen and into the "gathering room", as the music continues to get louder. And as I get closer, I realize it's a favorite song of mine, and it's coming from downstairs.

I walk quietly down the steps and into the living room where I find Ethan playing the guitar.

His back is to me, so I stay at the bottom of the steps for a moment just watching and listening. He looks irresistible, sitting there in a plain white t-shirt and gray cotton pajama pants, and my chest swells with pride at the thought that he's mine.

"Hi," I breathe, as I move to sit by him on the couch.

"Hi," he says, surprised to see me. "Did I wake you?"

"No." I lean in to give him a kiss. "I missed you beside me," I confess. "It was your idea to be continuously touching all weekend, remember?"

"I'm sorry, love." He smiles at me. "I will have to spend some time making that up to you."

"I'll hold you to that."

"You won't have to twist my arm too hard." Ethan puts the guitar down so he can hold me, and I move eagerly into his arms.

"I thought you said you didn't play well," I remind him. "That sounded pretty good to me."

Ethan laughs. "I don't play very well. I just like to play some times to clear my head."

"That was one of my favorite songs," I tell him. "Did you know that?"

"No, but I'm not surprised," he says. "It reminds me of you. That's why I was playing it."

I sit up a bit so I can see his face. "Why do you need to clear your head?" I ask. "Is everything okay?"

Ethan's face turns sad, which makes my stomach hurt. "I have some bad news," he says. "I got a call last night at some point. I'm not sure when and..."

He doesn't immediately continue, and I watch his face turn from sadness to anger, as he stares out the windows in front of us.

"And what, Ethan?" I say, getting anxious now. "What's wrong?"

Ethan finally looks back over at me. "We may have to cut our trip short," he says. "I'm so sorry, Samantha."

I sit up, so I can see his face clearly. "What do you mean? What for?"

I'm trying hard not to show the disappointment on my face that I feel in my heart. It's not his fault, but it's still hard to hear.

"I'm so sorry," he says again, as he stands up to move away from me. "It's Vick," he starts. "He was supposed to attend this award show on Sunday night, and he can't make it. So, I have to go in his place."

"Why?" I'm having a hard time fighting back the tears, thinking about our fabulous weekend coming to a close. "Why you?"

Ethan comes and sits back down beside me. "I'm contractually obligated. We're the lead actors, so when one of us can't attend something like this, the other has to show, as the only suitable replacement."

"But you're busy too, right?" I know this won't fly, but it's worth a shot. "It's not like you were sitting at home with nothing to do."

"Unfortunately, as much as I wish it was, a weekend alone with my girlfriend isn't a viable excuse."

"So," I say quietly, hanging my head, giving up on trying to hide my heartache, "when do we leave?"

Ethan grabs my hand. "I'm sorry, Samantha. I really am."

"It's okay," I say, trying to make us both feel better. "It's not your fault."

"You don't have to pretend to be understanding. I know you're upset about this," he says. "I am too."

"It will be okay," I say, squeezing his hand, realizing I need to be the optimist here, as hard as that might be. "We had yesterday, right? And there will be plenty more to come."

"Stop it," Ethan says, putting his head in his hands. "Just let me feel bad about this, okay?"

"No." I grab his face so he'll look at me. "Of course I'm disappointed, but this is your job."

"It's not worth it," he says, with sad eyes. "This is what I meant. All of this...it's just not worth it."

"Yes it is," I tell him. "Because you're brilliant at it. It's what first made me fall in love with you, and that talent and creativity is still a large part of what I admire most about you."

"Why don't you come with me?" His eyes are shining with his new revelation. "We can fly into L.A. tonight, spend the day together tomorrow, and then you can come to the awards show with me."

It sounds wonderful, but I know I can't. "I can't miss work on Monday, and I need to get back to Jake," I say. "But we will see each other again soon, right? If anything, I'll see you on set."

"It's just so hard," Ethan says, getting up from the couch again to pace in front of me. "I want to say no to them so badly, but I can't. Legally, I can't."

"You don't have to choose, Ethan." I stand up to stop his pacing. "This is not a choice between me and work. This is an obligation that happened to come at a bad time. It happens. It won't always be this way."

"What if it is?"

"It won't be," I assure him.

"But what if it is?"

"It won't be," I say again, as I put my arms around him. "It won't be."

Ethan sighs, I assume finally resigning to the fact that our weekend is over.

"I love you, Samantha," he whispers in my ear. "I love you so much."

"I love you too," I say. "And I'm always going to be here, Ethan, no matter what. Please don't worry about that."

Ethan pulls away to look in my face. "You promise?"

"I promise."

Ethan kisses me again, and I realize I'm a little more upset than I probably should be about our weekend getting cut short.

"We don't have to leave for another few hours," he tells me. "Wanna watch the sunrise with me from the hot tub? I think that's the only place we missed last night."

"Sounds perfect," I tell him, as I move to kiss his lips once more, fighting back tears the entire time.

&

"I have some bad news...I'm so sorry, Samantha...I have to go in his place."

Ethan's words from earlier this morning are circling around in my head as I feel the wheels of the plane touch the ground.

I look from the window to the man I love sitting across from me. At least I still have a couple more hours with him.

I close my eyes briefly and try to remember the hot tub full of rose petals; of my romantic Ethan and me having one more memorable moment before we left the house in Vermont. I smile at the memory.

"Hey beautiful," Ethan says sweetly when my eyes open again. "What are you thinking about?"

"Hmm...just hot tubs and roses," I say with a smile, and I watch as a slow smile spreads across his face.

I'm happy to see him smile. He's been so upset about having to cut our trip short, and no matter how many times I tell him it's okay, he just can't seem to get over it. I'll admit. It's hard for me too, but it's Ethan's job. It's his responsibility. I know all about responsibilities.

"Ethan," I sigh, as I reach across the small table between us and gesture for his hand. There is still worry and concern in those beautiful eyes. "Listen to me. For the hundredth time, I don't blame you for having to cut our weekend short. I know this all goes with the job and sometimes things don't work out the way you plan."

I sigh again. How many times have I told myself this over the past twelve hours? Saying it out loud still doesn't seem to make it any better, for either of us.

"I know you don't, but I wanted a weekend for you, with no interruptions," he says squeezing my hand. "I just wanted one weekend, where we could pretend like my crazy world doesn't exist."

I lean toward him to kiss his irresistible lips, while we're waiting for the plane to taxi into the hanger.

"Ethan Grant," I say as I break our kiss and see the worry still in there in his eyes. "This *has* been a special weekend. It's meant more to me than you'll probably ever know. And even if it was short, it was still priceless time I got to spend with you, and I think we made the most of it." I wink, in an effort to lighten his mood, but it doesn't work. Ethan doesn't even seem to notice.

"Samantha, I--"

I put my finger to his lips to stop him. "Ethan, please. Don't beat yourself up over this. I won't let you. Besides, everyone will want to see you at that event anyway instead of Vick, so really you're doing these folks a favor."

I try teasing him again, and this time seems more successful. Ethan laughs softly at my feeble attempt to poke fun at his costar.

"Yes, I'm sure Vick is doing something worthy, like saving a forest or getting a cat out of a tree," he adds, as our plane finally reaches the hanger.

He undoes his seatbelt and reaches over to take my face in his hands. "I love you so much. You know that right?" he says and kisses me before I even have a chance to answer.

I reluctantly pull away from the kiss when I hear Harold walking toward us, letting us know we can exit the plane.

"Of course I know you love me and I love hearing you say it," I say, as we both stand, and he takes me in his arms, "but we should probably go or we'll wind up putting our membership to the 'Mile High Club' back to good use."

I smile, before placing my lips on his again.

"And that would be a bad thing, why?" he murmurs as we kiss, and I sigh, wishing we had a few more hours on this plane.

"Because Lamont is probably ready to be off of Jake duty with my mom," I say, as Ethan takes my hand and we start to exit the plane. "I'll go back to your place and get my car, and then head home."

The thought of leaving him so soon makes me want to cry, even if it means seeing Jake a day earlier than expected.

As we exit the plane, we both take a moment to thank the pilot and Harold before heading to the car.

"Where's Lamont?" I ask Ethan as we make our way over to yet another limo.

I'm going to go into culture shock after this trip. Reality is going to be rough.

"I actually called him in Vermont before we left and filled him in." Ethan gestures for me to enter the limo first, and he follows close behind. "He said not to hurry back to your mom's because she has everything under control. And you know from speaking with Jake earlier, that he's having a great time," Ethan says. "Oh, and Lamont also said to tell you Happy Birthday."

I smile. "Lamont's such a sweetheart," I say, as I lean back in the seat feeling rather exhausted.

"Don't tell him that," Ethan says as he cuddles close to me and smiles his beautiful smile that I love so very much. "He'll deny it forever. Besides, it would ruin his reputation as a badass."

I laugh as Ethan takes one of my hands in his. "Happy Birthday Samantha," he says quietly as he places his other hand on my cheek. "It looks like it's just you me after all, if that's okay with you."

He leans in to kiss me, but I avoid him and start idly playing with the two buttons on his sweater, hesitant about staying.

Jake is having a great time, he assured me of that. But it just feels like I should probably end this weekend while we're ahead. It was fun while it lasted, but now it's time to get back to the real world.

"I know you really want to see Jake," Ethan says, as I move my arms around his neck, "and I understand if you want to go home, but I still haven't given you your birthday present. I would love for you to spend the night at my place. Please Samantha?" he begs, batting his luscious lashes at me. "I'm not quite ready to let you go."

He leans toward me and kisses my neck, nipping my earlobe in the process. *So sneaky.*

"You play dirty," I say smiling up at him, trying to catch my breath.

"Is that a *yes*?" he asks, winking at me knowing full well what my answer will be.

So, instead of answering, I take a moment to lovingly seduce him with my eyes, before reaching up to kiss him and nibbling a bit on his bottom lip. I do love our little games.

Ethan moans softly in reaction to my payback. "Your wish is my command," he says breathlessly, as we travel down the highway, finding ourselves once again completely lost in each other.

CHAPTER 22

"What's on your mind?" Ethan grabs my hand as we walk toward the lobby of his apartment building. Someone met us outside this time to get our luggage.

"Oh, I'm just thinking," I start, my mind racing.

"About what?" he asks, stopping me before we reach the door to his building, so he has my full attention.

I look up at his concerned eyes. I keep telling him to get over things, but if I'm being honest, I'm struggling too. I feel like I can tell Ethan anything, but can I really tell him this? I hate when my insecurities get the best of me.

"I was just thinking of you," I finally say, placing a hand on his beautiful face, "and how happy I am. You are the best thing that has ever happened to me, but sometimes..." I trail off, still not sure if I want to get into this right now.

"Sometimes what, Samantha? Tell me. Please."

"I just don't ever want to be a burden to you, Ethan," I say letting out the breath that I hadn't realized I was holding.

Ethan grabs my hand from his face and takes both of my hands in his. "Samantha, you are so many things to me, but a *burden*?" He shakes his head and smiles at me. "Why would you ever think that?"

I look down at our hands before answering him.

"I've just been thinking about your job a lot, especially on the plane ride back, and the paparazzi, and all the stress you have to endure for just being *you*, and I guess my insecurities got the best of me," I admit. "I started thinking that I might be...."

I pause again, but Ethan is quick to keep the conversation going.

"Samantha, look at me," he commands, and I obey. The urgency in his eyes is disarming. "I love you so much. I need you to understand that. You are the single most important thing in my life and you and Jake will never be a burden to me. Never."

He leans down to kiss me, but before he does, I pull my hands from his and place them on his chest to stop him. "Just promise me that if this gets to be too much – if *I* get to be too much – that you'll tell me. Okay?"

"I can assure you that won't happen. Please trust me."

I look into his pleading eyes and surrender. I do trust him, and I know he loves me. He's proved it time and time again.

I move my hands from his chest to around his neck. "Thank you," I say before kissing his cheek. "Thank you for this amazing weekend." I kiss his other cheek. "But most of all, thank you for loving me, too." This time, I kiss his sweet lips and Ethan pulls me close.

"It's all I ever want to do," he whispers. "And now we better get upstairs before I start taking your clothes off in the parking lot."

I smile. I had momentarily forgotten we were still in a public place.

Ethan lets me go, but keeps my hand to lead me into the lobby.

"So, was Jake upset?" he asks, as we get to the elevator.

I laugh. "Not at all. They're having movie night tonight. It's a big deal."

"Movie night sounds fun. We should try that."

I look at him out of the corner of my eye and smile. "Ethan Grant, when I'm with you at night, the last thing I want to be doing is watching movies."

"Oh, really?" he pushes me gently against the glass wall of the elevator. "What did you have in mind?"

He goes for my neck, and I'm once again putty in his hands. The man already knows me too well.

"You'll see," I say, as I wrap my arms around him.

We finally make it inside, and someone shows up barely a minute after with our luggage. Ethan pulls our bags into the bedroom, and I follow him. My feet are killing me, so I sit down trying not to get too distracted by the bed. I really would like a shower first.

As I lean down to unlace my boots, Ethan bends down in front of me and moves my hands out of the way.

"Let me. It's your birthday," he says smiling as he takes one boot off, and then the other.

Next come my ugly socks — my thick, gray, very unattractive wool socks that I took for the trip. I laugh, embarrassed that Ethan even has to see them, let alone touch them.

"Thank you for enduring my socks," I say, still smiling.

"I love your socks."

"You lie."

Ethan grins at me before wrinkling his nose. "They *are* kind of hideous," he admits.

"That's more like it," I say before leaning down to kiss him.

"There's something I want to show you," Ethan says with a

mischievous grin.

He stands and I notice he's already barefooted. I smile. There's not one part of this man's body that doesn't turn me on.

"C'mon," he says as he pulls me to my feet.

He's so excited that I start wondering if maybe my birthday present is in the next room.

We walk out of his bedroom and head down the hall towards a door that's painted deep green. I look at him suspiciously.

"Where are you taking me?" I ask smiling.

"My bathroom," he says, as he continues to lead me down the hall.

I've never been in this room, in the few times I've been to Ethan's place. We typically spend the majority of the time in his bedroom, which is fine by me. I've never even bothered to ask for a tour.

"I've been to your bathroom," I tell him, as we stop in front of the door. Ethan grins, moves behind me, and covers my eyes with his hands.

"Not this one. No peeking," he says into my ear, and I hear him opening the door. "I think this will be welcome after all of the traveling," he says softly and leads me inside before moving his hands to my shoulders.

I take a moment to look around before I speak. "Ethan, it's...incredible."

I feel myself relax instantly as I walk through the door.

"It's the only major renovation I did to the apartment when I moved in," Ethan says. "It was another bedroom, but I wanted a place to relax."

The walls are deep mahogany with little faint specks of gold that make it look like the room is sprinkled with pixie dust. Along the left side of the room is a marble top vanity with two sinks on either side, and above that is a wall of windows overlooking the skyline, with two mirrors seemingly floating on the glass above the sinks.

"Tinted? I assume?" I gesture toward the windows, and Ethan smiles.

"Of course."

On the right side of the room there are a couple of floor-to-ceiling cabinets painted the same color as the bathroom door, sitting next to a small room made of wood.

"It's a steam room," Ethan explains, watching me look around. "We can try it later, if you want."

I just look up at him and grin. I've never been in a steam room.

I turn back to the enormous bathroom and notice the biggest shower I've ever seen in my life is in the corner, complete with a stone bench that wraps around the inside. There are so many shower heads that water must come at you from every angle.

"Do you always have fresh flowers in your bathroom?" I ask, smiling at the vases full of red roses placed decoratively around the room.

"No," Ethan says, as he pulls me toward him, my back pressed firmly against his chest. "I wanted to keep Vermont fresh in your mind, so I thought we would just start where we left off."

"I will never forget that trip," I assure him, thinking again now about red rose petals and hot tubs. "I promise."

Ethan pushes the hair from my neck and starts kissing me. I'm about to be lost in the moment when something catches my eye at the back of the long room, directly in front of us.

It's a chaise lounge, but not just any chaise lounge. It's a prop from the show, and the fangirl in me instantly surfaces. I can't resist. I have to sit on it.

As I step off of the plush carpet in the doorway onto the tile floor, I brace myself for the cold, but instead, the floor is actually warm and toasty.

I turn to Ethan in shock. "Is the floor heated?"

Ethan smiles and nods. "Cool feature, right? Do you like it?" he asks, as he puts his hands back on my shoulders.

"What's not to like?" I say excitedly, before making my way over to the lounge.

"I can't believe you have this." I sit down and run my fingers over the deep green suede.

"It's one of my favorite props from the show and they were going to replace it. I thought it might work well in here."

"I agree." I smile up at him. "I may never move from this spot, even though I'm dying to take a shower," I say, as my eyes wander over to the impressive shower again.

Ethan walks slowly towards me and straddles the end of the lounge. He sits down, facing me, and I start to think about how many times I've acted out this scene in my mind.

But this is not a fantasy. This is real.

"How about a bath instead?" Ethan moves closer and brushes a stray lock of hair from my face, "With me, of course."

His eyes are blazing, and I stop breathing.

"Now that's an offer I can't refuse," I manage, lost as usual in his beautiful eyes.

"Perfect," Ethan says before grabbing and kissing each finger on my hand. "You stay here."

He stands up and walks over to an old fashioned claw-footed tub and starts the water. It's between the shower and steam room, but I barely noticed it before.

His back is to me as he stands and he slowly pulls his sweater up over his head.

I lean back into the longue and admire my view, as part of his t-shirt rises with his sweater, revealing his smooth, muscular back.

The next thing I know, he's at my side again, pulling me up on my feet. He's a sight to behold – barefoot, in faded jeans, a white t-shirt and his hair a mess from taking off his sweater. He's my birthday present, all ready for me to unwrap.

"Samantha, I think you're a little overdressed for our date tonight," Ethan teases.

"I think you may be right." I trail a finger along his perfect jaw line. "What are you going to do about it?" My turn for teasing.

"Well, I think we'll start with this," Ethan says smiling, as he tugs at the bottom of my sweater, and I lift my arms to oblige.

I start to take off my t-shirt, but Ethan stops me. "Oh, no you don't," he smirks. "That's my job."

I smile and raise my arms again so he can take off my shirt. His playful moods are my favorite.

"Are you cold?" he asks, as I shiver when his hands graze my bare skin.

"Not quite." I smile and give him a quick kiss. "Please, don't let me stop you from your work. You're doing such a great job."

"Well, if you insist." He grins. "Turn around, please."

I turn around and he pulls me against him. "Silky smooth," he whispers in my ear, as he caresses my bare stomach. "Like...*rose petals*," he teases, once again reminding me of our very memorable tryst in the hot tub in Vermont.

"You are horribly corny."

"But you love it."

"Yes," I say, smiling. "I most certainly do."

I lean my head back against his chest and wrap an arm around his neck. "You know, you might want to turn the water off before we have a lake in your bathroom," I say as I turn my head to look at the tub.

"No worries," Ethan says matter-of-factly. "It has a sensor."

I feel his mouth move into a smile against my hair, as his fingers move slowly to unbutton and unzip my jeans. He pushes them down my legs, and I step out of them before he spins me around and gathers me back into his arms.

"So, do I get to unwrap my present now?" I smile eagerly up at him.

Ethan looks confused. "Um, well....I was going to--"

I stop him with a kiss. "I don't mean whatever present you bought me. I was referring to *this* present," I say, as I spread my hands against his chest.

His answering grin is breathtaking. "Be my guest. I'm all yours."

I grab the bottom of his shirt, pull it up over his head and toss it on the floor. I feel Ethan shiver now, as I run my hands over his bare chest.

"Cold?" I whisper, as I reach to kiss his neck.

"Hardly."

I move my fingers up and through his hair, down the sides of his face, as I pull him to me, kissing his eyes, his nose, his jaw.

Ethan groans as I continue my assault, kissing along his neck to his collarbone, moving my hands slowly up and down his arms until they find their place back on his chest.

I lean down and replace my hands with my lips, kissing his heart. I look into his eyes as my hands travel slowly down and linger on his tight stomach a bit before moving toward the top of his jeans.

I turn him around the same way he did with me and place a few kisses on his beautiful back. I move my hands down, beneath his waistband and over his hips before I unbutton his jeans and pull them down. He turns to face me, and I smile. My present is now standing before me in nothing but a pair of boxer briefs. I have to take a deep breath to steady myself.

Ethan steps out of his jeans, and then leans down to get something out of his pocket.

"What's that?" I ask curiously.

Ethan looks lovingly at me. "Your birthday present. Do you want to open it?"

He moves toward the chaise, and I follow. He gestures for me to sit, and he sits beside me, holding a little square blue velvet box in his hand.

Oh dear God. My heart stops for a split second. Is this a ring? Is he going to propose?

So many thoughts run through my head all at once – thoughts of marriage, of being with Ethan forever, of him being a permanent fixture in Jake's life. I snap quickly back to reality, knowing Ethan wouldn't do that...at least, not yet.

"Before you open this, I need to tell you something." Ethan's face is soft but his eyes are serious as he turns towards me. "It's a little corny, but you'll love it."

I smile widely, as he continues.

"You know I'm not close to my family, but there's one family member that I actually used to enjoy when I was younger – my grandmother."

His face is so sweet and innocent at just the mention of her. I want to reach out and hug the little boy inside him.

"I haven't told you about her because I knew if I did, I may start crying like a baby or something and drop a few more points on the masculinity scale."

"Vulnerability can be very sexy, you know." I lean over and put my hand on his cheek.

"In that case," he smiles, "I can probably try and work up some tears later."

I giggle and give him a quick kiss. "Please continue."

Ethan grins and takes a deep breath before starting again.

"My grandmother was amazing – one of the few people in my family that was actually decent to me – and I used to love hanging out with her in her kitchen, eating her famous tiramisu." I watch him smile at the memory. "She's actually the one who taught me how to cook."

"I would like to thank her for that," I say, remembering the fabulous dish he made for my friends and me.

Ethan smiles and looks down at the little blue box in his hands.

"My grandmother was one of the few people I felt like I could be myself around when I was growing up," he continues, "and as I got older, we would talk about everything. She had some great stories." Ethan looks up at me again with sad and wistful eyes. I can see he misses her. "I asked her one day about my grandfather because I never knew him. She told me he was the love of her life, and the day before they got married, he gave her this." He spins the box in his long fingers. "It's been passed down through five generations of men in my family, but instead of giving it to my father, she gave it to me. She said I should only give this to the person I fall madly in love with – the person I want to be with forever." He places the blue velvet box in my trembling hands. "That person is you. Happy Birthday, sweet Samantha."

I hold the box in my hands and look up at him before I open it. The love in his eyes is all the encouragement I need to accept such a priceless gift. I slowly open the box, still not sure what I may find.

"Ethan, it's..." There are no adjectives worthy enough to describe the gift, or how I feel right now.

Inside the box is a delicate gold necklace with a pendant in the shape of an infinity symbol, and two small diamonds are placed where the lines cross in the middle. It's simple and beautiful and absolutely perfect,

I run a finger over the pendant as I think about how much love it's seen through five generations. Tears come to my eyes and I throw myself into Ethan's arms.

"I'm glad you like it," he laughs, running his hands up and down my back, hugging me close.

Wrapped in his strong arms, I try to control my tears. "I love it Ethan," I admit, "and the fact that you gave this to me — and what it meant to you and your grandmother — I'm speechless."

Ethan pulls me onto his lap and kisses away my tears. "You're very welcome," he says as he grabs the necklace and fastens it around my neck. He smiles at me, and I place a hand on my favorite spot – his beautiful face. "My grandmother would have loved seeing it on you. She passed away about a month after I left home."

"Ethan," I curl up in his lap letting my face settle in the crook of his neck, "I'm so sorry, but at least she's with your grandfather again. I would've loved to have met her."

Ethan pulls my face to his and looks down at the necklace. "She would've loved you," he whispers before kissing the pendant, resting close against my heart. "Almost as much as I do."

I smile at him, and place a hand on my fabulous new necklace. "So, how does it look?"

Ethan's wicked grin returns, to my delight.

"Hmm...all of these clothes you're wearing are a distraction – really taking away from the necklace."

I look down at myself in only a bra and undies and then smile back up at him.

He lays me down gently on the lounge and starts trailing kisses from my forehead, down to my neck where he lingers a while, knowing it's my favorite spot. Little does he know anywhere he kisses me is my favorite spot.

"Think the water's cold yet?" I ask, trying to catch my breath.

"Let's go find out," he says smiling, as he takes my hands in his and lifts me from the lounge.

I'm glad I have Ethan to hold on to, because my legs are like Jell-O, thanks to exhaustion and Ethan's relentless attack on my body a moment ago with his mouth.

"So, it looks like in all the excitement, you missed a present," he says, when we reach the tub.

"Are you kidding?" I smirk up at him. "I've been dying to open this gift for hours."

My eyes excitedly roam up and down his near naked body. I lean in to kiss his chest, as I place my hands on his hips and remove his underwear, unwrapping the last of my gift.

Ethan quickly returns the favor, by removing my bra and undies, and gives me a soft kiss on the lips.

"Ladies first," he says, and I place a foot in the tub. I'm delighted to see it's still very warm.

"Scoot forward," he says, and I comply as he steps in behind me. He sits down and pulls me between his legs, then wraps his arms around my waist. I lean into him, feeling safe in his arms, as we sit in comfortable silence, letting the water warm us.

"This room is fabulous," I tell him, eventually, as I run my fingers up and down his arms. "Let's stay in here forever."

Ethan laughs. "Sounds like a plan," he says, as he bends down and kisses my neck.

"Why have you never shown me this before?"

Ethan laughs again. "We typically stay locked in the bedroom when you visit, which I'm not complaining about, by the way."

I laugh too. "True. Very true."

Ethan pushes my hair to the side and starts kissing my neck again, then my shoulder. I moan softly, as he continues his kisses, his hands starting to explore parts of me below the water. *Mmmm.*

I lean back into him, and wrap an arm around his neck, wanting his lips on mine.

"I will never forget this birthday," I say to him, as I reach down and touch my necklace.

"You're welcome," he whispers. "I love you, Samantha."

"I love you too."

"What do you say we take this to the bedroom?" he says, with his eyes now trained on my mouth.

"I like the sound of that," I murmur onto his lips, never able to resist them so close to mine.

Ethan stands up first and then pulls me up beside him. He holds my hand, as I get out of the tub, and he follows.

"Over here," Ethan says, as I'm looking around for a towel.

He grabs my arm and moves me over to what looks like an upright tanning bed hanging on the wall. He flips a switch, and all of a sudden, I feel heat and warm air blowing me dry.

I smile up at him. "You celebrities and your modern conveniences."

"Maybe so, but you have to admit this is pretty cool."

"Seriously cool," I admit. "It may be a toss-up between you and the full-body blow-dryer."

Ethan smiles down at me. "I'll take that challenge," he says, as he starts moving his hands purposefully over my body. His touch, mixed with the warm heat and air from the dryer is a remarkable sensation.

Before I know it, he sweeps me up in his arms and carries me to his bedroom. He lays me gently down on the bed and slides in beside me. We both turn on our sides to face each other.

"You know," I say to him seductively, as I move my fingertips down his chest, over his stomach, "there's something I've always wanted to do," I whisper on to his lips, and Ethan shivers once again, as my fingers continue their path.

"Oh really?" he's breathless, his eyes full of anticipation. "Well, birthday girl, what exactly would that be?" And the wicked grin returns.

I sit up and then lean down so my lips are just inches from his. "Oh, nothing too crazy," I whisper again. "Just this."

I start tickling him mercilessly all over his body. I tickle his ribs, behind his knees, under his arms, and anywhere else I can find, as Ethan laughs and writhes beneath me, trying futilely to swat my hands away.

When he finally has enough, he sits up and pins me underneath him with his hands clasped in mine above my head. I'm laughing so hard at this point, my sides hurt.

"I wish you could have seen your face," I tell him through my giggles. "So adorable."

"You got me that time," Ethan says, smiling, trying to catch his breath. "It won't happen again."

"Oh, you loved it. Admit it."

Ethan leans down to kiss me. "I love *you*."

"And I love you," I say, as he lets go of my hands, but stays hovered above me. I reach my arms up and wrap them around his neck. "I have one final request for my birthday," I whisper.

"Anything for you."

I look into his eyes, dark and thrilling, as his hands start to caress my body again.

"You," I whimper, and close my eyes, as he trails a finger slowly up my inner thigh. "I just want you."

I open my eyes again to find Ethan smiling widely. "I think we can manage that," he says with confidence, as his fingers continue their pleasing journey, higher and higher, closer and closer, until...

"Yes," I hiss through my teeth. *Happy Birthday to me.*

戇機

The next morning, I wake up freezing. I roll over, wanting Ethan to keep me warm, but I quickly realize he isn't next to me.

There's a note lying on his pillow, with a single red rose on top. I'm really starting to love roses.

I untie it and hold the rose to my cheek, remembering last night. I read the note with a smile:

Good morning, my love.

Leaving you this morning, so beautiful and tempting in my bed, wasn't easy, but duty calls. These past few days have been some of the best in my life, and even though it was technically your birthday, I feel rather spoiled as well. Thank you for that.

I love you and will be thinking of nothing but you to get me through the day.

Call you later.

All my love,

Ethan

I sigh. I hate that I missed him, but I'm thankful I was able to spend one more night in his arms. I smile, as parts of last night start to trickle back in my head, and eventually, I fall back asleep holding my necklace in my hand, smiling and dreaming of Ethan.

CHAPTER 23

"I don't think I've ever hated Monday this much in my life," I tell Rose as we walk in to the coffee shop for my morning break.

"You're just coming off a romantic get-away weekend with your dreamy boyfriend," Rose says, as she rolls her eyes lovingly at me. "Of course this Monday sucks."

I smile at her and order my coffee. "So, are you going to tell me about it?" Rose asks after she places her own order. "When did you get in last night?"

"Well, actually..." I pause, not really wanting to rehash this, but knowing it will feel better to get it off my chest, "I got home Saturday."

Rose looks at me sharply. "What do you mean?" she asks in a panic. "Did something happen? Are you okay? Is Jake okay?"

"Everyone's fine," I say, waving off her concerns. "It was Ethan. He had something come up and we had to cut the weekend short."

Rose smiles. "Well, I hope you at least got some fabulous gift and a birthday cake."

"We had my cake for lunch on Saturday before we left," I tell her, and I'm a little bothered by how this doesn't seem to upset Rose as much as it upsets me.

"And I got this." I pull my new necklace up for her to see.

"Oooo! Very nice!" she says excitedly.

I stare at my friend, waiting for her to feel the same way I do, but she just looks confused by my stare.

"You're really upset about this," Rose says, finally figuring it out. "You're upset about Ethan having to work and having to cut your weekend short?"

"Of course I am," I say, trying not to whine like a child. "I was looking so forward to the trip. I never expected it to be over so soon."

I had all day yesterday to pine over this. Once Ethan left, my happy mood from the weekend wore off quickly.

"Well, of course you didn't," she says. "Why would you? If you were dating a normal guy, that wouldn't have happened. But Ethan Grant is far from *normal*."

We pick up our coffees and sit down at one of the tables near the window. I hate that Rose is right, but what I hate more is how okay she seems to be with it. Why can't I be okay with all of this?

"I'm too selfish," I admit, now feeling awful, like my pity parade isn't warranted. "I'm just spoiled I guess. I'm not a good sharer."

Rose laughs at me. "You love him," she says. "You hardly get to spend any time with him, so it's no surprise that you're a little put out by what happened." Rose takes a sip of her coffee. "Does Ethan know you're upset?"

"Maybe a little, but I tried to hide it."

"That's good then."

"I'm worried I may not be cut out for this, Rose."

"What do you mean?"

"I don't know if I'm the type of person that can deal with all of this Hollywood stuff," I tell her. "I'm a small town girl, who works in the county courthouse, and the extent of my weekend excitement is typically Chuck E. Cheese with Jake." I laugh. "And what about the paparazzi? I'm not meant for the spotlight, Rose."

"You used to be," Rose whispers, under her breath, as she sips her coffee.

"What did you say?" I ask, not believing my ears.

Rose rolls her eyes again. She puts her coffee down and stares hard at me. "Do you love him?"

"What?"

"Do you love him?" she asks again.

"With everything I am," I admit. "But does that really matter?"

"That is *everything*," Rose tells me, her eyes fierce. "If you love him, you have to fight for it, Sam. It may not be easy, but nothing that's worth it ever is." Rose grabs my hand. "Don't give up on this, Sam."

"I'm going to try," I tell her.

"Good," she says smiling as she pats my hand. "Now let's get to the good stuff. Tell me all about your weekend!"

❧

Here I am again, sitting in my bedroom, preparing for a long-awaited date with Ethan, and I barely remember how I got here.

I can't believe it's already springtime. I hardly remember the in between. So much, since I've been with Ethan, has gone by in a haze. I guess this must be what it's like to be in love. I just hate that everything seems to go by so fast. So much has happened since our trip to Vermont.

I love that Rose is living across the hall from me now. It turns out there *was* another girl for Danny. It happened to be an old high school flame. I'm not sure that Rose ever had a chance.

She's actually learning to be okay with it, and she loves her new job – waiting tables at a restaurant in Bristol. It's quite a drive for her back and forth, but believe it or not, it's better pay, and according to Rose, a better opportunity.

I'm thankful that Sydney and Liz still work with me at the courthouse. Liz and Bill got engaged, which made me feel a little better about mine and Ethan's rush to the "I love yous". They're planning a fall wedding here in Delia.

And I'm happy that Sydney and Scott are still going strong as well, which is a record for Sydney. The longest relationship she had before Scott lasted about six weeks. At six months, they may as well be an old, married couple.

As for Ethan and I, I'm more in love with him than ever. But unfortunately, it hasn't gotten any easier like I hoped it would. His schedule is still crazy and unpredictable, but I'm trying to deal with it, like I promised Rose I would when we spoke after my birthday.

The moments Ethan and I do get to spend together are so amazing that they almost make the bad stuff seem small and insignificant. Almost.

I think I have finally succumbed to the fact that flashes will be going off in my face every once in a while. I will never be fully okay with it, and it can still be scary, like when they came to Jake's school a second time. I shudder at the thought.

These guys were smart enough to stay off the school grounds, but they waited for him outside, thinking Ethan was picking him up from school that day. They never touched him, but they surrounded him in the street and the principal had to come out to break it up and bring him back onto the school property. It shook Jake up pretty bad this time, since he had to face it alone, and I felt horribly guilty for not being there.

"It's okay mom," Jake assured me after it happened. "I didn't get hurt or anything."

I knew he was putting on a strong face for me, which made me feel even worse.

Another fun thing I now have to deal with is the good *and* bad commentary that Ethan's fans and reporters have started up. There's new stuff every week, and the bad stuff can be especially painful. It's hard to think that there are people out there that want nothing more than to see us apart. I just can't understand it. Relationships are hard enough without all of these outside obstacles.

I've read things like "How could Ethan date her? She's so plain!" or "He deserves so much better than that hick!" or "Seriously Ethan? Are we scraping the bottom of the barrel now?"

Ethan always tells me not to worry about what other people say, so I try to push it aside, but it's not easy. My already fragile ego is taking a beating.

It's April now, and Ethan just finished filming the final episode of season two for *Stephen's Room*. He doesn't start filming again for season three until August, which would normally mean he has some time off. However, Ethan has found a new appreciation for his work over the past few months. He says he has me to thank for this.

"Now that I've seen I can have a personal life and acting, I think I can learn to love it again," he told me recently.

Of course I'm happy for him, and I'm happy that I've somewhat successfully managed to hide my questionable feelings about the spotlight from him. He asks me about it every once in a while when a particularly troubling headline comes out or when we have a paparazzi incident. And it's unfortunately sparked a couple of feuds between us when I let my stubborn insecurities get the best of me.

I usually just tell him everything is fine, but he knows me well enough now to know when I'm not being truthful. I know he hates it and it worries him too, but there's nothing he can do about it. That's the problem. There's nothing anyone can do about it.

Despite all of this, Ethan really is a different person now, and the media has noticed as well. Most of the good stuff written about me is on how I've brought out the best in Ethan.

Of course this is nice to hear, but I can't take all of the credit. I think Ethan was ready for a change, and I served as a catalyst.

He still doesn't seem to be truly comfortable with the spotlight any more than I am, but I think he's getting better. I wish I could say the same.

I'm planning to see him tonight, and I can hardly wait. It's been nearly three weeks this time, and the time away has been hard.

Ethan's been extremely busy, either filming or touring to do promo work for the end of the season. He's also getting ready to work on a new film he was cast for a few of months ago, so he's traveling back and forth to New York City a lot working out the details.

He's also been really edgy for the last few weeks, which makes the distance even harder. His mood swings come and go, and he keeps assuring me it's job stress. I only wish there was something I could do to help.

I'm driving to meet him at his place tonight, and we're supposed to go to dinner and then catch a show at the Fox. As I start putting on my dress, my phone rings, breaking me from my reverie.

"Hi beautiful," Ethan says when I answer, and I can already tell something's wrong.

"Hi." I still smile, as usual, at the sound of his voice.

"What are you doing?" he asks.

"Slipping on my dress. What are you doing?"

Ethan lets out a long sigh. "I have some bad news," he says, his voice full of regret. "I have to cancel."

My face falls, and I feel the now familiar sinking heart feeling I get when this happens. I hate that I'm getting so used to disappointment. This is the second time in a row he's cancelled.

"Why?" I ask, trying not to sound too whiney.

"I promise I'll make it up to you," he says, in his most persuasive voice. "I have to make an unexpected trip to New York tonight to be there for a meeting in the morning. Mick just called me."

Mick is Ethan's manager, and he doesn't like me. The feeling is mutual. I think he's a scumbag, and he hates the fact that Ethan is dating a "commoner". Ethan is loyal though, and Mick has been with him from the beginning. It isn't worth it to get upset with Mick around Ethan, and Ethan doesn't seem too influenced by Mick's opinion of me, so I let it go.

"I'm sorry to hear that," I say, plopping myself down on my bed, my dress still unzipped in the back. "I was really looking forward to seeing you."

"I completely understand," Ethan says, sounding pretty upset himself. "I was looking forward to this too."

"When will you be back?"

"I'll be back in a couple of days. I have a charity thing to go to in San Francisco on Monday, but I'll be back here on Tuesday. I promise you we'll see each other then, okay?"

"Okay." It's so hard not to take the rejection personally some times.

"Please don't be upset," Ethan pleads. "I love you," he adds, and I wish that helped make it easier.

"I'll be okay." I try to sound reassuring, like always. "Have a safe trip, and call when you can, okay?"

"Every day," he promises. "I love you, Samantha."

"I love you too."

When we hang up, I slide my little black dress off and put it back on its hanger. I then trade my lacey undies set for cotton, my stockings for sweat pants, I add a t-shirt and then go and knock on my neighbor's door.

"Aren't you going to be late?" Rose says, looking confused about my outfit as she answers the door.

"He cancelled," I say, pushing past her to go throw myself on her couch.

"Again?" she asks, as she shuts her door. "How about a movie then?" she says, coming to sit beside me.

"And Ben and Jerry's?" I ask hopefully.

"I have two pints with our names on it in the freezer." She puts her arm around me.

"Sounds perfect," I say with zero excitement.

"What was it this time?"

"Some meeting in New York City and then he has a charity ball in San Francisco on Monday."

Rose is quiet, and I feel bad for complaining to her again, but I don't have anyone else to talk to about this. I do my best to hide the majority of my disappointment from Ethan, which means Rose unfortunately gets the brunt of it.

"I just keep thinking it will get easier," I tell her. "I love him so much, but sometimes I can't help but wonder if it's worth it. All of the terrible stuff I have to read, the reporters stalking Jake and me all the time, just waiting for one of us to mess up. Plus, I know this is stressful for Ethan. He has so much to worry about already. I hate adding Jake and I to the mix."

"I wouldn't worry about Ethan," Rose says confidently. "I don't think he minds the extra worry, as long as he gets to have you and Jake in his life."

"I guess," I tell her, but I'm not so sure any more.

Ethan has never made me think otherwise, but I know it had to be easier for him before we came along. Maybe he was a little lonelier, but it was probably easier.

"I just wish I was more confident about all of this," I confess. "The internet doesn't make it any easier. I need thicker skin."

Rose releases me and pulls me up to meet her eyes. I'm surprised to see she's angry.

"Look, pardon my French, but I think it's time you shit or get off the pot."

"Ouch," I say, wondering what in the world I did to deserve the animosity.

Rose looks like she regrets her crass statement, but only a little. "I'm sorry," she says. "I ultimately want you to be happy, Sam, but you need to start facing the facts that this is the way things are going to be with Ethan."

"I know." I hang my head. She has a point.

"Do you?" I'm surprised to see she still looks a little frustrated with me. "You keep talking to me about how much you love him and how important he is to you. I know the celebrity stuff is a lot, but you either need to accept that part of it or move on. Things aren't going to change."

"Are you upset with me?" I'm on the brink of tears now. I didn't expect this, not from Rose.

Rose sighs. "I'm not upset, but sometimes I just wonder what the hell has happened to you?"

"What do you mean?" Her mood is completely throwing me off.

"Who is this person?" she asks, pointing at my chest. "You used to be so full of life! You used to have more confidence than anyone I've ever known. Every girl in town wanted to be you. What happened to *that* girl?"

I sink back into the couch. "She's gone," I say quietly, and suddenly, this conversation is no longer just about Ethan and me.

"No she's not!" Rose says, pointing her finger into my chest again. "She's still in there, Sam. You've just suppressed her so you don't have to feel the pain, but pain is not always a bad thing. Trust me." A tear comes to her eye. "You need to go through the pain. Holding it in is making you weak. Let it out, Sam. Let. It. Out."

I'm crying in earnest now because Rose is right, as usual. My indecisiveness with Ethan, my constant pity-parties and all of those years feeling sorry for myself knowing I could do something if I wanted to, but never having the guts. How could I be so selfish? I've used my situation as an excuse to be miserable, and it's changed me. Jake brings out the best in me, but without him, I'm just a shell of the person I once was. I've relied on everyone but myself to get by for nearly a decade. I think it's about time I change that.

"I didn't mean to upset you," Rose says, hugging me to her. "I just hate seeing you like this."

I don't say anything. I just cry into her shoulder, trying to remember who I used to be, and trying to figure out a way to get her back.

࿐

My phone startles me awake around six thirty. Jake comes to mind initially, but then I remember that I went to pick him up from my mom's last night after Rose and I ate a pint each and then, feeling totally sick, decided to skip the movie.

I rub my eyes and think maybe it's Ethan. He didn't call me last night as promised, and I didn't call him. I know he was probably busy. I know there had to be a good excuse. He would never just forget to call.

It only rings a couple of times before hanging up. I look at my phone to see the missed call. My heart flutters anticipating a call from Ethan, but stops dead when I see it's Luke's mother. What could she possibly want?

I get out of bed to go check on Jake. He's still asleep, so I close his door and go back to my room to return my phone call.

"Samantha?" Luke's mother answers and I can tell she's been crying.

"What's wrong Helen?" but somehow I already know the answer.

"It's Luke," she sobs. "He's gone."

I sit back in my bed, tears instantly rolling down my face. I have no idea what to say.

"Are you there?" Helen asks, when I don't respond immediately.

"I'm here," I sniffle. "How?" I manage to get out.

"His truck ran over some kind of bomb while he was on patrol. It was in the middle of a city street!" she exclaims. "Can you believe it?"

"No," I say quietly. "I can't believe it."

"We knew something was wrong. We hadn't heard from him in a few weeks, and I called and called, but I couldn't get any answers. They just got back to us last night."

"I'm so sorry Helen."

My feelings for Luke may have changed over the years, but he's Jake's father and so many firsts for me. I can't believe he's gone.

"Me too, dear." Helen's sobbing. "Me too."

Helen proceeds to tell me that she'll call me later with funeral details and asks that I let a few other people know. I decide I'll wait until a little later to call my short list. It's too early to bother anyone else this morning.

I walk slowly into the kitchen to make a cup of coffee. There's no way I'm going back to sleep after that news.

I sit at my kitchen table with my coffee and quietly cry my eyes out. What am I going to tell Jake?

I want to talk to Ethan now so badly, but he still hasn't called, and I don't feel right calling him for some reason. I finally decide I don't care and pick up my phone to dial him. It's still early, but maybe he'll answer.

"Hello?" I'm startled by the voice that answers. It sounds freshly awake, and even more troubling, it's female.

I look at my phone to make sure I dialed correctly. "Hello?" I question.

"Who is this?" the female voice asks, thick with sleep.

"Is Ethan there?" I ask, closing my eyes, waiting for the response.

"He's...unavailable right now," the voice teases. "Could I take a message?"

"No message. Thanks," I say quickly before hanging up.

This isn't happening. There is no way in hell this is happening.

I toss my phone toward the living room and shove myself away from the table. I start pacing in my kitchen, tears pouring again down my cheeks.

Jake walks into the kitchen a few minutes later. I'm still pacing. "What's going on mom?"

His sentence triggers something inside me. That's who I need – my mom. "Get dressed buddy. We're going to see grandma."

"But what's the matter?" he asks, obviously confused about my tear-stained face.

"I'm all right," I lie. "We'll talk about it later, okay?"

Jake doesn't look too satisfied with this plan, but he follows orders any way and goes back to his room to get dressed.

I go into my own room and change. I'm ready before Jake, so I pace some more in the kitchen waiting for him.

Once Jake is ready, I quickly usher him out the door and I find myself speeding to my mom's house. Jake keeps asking me what's wrong, and I keep avoiding the question. I still have no idea how to tell him about his dad.

I called my mom before we left. She heard the sorrow in my voice, but I told her I would explain when we got there.

"Jake, I need to talk to grandma a minute," I tell him as we arrive, and walk to meet my mom on the porch. "Go inside, and I'll be right there."

Once again, Jake follows orders, but he doesn't look too excited about it.

"What in the Sam Hill is going on?" my mom asks, as soon as Jake is safely inside.

"Luke's dead," I say quietly, afraid Jake will hear. I sit down on the porch swing, with my head in my hands.

"Oh, dear Lord." My mom comes and sits beside me. "How'd it happen?"

"His mom called this morning," I get out between sobs. "She said he ran over a bomb while on patrol."

My mom covers her mouth in shock. "I assume you haven't told Jake?"

I shake my head. "I don't know how."

"Well," my mom thinks for a moment, "he may have not be close to him, but he was his father nonetheless. I'm sure he'll take it badly."

I start sobbing again. "It's too much," I wail. "It's too much for an eight year old to go through."

"It's life, hun." My mom puts her arms around me. "It's life."

I cry into her chest for a couple of minutes, feeling awful because I'm not sure what I'm more upset about: losing the father of my child, or possibly losing the love of my life.

CHAPTER 24

Jake took the news about his dad surprisingly well, but he was still upset of course, just like everyone else. The town lost a hero, as far as Delia is concerned. Luke was always a hero, even in high school – captain of the football team, community volunteer, great student – and now he's died for his country. He's practically royalty.

The funeral was this morning, and Jake cried his tiny tears, but he's doing better than expected. Luke wanted to be cremated, and I'm secretly thankful for that. Now he's preserved in my memory the way he should be – eighteen and ready to take on the world.

It was a beautiful day today, and I think the entire town was at his funeral. Everyone has been asking how I'm holding up, assuming I still have feelings for Luke. I just keep answering "fine" and give smiles accordingly, not wanting to upset the herd.

The truth is, I'm dead inside, and it has very little to do with the death of my son's father. I haven't spoken to Ethan now in two weeks.

He eventually called me later that dreaded Sunday morning while I was at my mom's, and even thinking about it now makes me shiver.

He explained that someone had stolen his phone from a restaurant that Saturday night, and he didn't call that night because it was too late when he got to his room. He was ashamed to say he didn't have my number memorized. He had Mick find my number, and Mick passed it on only minutes before Ethan called.

Ethan apologized a million times, and I believed him. The thing is it just wasn't enough. Rose was right. As long as Ethan is a celebrity, his life will be an open book. That's just the way it is.

I still love Ethan, very much, and probably always will. But his lifestyle is just too much for me, and I was worried that it would eventually be too much for Jake as well.

"I can't do this anymore, Ethan," I tried to explain to him for the hundredth time on the phone that Sunday, tears streaming down my face. "I'm not happy."

"Why are you not happy? What have I done?"

I close my eyes now, remembering the panic in Ethan's voice.

"You haven't done anything. Don't you understand?" I told him. "I'm not suited for your life Ethan, and I think we've both known that all along. Jake and I are simple people. We lead normal, boring lives, and we like it that way." I could barely speak through my sobs, and I could tell Ethan was losing it on the other end. "I can't take any more cameras in my face, or in Jake's. I can't handle any more broken promises or false hopes. I can't handle it."

"You still love me?" he asked in a small voice.

"Yes," I reluctantly admitted. "Always."

"Then that's all that matters!" he said, at the height of his desperation. "*Please.* Please Samantha, don't do this. You promised," he said, reminding me of our trip to Vermont, which was nearly my undoing. "You promised this wouldn't keep us apart. Please."

I remember suddenly feeling the truth in the phrase, "dying from a broken heart". I felt mine split in two in that moment, and it has continued to break and shatter, slowly, piece by piece, since I last spoke to him.

"I have to Ethan. It's the only way," I told him, and I hung up the phone.

I had no idea that Ethan wasn't going to give up that easily. He called me what had to be a million more times, but I never answered. I just curled up on my mom's bed and cried my eyes out.

Shortly after I hung up with Ethan, my mom came into her bedroom, only to find me in a fetal position, barely coherent.

"It's okay, hun. It'll be okay." She sat next to me, and rubbed my arm. "You just need some time."

I could barely hear her. All I knew was, from that day forward, my life would once again be changed forever.

"Mom?" Jake came walking in, probably hearing my sobs, his eyes wet from his own tears after hearing about his father. "Mom, are you okay?"

"She's okay." My mom thankfully answered for me, since I was unable to speak. "She's just had a rough day."

Jake climbed on the bed behind me then and wrapped his little arms around my waist. "You said all you needed was me to be happy, mommy," he whispered in my ear. "You said I was all you needed to be the happiest person in the world, right? I'm here mommy. I'm here." He was crying, and I turned and took my precious angel in my arms.

"You are everything, baby," I told him. "Mommy is just sad, but I'm feeling much better now that you're here."

"Really?" I watched Jake's face brighten.

"Absolutely," I said, brushing his hair from his face, wishing I was telling him the truth.

So, now here I sit, at Helen's house, remembering that horrible day, remembering how I thought I would never lose that empty feeling I had after my conversation with Ethan, and unfortunately I was right. It's only gotten worse.

Ethan skipped his charity function, and came to see me that Sunday night. It was really late, and I was already in bed, but obviously, sleeping was near impossible.

He texted me to let me know he was there, but I couldn't bring myself to come to the door. I couldn't see him again, because I knew if I did, I would never let him go. I'd surrender everything, if given the opportunity to stare into his green eyes again, and I had to stay strong. I felt I'd made the right choice, no matter how badly it hurt.

Ethan stayed in my parking lot until almost dawn, texting and calling me the entire time, begging me to let him in. I remember lying on my bed, reading his texts and shaking horribly from all of the crying.

I snuck a look out my window once, and I could see him sitting on the curb. His head was down and his hands were pulling anxiously at his hair.

As if he could feel me watching him, he looked up and I hurriedly ducked down so he couldn't see me. But I caught a glimpse of his face. It's still haunting me.

I'm not sure what made him finally leave, or when he actually did.

Surprisingly, I eventually dozed off for a few minutes before the sun came up but woke suddenly in a panic. I ran to my window, but he was gone – like a dream that never really happened.

My resolve is weakening every moment I'm away from him. I know it won't be long before I give in and call him, but I also know it will be too late. I haven't heard a word from him since he left my parking lot early that Monday morning, and I have a feeling I will never hear from him again.

"How are you?" Rose's voice breaks me from my never-ending nightmare, as she comes and sits next to me on the porch steps at Helen's house.

"I'm okay." I'm starting to get pretty good at this lying stuff.

"Liar."

Okay, maybe not around Rose, but thankfully she decides to move on. "How's Jake holding up?"

"He's actually doing pretty well. I know this is hard for him, but since he has never really known his dad, it's not as hard as it would be for most."

Rose nods her head in understanding. "Want to come over tonight?" she asks. "Sydney and Liz are coming over, and I'm stocking up on Cherry Garcia."

I smile at my friend. "Not tonight. I think I'll spend it with Jake."

"Are you sure?"

"Are you mad with me?"

"Maybe a little," she admits, with a sigh, "but I'll recover. I just don't like seeing you like this."

"I don't like being like this," I agree. "But I'll get better eventually." I look down at my feet. "I did the right thing didn't I, Rose?"

I've asked this question to everyone I know multiple times over the past two weeks, and even though everyone agrees I was right, it still doesn't help ease my mind in the slightest.

"You did what you felt you had to do," Rose tells me, and I shake my head at her.

"That's not a real answer, Rose."

Rose exhales in a huff. "What do you want me to say, Sam? That I think you're crazy for leaving him? That I think you ran scared for the millionth time in your adult life when things got too hard? Do you want to hear that?"

Rose rarely gets upset with me, and since I've already been crying for most of the day, the tears spring easily. Rose puts her arms around me.

"I'm sorry," she whispers.

"Don't be. You're right."

It's what I need to hear, as hard as it is. It only confirms what I already know.

"You're my best friend, Sam. I'm tired of seeing you like this. You're miserable, and for no good reason. Everything you want is within your reach. You're just too scared to put a hand out."

I cry into her shoulder. "I thought leaving him was the right thing to do. I thought I would be helping him *and* me in the long run," I say through my sobs. "I wanted to find independent, headstrong Sam again, but I need him too much. I need everyone too much."

"That's not true," Rose says. "*Wanting* and *needing* are two very different things."

"I gave in to my doubts with him, Rose. I quit the one thing other than Jake that ever mattered to me."

"It's going to be okay," Rose says, pulling away so she can look in my face. "You still have me, Liz, Sydney, your family. Everything is going to be fine, and if things with you and Ethan are meant to be, they will be."

"I miss him," I add quietly, "so much."

"I know." Rose pushes a piece of stray hair behind my ear. "I know girl, but maybe things will come back around."

"Doubt it," I huff.

Rose smiles at me. "You never know," she says. "You just never know."

As always, this makes me smile. "How about I have everyone at my house tonight?"

I wipe the tears away with my ratty tissue I've been carrying around all day. It's amazing I even have any tears left.

"Really?" Rose is surprised as she checks my face for the truth.

"Really," I say smiling. "It's time I found the old Sam again, and it starts with ice cream."

"Sounds perfect." Rose puts her arms around me. "I'll see you later then," she says, as she gets up and walks back inside. "And I'll let the girls know. Sevenish?"

"Sounds good."

I know it will take a long time for me to get back to where I want to be, but Rose is right. You never know. There is always hope.

⁂

The girls show up right on time, everyone wearing sweats, and everyone toting a pint of their favorite...ice cream that is.

I let Jake invite Sean over, who brought his Xbox, so they'll be busy in Jake's room for the evening.

"I'll order us some pizza for dinner," I tell him as the girls show up.

"Awesome!" he says, before running back to his room with Sean. I wish it took that little to make me happy these days.

"So what's on TV tonight?" Liz asks me, looking elegant in her black velour sweat suit.

"I was thinking we would do *Gone with the Wind*. What do you think?"

"Perfect!" Sydney says, dropping her ice cream on the coffee table and plopping down on the couch. "I get to be Scarlett!"

"You're always Scarlett!" Rose whines. "I want Scarlett this time."

"Fine," Sydney huffs. "I'm Melanie then. Don't even think about it, Liz."

"You know I'm always Rhett," Liz smirks.

"Sam?" Rose asks. "Who will you be reciting this evening?"

My friends and I have seen this movie so many times that we know it by heart. So, any time we watch it, we choose a character and do our best voice-overs throughout the movie. It's a blast, even better sometimes when drinking is involved, but we'll be keeping it to ice cream this evening with Jake at home.

"I'll take Ashley," I say. "Ooo, and Belle," I add. "I'm feeling a little Belle tonight." The girls laugh.

"Rose, you'll be doing Mammy too I hope?" Sydney asks. Rose does a spot on impression and it's awesome.

"You know I will, Ms. Melanie," she says in her best Mammy voice.

"Awesome! Let's go!" Sydney says, rubbing her hands together. "Sam? Spoons?"

I get up to get the spoons, as Liz flips through the channels before we put in the movie.

"Turn it to the *E!* Channel," I hear Sydney request, as I continue my mission for spoons. "I need to catch up."

"Contrary to popular belief, that is not a legitimate source for world news," Liz remarks.

"Shut up Liz, and turn the channel please?" Sydney's huffs and I giggle to myself as I picture Sydney wearing her very non-threatening bitch face.

I hear his name, but I don't turn around to look at the television. I've been diligently avoiding all things "Ethan" for the past two weeks.

However, I start to feel a little nervous when the girls suddenly go silent. Is something wrong?

"Umm....Sam? You're gonna want to see this," I hear Sydney say, and her voice makes me so anxious I run into the living room, waiting to see some headline about him being killed in a plane crash or something. My heart is beating through my chest.

But when my eyes finally find the television, there he is, sitting in a chair at a press conference of some kind, as beautiful as ever and thankfully alive. I put my hand to my chest.

"Why did you call me in here?" I ask Sydney, not even trying to hide the irritation in my voice.

"Look at the bottom of the screen," Rose directs me.

I look, and then I feel faint. "Ethan Grant to Retire" is in huge white letters at the bottom of the screen.

Suddenly, the room starts to spin. I feel cold and the forgotten feeling of being trapped in a glass jar comes rushing back to me. I no longer *think* I'm going to faint. I do.

All I can see is black, but I keep hearing Rose's voice. "Don't leave us!" she keeps shouting at me. "Please stay with me, Sam!"

I feel very anxious as I start to slowly open my eyes. I want to know what the hell is wrong with Rose, but it's Liz standing over me, waving me with a magazine from my coffee table. She's smiling.

"How long was I out?" I ask groggily.

"Not too long, but it's over," she says, nodding toward the television.

It takes me a couple of seconds, but everything finally starts coming back. "Rose, why were you telling me not to leave you? I just fainted, right?"

"Did you hit your head?" Rose asks, as she comes to my side and starts examining my head.

"You weren't yelling at me?" I ask her, feeling very confused.

"Nope," she smiles, apparently happy with her examination results. "Wasn't me."

I shake it off and rub my head myself. I don't feel any bumps either, at least not yet. I look at Rose then, the rest coming back to me now. "He really quit?"

Rose is smiling at me. "Seems that way."

"Here it comes again!" Sydney yells still in front of the television. She grabs the remote and quickly pauses the screen.

Rose and Liz help me carefully to my feet and sit me on the edge of the couch next to Sydney.

"Ready?" Sydney asks excitedly, looking at me.

I slowly nod my head, still very foggy from my fainting spell.

"You heard it first ladies and gentleman, right here on the *E!* Channel," some tacky blonde is saying. "Ethan Grant has dropped his acting career like a bad habit. We have our suspicions why, though Ethan, in his typical closed-lipped style, didn't give us any details today."

Then they show a part of the press conference with Ethan. My chest instantly starts to ache from just seeing him on the screen.

"What about your movie this summer?" one reporter asks.

"I've negotiated my way out," Ethan answers, moving on to the next question.

"Tell us about *Stephen's Room* again? What exactly will happen to the show now that you're leaving?"

"As I explained before," Ethan starts, with his calm "for work" face that I've come to know and appreciate, "they will begin casting soon for a replacement, and I am confident the show will go on without a hitch. The writing is excellent, and it's only been through two seasons. It's sure to continue its' well deserved success."

I'm shocked. I have no idea what he's thinking. It feels like I barely know him anymore, even though it's only been a couple of weeks.

"Some would say you're the reason for that success, Ethan," another reporter comments, which is followed up with lots of nods and mumbled agreements from the other reporters.

"That's a matter of opinion," Ethan says smiling, "and not a very good one."

The audience laughs before another reporter rises to speak. "Most people would speculate you're abandoning your career for a certain someone, Ethan. Care to elaborate on that?"

Ethan smirks. "It seems my personal life is no longer your business."

The audience laughs again, and then the same reporter asks another question.

"Will we see you in Hollywood again someday, Ethan? Will you make a return to acting?"

Ethan looks down and laughs to himself. When he looks back up, a smile slowly stretches across his face.

"You never know," he says. "You just never know."

"And there you have it ladies and gents!" The annoying blonde is back. "Ethan Grant is out of our lives for good, or is he?"

Sydney clicks the television off, and turns toward me. "What say you?"

I feel faint again. "What are you talking about?" I rub my temples. This seems like good news, but I just can't make heads or tails of it.

"Sam, he is obviously doing this for you. You heard what he said at the end." Liz is giving me her best lawyer eyes. She uses them to persuade the jury to believe anything she says.

"I'm kind of confused," I say, putting my hands over my eyes. "How could he leave acting? He loves it?"

Doesn't he? He told me once he was losing the passion for it, but that was a long time ago. He had found his way again, happy once he found out he could have me *and* his career.

For a second I start to believe. He no longer has me, so is he really giving up his career – a career he's worked so hard for – to be with me? It's not possible. It can't be. It's over between us. I unfortunately made sure of that.

"What are you thinking?" Rose asks me.

I run my fingers through my hair and notice my hands are shaking. "I have no idea what's happening," I say dazed, as I try to get a hold of myself. "But we know nothing for sure. He could be doing this for a million reasons."

"She has a point," Sydney says, nodding her head in agreement.

Liz directs her attention to me. "Look, I would be willing to bet a lot of money that this is about you, and you need to realize it. I have a strange suspicion your phone may be ringing any minute, and you need--" but Liz is interrupted by the doorbell.

We all look at each other in a panic. The truth is we were all so involved in Liz's speech that the doorbell scared us to death.

"Who's at the door?" Jake asks, as he and Sean come into the room. "Pizza here already?"

"I have no idea. I haven't even ordered the pizza," I say, looking from the door to my friends. They are all in different modes of anticipation, some standing, some sitting, but all rather jumpy.

My legs are still wobbly as I walk to the door. I didn't really expect to see Ethan, so I'm not too disappointed when I'm met with a delivery guy. He's holding the largest bunch of red roses I've ever seen in my life.

"Ms. Harper?" the delivery guy asks. He's kind of scrawny, and the flowers look like they may overpower him at any minute.

"Yes?"

"These are for you," he says, as Liz shows up beside me and takes the flowers from his hands. He looks very relieved. "Sign here, please."

I sign and shut the door. I turn to find Sydney plowing through the enormous bouquet trying to find a card. "Got it!" she says triumphantly, as she lifts the small card in the air and hands it to me.

"Wow!" Jake says, staring at the huge display. "Who are they from, mom?"

"I'm about to find out," I say quietly, holding the card in my hand. My palms are sweaty, my knees are shaking, and I feel like I could definitely faint again at any moment. I open the card slowly – Sydney is about to come out of her skin – and read the words to myself first.

This is the first attempt of many. I'll do whatever it takes. Please come back to me.

Love,

Ethan

I read and reread the words several times before I can even manage to look up again.

"I'm dying over here!" Sydney whines. "Please!"

"It's from Ethan," I say, a tear dripping on to the small card in my hands. "It's from Ethan."

I pass the card on to Sydney, knowing I would never be able to read the words aloud.

I watch her read the card, waiting to see the look on her face. Maybe I misread it. Could this really be happening?

Sydney passes the card on to Rose and Liz before looking back at me. She has her hands over her mouth, and she comes to hug me.

"I knew it!" she says as she hugs me tightly. "You're so worth it," she whispers in my ear.

"Thanks," I manage, and squeeze her back. Then the other two girls come to hug me as well. We are about to have a pathetic crying fest when Jake and Sean interrupt.

"Will someone *please* tell us what's going on?" Jake asks, his hands on his hips.

I laugh and go to pick him up. "It's from Ethan, buddy."

"Wow!" Jake says, eyeing the flowers. "He loves you again?"

"I think so," I tell him, silently wondering if you can die from happiness.

"When can we see him?" Jake asks excitedly, as he hugs me in my arms. "And Lamont, too? When can we see them again?"

"I don't know," I say. "Let's see how it goes. I'll keep you posted."

I put Jake down, and he and Sean start back toward his room, probably eager to get away from the emotional females.

"Are you going to call him?" Rose asks me.

"I think I might."

"Sweet!" Sydney is beside herself. "We'll start the movie. You go call Ethan, and then you can tell us all about it!"

I roll my eyes, but my perma-grin is here to stay. "Fine. I'll be back in a few."

My head still feels a little cloudy, probably from my earlier fainting episode, but now mixed with excitement and pure glee. He loves me. I can't question that fact any longer. My vision starts to blur, as my eyes fill up with tears. He truly loves me.

When I get to my room, I fall onto my bed and hold my phone close to my chest. What am I supposed to say to him? I owe him an apology. That's one thing I know for sure.

I decide to call, without another thought. I'm so eager to hear his voice again; I can barely control my trembling fingers as they search for his number.

I'm startled when Ethan answers after the first ring.

"Hi," he says, his voice understandably tentative.

"Hi," I breathe, as his voice slowly brings back emotions I've been working so hard to repress. Tears are now streaming down my face.

"Samantha, I'm so--" Ethan starts, but I cut him off.

"Ethan, please let me go first," I beg.

"Okay," he agrees, hesitantly.

"Ethan, I just want you to know how very sorry I am," I tell him, but Ethan interrupts me this time.

"Samantha, don't."

"I have to get this out," I say. "It's important."

"No it's not," Ethan interrupts me again. "I don't need or want your apology," he tells me. "You've done nothing wrong."

"Yes, I have," I try to explain. "I gave up on us, Ethan. I gave up, just because things got a little tough. That's not like me, and I hate myself for it."

"Do you still love me, Samantha?" Ethan asks quietly.

"What?" I'm appalled. I can't believe I made him question my love for him.

"Do you still love me?" Ethan repeats, and I smile, solely from hearing him say the word "love" again.

"Of course I do," I happily admit. "I will always love you."

Ethan sighs. "Then that's all that matters," he says, sounding relieved.

"Ethan---" I start, but only to be interrupted once again.

"Samantha, I don't care what happened," he says. "All I care about is that you still love me. As long as I know that, I know there's hope that one day, we can be together again. And I will do anything. I will try every day, whatever it takes to get you back. I just hope you don't get sick of me before I finally get you to cave."

I laugh quietly through my tears. "Not a chance," I assure him. "And I don't think you're going to have to try very hard."

Ethan is quiet, which makes me nervous. "Ethan?" I say his name softly, after he doesn't speak for a while. "Ethan, are you still there?"

"Samantha," he finally speaks up. His voice is hushed and serious. "Samantha, don't play with me," he rather sternly demands. "Are you saying....are you saying that you'll take me back?"

I laugh out loud. I can't help it. As usual, things are completely backwards. I should be the one begging him back, not the other way around.

"Only if you say I can see your gorgeous face in the next five minutes," I tease. "Otherwise, the deal is off."

Ethan laughs this time. "Actually, I'm in your parking lot."

"What?!" I scream, as I jump off my bed and go to my window. I watch him get out of his car and wave to me, a beautiful smile on his face.

I smile and wave back before tossing my phone on my bed, not even bothering to hang it up, and run out of my room toward my front door.

"Where are you going?" I hear someone say as I pass through the living room, but I don't stop. Nothing or no one can derail me. The thought of being in Ethan's arms again is overpowering everything else.

I start to run down my stairs, and Ethan is there as I turn the corner after only one flight. We stop and stare at each other for a moment, neither of us speaking; both of us smiling like kids in a candy store.

"Samantha," Ethan whispers, with tears in his eyes.

I watch as his face turns serious and unsure. My entire body begins to shake with the need to be next to him. I run confidently into his arms, and he holds me so tight, I can't breathe...and I don't care.

We stand in the stairwell for a long time, holding each other. Ethan is the first to break the silence.

"I will never let you go again," he promises. "I can't be without you, Samantha."

"I understand," I whisper, my face buried in his neck. I can't stop crying or smiling. "I feel the same way about you."

"I love you," he says, as his lips touch my hair. "I love you so much."

"I love you too," I say. "Always."

CHAPTER 25

Ethan and I finally make our way back up to my apartment. The girls are still watching the movie, though I doubt they've been paying much attention.

All eyes are on Ethan and me as we walk in the door. Everyone is smiling, but no one says a word. I finally decide to end the awkwardness.

"Everyone," I say, wondering if I will ever stop smiling, "look who I found."

Rose gets up then and rushes over to give me a huge hug. I only have one arm to spare, since I'm unwilling to let go of Ethan's hand.

"I'm so happy for you," she says to me, before looking at Ethan. "I'm happy for you both."

"Thanks Rose," I say to her. "Thanks for everything."

"Anything for you."

I'm not surprised to see Rose getting teary eyed now too.

"We should get going," Liz says, rising from her chair. "You guys probably need some time to chat."

Even though Ethan and I definitely have some catching up to do, I feel bad for ditching my friends.

I look over at Ethan, and like always, as if we never missed a beat, he reads my mind.

"I don't know. *Gone with the Wind*?" he asks as he looks at the television. "It's one of my favorites."

He looks back at me and smiles as he moves toward the couch to take a seat. I hate that he let go of my hand, but I love what he's doing. He is perfection. And he is all mine.

Liz smiles at me as she sits back down, and I notice Sydney is nearly bouncing up and down in her seat next to Ethan.

The next thing I know, Jake and Sean come barreling into the room.

"Ethan?!" Jake calls as he runs toward him.

My smile grows even wider. Jake seems almost as excited to see Ethan as I am.

"Hi Jake. I've missed you," Ethan tells Jake, and my eyes are watery once again, along with the other females in the room.

Rose and I stay by the door giggling with each other like thirteen year olds, as Ethan and Jake spend a minute catching up.

"Why don't you get back to your video games," I finally tell Jake, after he's gone through basically every minute of his life since the last time he saw Ethan. "You can chat more with Ethan later on, okay?"

"I'll be here," Ethan assures him, and my heart swells hearing that promise.

Jake pouts at me and gives Ethan one last hug before he and Sean reluctantly make their way back to Jake's room.

After Jake and Sean leave, Rose and I re-join the group. Rose sits on the other side of Ethan on the couch, and I sit on the floor, my back resting between Ethan's legs.

"It's nice to see you again, Ethan," Liz says, with her typical, confident air.

"Thanks. I appreciate the second chance," Ethan says.

I look up to see his face is sincere...and absolutely beautiful. Ethan smiles at me as he runs his index finger along the bottom of my chin. I briefly close my eyes. It feels so good to be close to him again.

"I'm not sure we should be giving you a second chance," Sydney adds in a snarky tone, and I feel like decking her before I notice the grin on her face.

"Why's that?" Ethan asks, as he looks around at each of us, obviously wondering what joke he's missing.

"Sam deserves better than some unemployed loser, you know." Sydney continues grinning widely. I punch her lightly on the leg, and we all start to laugh.

"Leave it to Sydney," Rose says quietly under her breath, but I hear her and smile.

"Good point," Ethan says, smiling at Sydney. "Are they hiring at the courthouse?"

"Very funny," Sydney says. "But seriously, what are you going to do now?"

Ethan looks uncomfortable, and I start to feel a little uncomfortable myself.

"We don't have to talk about this right now," I interject, and Sydney rolls her eyes at me.

"Well, I'm honestly not sure," Ethan confesses, deciding to answer. "I hadn't gotten much past the quitting part...and of course my diabolical plan to get Samantha back."

"That didn't take quite as much time as you thought, I assume," Liz says, still smiling at me.

"Thankfully not." Ethan looks down at me as I lay my head on his knee. He starts to lightly stroke my hair.

I doubt my friends are enjoying our public display of affection, but I couldn't care less at the moment.

We spend a few more minutes chatting and then Rose decides we should showcase our talents and indulge Ethan with our little *Gone with the Wind* game for a while.

Ethan is pretty impressed by our impersonations and teases that he thinks we would all have a bright future in acting.

When the movie is over, everyone starts getting ready to head out. I stand up and Ethan helps me take the empty ice cream containers and spoons back to the kitchen, as everyone else gets their things together.

"Okay, I don't know about you ladies, but I'm ready for my bed," Liz says as she stands up and grabs her purse.

"Same here," Rose agrees.

I see that Sydney actually looks a little disappointed she has to go, but her smile tells me it's only because she's so happy for me and that she isn't ready for the excitement from tonight to end. I can't blame her.

"Goodnight ladies." Ethan gives everyone a wave as they make their way toward the door. "It was good to see you all again."

"Goodnight Ethan," they all say in turn.

"It's nice to see you again too," Liz adds, but she's looking at me when she says it.

Rose gives me one last hug before she heads out. "I'm so happy for you," she whispers in my ear.

"Thanks Rose," I say, trying not to cry again tonight.

To my surprise, Rose gives Ethan a hug too. To my greater surprise, he gladly accepts and by the look on his face, I think he may be holding back tears as well.

After everyone leaves, I turn to Ethan.

"Mind if I stay a while longer?" he asks.

"I was hoping you would," I admit.

Ethan walks slowly toward me, and once again, the ache to touch him is overwhelming.

I reach instantly for his face when he's close enough. Touching his perfect face is like coming home. I feel complete once again.

Ethan wraps his arms around me and pulls me close. I leave my hands on his cheeks for a little longer as we gaze into each other's eyes. I realize then how much I've truly missed him.

I wait for him to kiss me, but I'm surprised to see hesitancy in Ethan's eyes. Could he still be questioning my love for him?

For the first time in our relationship, I feel completely confident, as I let go of his face to wrap my arms around his neck. I lean in slowly, cherishing every second before my lips meet his.

Ethan's uncertainty seems to melt away immediately as we kiss. I feel his body relax into mine as I run my fingers slowly through his hair.

I'm the one to pull away first, but only because Jake is a room away. Plus, I know there will be plenty of time for making up.

"Maybe I should have made you work for it," I tease. Our arms are still wrapped tightly around each other.

"I would have done anything," he says softly as he reaches a finger up to caress my cheek. "No matter how long it took."

"Exactly," I say. "Just think of how I could have milked that."

Ethan smiles at me, and pulls me closer. "I am still willing to beg, if you'd like."

"Maybe later," I say, before stealing one more kiss.

Ethan decides to make the kiss a little longer than I intended, but I don't complain.

"I can't believe you quit," I say, after reluctantly pulling away once again. "I would be lying if I said I didn't feel a little guilty about this. I mean, you can always go back to acting, right?"

"I don't want to," Ethan says confidently.

"What do you mean?" I ask, feeling confused. "You were starting to love it again. Everyone could see it. You were so happy."

"I thought so too," Ethan laughs, "until you left. Then I realized that it wasn't my job that was making me happy at all."

"But you love it, Ethan," I tell him. "I know you do, and you're an amazing actor. I don't want you to give up something like that for me. You shouldn't have to. It's not right."

"Whether I'm good at it or not, is irrelevant," he says, his face completely serious. "I've spent my entire life trying to find something, anything that makes me feel the way you make me feel. You think I'm going to let a career, or anything else for that matter, get in the way of that?"

I smile at him. "You really love me, don't you?"

Ethan smiles back. "You have no idea."

"I'm sorry it took you losing your job for me to realize that."

"I'm not." Ethan laughs again. "I told you. I'd do anything for you, Samantha."

"I just want you," I declare. "Just you."

"That's easy," he whispers in my ear, as he lightly pushes a piece of hair off my shoulder. "I'm yours."

We kiss again for a moment longer, still standing by the doorway.

"I heard about Jake's dad," Ethan says solemnly. "I'm so sorry."

I feel a little twinge of guilt. I had momentarily forgotten all about Luke. How does Ethan know?

"It's okay," I tell Ethan. "Jake was upset, of course, but he's never been close to him."

"Are you okay?" Ethan asks.

"I'm fine." I smile to reassure him. "I will miss him in my own way, but Luke hasn't been a part of my life for a long time."

"I truly am sorry for your loss."

"Thank you," I tell him.

Ethan grabs my face and kisses my forehead. "What are you doing tomorrow?" he asks as he leads me to the couch.

I curl up next to him before I answer. "Well, I had planned on the usual: church, then lunch with the ladies. Why?"

Ethan grimaces. "I hate to ask you to miss church, but I would like to spend the day with you tomorrow, if that's okay."

I pretend to ponder the thought for a moment. "I'll beg for forgiveness next Sunday. Where are we going?"

"I have a place in mind."

"Okay," I say excitedly. "I'm sure mom wouldn't mind keeping Jake."

Ethan looks upset all of a sudden, which sets my nerves on end. "What's wrong?" I ask, sitting up a little so I can see his face clearly.

"Exactly how much trouble am I in with your mother?"

I giggle. "I think she was more upset with me than you, like everyone else," I promise him. "I don't think you have anything to worry about."

"Good." Ethan exhales, as I laugh at the legitimate relief on his face. "She can be kind of scary."

"She can indeed," I agree. "But she's happy if I'm happy."

"And are you happy?" Ethan asks quietly.

"Happy doesn't even begin to cover it."

"That's good to hear," he says smiling now. "But just so you know... I understand why you did it, Samantha," he adds, which surprises me. "I can't say I liked it. I obviously didn't like it at all, but I understand."

"I know." I touch his perfect face again and kiss him. "But it will still be number one on the list of the dumbest mistakes I've ever made."

"Should I feel privileged?" he asks, still smiling.

"Probably so. It's a pretty long list."

"So, your mom wouldn't mind keeping Jake tomorrow?" he starts again. "I would love to spend some time with Jake too, but for tomorrow, I wanted it to be just the two of us."

"That sounds nice," I say. "And I don't think she'll mind."

"I'll pick you up tomorrow morning then? Around ten?"

"Okay and where are we going again?" I prod, trying to get him to tell me, but really not caring at all. Anywhere with Ethan sounds wonderful to me.

"Don't even try it." His smile is breathtaking. "Just wear comfy shoes."

"May I at least know what we're doing?"

Ethan sits me up and pulls me close so that my face is inches from his. "Let's just say that...I think it's time I cashed in my fifth question," he says before kissing me again.

The kiss is nearly successful in making me lose my train of

thought, but not quite.

"What question?" I ask.

Ethan looks disappointed. "Don't you remember? In Vermont?"

Vermont seems like a million years ago, and I've been trying not to think about it too much for several reasons, but now that he mentions it, I remember our game of "Five Questions" while we sat on the dining table in that incredible house.

"Right. I remember," I confirm. "You said you were saving your last one for a rainy day."

"Well, I don't think it's going to rain tomorrow, but either way, I have something I want to ask you."

There's something innocent and child-like in his face that's making me fall in love with him all over again. My smile is so wide my cheeks hurt. I have a feeling I know what his question will be, and I also know my answer will be *yes*.

"Let me try and call my mom before it gets too late. Okay?"

"Sure," Ethan says before giving me another kiss.

"And I'm going to go check on Jake as well," I add. "I'll be right back."

"I'll be here," Ethan promises with one last kiss before I get up and walk toward Jake's room.

"Everything okay in here?" I open Jake's bedroom door to find Jake and Sean lying on his oversized beanbag chair, still happily playing video games.

"Yep. We're good mom," Jake tells me, after pressing "pause", of course. "Is everyone gone?"

"Ethan's still here," I tell him, and Jake's happy smile matches mine.

"I'm glad," he says softly, and I have to fight off tears for what feels like the millionth time this evening.

"Me too, angel. I'll be in the living room if you need me."

"Okay mom. I love you."

"I love you too."

I start walking slowly back toward the living room, but I pick up the pace, remembering who's waiting for me.

It's no wonder I miss the toy car. My left foot hits it at the same time I notice it in the hallway. I try to correct myself, but my head is still a little foggy from my earlier fainting spell and all of the excitement since. I fall forward, as the car rolls out from under my foot. I feel my ribs crack against the small table at the end of the hall, and the next thing I hear is my head hitting the same table on my way down. Then everything goes black.

CHAPTER 26

Beep. Beep. Beep.

"Please stay with me, Sam. Please." I can hear Ethan's voice calling to me, but his face isn't quite clear.

I'm in the confusing glass jar again. Suddenly, I can see Ethan's face, which makes me feel a little better, but to my dismay his voice starts fading.

Beep. Beep. Beep.

I want to touch him so badly. Why isn't he holding me? I'm so scared. Why isn't he comforting me? I try to reach his face, but I can't move.

Beep. Beep. Beep.

"Please don't leave," he pleads, barely a whisper now. "Stay with me."

I know I should say something, but I can't get the words to come out. Why does he think I'm leaving him? I want to tell him I will never leave him again. I want to tell him how much I love him, but his voice is so far away and fading fast.

Beep. Beep. Beep.

I start to panic as his face begins fading as fast as his voice. I can feel my heart quicken as I start recognizing new sounds and smells that are strange and unfamiliar.

I'm happy to finally feel my arms and hands, and I reach quickly to touch Ethan's face. But when I'm only inches away, his face disappears completely.

I gasp as my eyes fly open in shock.

"Oh thank God. I was worried sick." This voice is clear and very familiar, but not what I expected.

"Mom?"

My mom's presence is comforting, but I'm so confused, and my head is throbbing. I close one eye to try and focus on her.

"How do you feel baby?" My mom pushes some hair from my forehead.

"Not so good," I admit.

My head is killing me, and when I try to move into a sitting position, I feel the pain in my side. It feels like I've been kicked by a bull.

The accident starts to slowly come back to me. I can remember falling now, hitting my head and my ribs cracking. But I look down to see my leg in a cast as well. *How did that happen?*

My mom startles me with her laugh. "I'm just so happy to see you awake finally," she says, relief evident in her voice. "The doctors said you would wake up eventually, but you know I don't put much faith in hospitals."

I laugh weakly at my mom, which feels like knives are jerking around inside me. "How long have I been out?" I ask. My mom is acting like it's been a while.

"Just a few days."

"A few days?" I panic. "Has Ethan been by? Does he know?"

My mom smiles at me, but her face is wary. "You need some more rest, hun. Let me get that nurse in here."

I sink back into the pillow trying – with futility due to my injuries – to take some deep breaths so I can get my bearings. Things definitely do not feel right.

The nurse comes in my room a few seconds after my mom pushes the call button. "Yes ma'am?" I hear her say from behind the curtain hanging in front of my bed. I watch as my mom gets up to go meet her.

"She's awake, and I think she may need some more pain medicine," my mom tells her. "And could you turn the heat up in here? It is November for goodness sake."

The nurse mutters something before she leaves, and my mom comes back around the curtain. "Incompetent fools," she murmurs. "I've been freezing my tail off for the past three days."

I rub my eyes. Surely I didn't hear her correctly. "Mom, what month did you say it is?" I look over and notice for the first time what my mom is wearing – her huge fleece pullover, jeans and sneakers – definitely not dressed for spring. My heart starts racing, and I can hear the results...*Beep. Beep. Beep.*

My mom looks at me. "November?" she laughs. "What month do you think it is?"

"That can't be right." I smile, trying to shake off the overwhelming sense of panic that is now brewing inside me. "I must be dreaming."

I close my eyes, hoping to wake back up in my living room, and then I feel a pinch on my good leg. It makes me jump.

"Ouch!" I shout, not so much from the pinch, but more from the pain in my side when I jumped.

"Not dreaming," my mom says smiling, obviously still just happy to see me awake.

I hear the door to my room open and I quickly look to my left, hoping Ethan will walk in. To my dismay, an older gentleman peers around my curtain.

"I hear she's finally awake," he says cheerfully, but his face is drawn and tired-looking.

"Hi, Mr. Spovak!" my mom greets him with a smile. "Yep, today is a day for good news."

I close my eyes again. Mr. Spovak? Why does his name sound familiar to me?

"Let's hope so for my Juney as well," I hear the old man say, and then I open my eyes to see him making his way back over to the other side of the room. Obviously, there is another patient next to me.

"Poor Juney," my mom says, shaking her head. "Been praying almost as hard for her as I have been for you."

Finally I realize why Mr. Spovak's name sounds familiar. I heard it being paged over the loud speaker at the fundraiser last year. It is not a very common last name, especially around here. I smile as I think of what a coincidence it is that there is more than one Spovak....then it hits me.

My mom's right. I'm not dreaming. Not anymore.

I realize now I have just come from one. My head is fuzzy from all of the pain meds, but it's clear enough to make sense of what's happening. I didn't fall in my apartment.

Suddenly the smell of alcohol and sanitizer are all too familiar. I've been smelling them in my apartment for months, but thought nothing of it.

"What happened?" I ask my mom, tears starting to stream down my face.

Of course it was a dream. Of course *he* was a dream. Ethan was always too good to be true, and deep down, I should have known.

My mom starts patting me, trying to find the source of my tears. "Are you okay? That dumb nurse is coming back with pain medicine in a minute."

I push her hand away. "I don't need pain meds." I put one arm over my eyes, the ominous florescent lights suddenly to bright. "Tell me what happened."

I can hear my mom sit back down in her chair. "Well," she starts, "you got hit on your way home from my house last Thursday. They determined the guy was drunk as a skunk." I uncover my eyes to see my mom shaking her head in disgust, and then an empty crushing feeling comes over me.

"Jake?" I nearly shout, as I try to jump out of the bed, but the pain and my cast won't let me get far. I lie back into the bed, trembling with pain, as the nurse walks in to my room.

"You okay dear?" she asks. She's a tiny lady with bleach blonde hair, blue eye-shadow and a strong southern accent. I'm not sure why, but I don't like her.

"Can we hold on that pain medicine for a while?" I tell her, as I try to catch my breath from my recent attempt to get out of the bed.

I see my mom nod at the nurse, giving her the okay to come back later.

"Jake's fine," my mom says to me. "He's totally fine, and he's at Sean's house tonight. He barely even had a scratch."

I try to breathe a sigh of relief, but it is rather shallow, as I become more aware now of my injuries. My mom sees me calm down.

"You got the worst part. The car hit on your side."

After hearing Jake's okay, I'm suddenly back to Ethan. I try to come to grips with the fact that it's over. I try to come to terms with the fact that none of it was real, but this is all hitting me like a freight train at full speed, and it hurts so much. The pain from the accident is nothing in comparison.

I start crying again. I just want to go back. I want more time with him. I want to kiss him again. I want to tell him over and over how much I love him.

My tears come harder, as I realize that it doesn't matter. It was only a dream – a beautiful, perfect dream.

"Are those tears of joy?" I can tell my mom is nervous.

I don't respond at first. "I think I'll take those pain meds now," I finally say.

Maybe if I go back to sleep, maybe I'll pick up my dream where I left off. Or maybe I will realize *this* is a dream. Either way, I want Ethan back, and I want him back now.

☙❧

It's been three weeks since the accident, and I'm still pretty much a zombie. No matter how hard I try, I can't get Ethan or my dream out of my head.

For a while after the accident, I felt like I was stuck in limbo between reality and some alternate universe. This world is so different from the one I apparently dreamed up.

It was hard at first to get back to the day-to-day. Obviously, nothing that happened in my dream is real, so it's been hard to make sense of things. There is no Scott and Sydney, no Bill and Liz, and Rose and Danny are still married, at least for now. Rose

confided in me just last week that they're having some problems.
Even though I know the truth, I keep hoping that maybe I have it
backwards, and what I thought was a dream is actually reality. But
I can't seem to wake up. My life has become a living nightmare.

Everyone is going set stalking tonight, but I'm done with that part
of my life. There's no draw there for me anymore, but no one
understands why. I haven't told anyone about my dream and don't
plan on it.

"Won't you come out with us?" Rose asks, as we leave the
courthouse. "Just come spend some time with everybody."

"I can't," I say, in the monotone, lifeless voice I've adopted since
the accident.

"Are you okay?" she asks tentatively.

"I'm fine."

"No, you're not," she says quietly. "Why won't you talk to me?"

I stop and look up at her as we reach our cars. "I'm fine, really," I
lie.

Rose gives me a look that says "I'm sorry" but she doesn't say
anything. I've been a ticking time bomb since I got out of the
hospital, and people are starting to learn not to cross me.

I grab at my chest. My injuries have pretty much healed, but I still
feel the sharp pains at times from my shattered heart.

"See you later then?" Rose asks, as she pulls her folding chair from
her trunk.

"Yea, sure," I say, before getting in my car and driving quickly
away.

I drive straight to mom's house to get Jake. He's the only thing
that makes me even slightly happy lately, so he's become my
security blanket. I'm happy to see he's there to meet me at my car,

when I pull up.

"Hi mommy!" Jake runs toward me as I make my way to the porch.

"Hi, sweet angel," I say, and give him a hug. "How was your day?"

"Pretty good," he says, as we walk to my mom's front door. "I got an 'A' on my math test."

"Excellent." I know I should be more excited for him, but it's tough.

"Hey there, hun." My mom kisses my cheek when I walk in the door.

"Hi mom."

My mom looks at me with disgust, the same way she's been looking at me for the past couple of weeks now.

"Jake, how about you go play outside. Your momma and I need to chat about Christmas," she says excitedly, to get him roused up.

"Sure!" Jake willingly complies, and starts toward the back door. "Remember, I keep my list for Santa under my bed at home, if you plan to talk to him or anything."

"Got it," my mom says with a wink.

I watch Jake take off out the back, and then look over to see my mom gesturing for me to sit down at the kitchen table.

I'm not really in the mood to hear another one of these lectures, but I know I'll be forced to listen.

"What's the problem today?" she asks condescendingly. "What unlucky creature has crawled up your behind this fine afternoon?"

I look at her in disbelief, wishing she was more understanding, but quickly realizing why I can't expect that from her. "I'm fine," is all I say.

I want to tell her the reason for my moods lately, but I can't. It sounds crazy, even to me, so there's no way I can tell anyone else.

"I'm fine," she says, mocking my tone. "I'll just walk around all day, in my own sad, pitiful little world, hoping nobody talks to me so I can mope and cry for the rest of my years."

"Nice, mom." I roll my eyes.

"Look, baby girl," she comes to sit down next to me at the table, "I'm not telling you what to do."

"Yes you are," I interrupt her.

"No, I'm not," she says. "I'm your mother, and I have every right to tell you what to do, but I'm only going to give you advice – and good advice at that."

I don't say a thing. I just cross my arms, waiting for her life changing advice.

She studies me for a moment. "I think you should move away."

"What do you mean move away?" I choke, completely surprised by this idea.

"Move away from Delia," she continues. "I don't think this place is any good for you anymore, and I think you need to get away. You spend all your time either at work or watching them film that dumb television show. There's a whole world out there, Sam. Maybe you should go explore a little."

"But this is my home. This is Jake's home." I start getting defensive. I think maybe I should tell her the truth now, but I don't even know where to start. "You're here. Why would you want us to leave?"

"I don't want you to leave," she clarifies. "But it's not about what I want." She takes my hand in hers. "You've wanted to get out of here for twenty six years. Don't tell me you haven't."

I can't confirm or deny that statement, so I decide to leave it alone.

"I think it's time you realize it's not Jake that holds you back. It's you. You have to make a change, and I think the first step is getting away from here."

I start crying, which doesn't take much these days.

"What about my friends?"

"You can make new ones."

"What about Jake's friends?"

"He can make new ones, too."

I stare at my mom. "You're serious?" I ask her, not sure I want the answer.

"As a heart attack."

"I can't believe you're saying this."

My mom sighs. "I'm not sure what happened, but you haven't been in a good mood since your accident. And if I'm being honest, you haven't been in a good mood for several years now. I just want to see you happy again, baby, and I think you need a change to make that happen."

"But I don't want to leave." I put my head in my hands. "I don't want to be alone."

My mom puts a hand on my head to soothe me.

"I'm not sure I follow," she says, and I sigh in frustration.

"I'm tired of being alone. I know I have Jake, but it's not the same. I don't want to do this by myself anymore."

My mom raises her eyebrows at me, like a light should have went off with my last statement, and it does.

My selfishness knows no bounds. It was a dream, and this is reality. I better start getting used to that fact.

I'm isolating everyone I love with my selfish ways, but they've been there for me all along. I haven't been alone. I've just been pushing everyone away, wallowing in self-pity for nearly a decade. Everything I need has always been right in front of me. Isn't that always the case?

It's time I stop whining about my past and start looking toward my future. It's time I start living my life with no excuses.

"I love you momma," I tell her, drying up the tears and managing the first real smile I've had in weeks.

My mom smiles back. "I love you too, baby, and I'll miss you."

CHAPTER 27

Here it is, April now, and as I sit at my tiny breakfast table to enjoy some lunch, I start thinking about how much things have changed since the accident – how most everything has changed for the better.

I still can't believe I took my mom's advice and moved away from Delia, but it was time. She was right. There was no future there for me. Jake and I found this great apartment in Atlanta and Jake loves his new school – no more "Mean Johnny".

And I can't believe I'm in school as well. I enrolled at the Art Institute of Atlanta in January, and I'm working on a degree in Culinary Arts. I've always loved to cook, and since I've been working at a restaurant here in town, I've learned I'm actually pretty good at it.

I'm only taking classes one at a time, due to a lack of funds and my mom not being readily available to watch Jake, but I'll make it through.

My roomie, Rose, helps me out when she can. She and Danny divorced officially a couple of weeks ago, but she moved in with me back in February. I smile as I think about how happy I am to have her here. Even though I told her she didn't have to, she insists on helping with the bills. She is truly a Godsend in more ways than one.

The front door of the apartment opens, causing me to nearly jump out of my seat.

"Sam?" Rose calls from the door. "Anyone home?"

"I'm in the kitchen."

Rose walks in to the kitchen, her arms full of groceries. I get up to help her.

"Just got a few provisions for this evening," she says. "Are you excited?"

Rose is smiling. I am not.

"Rose," I start helping her put some of the groceries away, still feeling thoughtful, "did I ever tell you that Jake and I saw Luke at Christmas?"

Jake and I had a huge surprise at Christmas before we left. Luke came home for the first time in over eight years.

"No!" Rose shouts at me in surprise, as I continue putting groceries away. "Where did this come from?"

"He contacted me and wanted to meet Jake," I tell her. "Jake agreed to it, and it was a little awkward at first, but Luke was persistent and spent at least a little bit of time with him every day when he was home. By the time he left, after his two weeks were up, he and Jake had bonded pretty well. They agreed to write each other until Luke came home again."

I turn to look at my friend, nearly in tears, with no idea why. Rose looks confused by my sad expression.

"Well, that's good, right?"

"Yes," I say, as I put away the last of the groceries. "It was really nice. Luke and I even managed to hash out a few differences between the two of us. He let me vent my frustrations about him leaving, and I let him explain his reasons."

I look over at Rose again, as she moves to the breakfast table. She gestures for me to sit with her. "What did he say?"

"He told me he was scared," I say, as I sit down at the table. "He said he was a coward and that he was eighteen and didn't have any excuse good enough to make up for what he'd done. He just hopes one day we can forgive him."

Rose grabs my hand, and I'm crying now, but I continue. "Luke told me he was taking his leave at ten years. He got his degree in computer science, courtesy of the Marines, and he plans to try and find a job in Atlanta when he gets out. I told him we could discuss joint-custody when the time came," I tell her. "He is Jake's father, after all."

"Why haven't you told me any of this?" Rose asks quietly. "I saw you over the holidays. How did I miss this?"

"You were busy with Danny, and Luke didn't really tell anyone he was home," I explain. "He told me he came home specifically to see Jake and me."

"Wow." Rose looks shocked. "I was in a different frame of mind then. I'm sorry for not being there."

"Rose, please." I laugh and wipe my eyes. "It ended up being fine and you had much more important things going on."

"Why are you just now telling me about this?" Rose asks, and I pause before answering.

The real reason is that I was thinking of my dream before Rose walked in, and I was thinking about Luke's part in it. Even though I haven't been romantically involved with him in a long time, realizing he was alive and well was a huge relief – one of the only good things that came from waking up in the hospital that day.

"It was just on my mind," I finally say. "I just wanted to share it with you."

"Okay, so why are you upset?" Rose asks. "That all seems like good news."

"It is," I admit, but then I get another vision from my dream.

It happens a lot, but this one is from mine and Ethan's night together in the house in Vermont. It's been popping in and out of my head all day, and I suddenly have the overwhelming urge to tell someone about it.

"I'm not crying because of Luke," I confess. "I'm crying for another reason."

Rose leans in and grabs both of my hands now. "You can tell me anything," she says, and I know she means it.

I close my eyes for a moment and bow my head. Should I tell her? *Can* I tell her?

I've been trying so hard to forget about it for months now, but randomly, a piece of the dream will seep into my head and it's as clear as if it happened yesterday. *He* is so clear, so beautiful, so perfect.

"Rose," I look up at her, and she looks so worried, "I have something to tell you, and you will probably end up laughing at me."

"Never," Rose interjects.

I smile. "Yes, you will, but that's okay. I just have to get this off my chest."

I proceed to tell Rose about my dream. I tell her all I can remember, which is basically everything.

I tell her about the party in Atlanta, where I first met Ethan. I tell her about him texting me on set. I tell her about our first date, our first kiss, even the first time we made love.

I tell her how real everything felt, and how reality has been crushing me ever since I woke up.

I'm crying the entire time I'm relaying my pitiful story, but Rose never interrupts. She just holds my hands and listens, like the wonderful friend that she is.

After I finish, I'm glad to say I feel better instead of worse. And I'm glad I chose to tell Rose over anyone else.

"That's some dream," she finally says, as she lets go of my hands and smiles at me.

"Yep." I nod as I wipe the tears from my face with a napkin.

"No wonder you gave up the set stalking for a while," Rose says, handing me another napkin.

"I just couldn't do it," I tell her. "I know it's ridiculous, but I couldn't see him after that. My heart is broken, even if it was a stupid dream."

"It's not stupid." Rose shakes her head at me. "It was a beautiful dream, and I've had dreams that seemed real like that."

"You have?"

"Sure. Maybe not with that much detail, but I've woken up disappointed before when reality set in."

"The crazy thing is," I sigh, "I think I'm still in love with him Rose, and I don't even know him, at least not in real life."

"You've always been in love with him." Rose smiles at me. "But maybe it was always more the *idea* of him."

"What do you mean?"

"Like an escape," she explains, "a way out. I mean, isn't that what fangirling is all about?" she shrugs. "Idolizing someone you've put on a pedestal? Someone you've made perfect in your head? But he is not perfect, Sam. No one is. And you can't run away from real life. Prince Charming does not exist."

"I know," I nod. I know that more than ever now.

Rose takes my hand and leans in again.

"Sam," she starts, "you are a very strong and confident woman, but I'm not sure you've ever believed that about yourself." I can feel the tears surfacing again, as Rose continues. "And you've never liked being alone," she adds.

"I know," I say again, but Rose interrupts.

"Let me finish," she says, squeezing my hand. "I just want you to see it. I just want you to see how far you've come. I want you to see what an amazing boy Jake is and know that you've done that all on your own. I want you to see what you've accomplished in just a few short months since you've moved to Atlanta. You're in school to be a chef, for goodness sake!"

I smile through my tears. "I think I get it, Rose."

Rose smiles too. "I hope so," she says. "You've always said you can't do this alone, but you can, and you have. I just want you to understand how strong and capable you are, Sam. You have been such an inspiration to me with everything I've gone through with Danny. I look at you and Jake, and I know that everything will be alright."

"Stop it," I tell my dearest friend as I smile and push her hand away. Rose is crying now too.

"You're the inspiration," I say. "You always have been."

We just sit and smile at each other for a second as we dry our faces.

"So," Rose starts, as she stands to go get ready, "you're still going tonight, right?"

I look down, still feeling a little unsure.

Rose walks over to me and sits back down at the table. "Sam, the dream wasn't real. It didn't really happen."

"I know that," I wince.

"I didn't mean to hurt your feelings," Rose says, obviously noticing my chagrin. "What I was trying to say is that you can go watch filming with us because technically, nothing has changed. I'm sure it will be weird to see Ethan again," she adds, "but he's still the same person he was the last time you saw him. He doesn't know about your dream."

I smile, thanking God for that one. "It will be a little weird, but I'm going," I say. "Besides, Liz will probably beat me up if I don't."

Rose smiles too. "Probably so."

Rose gets up again to go get ready, but I stop her.

"Rose?"

"Yes?" she turns to face me.

"Thank you," I say sincerely. "For everything, and for not thinking I'm crazy."

"Who said I didn't think you were crazy?" she says smiling. "And you're welcome."

I get up then to go get ready myself. Perhaps tonight won't be so bad after all.

CHAPTER 28

I'm in Delia quite a bit to see mom, but I haven't been to watch filming since the accident. However, after my conversation with Rose earlier, I feel better than I've felt in months.

Rose is right. I know now more than ever that I can make it on my own. And when I feel like I can't, I have friends like Rose, and people like my mom, who will help me get through. I will keep on living; keep on surviving, just like I always have.

I look forward to the day when I can have someone like Ethan – or at least my perception of Ethan – in my life, but for the first time in a long time, I know that if that never happens, I will be okay too.

"You ladies have a good time!" my mom calls to us as we're leaving.

We had to stop by to drop off Jake. He's so excited to see my mom, especially since he doesn't see her as often any more.

"We will!" I call back and wave.

Rose and I get in the car, and my nerves start inching up again.

"Are you excited yet?" Rose asks. "I know I am! Vick is going to be there!"

I smile at her. "I'm excited," I admit, "but still a little nervous."

"Remember, you have nothing to worry about," she tells me.

"You're just there to have a good time with friends."

"Got it," I say, nodding at her.

Rose told me earlier this is the last taping for the season finale of season two, and most of the cast will be here tonight...including Ethan.

I'm trying not to think about him, and especially not the dream, but it's hard. I just try to think about seeing the girls again, and that makes me happy. It's been a while.

Rose and I are downtown in no time, and the square is crowded. Everyone seems to be out tonight to see the filming. I have to park kind of far away, but it's nice out, so neither of us mind the walk.

We finally get to our friends, and they look very happy to see us both.

"Sorry we're late," I say, smiling.

"Sam!" Sydney squeals as she rushes to hug me. "It's good to see you!"

"It's good to see you, too!" I tell her, and then the hug fest begins.

"When are you two moving back?" Liz asks. "I am getting bored with having to keep Sydney in line," she says, as she smiles at her friend.

"Whatever!" Sydney glares at Liz, but she's smiling as well.

Rose and I unfold our chairs, and once the filming starts, I'm reminded of the things I love about this experience that don't have anything to do with Ethan.

It really is exciting to see the inner-workings of Hollywood in our tiny little town, and as we sit and chat, I realize how much I've missed my friends.

We proceed to sit outside for hours – just like old times. I'm getting increasingly nervous as the night goes on, but I try to hold it together. I keep reminding myself of what Rose said earlier. No one knows about the dream. Nothing has changed.

I'm telling Liz all about school, when Sydney sits up suddenly.

"Wait a minute, is that...?" Sydney is perched on the edge of her seat and pointing at something in front of her. We all look in the direction of Sydney's well-manicured finger.

One of the white passenger vans has pulled up near the curb, and a couple of people are getting out.

I've seen it in on TV several times. It's that moment where time seems to stop and everything around you gets fuzzy and eventually ceases to exist. All that's left is you and the object of your desire.

It's him. It's Ethan, and as I look at him everything comes back to me. He's no different than he was in my dream. Reality suddenly starts to blur again. I remember how it felt when he held me, how his lips fit perfectly with mine, how it felt when he said he loved me.

He's just as beautiful as I remembered. He is of course wearing make-up for filming, and he's in his standard dark colors for the show – black jeans and a black t-shirt – but he looks gorgeous. I'm frozen in my seat staring at him.

"Sam, are you okay?" I hear Liz ask, but I can't speak or take my eyes off of Ethan.

I watch as Ethan starts walking toward the director's tent, but then I'm shocked as he looks over and starts scanning the crowd.

"What's he doing?" I hear Sydney ask. "Is he looking for someone?"

"I've noticed him doing that a couple of times before," Liz adds. "I wonder who he's looking for."

Liz and Sydney's conversation seems distant in my ears. I can't peel my eyes, or thoughts, away from Ethan.

I continue to watch as he begins to step closer to the crowd, still scanning, and then my heart stops as he suddenly zeros in on someone. His eyes meet mine, and I instantly look away, embarrassed for being caught gawking.

"Umm, Sam?" Rose whispers. She's leaning in close to me, which is the only reason I hear her.

"Yes?" I turn to her to find out why she's whispering. "What's going on?"

She doesn't say another word. She's looking straight ahead, so I follow her line of sight and I see it – or him rather – walking toward us. This would mean nothing really except his eyes are still fixed on me.

My heart starts pounding furiously. The crowd is going wild. If he's coming to sign autographs or take pictures, it would be a first. From whispers to full out screaming his name, I can tell people are just as confused about what he's doing as I am.

"Excuse me?" he yells suddenly from the center of the square, across the street from where we're camped out.

The commotion among the crowd abruptly ceases at the sound of his voice. They all look around at each other – everyone smiling at the possibility he's referring to them – except for me. My eyes never leave Ethan's.

"Excuse me, Miss?" he repeats, gesturing now with his finger, which with another hard pound of my heart I realize is pointing at me.

Within a second, all eyes are on me. My heart's going so fast now I fear it may tire itself out and eventually quit. I grab my chest and stare at him.

Out of the side of my eye, I see Sydney get up and come to stand beside me. The next thing I know, she grabs my arm, pulling me toward him. I resist.

"I can't," I whisper.

"Oh yes you can!" Sydney tugs me toward him, stronger than her tiny frame may have you think she's capable.

Sydney leaves me in the middle of the street, and goes back to watch with the other girls, forcing me to walk the last few steps alone.

Ethan comes out to meet me halfway, and offers me his elbow. I put my arm through his, still unable to speak.

He ushers me to where he was just standing at the edge of the square and drops my arm to face me. I look over at my friends for reassurance, but Rose and Liz are still in their seats, eyes and mouths wide open. Sydney is jumping up and down and waves when she sees me look over.

"I've seen you here before, but it's been a while, right?" Ethan asks with a smile. His voice startles me.

"Y-Yes," I manage to stutter out.

"Forgive me for being blunt," he laughs nervously, "but I've been meaning to talk to you. I just haven't had the nerve. I saw you here tonight, and I thought I better take my chance."

"You wanted to talk to *me*?"

There's no possible way this is happening to me. Where is my mom to pinch me when I need her?

He laughs. "I could swear I've met you before," he says, still smiling but with a furrowed brow. "But that's impossible, I guess."

My turn for nervous laughter.

"Pretty impossible," I confirm.

"Maybe in another life or something."

"You never know," I say smiling.

Ethan smiles his own gorgeous smile. The one I remember from my dreams.

"Would you like to have dinner with me tonight?" he laughs again. "Okay, so blunt and maybe a little forward," he adds.

I look over at my friends once more and smile, and then I look back at Ethan. "I would love to," I say with confidence.

"Great," he says, still smiling. "I think I'm having some kind of Italian food, maybe?"

"Sounds....dreamy," I say smiling widely now too.

"I'm Ethan, by the way." He offers his hand to me.

"My name's Samantha." I take his hand, happiness crashing through me in waves. "It's nice to finally meet you."

"Samantha." Ethan repeats my name as he shakes my hand. "It's great to meet you too."

EPILOGUE

A rather dream-like three years later...

"I cannot believe you're in sixth grade!" I squeal as I hug Jake. "Middle school! You're growing up so fast."

"Don't freak out mom." Jake smiles at me, while rolling his eyes. "You gotta watch out for this one," he says pointing to me and speaking lovingly to my growing belly.

"Hey!" I tease him. "You may be as tall as me now, but I'm still your mother."

Jake laughs. "Bye mom. I'm going to be late."

"Bye, my angel." I wave as he rushes out the front door.

The fact that I cry easily, plus the emotions brought on by my raging hormones, means that the tears start before Jake is even officially out the door. I can't believe he's another year older. My sweet baby. Has it really been twelve years?

Finding out I was pregnant with him seems like yesterday. If someone would have told me then how my life would turn out, I certainly never would have believed it. What I would have believed is what an amazing boy, or young man I should say, that Jake has turned out to be. I remember loving him more than I loved myself before he was even born. Just one kick from inside my belly, and I was smitten. It's been a wild ride, and he's changed my life completely, but I wouldn't change one thing. Not one.

To my surprise, Jake comes bustling back in the door, pulling me from my trip down memory lane.

I quickly rub at my eyes, not wanting him to know I'm crying. "Did you forget something?" I ask him.

"Yea," he says, and then leans in to kiss me on the cheek. "I love you mom."

"I love you too," I say, as I reach to hug him once more. He will always be my baby angel, no matter how old he is. "Now go," I tell him. "You don't want to be late on your first day."

"Bye mom." He waves as he rushes out the door for the second time. I wave back, and wipe my eyes again.

"Lamont taking Jake to school?" my loving husband asks as he enters the kitchen.

"Yep. He told him he would as long as he keeps his grades up this year. Otherwise, it's the dreaded bus."

"And how are my other two favorite people this morning?" Ethan comes up behind me and puts both arms around my now non-existent waistline, one hand gently caressing my belly.

"We're doing just fine," I say, leaning back into him. He's freshly showered and smelling lovely.

"Glad to hear it." Ethan nuzzles into my neck, and I let out a contented sigh.

"Are you sure you have to leave?" I whine. "I'm going to miss you terribly."

"I will miss you too, of course, but yes, I have to go. Someone has to pay the bills around here," he teases.

Ethan left acting a couple of years ago, but he couldn't deny his passion for the industry for long. He spends his time behind the camera now. I still can't believe it – Ethan Grant, Director.

"We're almost done shooting this episode," he continues. "I shouldn't be late tonight."

"Good. I'm making lasagna."

"Sounds delicious." He smiles, as he spins me around and then kisses me softly on the lips. "Makes me think of our first date."

I laugh. "It wasn't lasagna. It was spaghetti." I smile just thinking about that night. It ended up being more magical than anything I could have ever dreamed up.

"Right. Spaghetti," Ethan says as he remembers. "I was close."

"That was a good night."

"Yes it was." Ethan smiles at me. "I remember being so happy to finally see you there in the crowd. I never thought I'd see you again. I'm still kicking myself for not talking to you sooner."

"It doesn't matter. If not that night, I'm convinced we would have eventually found each other," I say with confidence. "My heart belongs to you. It always has, and it always will."

"Yes it does," Ethan says, placing a hand gently on my cheek. "And mine to you."

Ethan leans down to kiss me again, this time less gentle than before. I'm breathless, as we break away and I smile up at him.

"Do you have time for breakfast?" I ask, hoping to get a few more minutes with him before he leaves for the day.

Ethan got a job directing a television show that's filmed in and around Atlanta. He's been working on the show all season, and his days are packed, but he's been home every night. I know we won't always be this lucky, so I'm enjoying it while I can.

"Of course," he says. "I wouldn't miss it."

I smile as I turn back to the omelets I started for us before Jake left, and Ethan heads for the breakfast table.

"So, have you thought any more about names?" Ethan asks once he sits down and pours himself a glass of juice from the pitcher on the table.

"I'm still firm on my decisions. I'm just waiting for you to cave."

Ethan laughs. "I love you baby, with all of my heart, and I am all for naming our child after a beloved family member, but are you serious about the boy name?"

I try to hide my smile. "Totally."

Ethan laughs again. "Okay." I see him shaking his head out of the corner of my eye. "Napoleon it is. I'm not going to lie. I kind of hope it's a girl."

I gasp in mock horror. "Are you making fun of my father's name?"

"Of course not."

Ethan knows I'm kidding, but he still looks torn, like he doesn't want to hurt my feelings. God, I love this man.

"Perhaps we can compromise, come up with something similar, or maybe make it a middle name?" he asks, and I smile at my beautiful husband. I still love saying that...*my husband.*

"Baby, I am totally fine not using Napoleon. I just love to tease you."

"Yes, you do," Ethan agrees smiling at me, "but I still love you."

"Thank goodness," I giggle.

"How could I not?" Ethan gets up and moves toward me again. "I mean, look at you." He grabs both of my hands, pulling them away from my chopping and holds my arms out, admiring me. I blush.

"You're the most beautiful thing I've ever seen," he whispers, as he drops my arms and pulls me close.

I stare into his gorgeous green eyes. "You're going to make me cry," I tell him. "You know it doesn't take much, especially lately."

Ethan smiles at me before leaning down and kissing me again. "I just can't seem to get enough of you."

"Ditto, my love."

"What about girl names?" he asks, still holding me close.

"I like your idea."

"*Hope*? You like it?" Ethan smiles.

"I do. Very much."

"*Hope* it is then." Ethan kisses me once more before letting me get back to my veggies. "We can hammer out the boy names later."

"Sounds good," I tell him. "But honestly, I like your idea there too."

"Really?" Ethan is beaming. "It will make him so happy."

"I know it will, and he deserves it," I say. "Lamont is a wonderful person. I'd be proud to name a son after him."

"Me too," Ethan says, and the look on his face makes me very glad I agreed on his boy name too.

"Now I kind of hope it's a boy." He shakes his head. "But of course, at the end of the day, I could care less. I just hope he or she is happy, healthy and gets all of mommy's good looks and charm."

I smile at him. "I hope he or she gets your eyes, and those ridiculously long lashes. It's sinful how beautiful they are."

Ethan smiles back at me. "So, I feel awful for missing the first doctor appointment, and I know you're all against finding out the sex, but what do you think it will be? Boy or girl?"

I can barely contain my excitement. Keeping this secret from him has been brutal.

"Could be a boy, could be a girl..." I grin down at my veggies before looking back up at Ethan. "...could be both. You just never know," I wink.

Ethan regards me intently for a moment. "Twins?" he asks in a whisper. "Are you serious?"

"Twins," I confirm, a wide smile stretching across my face.

The next thing I know, Ethan pulls me into his arms, holding me so tight it nearly takes my breath away.

I know the feeling well after these past few years. Ethan has a tendency to take my breath away on a daily basis.

"You make me so happy," he whispers into my ear. "I love you, Samantha Grant."

"I love you too." And oh how I do love him.

Ethan lets me go, but only to pull my face to his. This kiss is full of a burning desire I have also come to know and love. I quickly drop my knife on the counter as Ethan's hands start moving slowly up the back of my shirt.

I feel Ethan smile onto my lips. "Breakfast can wait," he breathes, and I couldn't agree more.

The End

Dearest Reader,

First and foremost, I want to thank you from the bottom of my heart for taking a chance on me. I wish there was some way for me to express my gratitude to each of you personally, but the best I can do for now is just say thank you, thank you, a million times THANK YOU!

I have had crazy stories zinging around in my head for as long as I can remember. While on maternity leave with my son, I decided to spend some down time putting one of those stories on paper. Within a few months, *You Never Know* was born.

I had zero intentions of ever letting anyone read it, much less publish it. But almost a year after I finished the book, I met someone who changed my mind. An unexpected friendship with a fellow fangirl (and future soul sister!) gave me the courage to release Sam and Ethan to the world, and I couldn't be happier.

The unfortunate dark cloud is that, like most self-published authors, I could not afford professional editing. I tried my best to get this story as perfect as possible for you, but I am confident you will still find errors, and for that I am deeply sorry.

But despite the book's imperfections (and mine!), I hope you will continue to take chances on me and my crazy stories, as I look forward to sharing more adventures with you soon.

All of my love,
Melinda

ACKNOWLEDGMENTS

I'll try and keep this short, but there are definitely a few people that need to be recognized...

First, thank you to my husband for...well, everything. Your love (and unbelievable ability to put up with my crazy arse) is all the inspiration I will ever need. I love you, H, with everything I am.

Next, I have to thank my entire family for all of their encouragement and support of not only my writing, but of everything I do. We may be big and loud, but so is our love, and I wouldn't have it any other way.

Thank you to my dear friend, Kara, for the beautiful cover art. Even though I was probably the most difficult client you've ever dealt with, know that your creative genius astounds me, and no one could have captured my vision like you did. No one.

And I have to give a very special thank you to my soul sister, Kristi. I would never have had the courage to share this story without you. I will be eternally grateful to you for taking this journey with me and for loving Sam and Ethan as much (if not more than) I do. Forever soul sisters, we will be.

And last, but certainly not least, to all of my fangirl soul sisters out there – especially Dana, Dawn, Maya, Summer and Shelley – thank you for always being there for me, armed with good times, zero judgment and huge hearts. You have changed me forever and most definitely for the better.

ABOUT THE AUTHOR

Melinda Harris is an inspiring author and a professional fangirl. She currently resides in the great state of Georgia with her family, and when she's not writing, she likes to spend rainy nights with her nose in a good book and sunny days on a playground chasing her son. And most anytime – rain or shine – she can be found engaging in her favorite pastime, which of course is eating ice cream...lots and lots of ice cream.

37589649R00224

Made in the USA
Charleston, SC
12 January 2015